The Muse

JESSICA EVANS

Meryton Press
Oysterville, WA

This is a work of fiction. Names, characters, places, and incidents are products of the author's imagination or are used fictitiously. Any resemblance to actual events or persons, living or dead, is entirely coincidental.

THE MUSE

 For information: P.O. Box 34, Oysterville WA 98641

ISBN: 978-1-936009-39-8

Front cover ballerina: iStock contributor joshblake
Back cover ballerina: iStock contributor myshotz
Cover design by Zorylee Diaz-Lupitou
Layout by Ellen Pickels

Dedication

To my parents, for their unconditional love and support

Acknowledgments

This novel was several years in the making, and I am grateful to many who helped make it a reality.

First, I am truly grateful to my fabulous editor at Meryton Press, Debbie Styne. As this story's original beta editor and then as my friend, Debbie has always been my loudest and most enthusiastic cheerleader. Thanks also goes to Michele Reed at Meryton Press for her help and support, to Zorylee Diaz-Lupitou for her patience and talent in cover and web design, and to Ellen Pickels for her sharp eye with edits.

Thank you to fellow Austenesque writers Abigail Reynolds and Jan Hahn for giving me valuable advice on publishing this story. My friend Keiko Fernandez gave me much insight into the world of professional ballet dancers. I am also grateful to Erica Silberstein for being not only my friend but also the photographer of my author picture. In addition, I owe sincere appreciation to the many readers of an earlier version of this story who, on various websites, gave their time and interest, their support, and their encouraging feedback.

Many have said before that writing is a lonely job; it is all too easy to get sucked into self-doubt. That is why I am grateful most of all to my family, my friends, and all of the special people in my life who believe in my writing and me. Your support and love give me the courage to write.

Mr. Darcy stood near them in silent indignation at such a mode of passing the evening, to the exclusion of all conversation, and was too much engrossed by his own thoughts to perceive that Sir William Lucas was his neighbour, till Sir William thus began.

"What a charming amusement for young people this is, Mr. Darcy! — There is nothing like dancing after all. — I consider it as one of the first refinements of polished societies."

"Certainly, Sir; — and it has the advantage also of being in vogue amongst the less polished societies of the world. — Every savage can dance."

— *Pride and Prejudice*, Jane Austen

Dancing fools and watching fools. Both are the same fools, so why not dance?

— Japanese folk song

Chapter 1

A dancer's life is a series of small routines. The same exercises in the same order: *pliés, tendus, battement jetés.* Bandages wrapped around the same toes, the ones that, despite dime-sized calluses, always rub and blister by afternoon rehearsals. The same faces in company class, the same bodies with their minute variations. The same schedule: company class, rehearsal, performance. Repeat. The programs may change, the casts may change, the audiences may change, but the routines endure.

That morning, however, was different. That morning the dancers of Ballet Theater of New York walked into the studio fresh and alive. They danced the first exercise, *pliés,* with the grace of *Swan Lake.* Legs sliced crisply through during *tendus* and *jetés.* By *rond de jambes,* sweat beads trickled down foreheads and fell in droplets to the floor. A man sat at the front of the studio, arms folded across his chest, blankly looking out at the company of dancers. Every so often, he glanced down, scribbled in a notebook with a thin black and gold pen, and then looked up, expressionless.

He was William Darcy, the Ballet Theater legend, the one in the company's old promotional poster hanging in the lobby downstairs. William Darcy, back at the company in a new capacity: to create dance.

He was casting for his new work, and class was his audition. All of the dancers knew it. All of them wanted a part in his next piece—the one that already had the critics buzzing, the one that had yet to be choreographed.

The music ended, and the dancers brought their arms down to the finishing pose, holding their heads still as the piano quieted. Then, they relaxed. The ballet mistress nodded and began demonstrating the next exercise, *frappés.*

From the back of the room on the *barre* against the wall, Elizabeth Bennet slowly mirrored the teacher's movements, committing the exercise to memory. She'd only been dancing with the company for six months, and her stomach had only just stopped fluttering throughout class. She'd just grown accustomed to her idols, Caroline Bingley and Louisa Hirsch, dancing a few *barres* down.

The exercise began, and the ballet mistress paced around the room, correcting the dancers. She walked next to Elizabeth, stared blankly, and then paused. The old woman tapped Elizabeth's right hip twice.

"You're sinking."

Elizabeth pulled her torso up to correct the misalignment of her hip. With just a raised eyebrow, the old teacher nodded and continued on. Elizabeth's heart pounded. It was her first personal correction from the ballet mistress, who recognized no one except for her dozen pet dancers. With a concealed smile, Elizabeth took this correction as proof that she might be on her way to belonging there.

Class proceeded uneventfully. William Darcy remained stoic at his seat in the front, scribbling notes to himself. Many of the dancers tried to catch his eye during *révérence*, but he refused to acknowledge them. When class ended, he stood and nodded curtly to the ballet mistress and the dancers, and then he strode out of the studio.

Many of the dancers grabbed water bottles and the discarded remains of their warm-up clothes. Some stayed in the studio to stretch, Elizabeth Bennet among them. She splayed out in a small group of some other *corps de ballet* dancers, which included her sister, Jane.

Jane exhaled as she stretched out her calf. "So what did you think of Darcy?"

"Scary," replied Elizabeth. "Did you see his face during class? He could be one of those human statues that perform for the tourists in Times Square. He didn't blink once throughout *adagio*. I watched him the whole time."

"He was hot," said Charlotte Louis, jumping in place to break in a new pair of pointe shoes. A tall, lithe dancer with ebony skin and sharp cheekbones, Charlotte had entered Ballet Theater that year like Elizabeth, although she had danced for three years previously at Atlanta Ballet.

"What rehearsals do you have this afternoon, Lizzy?" Jane asked.

"Just Act II of *Swan Lake*." Being a new member of the company, Elizabeth was rarely cast in ballets. She performed at least every other night.

"Cheer up," Jane said, patting her sister's leg. "It takes a while."

"Easy for you to say."

Jane furrowed her eyebrows but didn't reply. Long-limbed, blonde, and graceful, Jane seemed poised to rise up the company ranks. She'd been in Ballet Theater for a little over five years since graduating high school, and she'd become a casting favorite of Charles Bingley, the company's Assistant Artistic Director. In the last few months, she'd also become his girlfriend. Lately, Jane had begun dancing soloist roles, although many wondered whether this was due to the burgeoning romance between the two.

Sighing, Elizabeth plopped to the floor. "I desperately want to be in Darcy's piece."

Just then, another dancer, Lydia Lopez, leaned over to their group and interjected, "I've heard he's an asshole but a brilliant asshole. Did you see his last piece at San Francisco? It was beautiful. If he doesn't cast me, I'll die."

"I just want to stare at him for a few hours every few days," Charlotte joked. "Asshole or not, the man is hot."

"I'm having déjà vu," Elizabeth joked.

"Shut up," replied Charlotte, poking her friend. "He's hot. It's a fact."

Elizabeth winked. "Worth repeating over and over and over again."

A few other *corps* dancers giggled.

"Do you want to eat lunch or what?" Jane asked as she stood. She extended her hand to her sister and hauled her up.

"Lead the way," Elizabeth replied. "Charlotte?"

Grabbing the remainder of their things, they hurried down into the locker room to grab protein bars, yogurts, and baby carrot sticks before afternoon rehearsals.

After observing class, William Darcy headed upstairs to Bingley's office.

"Hey, Will," Charles said, smiling and leaning back in his chair when William strode into his office. "How was class? What'd you think?"

William sat down in one of the old leather chairs on the opposite end of the desk. "Fine. It was company class. Not too different than how I'd remembered it."

Charles laughed. Only William Darcy would think company class at Ballet Theater of New York was just "fine." Not only was it one of the best ballet companies in the city, Ballet Theater of New York was also one of the oldest and most highly regarded in the country. Founded at the turn of the century by a choreographer from Russia, Ballet Theater had quickly become known for its uncompromising productions of classical ballet standards: *Swan Lake, Giselle, Cinderella.* Technically precise and relentlessly talented, some of the best dancers in the ballet world belonged to its ranks, and William knew it. Hell, he'd been one of them for years.

He laughed with Charles, some of his nerves dissipating. It was good to be working with his friend again. William and Charles went way back. They'd known each other since they'd entered the company together as teenagers. Unlikely friends, Charles was sunny and gregarious, friends with *corps de ballet* and principal dancers alike. William, on the other hand, had been a cocky know-it-all, a privately schooled Manhattan blue blood who only deigned to interact with those worth his notice. Still, they'd bonded. Call it their similar ages, their similar sexual preference—they were among the few straight guys in the company—or their similar upper-crust upbringing. Whatever the case, somehow the friendship had lasted.

Seventeen years later, now both retired from Ballet Theater with Charles at the helm of America's best dance company and William Darcy a rising choreography star, it seemed only right that they were reunited. Same place, different roles.

For William, it was the career opportunity he'd been waiting for. Only legit choreographers created dance for Ballet Theater. For Charles, it was a chance to breathe new life into a company that had seen its ticket sales dwindling season after season and its fundraising pool drying up as its donors continued to die off.

"So"—William smiled at his friend—"when can I start?"

"Next week?"

Nodding, William opened up the manila folder on his lap. "I suppose you'll insist that Caroline dance the lead."

Caroline Bingley, Charles's younger sister, was the star principal dancer in the company equally famous for her crisp double *fouetté* turns as she was for her hissy fits.

"I won't insist, but I'm sure she won't leave you or me alone unless she does."

"She's a fabulous dancer, but I don't know about her for this piece."

"I know what you like, Will. She's got the technique. Perhaps with coaching, she can give you what you want."

William stared absently out of the window behind his friend. "She's not expressive."

It was an excuse, of course. He knew Caroline would throw a signature tantrum if she weren't cast in the piece. She would run to the artistic director, Sir Webster Lucas, and threaten to quit and join New York City Ballet as she always did. And Lucas would appease her as he always did. It was no use fighting them. Charles had tried it several times already and lost.

"I'll beg if I need to," Charles half-joked, his desperation palpable.

William smiled in sympathy. He knew how these things went. He also knew enough about Caroline to know that he didn't want his best friend to suffer her wrath. When a person had equal degrees of wealth, beauty, and talent, as Caroline did, perhaps she couldn't help becoming a spoiled brat.

"So Caroline for the A cast and Louisa for the B cast. And them," he said, throwing the roster of headshots on the table. A few faces were circled in red.

Charles sighed and smiled warmly at his friend. He plucked the headshots up off the desk and flipped through them, nodding in approval.

"I'll send these up to Lucas and post something on the boards today."

"Thanks, Charles," William said, standing and stretching out a hand. Charles shook it and grinned.

"It's great to be working together again, isn't it? Does being back here inspire any nostalgic feelings?"

"A few." William looked around. Being at Ballet Theater brought back too many nostalgic feelings, in fact. Every corner, every hall, every studio teemed with memories of his too-short dancing career.

Charles slapped his friend on the back. "If you thought it was bad when you were a dancer, you should see what it's like on the administrative side of things. Good luck, Will. You're going to need it."

Snapped back into reality, William smiled and shook his head. It was kind of Charles to say, but William Darcy didn't need luck. He had talent.

Leaving the office, he headed to the studio to work out some of the choreography before the next day's rehearsal. Downstairs, a few stray *corps* members were stretching and gabbing in the hallways, warmers and T-shirts pulled on over their leotards and tights. Their chatter faded as he breezed past them into Studio B, the one without windows, before he closed the door with a thud.

Elizabeth feared cast lists. The unfeeling white computer paper, the staid Times New Roman font, and the columns—only two words per line, a first name and a last name—always let her down. Mania followed in the wake of their posting and disappointment in the wake of seeing her name towards the bottom of the paper or not at all.

The fear began when she was twelve years old and Jane thirteen. It had been *Nutcracker*. Jane's name had been at the top as Clara, Elizabeth's further down as Child #3. Her sister and mother had hugged each other and squealed. Elizabeth tried to squeal, too. It was hard, though, to feel delight when her heart had fallen with a dull thud into her stomach. She remembered turning back and running her index finger up the paper again, cursing each letter on the page.

Such scenes would become commonplace through the years, playing out in summer dance recitals, *Nutcrackers*, and *Swan Lakes*. Slowly, Elizabeth's name had risen up on those lists, but it had never surpassed her sister's.

So, no dancer was more surprised than Elizabeth to see her name on the cast sheet for William Darcy's piece. After the list went up, she stared at it in shock for several seconds. Perhaps there had been some mistake. There was a soloist in the company: Elisabeth Sweeney. Perhaps they had meant her instead.

Jane, Lydia, and Charlotte, all cast in the piece, told her to shut up and snap out of it. They celebrated that evening with drinks, but Elizabeth still couldn't be sure. Was this really happening? Would she really get a chance to work with superstar William Darcy? It didn't feel real.

Ten minutes before the start of his first rehearsal, it started to feel real. The twenty other dancers in his piece waited for the choreographer to show up in Studio B. Several did *relevés* at the *barre* to warm up their feet. Others clustered together chatting. But all eyes remained fixed on the doorway. Anticipation crackled throughout the room.

At two-thirty sharp, Darcy walked in. The chatter ceased, and a few dancers applauded. He barely acknowledged the greeting, preferring to head wordlessly over to the stereo to plug in his iPod.

Lydia leaned over to whisper to Elizabeth. "Nice introduction, huh? Guess he doesn't like formalities."

Elizabeth shrugged.

"Close the door, please," Darcy barked to whichever dancer was nearest to it.

"At least he said 'please,'" Elizabeth said back to Lydia.

Several dancers cast looks at the others around the room. Elizabeth raised her eyebrow to Charlotte, who stood a few feet away. They held their collective breaths, waiting for a smile, an acknowledgment, any sign of interest from the famed dancer-turned-choreographer.

Ignoring them, Darcy shook hands with Ben, the male lead in his piece, and made a few words of indecipherable small talk with him. He cracked a wry smile, shook his head, and glanced around the room. Elizabeth heard Darcy ask something about Caroline, and hearing Ben's reply, the choreographer's face went black. Ben laughed nervously, and their conversation finished.

"Let's begin," Darcy said. "You," he snapped to Charlotte who jumped when he acknowledged her so suddenly. "You'll come out from stage left."

Charlotte scurried to the other side of the room.

"You'll also come out stage left." Darcy pointed to another *corps* member standing at the back of the room, who followed Charlotte.

Just then, the door creaked open, and they heard the titter of Caroline Bingley's laughter before she stepped in.

"I'll call you," she chirped to someone in the hall. Flashing a wide smile, she set her bag down in the corner and strolled to the middle of the room.

"You're late," Darcy said, glancing at the clock in the back.

Caroline smiled. "Sorry about that."

"Rehearsal starts at two-thirty sharp, not when you decide you'd like to show up. I expect you to be on time from now on," he said. The smile melted off her face.

Caroline was infamous for her temper tantrums. Had any other ballet mistress or choreographer made that remark, Caroline would have cursed him out and left the stunned room to their own devices. Once she'd cursed out a rehearsal director because she'd mistakenly called her "Catherine" instead of "Caroline." She got away with it because she sold tickets. The *prima* was a whirlwind and virtuoso. Her hyperextensions made audiences gasp, and her leaps and turns defied physical laws. These tricks had catapulted her from *corps de ballet* to prima ballerina in three years and had kept her at the top of the Ballet Theater food chain in the six years since.

Of course, her family's wealth helped, too. Caroline and Charles came from old New York money. Their parents and grandparents had concert halls and museum wings named after them. Besides being a famous principal dancer, she was a darling of the New York social scene, dated Hollywood actors and Italian models, and often appeared in the tabloid gossip pages.

She'd grown up spoiled and now lived a charmed life. No one, not even Sir Webster Lucas, dared chastise her in front of the other dancers as Darcy had just done. Tension crackled through the air.

Then she broke into a plastic giggle. "Yes, sir," she said, saluting. She even winked.

A few of the dancers tittered. Darcy glowered until Caroline shirked back, allowing him to finish placing the rest of the dancers. Elizabeth found herself in the back row, all the way stage right.

He began to show the first steps, offering corrections and suggestions.

Caroline, whose entrance came later than the *corps de ballet*, stood off to the side, leaning with both elbows on the *barre* and sending a text message on her phone.

Midway through a *pas de bourrée*, Darcy looked up at her reflection in the mirror and stopped.

"Ms. Bingley, put the phone away."

Stunned, everyone including Caroline could only stare at Darcy.

"I'm sorry?" she replied.

"Professionals don't text during rehearsal. Put your phone away."

Straightening herself, Caroline raised her chin and replied, "Mr. Darcy, I believe texting during rehearsal is not specifically forbidden in my contract. Perhaps you should discuss it with Charles."

Darcy reddened. Elizabeth watched the scene unfold, and her heart began to pound. She admired both dancers, although Caroline could often be a tad spoiled, she thought, but watching them fight was beginning to topple her image of the ballet idols.

"Ms. Bingley," Darcy said, his voice lowered to a chilling monotone, "your contract is the administration's concern, not mine. In my rehearsals, I have my own rules. If you don't like them, I welcome you to discuss them with Lucas."

Elizabeth knew Darcy would win that one. If there was one thing everyone including Caroline knew, it was that Sir Webster Lucas would choose Darcy over her. Caroline might be great, but Darcy was golden. The two stared at each other in a momentary standoff. The second hand of the wall clock ticked loudly, and stray voices echoed from the hall. The dancers' eyes darted from the choreographer, his face frozen in indifferent calm, to Caroline, whose eyes flashed with insubordination. Finally, Caroline, with a melodramatic huff, shoved the phone into her dance bag and glared at Darcy.

Elizabeth marveled at the choreographer's contained power. Even Sir Webster could not force such obedience out of the *prima*. None of them had ever seen Caroline Bingley silenced so thoroughly with just a slicing glance of those dark eyes. Although she had done nothing wrong, Elizabeth shrunk into herself, vowing never to do anything that might warrant those eyes to look at her that way.

"The opening sequence. Again," Darcy said. He paced back and forth, slowly inspecting the dancers.

"You, elbows up."

"Right side!"

"*Glissade*, not *pas de bourrée*."

He had marked the steps twice already and was clearly exasperated that the dancers hadn't yet picked them up. He ordered them to go through the sequence again, threatening that he would keep them as long as it took to get it right, union rules or no.

Stopping at Elizabeth, he stared at her feet.

"Heels down." The steps, however, were too fast for Elizabeth, and she had to sacrifice a succinct landing after the jump series in order to move on to the subsequent *pas de bourrée*. "If you value your Achilles tendon, you'll get those heels on the floor after you jump," he said.

Furiously trying to keep up, Elizabeth missed a step, pausing to see where the others dancers were so she could catch up.

"Don't stop!" he growled.

Elizabeth caught up just as the sequence ended. She saw Darcy look heavenward before he yelled to all the dancers, "Once more, until *everyone* gets it right."

Too afraid to sigh in exasperation, the dancers walked back to their initial spaces, panting and tired.

Despite it all, rehearsal ended promptly. The sweaty, exhausted dancers flung off their pointe shoes and trudged back to the locker rooms. Charles greeted them as they left, then entered the studio and looked expectantly at William.

"Well, how'd it go?"

"Fine, except for your sister." William scribbled notes while he spoke.

"What'd she do this time?"

"Came in late, texted during rehearsal, openly challenged me."

Charles shrugged. "Sounds tame for her. She challenges everyone."

William narrowed his eyes. "Her behavior isn't professional, Charles. She acts like a child. Do me a favor, and tell her to cut the crap."

"I'm not telling my sister that! She'll rip out my insides and feed them to the vultures," Charles joked.

William shook his head and removed his iPod. "Who's the one you're seeing?"

"Jane Bennet. Tall. Blonde. Gorgeous. She's good, isn't she?"

William nodded. "A very respectable dancer. But are you sure you should get involved with her?"

"Why not?" Charles protested. "It never stopped you when you were in the company."

"It's one thing when you're a dancer and another when you're their boss."

Charles frowned in response.

"Take it from experience. If she hasn't asked you for a better part yet, wait. It's coming."

"She's not like that, Will. I've dated women like that. Jane isn't one of them."

William was doubtful. "Just be careful. Dancers in *corps de ballet* will do anything not to be in the *corps de ballet*."

Charles stared at his toes. The two remained silent for a time before Charles smiled and spoke. "But, hey, I've been dying to know what you think about the *corps*. They're pretty good, aren't they?"

As associate artistic director, Charles oversaw auditions and chose new members for Ballet Theater. He felt responsible for the *corps de ballet* dancers he hired, as they'd be the future stars of the company.

William returned Charles's smile and nodded slowly. "Yes, they're good. Strong technical dancers, most of them. But it's obvious you were the one who chose them."

Charles laughed. "And why is that?"

"They all reek of that Balanchine standoffishness that I hate," William explained, knowing his friend trained at School of American Ballet, founded by George Balanchine. "Their faces are dead. Bent elbows and wrists. They have no expression, Charles."

"And here I thought you were 'following in Balanchine's footsteps,'" Charles teased, quoting a recent article in *Dance Magazine.*

"The man was a brilliant choreographer, and I respect him artistically, but he had a horrible sense of casting. All limp and dull dancers."

Charles laughed again, more amused than offended by his friend's characteristic grouchiness. "Okay, but what about... what about Lydia Lopez? She's fabulous. Fiery and quick feet. A real Firebird."

"Yeah, and a frozen face that's painful to watch, even if she is fast."

"She's young, Will! You have to grow into that kind of expression." Charles shook his head. "Okay, okay. There's Jane's sister, Elizabeth Bennet. She's quite good... the kind of dancer with the expressiveness you like."

"She's Jane's sister?" William asked.

"Yeah, Jane said she'd be great for the company and so I—"

"Charles, are you listening to yourself? You're already whipped."

"But, Will, she's good! If she was a terrible dancer and I still hired her, it would be one thing—"

William snorted. "Right."

Elizabeth got halfway down the stairs before she realized she'd left her water bottle behind in the studio. Face drenched with sweat, mouth pasty and vile-smelling, she needed it desperately. She huffed in annoyance, told her friends she'd see them in the locker room, and then walked back to the studio. She heard voices as she approached.

"Charles, are you listening to yourself? You're already whipped," came a baritone she recognized as William Darcy's.

Elizabeth froze when she heard her sister's name.

"But, Will, she's good!" Charles replied. "If she was a terrible dancer and I still hired her, it would be one thing—"

Darcy snorted. "Right."

Elizabeth narrowed her eyes. Charles didn't hire Jane. He wasn't the AAD then. So then who *were* they talking about?

"Which one is she, anyway?" asked Darcy.

"Little bit darker hair than Jane and shorter."

Her heart clenching, Elizabeth realized they were talking about *her.*

"There are four dancers who fit that description."

Charles sighed. "She's the one with the..." He said no more.

Elizabeth frowned.

"Oh. Uh-huh," came the reply from the choreographer. "She doesn't put her heels down in the jumps. She'll get Achilles tendonitis in a couple of years, and you'll be out a dancer."

Elizabeth started. She clutched the wall for support and felt her heart rate spike.

"I can talk to her about that. That's a habit easily fixed."

"And this . . . " Darcy paused. "You don't find that a problem?"

Elizabeth's heart thundered in her chest, terrified and desperate to know what "this" meant.

"She's curvier than the other dancers, yes," Charles said. Elizabeth's jaw fell open. She glanced down at her chest.

"Not a typical ballerina body, but she's thin enough," Charles continued. "What's the problem? You cast her."

Darcy was silent for a long moment. "That's not the point, Charles. Would you ever have hired the other Bennet if not for your affair with her—"

"It's not an affair."

"Okay, fine. Your *relationship* with her sister. She's short, she's got tits, and she'll have full-blown tendonitis in a few years if she doesn't already."

"Oh, Will, come on. You cast her."

Elizabeth's mind went white, and her heartbeat stopped up her ears as if she were under water. She felt her throat constrict with humiliation and rage. She didn't want to hear any more.

Abandoning her water bottle, Elizabeth spun on the balls of her feet and stormed back to the locker room, her heart pounding through every vein of her body. She stomped past her friends in the changing room and threw her locker open with a clang. In her wild rage, she had to stare into her locker to remember what she needed.

Jane cast her a quizzical glance, which she ignored. Stripping off her leotard and tights and yanking her hair out of the bun, Elizabeth strode over to the showers and turned the water on cold. She stepped in, feeling the freezing water fall over her shoulders and neck. She shivered and replayed the conversation.

You never would have considered this girl if it hadn't been for your little affair . . . She's short, she's got tits, and she'll have full-blown tendonitis in a few years if she doesn't already.

That was all it ever came down to, wasn't it? Her body. What it looked like. Never about how she moved. Never about anything else but her breasts and her height. Elizabeth knew she was a good dancer. She didn't have Jane's extensions, Lydia's quickness of feet, or Charlotte's height, but she was a damn good dancer, and no one ever saw it because they couldn't look past her body.

She's short, she's got tits, and she'll have full-blown tendonitis in a few years.

How many times had she heard some version of that? Always from men! The artistic directors. The choreographers. How many times had she been excluded from cast sheets because her body didn't conform to their picture of perfection?

Elizabeth was done sobbing in showers over that one. She stared blankly at the tiled wall in front of her, paralyzed by fury. Finally, when her skin began to pucker into goose bumps, she turned off the shower and toweled off. The freezing water had done nothing to cool her anger.

Charlotte lounged on the bench by the lockers, winding a bandage around a bleeding blister. "What's up, Liz? You look like you're ready to kill."

"I probably could."

"Ooh, who's Lizzy going to kill?" Lydia asked.

Jane stared nervously across the locker room at her sister.

"That bastard, William Darcy."

A few chortles went up across the locker room.

"Get in line," called out another dancer from across the room.

"Give us the gossip!" Lydia cried, squeezing Elizabeth's shoulders. "What happened? Did you talk to him when you went up there?"

Elizabeth looked at Lydia and then around the room. Nearly a dozen pairs of *corps de ballet* ears had perked up, ready to hear whatever gossip fell out of Elizabeth's lips.

Did she really want the entire dance company to know that Darcy thought she was a lousy dancer? That she had only gotten in the company because her sister was sleeping with the AAD? Elizabeth sobered. Hooking her bra, she sighed into the depths of her locker.

"Just a long, exhausting rehearsal," she muttered. "He's rude."

Charlotte frowned and wrapped her arm around her friend's shoulders. "Yeah, he's a jerk. But don't let it get you down, Lizzy. You're better than he is."

It wasn't true, but she thanked her friend for the support anyway.

"Yeah, and I'm sure he's not *that* bad," Jane offered. "It was his first day. Maybe he was nervous."

Elizabeth shot daggers at her sister and then threw on her sweatshirt. Holding up her hands in defense, Jane added, "And he's Charles's friend. I'm sure Charles wouldn't be friends with someone who was genuinely a horrible person."

"Right, Jane. Okay, let's just forget about it."

"I'm going to grab a sandwich before the show tonight," said Lydia. "Anyone want to come?"

"I'll go," replied Elizabeth. "Just give me a sec? I really do need to get my water bottle."

Lydia nodded. Elizabeth jumped into her jeans and sneakers and dashed upstairs to the studio.

The lights were still on, but she heard no voices from within. Emboldened by anger, she entered and spotted Darcy by the stereo, scribbling into his notebook. Her sneakers squeaked on the wood floor, and he peered up at her.

Elizabeth met his gaze, but her expression remained hard. She cursed him inwardly as she retrieved her water bottle. He said nothing to her, and it made her even angrier. Water bottle in hand, Elizabeth raised her eyes to him, glittering and cold.

"See you tomorrow," she said flatly. As she spun around, her sneakers shrieked against the floor.

Chapter 2

With the dancers now acclimated to his demands for punctuality, William strode into rehearsals at exactly two-thirty, knowing that they would be there waiting for him—even Caroline.

He modeled his rehearsals after his favorite dance teacher, an old-school Russian, hard as granite. Mr. V they'd called him. He never smiled and often yelled, ruling over the studio with cutting stares. Praise came rarely, particularly for his favorites. It was said that the crueler he treated a student, the more promise Mr. V saw in him. Mr. V yelled at William often, told the young dancer he had no future, and made William repeat steps until he got them right while the other students in class watched. In turn, William had become a technically flawless dancer.

William emulated that: The dance was the important thing; everything else was secondary. His unwillingness to compromise, he believed, made him a great dancer and choreographer. Yes, he was talented. But ballet teemed with talented artists. The difference was that William had both talent and drive, and that made him an outstanding choreographer. A lot of dancers didn't understand that. They wanted a bouquet of roses for simply putting on their pointe shoes.

William knew that he wasn't the nicest guy in the studio. He felt dancers shirk away when he gave them a certain look. He had been called draconian, but that didn't bother him. He saw no need to become best friends with the dancers as Charles did. They were just dancers, and they would come and go. His choreography, however, would be remembered, and he wanted it to be remembered well. As such, William didn't doubt himself, and he didn't feel guilty for some of the things he said and did in the studio.

But something from the other day was on his mind: that conversation with Charles about the *corps* girl, Elizabeth or whatever her name was—Jane's sister. Charles swore that she was a lovely dancer, that she had a certain something that would make her a star. When William had cast his piece, he'd chosen dancers he liked, although none of them seemed particularly star-worthy except for Caroline. Everyone in the *corps de ballet* was good. This was Ballet Theater after all.

Then he had a chance to study Elizabeth in his second rehearsal. She still fumbled through the jump sequence, but William looked further up, ignoring her legs and focusing solely on Elizabeth's torso.

From the movements of her upper body, he never would have been able to tell how much she struggled. Her arms floated through the *port de bras*. Her head turned this way, craned slightly that way. Her eyes focused on the tips of her fingers and then far away to the imagined audience. They didn't stare nearsightedly into the mirror like the other dancers'.

From the waist up, it was exactly as he envisioned the movement. Exactly. But from the waist down, things fell apart. That was okay, he thought. He could work on that.

"You, in the back," he called out, pointing to Elizabeth, "switch with her."

Any dancer should love being promoted from the back row to the front. But Elizabeth walked to the front, expressionless. It was unexpected, and he wondered why.

"From the beginning," William said, walking over to the stereo to restart the music. He crossed his arms over his chest to watch. Four *corps* members bounded on stage in a series of fast-paced jumps, merging and rebounding to create the last diagonal formation.

"You need to close your *glissades* more definitively. Attack the descent," he barked at Elizabeth.

She tried it, but she ended up looking like a wobbly fawn.

"Now you're short-changing the jump. Try again."

She looked blankly in the mirror and jumped.

"No," William said, waving his hand. "Okay, everyone from the beginning."

He turned back to cue the music, when he heard her say, "Excuse me, Mr. Darcy, can you show me the exact rhythm you want for that phrase, please?"

He turned back and stared. Did she realize whose time she was wasting?

He had three movements to choreograph and only two months of rehearsals, three days a week and two hours each day in which to accomplish that, and this *corps* dancer wanted private lessons? He blinked, amazed at her lack of decorum.

"No," he said, "go back there and figure it out for yourself. That's what professionals do."

Straightening her spine, she retreated from the center of the studio to stand at the back.

Rehearsal finished with Darcy proclaiming, "This choreography is about *artistic expression*, so I need to start seeing some from you!"

Not a positive end to two hours of grueling drills. A few dancers trudged out. Elizabeth stayed behind.

She had no clue what Darcy had meant. *Attack the descent but don't shortchange the jump.* Was she supposed to defy gravity? In the back of the room, Elizabeth studied her *glissade* in the mirror. A few other dancers honed steps around her as well, but the choreographer's eyes settled on her. She noticed him pacing towards her—studied, cat-like.

"Your rhythm is off," he said, when he was no more than a few feet away. "*Duh*-duh, *duh*-duh," mimicking the music with his voice and the rhythm of the jumps with his hands.

She tried again, and he shook his head. Elizabeth placed her arms akimbo and looked down in frustration. Head still down, she cut her eyes up to the choreographer. "I must be having an off day all around."

He looked annoyed. Rather than frightening Elizabeth, it made her feel triumphant.

"Don't go for height. Go for movement. Imagine that someone's carrying you across in the air. Both legs out."

Unlike Caroline or even Lydia, Elizabeth did not have the quickness of feet to be a virtuoso jumper. She tried once more, and Darcy looked as if he was ready to give up and leave. Her temper flared. She suspected he was giving her BS corrections and nit-picking just to be a jerk. Well, she could be a persistent jerk right back. Elizabeth cocked her chin and looked him square in the face in a wordless challenge to show her the right way.

Sighing, Darcy suddenly walked behind her and grabbed her waist. Elizabeth sucked in a quick breath.

"*Glissade*," he ordered.

Heart thudding, she obeyed. His hands were strong but light on her back, gliding her over the floor. Then, she felt the pressure of his hands on her sides, guiding her down again. He had barely moved her off the floor, and yet the dynamics of the jump felt completely different.

"That," he said, "is what I want."

She tried it a few times herself. It pained her that the sequence now took on a different and vibrant musicality. Darcy looked at her smugly and then turned away. Success had never felt so defeating.

"Partnering a woman is like making love to her," Mr. V had once told William's *pas de deux* class in his heavily-accented English. They had been teenagers at the time, and most had chuckled with feigned knowing.

"You need to touch woman gently, but not too gently. You need to be strong but not *too* strong. Then the woman feels uncomfortable. You have to hold her just right. Good partner is good lover," his teacher had said. William had never forgotten that advice.

Was it the chicken or the egg, he wondered? Had he bedded so many dancers because he had been a good dance partner? Or had he become a good dance partner by sleeping with so many women? In any case, he thought of that advice often before he touched a woman on stage or in the bedroom. The thought had been in his mind, too, as he placed his hands around Elizabeth Bennet's waist and lifted her.

In his experience, the same truth held for women: The ones who let themselves be partnered were usually the ones who melted, molded, and danced under the sheets; the ones who blushed, flinched, or stiffened when a dancer touched her on the floor usually shriveled up in bed.

Although she had tensed initially, Elizabeth Bennet, he noted, had eased into him when he grabbed her. She had been light and pliant. A small detail, but one that was on his mind as he stood in the center of Studio B, staring at his feet, thinking of what came next.

In the choreography, he had reached a dead-end. He didn't know how to get his dancers off stage and get the principal dancer on. Well, it wasn't really a matter of not knowing how; it was more that he suddenly didn't care. Did it really matter? He could have his dancers clip their toenails on stage, and the critics would call it a brilliant feat of post-modern dance.

He knew he shouldn't complain. As a young choreographer creating dances for barely four years, William should have been grateful for the rebirth of his dance career. Life after his career-ending knee injury had been bleak, and choreography had resurrected him. For several years, he'd traveled to new dance companies, working with new dancers, pumping out new ballets, receiving ovations, and tasting glory again, even if it was from behind the wings. But over a year ago, choreography stopped being the panacea it had been. William began to feel empty again.

The door creaked open, interrupting his thoughts, and Caroline Bingley entered the studio. He inhaled, bracing himself.

"Hello, William," she said, dropping her voice.

He turned his head to acknowledge her. "Caroline."

She wore her street clothes, a beige turtleneck with tight jeans, and sashayed over to where he stood. His stomach lurched with desire. After all, Caroline was a beautiful woman, sleek and well manicured. He couldn't fail to notice that.

"We didn't start this off on the right foot," she said. "Which is a shame, really. Because I was looking forward to seeing you again."

He stared down at her with no intention of saying anything. Caroline's blonde hair hung down around her shoulders, and her cheeks were flushed with the remains of that day's exertions. She looked like sex.

"I was wondering if I could make it up to you. If you wanted to come over tonight. To catch up."

He swallowed and turned away, disgusted with himself and with her. "I can't."

"Tomorrow, then?"

"I don't think so."

Caroline smiled. "It would be fun, Will."

At one time in his life, it had been fun. They'd had a prolonged and satisfying physical relationship. He ended it when her late night phone calls had become a little too insistent, when she started staring at him with that look in her eyes, when her feelings spilled over from the bedroom into the dance studio. Although the affair ended years ago, Caroline had obviously not forgotten. William had. There were too many *Carolines* in his past to count, affairs that had ended badly. William finally realized the sex wasn't worth the fallout, particularly not sex with your best friend's kid sister.

"I'm trying to choreograph here," he said, encouraging her to leave.

"Can I be of any assistance?" she inquired, snaking a hand up his bicep.

"No. I choreograph alone."

"You're too uptight for your own good."

William glowered at her. "I'll see you on Friday in rehearsals."

Caroline chuckled. She raised the corner of her lip. "Call me if you change your mind." Then, she leaned up and planted a soft kiss on his lips, one that lingered a little too long. She squeezed his arm and then walked out of the studio, leaving William annoyed and more disoriented than when he began.

He stood in the center of the studio for a long time, his heart pounding. He hated himself for letting Caroline affect him like that.

He approached the mirror and studied his face. Lines had emerged at the corners of his eyes. Twice in the past month he had yanked out a stray gray hair from the mass of dark brown waves on top of his head. William frowned. He was growing old. Once he could no longer dance, he began to feel the heaviness of time dragging down the skin on his face. The wrinkles didn't show much now, but give them a few years. He sighed and sank into the chair at the front of the room.

After several minutes, William saw visions of his younger self bolting down the diagonal in a rapid series of leaps, turns, and beats of the leg. As a dancer, he had been a completely different person, cocky and brash. He had smiled more, charmed more. There had been nothing more ego-inflating than catapulting himself three feet off the floor in a *grand jeté*, whirling around in a quadruple *pirouette*. Nothing more gratifying than the explosion of applause after a perfectly executed variation. And now it was gone.

In envisioning his younger days, William suddenly thought of Elizabeth Bennet. He thought of her dancing. She was still clumsy in some of her movements, but she danced with an energy that he recognized: fierce and delicate at the same time. In her eyes, he recognized a passion for expression that he, too, had once felt. Elizabeth Bennet, he could tell, loved to dance.

William rose again and paced towards the center of the room. She definitely had a strength for *balancés*, those rocking steps done in a waltz rhythm. Perhaps less vertical movement and more horizontal would work better in this section. He attempted an impromptu phrase of *balancés* and *piqués*, and ending with a series of *chaînés*. It fit the music. It would work. Suddenly, William had direction. He got out his notebook and scribbled down the steps, imagining their execution by a petite *corps de ballet* girl with a penchant for haughty lifts of the chin and a pair of cold, glittering eyes.

Jane and Elizabeth Bennet waited for the last taxi to whiz past them before they jaywalked onto Columbus Avenue. They were on their way to the deli to grab a post-rehearsal snack before that night's performance.

"Darcy's an ass," Elizabeth declared. "Did you see his face after rehearsal? Ugh! God, I hate him."

"'Hate' is a strong word. You don't even know him, Lizzy."

Elizabeth narrowed her eyes at her sister. "Why are you defending him? He's not exactly nice to you, either. Just because he's *Charles's friend*." Elizabeth's voice rose an octave when she said that, and she fluttered her eyelashes.

Jane blushed. "Don't say it like that."

"Well, that's how you get whenever anyone mentions Charles."

"I like him."

"You *like* him?"

"I *care* for him."

"You're gone on him!"

Jane giggled and sighed. "Yeah."

"And you can tell he's head-over-heels for you."

"Really?"

Elizabeth gave Jane a look that said, *"Duh, are you crazy?"*

Jane's face melted into a smile. "He said he loved me the other night."

"What!" Elizabeth squealed. "Why didn't you say anything?"

Jane shrugged. "I felt a little guilty. It was the night you were upset... because of Mr. Darcy."

Elizabeth's face darkened again. She felt a sinking feeling in her stomach, the same feeling she always had when she remembered what she'd overheard a few days ago.

"Lizzy, I know something happened when you went back up there. C'mon, spill it."

Pushing open the door to the deli, Elizabeth spied a few other dancers picking up yogurts and bananas. She grabbed her snack—a bag of cashews and a fruit salad—and made small talk with the dancers while she waited in line.

Once she and Jane were back onto the noisy privacy of Columbus Avenue,

Elizabeth said, "I overheard Darcy and Charles talking. Darcy said something really rude about me." Elizabeth omitted the fact that he'd said something rude about Jane, too.

"What?"

"Let's see. I believe it was that I'm short, I have big boobs, I'm going to get tendonitis, and that essentially I'd be a crappy ballerina, and Charles should never have hired me."

Jane's eyes widened. "He didn't!"

"Yep."

Jane shook her head. "That was wrong of him."

"Yep."

They walked back in silence to the double doors of the building. Then, Jane said, "He couldn't have meant it, Lizzy."

Elizabeth snorted. "He meant it. He hates me."

"I don't think he hates you. He gave you a lot of feedback today. And he moved you to the front in the opening."

"He's picking on me."

"Why would he be picking on you?"

"I don't know! I just get the sense he's taunting me."

Jane snorted. "Let him taunt you then if it means you're going to keep getting better parts in his piece."

"Listen, Jane. Let's not talk about this now," whispered Elizabeth, glancing around. "I don't want the whole company to know how little Darcy thinks of me. It's embarrassing."

"Suit yourself." Jane twisted open the cap to her bottle of seltzer water. It hissed, and she took a timid sip. "I just don't think it's as bad as you're making it out to be."

Elizabeth waved her sister off. Leave it to Jane, ever the annoying optimist, to try to see the good in everyone, even arrogant jerk-offs who didn't deserve it.

Later that night, Elizabeth stood in the wings, rising up and down on the tips of her pointe shoes. Tom Hurst, as a grief-stricken Duke Albrecht, was sobbing at the grave of his dead lover, Giselle. Next to Elizabeth in the wings, also dressed as the spirits of dead women, Lydia and Charlotte were discussing the dresses they would be wearing to the after-party that evening. She tried to ignore them. The audience applauded as Louisa Hirsch, cast as

Myrna, Queen of the Wilis, darted on stage. Elizabeth waited for the wind notes signaling her cue. She inhaled deeply and adjusted the tulle shroud over her head.

It never failed to hit her: that buzz of excitement and fear before stepping on stage. The veteran dancers said it would pass. The steps, the music, the sequence of the dance would eventually bore into her muscles until they became rote. Her head would empty of doubt—empty of everything, really. The dance would turn into the ultimate nothingness, and eventually, the doldrums would set in.

Her cue arrived, and she walked on stage, wrists crossed over her heart. Soon, the tempo picked up, and bodies began to whiz around on stage. Elizabeth heard the musicians in the orchestra turning pages of sheet music. On stage, a dancer whispered through her teeth, "Slow down, Maestro." A bead of sweat tickled Elizabeth's temple as it rolled down her skin. For a frightening second, a tree of lights in the wings blinded her and she nearly forgot a step.

The opening continued, formations made, poses struck, until it was finally time to run back into the wings and throw off the tulle shroud.

Costume mistresses waited with outstretched arms. Elizabeth tore off her veil and threw it to one of them. Then she sprinted around the backstage to stage right for her next entrance in the grueling second act of *Giselle*, in which she and the rest of the *corps de ballet*, as vengeful spirits, would command the duplicitous Duke to dance until his death.

Despite the blinded vision, the exhausting series of *sauté arabesques*, the twenty minutes of holding a frozen pose on stage, the turns, the lifts, the jumps, and the fact that the maestro and his orchestra seemed to be playing a hair too fast that evening, it went as it always did: flawlessly. And with the audience's applause, the golden curtain of the theater closed, and the winter season ended.

Chapter 3

Rehearsals, however, had not ended.

On Tuesday, Darcy singled out Elizabeth in his rehearsal three times with corrections, each one growing sharper and more exasperated. He practically yelled the last correction he gave her—about the angle of her leg in an *attitude*—in her face, and her with a wave of his hand. When he turned and stalked off to the stereo, several dancers offered her sympathetic glances.

Elizabeth expected his wrath. She had crossed the king of Ballet Theater, and now he was out to make rehearsals hellish for her. Actually, it amused her in a sadistic way. Had she really irked him so much that he needed to retaliate that harshly? He was legendary, celebrated, and famous in the dance and New York social worlds. She was just some *corps de ballet* dancer. Did he really need to go to such lengths?

Wednesday's rehearsal played out very much like the day before.

"Ms. Bennet," Darcy called out over the music, "I've already told you —your hips!"

Maintaining her composure and continuing with the steps, Elizabeth jerked her right hip in line with her left.

She saw Darcy sigh and rub his eyes.

But he was not only severe with her. He treated many of the dancers harshly, and that day he focused his wrath on the other Bennet sister.

"Get a deeper *plié* before your *pirouette*!" he yelled at Jane.

Elizabeth fumed with righteous rage on her sister's behalf. Jane didn't deserve to be humiliated; after all, she treated Darcy with deference and respect, unlike Elizabeth who never bothered to conceal her disdain towards him.

Her face red with embarrassment, Jane nodded at Darcy's correction and prepared again for the turn. She bent her knees deeply, as Darcy had told her, and managed the turn gorgeously. From his chair, Darcy raised his eyebrows as if to say, "Told you." Elizabeth seethed. That turn had been Jane's doing, not his.

"Better. Let's try it again from the X formation," he said.

The four dancers scurried to the center of the studio, and Darcy cued the music. Elizabeth watched the dancers turn and jump away from the starting pose in the center of the room. The *en dedans* turn neared. Jane prepared, bent her knees deeply, whipped her leg in, and completed one and two turns flawlessly. But she had so much force going into the *pirouette* that she fumbled her landing. Coming off her supporting leg in an awkward position, she twisted her ankle and fell, the knee of her other leg crashing into the wooden floor. The noise was ghastly, and several of the dancers gasped, Elizabeth included. She cried out in sympathetic pain, her heart jumping to her throat.

The music continued. Darcy looked nonplussed from his chair in the front.

"Sorry!" Jane cried, attempting to stand up. But she yelped in pain and crumpled back to the floor, cradling her ankle.

Elizabeth rushed to her sister and knelt down next to her. "Are you okay? Can you move it?"

Jane's eyes filled with tears, and she winced as she tried to wiggle her ankle. "It hurts," she whispered.

A ballooning panic pressed against Elizabeth's chest. What had Darcy done? One fall could end a dancer's career forever! Jane was still young, only twenty-four, and a hair's breadth away from being promoted to soloist. She had been the one who urged Elizabeth to join the company; she was Elizabeth's rock. For her sister's career to end so early and because of someone so unfeeling and vicious—Elizabeth clenched her knuckles, feeling a surge of fury rise inside of her.

Suddenly, Elizabeth noticed a pair of male knees at her eye level. She glared at them and then Darcy knelt beside her. He looked at Jane's ankle for a few seconds and then stood and barked to a dancer who was standing in the back.

"Go get Ms. Crawford."

Ms. Crawford was the company's head physical therapist. The dancer scurried out of the room, and Darcy knelt back down to examine Jane. He smiled. "At least you hit the turn. Nice work."

Elizabeth snorted. He looked up at her. She glowered.

Jane sniffled, and Elizabeth could see her sister's determination to conceal the pain she felt. Everything in Jane's body seemed tense. Then Darcy held out his hand to her.

"Let's go. I'll take you downstairs."

Elizabeth was shocked when Jane accepted. He hauled her up easily and swept her into his arms. Elizabeth stood next to them, still speechless. She stared at Darcy who stared back with no expression.

Just then, Charles and the other dancer appeared in the doorway of the studio. Before Charles could ask, Darcy spoke. "She took a nasty fall. It's her...ankle?" He looked to Jane to confirm his assessment. She nodded, wiping the tears from the corners of her eyes.

"Are you okay?" Charles asked her with a tenderness that exceeded professional concern.

"Let's get her to the therapy room," Darcy said, breezing out of the studio with Jane still in his arms. Elizabeth and Charles followed. Once on the administrative floor, he carried her into the therapy room and placed her down on the massage table in the center of the room. Ms. Crawford asked Jane a string of questions while tenderly touching her ankle and foot.

Elizabeth peeked into the physical therapy room. If she wasn't supposed to be there, nobody seemed concerned enough to tell her to leave. Charles and Darcy were crowded around Jane. Elizabeth saw Darcy sigh impatiently and place his hands on his hips. His eyes darted around the room, settling on the clock above the door.

He just wanted to get back to his rehearsal! Jane might never dance again, she had no college degree, she was trained for nothing else, and all Darcy cared about was his rehearsals! She turned away, clenching her jaw.

Ms. Crawford looked up at the small crowd and smiled gently. "Thank you all for your concern, but I'd like a little privacy with Jane, please."

Charles frowned and reluctantly turned to leave. Darcy followed him, but before he walked out of the room, he looked at Jane and said, "You'll be okay."

Then, facing Elizabeth, he said, "Let's get back to rehearsal," before brushing past her into the hall.

Casting Jane a tender look, Elizabeth turned out of the room. She breathed shallowly. The tips of her ears burned. Elizabeth quickened her step to catch up with the choreographer just as they reached the stairwell.

"It's a good thing that we still have a few more minutes to rehearse," she said. "Wouldn't want to waste any more time than we already have."

"The show must go on, as they say."

They both descended the stairs, Elizabeth lagging because of her clunky pointe shoes.

"My sister's dancing career may be finished."

Darcy paused on the stairs and turned to face her. "She won't be the first, Ms. Bennet."

Elizabeth started. Opening her mouth to form a reply, she found no words. Couldn't he at least attempt to comfort her with false promises that Jane would be fine?

Darcy continued down the stairs. Elizabeth stayed a moment alone, moving only when she heard the door two flights down open and shut coldly.

Inside the studio, all of the dancers, including William, were jittery and unfocused. He was bad at stuff like this. Emotional stuff. His dancers looked to him to set the tone after the day's frightening events. *What now?* their faces asked. He didn't know. What kind of rehearsal could he have, really?

He remembered what it felt like, watching a friend die on the battlefield. And he didn't want to rally the troops. He didn't want to tell them to sally forth for the greater good. He, too, wanted to be alone. Putting on a straight face, he pronounced rehearsal for that day finished. The dancers quickly gathered their things and left.

When he was alone, he slumped into the chair at the front. The sound of Jane's knee on the wooden floor made the fall sound horrific, yet bone, he knew, was far stronger than ligaments or tendons. She would be fine. Even if she were injured, Ballet Theater employed capable physical therapists who would heal her with proper treatment. And yet... her injury had been the result of his relentless pushing. He had never injured a dancer before and certainly never ended one's career. Rubbing his eyes, he leaned his head back against the mirror, hearing only the whir of the heater.

He thought of her fall: her arms flailing, her face twisting in fear, the reverberation of bone meeting wood. William remembered the sickening pop of his own knee; his leg crumpling, the hollow sound of his body meeting the wood floor. And then it had been over. The ligaments in his knee were gone and, with them, his career.

The soft clod of pointe shoes snapped him back to attention. Elizabeth Bennet had come back to retrieve her things. He could see that her nose was red, and she had obviously been crying. She forced her shoulders back as she stepped into the studio, her chin up but tilted away from him. William sat in silence, watching her shakily kneel down and reach under the row of *barres* for her warmers, water, and towel.

He felt a twinge of guilt but not for Jane. Injuries happened. William never blamed Sir Webster for his injury, although it had happened in the artistic director's rehearsal. Rather, William felt guilty about his words in the stairwell, his hardness. As someone who had experienced all of the pain and frustration of losing a ligament and dance career, William knew that he should have at least attempted sympathy.

Elizabeth was trying hard to ignore him. He heard her sniffle twice. Pushing himself off of the chair, he strode to where she now stood.

She turned her icicle eyes to him as he approached. Suddenly, in the face of this petite, *corps de ballet* dancer, thirteen years his junior, William felt shy and small. He swallowed and leaned his hand against the row of *barres*, unable to think of anything to say.

She waited for him to speak. After several moments, she asked with that barbed politeness he'd begun to recognize, "Did you want to say something, Mr. Darcy, or should we just continue to stare at each other?"

It annoyed William, and he finally found his voice. "You're overreacting. She'll be fine."

Elizabeth smiled bitterly. "Thanks for the reassurance."

"I do have a bit of experience with injuries, Ms. Bennet."

Elizabeth made no reply. After several moments of silence, she glanced at the choreographer one last time. "It's been lovely chatting. But since rehearsal's over, I'm going to check on Jane."

"Actually," William interrupted, "we still have thirty minutes."

Elizabeth's eyebrows flew up. "There's no one here!"

"I need to work out some things for the *pas de deux*. Any body will do."

Her eyes blackened, and he saw a vein bulge on her forehead. She was silent, but he could hear the cacophony in her head. Then, she threw her towel over the *barre*, dropped her water bottle, and muttered, "Fine."

"You should do a few *relevés*," he said, before turning away to cue the music.

Violins suddenly blasted from the speakers, and Elizabeth jumped. Darcy lowered the volume.

Any *body* would do? He couldn't even grant her the dignity of personhood?

Elizabeth marched up and down onto her toes to warm up her feet, glaring in the mirror at Darcy all the while. Her fingers trembled. She didn't want this. She didn't want to be alone with him, much less touch him. He intimidated her with his steel looks, his height, and his air of hauteur. He was not the kind of choreographer with whom one could be collegial or even personable. He made no effort to converse or put her at ease. Even his soothing music did nothing to soothe. Despite doing a series of *pliés* and *relevés,* Elizabeth's body felt cold and tight. Her face was the only part of her that was warm.

After listening to a few bars, Darcy stopped the music and turned around. "Okay," he clipped, walking to the center of the room.

Elizabeth turned from the *barre* and made her way to him. "*Piqué arabesque*, both arms forward."

She unfurled her right leg and stepped onto the tip of her pointe shoe, her other leg extended to the back.

"Your hip, Ms. Bennet."

She twisted it forward. Darcy shook his head.

"You'll need a hip replacement by the time you're forty if you keep doing that."

Elizabeth collapsed off her pointe and put her hands on her hips.

"*Tendu* back," he said

Elizabeth complied, assuming a similar position to the *arabesque*, only with the tip of her toe touching the floor. Darcy lowered his hands to her hips and held onto them firmly. It was not his touch that sent Elizabeth's pulse racing; she was used to hands on her body. It was the way he stared at her and the low timbre of his voice. "Now, *arabesque*."

Without thrusting one hip back out of alignment, Elizabeth struggled to create a 45-degree angle with her legs. She could normally get her leg up over 90 degrees.

"There," Darcy declared, releasing her hips. "That's your true *arabesque*."

Elizabeth gawked. That was the line of a girl in beginning ballet, not a professional dancer. An *arabesque* like that would get her fired. She laughed. "I'm sure Sir Webster wouldn't like to hear that."

"The more you work on it, the more flexible your hips will become. Eventually, your *arabesque* will go back to where it was," Darcy explained. "But you're better off sticking to this. Your hip sockets will thank you."

Elizabeth's mouth hung open, and she laughed again. "I'm sure you've danced long enough to know that no teacher, choreographer, or director will let me get away with an *arabesque* this low."

"Then you'd better work at getting it higher. I don't want to see crooked hips again."

Elizabeth's pulse thundered. She felt disgusted with herself because she had let him do the thing she said she wouldn't let Darcy do: intimidate her.

"Let's try the choreography again," he said.

Elizabeth nearly choked on her own breath when she stepped onto the tip of her shoe and reached for his hands for balance. She wobbled, but his hands tightened under her fingers, steadying her. Thinking of the next movement, he raised her arms.

"*Fouetté* now so that your leg is in front," he said. Still *en pointe,* Elizabeth turned so that she was now facing the leg that had been behind her.

"Arch back. Fall into me," he said.

"What do I do with my arms?"

"Bring them around my neck."

Elizabeth attempted the step. Arching her back, she allowed the weight of her head to take her back until she felt his chest pressed against her. The difference in their heights made it difficult to find his neck. Glancing in the mirror, she used their reflections to guide her. His dark eyes locked with hers.

Elizabeth felt the rise and fall of his chest as he breathed, inhaled the spice of his shirt, and felt his breath somewhere around her ear. And then to her horror, she saw him close his eyes, turn his head towards her, and press his lips into the crown of her head.

Elizabeth's heart burst into a frenzied rhythm. What was this? Before she could open her mouth to protest, one arm wrapped around her waist, pressing her torso into him. With the other hand, he grasped the soft flesh under her bicep and proceeded to run his hand down her arm, her ribs, her waist, finally meeting with the other hand on her stomach.

She wanted to push him away. What was he doing? It was unthinkably inappropriate. His touch, like snake venom, had paralyzed her though.

They stood that way, Darcy's hands gripping her body to his, for a few more seconds. The panic finally subsided enough for Elizabeth to regain her sense of outrage. She was about to tell him to get the hell off when he released her and said indifferently, "Okay, I think that might work."

Then he strutted away. Elizabeth gaped as he jotted down notes in his notebook. She blushed.

"Let's try it again with the music," he said. She remembered his hand pressing down her body, and her stomach clenched.

"It's a pretty immediate cue," Darcy said. "Get ready."

Before she could reply, the violins of *Air in G* plucked out their first notes. Elizabeth stepped into the *arabesque* that brought her closer to him, but something inside of her flipped. The next time he ran his hands down her body, she resisted and arched away from him.

William frowned when she did it. He hadn't given her the next steps. Instinctively, he hooked his arm around her stomach, overcoming her resistance. When he looked, though, he liked the improvised step. He let the music continue.

Elizabeth lowered her leg and then whirled around, glaring. He started.

"I didn't tell you to do that," he said.

"It felt . . . right." She lifted her chin, which she did a lot. It irritated him.

He paused. Fighting his annoyance, he asked her to do it again, this time to *plié en pointe* when she whipped around to face him. Elizabeth narrowed her eyes. She repeated the step with less of the sharpness. It had looked better the first time.

"No," William said, "like you did it before."

Elizabeth repeated the step, half-turning on the tips of her pointe shoes to face him. She waited there. His hands still gripped her waist. William had choreographed an entire opening sequence last night, and suddenly, he decided to scrap it. What they had just done here had been far more intriguing.

Elizabeth's eyes darted up past him to the clock at the back to the room. She was checking the time. Although a perfectly natural action at the end of a long day of work, it made him more annoyed. They had seven more minutes, after all, and he intended to fully exploit them.

"Arch back," he said.

"And then what?"

"Just arch back, and then I'll tell you."

With a searing look, Elizabeth complied.

"Try it in *plié*. Wait. Like this."

William placed one hand behind her shoulder blades and one boldly on her breastbone. He bent her backwards as if folding back a rag doll. It satisfied him a little when Elizabeth's eyes widened in surprise. Still playing puppeteer, he straightened her back.

Their improvisations excited William. This way of creating dance felt fresh and living. He smiled.

"I like it," he declared. "Let's try the whole sequence."

He walked to the stereo to cue the music. When it began, he danced with one eye on Elizabeth and another on their reflections in the studio mirror. This was it—what he'd envisioned for his *pas de deux*. Granted, it was only the first twenty seconds of it, but their dancing had opened up a new, creative space in him.

At two minutes past five, he let her go.

"Thank you, Ms. Bennet."

It took careful restraint not to betray his exhilaration. William barely noticed that, after he dismissed her, Elizabeth did not look at him once, did not acknowledge his exclamation of gratitude.

Chapter 4

Back in her apartment, Elizabeth lazed, stomach down, on the secondhand, too-soft sofa, using bad television to blot out the day's events. Although the living room was lit only by the blue glare of the screen, she needed it that way to dull the pulsing pain behind her left eye. Her stomach grumbled, but she couldn't spare the brainpower to make dinner decisions. Elizabeth knew, despite a perfectly good chicken breast and an unopened bag of organic spinach that she needed to eat before it liquefied in the vegetable bin, she'd probably just end up eating raisin bran.

Darcy's rehearsal had walloped her. She couldn't stop ruminating over what had happened in the studio that day. It felt wicked. People at her level in a dance company didn't have *pas de deux* choreographed on them. Was it even allowed for a choreographer to create dance on someone he didn't intend to perform the role? It didn't seem right. Although she had no prior experience for reference, Elizabeth suspected he had taken flagrant liberties with her. She wished Jane were home so they could analyze what had happened in Studio B from every intricate side.

When her ruminations began to overwhelm her, Elizabeth grabbed her cell, typed out a message to her sister—*How are you?*—and sent it. She waited. Jane's reply didn't come. Rationalizing her disappointment, Elizabeth told herself that Jane was with Charles. A cry-for-help text message would just be intruding. If she had a boyfriend, Elizabeth reasoned, she wouldn't spend half the night gossiping through bubbles on her cell phone.

Elizabeth continued to think. She couldn't get that music, *Air in G*, out of her head. It made her pulse race in anger all over again, the way he'd maneuvered her like a rag doll. It was degrading.

And her own thoughts were even more degrading because she kept remembering the feel of his torso as it pressed solidly against the length of her back; when he murmured dance steps in her ear, it had sent sparks down her neck and arms. She wished it hadn't made her warm then and even now, but it did, despite his disgusting behavior.

Loneliness must be catching up to her. Perhaps she was just horny; it was pathetic, the images running through her brain. In particular, one made her melty—the famous one, the photograph from the Hermes ad.

Years ago, as a teenager, she had torn it from the pages of one of her mother's fashion magazines: a black-and-white photo of William Darcy, sinewy and naked, only shadows preserving his modesty. That ad had caused an uproar in the world of professional dance. Never had a classical ballet dancer been the spokesman for a commercial product. Never had a professional dancer been launched into stardom the way Hermes had launched William Darcy. Now, dancers posed for all kinds of ads: watches, cars, luxury brands. But William Darcy had been the first and, by far, the biggest.

And today, her body had been a t-shirt's breadth away from his.

Fortunately, at that moment, her phone chirped with a reply from her sister: *Doing better, thanks.* ☺ And then: *You?*

Elizabeth replied, nearly frantic with relief: Rehearsal with Darcy today was craaaazy!

Wow! What happened?

He used me like a doll to practice on.

Huh?

He choreographed the pas de deux on me.

OMG!!! Does he want you to dance in it???

Yeah, right. He spent the whole time lecturing me on my hip placement. Jerk.

Jane's reply took a bit longer to come through. *Hm. That's weird. Gotta run, Lizzy. We'll talk tomorrow. Can you bring me a clean leotard and tights? Thanks. XO*

Elizabeth was seized by disappointment and loneliness again. Didn't Jane care about what had happened that day in the studio? It felt overwhelming to Elizabeth, and she needed to share it with someone.

But that was her reality now. Jane was with Charles. He was her boyfriend.

She was spending less time with Elizabeth and more with him. And that was okay. Jane had found someone who made her happy, and Elizabeth was happy for her sister.

When Elizabeth had moved in with Jane several months ago, Charles Bingley was already tentatively in the picture as a good friend who clearly wanted to be more. Elizabeth had been suspicious of him at first as she was with any man who pursued Jane.

Beautiful, blonde Jane had never wanted for men to fawn over her. It had been that way since high school. But those men rarely understood her. They expected a bombshell personality to come with Jane's bombshell looks. Her sister, however, possessed an artist's sensitive soul and a kind of naïveté that didn't seem a match for the contemporary world. There had been a number of bastards in Jane's life—the kind who made promises only to get what they wanted and then stopped calling once they had.

But, to his credit, Charles had been patient and friendly. He had the same sunny personality as Jane, and even Elizabeth had to admit they were perfectly matched. With Charles, Jane never fell into melancholy as she could be prone to do. Things were calm. Jane was happy. It was hard to begrudge her sister that.

But Elizabeth couldn't help it; she envied Jane. Sure, Jane's Grecian goddess beauty had gotten her burned before, but she still looked like a Grecian goddess with a Greek god boyfriend. Classic, American, boy-next-door handsome man complete with the dimple, the sandy blonde hair, the clear brown eyes, and all that. Even more irritating, Charles was a good man, patient and affable. Elizabeth wouldn't call him clever, and sometimes his inability to catch her jokes or engage in her favorite sport, good-natured teasing, annoyed her. Still, it would be nice to have a boyfriend like him.

Elizabeth hadn't been on one date since moving to the city six months ago. At home in Michigan and even in Germany, she'd enjoyed her share of male attention. But in New York, she felt swallowed up. For a man to notice a woman in New York required the kind of primping and effort that Elizabeth just couldn't afford. During the season, she was exhausted all the time. During the off-season, she had barely enough money to make rent and buy food. Finding men to date at work was nearly impossible with the skewed gender ratio, made even more skewed by most of the male dancers' preferences for each other. And she wasn't beautiful enough like Jane for men to approach her in random places like the grocery store or the post office or other fabled meet-cute settings.

Elizabeth forced herself to feel happy for her sister. Jane was an extraordinary dancer with extraordinary looks and an extraordinary kindness to match. People like Jane deserved people like Charles. Elizabeth was a good dancer with pleasant looks and a personality that was a bit sharper around the edges. And if she had to choose between focusing on her career and focusing on the search for love, Elizabeth would choose her career. A dancer was only young once. Love could happen whenever.

Still, a woman had needs, and it had been a while since Elizabeth's had been met. And William Darcy had made her all warm and tingly when he'd laid his hands on her back and pressed her into his chest. That must have been why Elizabeth couldn't stop thinking about him as she sat alone in her living room with a bowl of cereal on her lap for dinner.

The next day the dancers glanced at each other in confusion and then up at the clock on the back wall. William Darcy had ended rehearsal thirty minutes early in a gracious, if uncharacteristic, gesture. Before he had a chance to take it back, they scrambled for their things and made their escape from the studio.

Smiling and raising her eyebrows at Charlotte, Elizabeth thought of all the things she could do with thirty extra minutes of daylight. She could stop at the supermarket, make dinner—

"Ms. Bennet, I'd like you to stay," Darcy called. Elizabeth's smile dissolved.

Charlotte furrowed her eyebrows in a silent question to her friend. After all, there would be no reason for the choreographer to see Elizabeth alone. Elizabeth waved Charlotte's look away in a gesture that said, *"I'll fill you in later."*

With her hands on her hips, Elizabeth turned to face Darcy, trying to conceal the frantic rhythm of her pulse behind a mask of annoyance. He waited for the last dancer to leave before he rose from his chair, walked past her, and closed the door.

Elizabeth waited for him to speak, unsure about finding herself, once again, alone in a dance studio with him. Darcy stalked past her to the stereo.

"Mr. Darcy?"

"Hm?" he muttered, swiping his thumb intently across the screen of his iPod rather than dignifying Elizabeth's presence with eye contact. Elizabeth's blood pressure spiked. Finally, with his music cued, he looked up at her with a gaze that made her stomach wobble.

"Are you going to fill me in on why I'm here?" she asked.

Darcy frowned. "You'd rather not work anymore today?"

"It's not that." Elizabeth folded her arms across her chest. "Mr. Darcy, are you trying to intimidate me? Or prove a point?"

"It's called choreography, Ms. Bennet."

"Is there a reason that I have, once again, been honored as the vessel for your creative genius? Caroline was in rehearsal."

"I'd have to teach her everything from the last time."

"This whole arrangement just isn't... normal." She folded her arms over her chest.

"I'm not a *normal* choreographer, and I don't believe you're a *normal* dancer either, Ms. Bennet. Normal is mediocre."

Unsure whether he'd just paid her a compliment, she looked at the floor. He showed no sign of relenting, so composing herself, Elizabeth swallowed down her annoyance and tried to make her voice sound light. "Okay."

But she found it was not easy. The dark timbre in Darcy's voice sent her flesh tingling. She hated herself for it. She hated the way she reacted to him. She hated that Darcy, despicable man though he was, made her quiver in fear, fury, and fervor.

"Let's go from the top," he said.

The music began. Her insides burning, Elizabeth danced the movements she knew, trying everything to avoid looking into his eyes because she didn't want him to look into hers. She stopped in Darcy's arms once the steps ran out, facing him.

"Lean your head back," he murmured. When he choreographed, his voice reverberated erotically. Everything in her body raced, sparked, and pulsed.

Elizabeth complied, keeping her gaze on his chin. She arched backwards. One of his hands snaked up her back, the other down her thigh, pushing her right leg behind her into an *arabesque*. He waited, perhaps thinking, but her back hurt from the prolonged arch. He did not tell her to, but she was angry and felt too vulnerable bent backwards in front of him. The fury-fervor took over, and Elizabeth straightened her spine.

Darcy's eyes widened. With her hands still supported in his, she leaned forward on the tip of her pointe shoe until she couldn't support her weight alone anymore. Despite his shock, Darcy's impeccable partner training took over, and he caught her. Elizabeth leaned into his chest, wrapping her arms around his neck for support. She thought that would be the end of it, but suddenly, he was twisting and lifting her. Her heartbeat surged in her ears. Her leg muscles melted. She responded to his improvisation, allowing herself to be swept into the music and his movements until the steps just naturally trailed off like a conversation.

They stared at each other.

"Let's t-try that with the music," Darcy stuttered, reddening as he walked away from her.

Elizabeth swallowed as she watched him. "I'm not sure I remember how it went."

"I'm sure we can figure it out."

The music began again, and they danced the choreographed portion of the *pas de deux*. Nearing the point of their improvisation, Elizabeth let herself be swept back into the music and his body. Neither seemed to want to stop dancing. Again, Darcy moved her, and she moved with him. Giving herself to the dance, Elizabeth became keenly aware of the smoothness of Darcy's hands, the solidness of his chest, his deep, controlled breathing.

She leaned into him, her arms around his neck, their noses inches apart. Elizabeth stared at the deep bow of his upper lip. The music continued but Darcy remained. She raised her eyes up to his to find them slowly searching her face. Like Eve after The Fall, she was suddenly aware of her "nakedness," and she blushed.

Pushing herself away from him, she rolled off pointe and looked away.

"I suppose we should try to figure that out," he said.

"Figure what out?"

"The steps?"

"Oh. Right," Elizabeth said.

For the next fifteen minutes, they walked slowly through their movements, careful not to look at each other too closely and replay the strange intimacy they had shared. Darcy choreographed several more bars, speaking little beyond dance terminology. Elizabeth was grateful for it.

Finally, he thanked her for rehearsal, and she backed away from him.

What the hell had that been? What had Elizabeth Bennet done to the minute and a half of choreography he'd labored over the night before? The minute and a half that had taken him nearly two hours to piece together—that had made him throw his notebook across the studio and yell obscenities? She'd just done away with it. William should have been livid; instead, he felt buoyant.

What they'd done just then had never happened to him before, either as a choreographer or a dancer. Those two moments of improvisation felt gifted to him by an unknown muse. No longer the stilted series of steps he'd eked out, the *pas de deux* felt filled with the breath of life. He was torn. Should he tell her never to usurp his choreography or beg her to make it happen again?

After he ended rehearsal, William stood in the corner of the room next to the stereo with his back to her, pretending to write in his notebook. His thoughts reeled. He tried to control his breathing the way he had learned in yoga class. If he could calm his breathing, then he could calm his thoughts. Today, the *prana* wasn't working.

Staring up into the mirror, he assessed Elizabeth as she unfurled the ribbons of her pointe shoes. Framed by lush eyelashes, her eyes revealed intense feeling. They were the feature he admired most about her. Her other features were sweet and pretty. Freckles dotted her nose and cheeks, and several wisps of hair were matted by sweat against her temples. But her eyes—a strange jade color—whispered alluringly.

When she pulled off her left pointe shoe, he noticed a wine-red stain on the toes of her tights. A burst blister. Elizabeth glanced up at him then, catching his gaze. And then she looked down and blushed. She did not look back up at him, and he said nothing to her, but he did continue to watch. She shucked off the other pointe shoe, rolled up the feet of her tights, and stood, walking to her dance bag by the wall. She was leaving, and he found he didn't want her to.

Reaching for something to say, he blurted out, "You know, I have this great Pilates teacher who I think could help you with your poor alignment." When Elizabeth said nothing, he added, "I'll give you her card."

"Thanks."

"I'm not sure she's taking any more private students, but if you tell her you know me, I'm sure she'll be able to fit you in."

Elizabeth turned to him. "Don't worry. I can't afford private Pilates sessions anyway."

The ingratitude in her voice annoyed him. He retorted, "For the sake of your career, you really need to do something about your alignment. Consider it an investment. Go shopping less."

Elizabeth snorted. "I don't go shopping."

"Or don't go out on weekends or whatever it is you do."

"Thanks for the free financial advice, but I hardly go out either."

He stared at her doubtfully. A young and beautiful woman, who lived in the most exciting city in the world, didn't go out on weekends? Not likely.

Unless she had a boyfriend. That hadn't crossed his mind. The image of Elizabeth and some faceless man curled up together on the sofa watching movies suddenly made his mouth go bitter.

Fortunately, the creaking of the door hinges broke their standoff. Charles poked his head through, looking puzzled. Neither Elizabeth nor William offered any words of greeting. Opening the door wider, Charles entered the studio and smiled.

"All of the dancers were out. I thought rehearsal might be over," he explained.

"It is," William said gruffly, turning back and heading towards the stereo.

"Hello, Liz," Charles said, smiling at her.

"Hey," she said cheerfully. It only annoyed William more.

"This is perfect!" Charles exclaimed. "Just the two people we wanted to find!"

"Who's we?" asked William.

"Jane and I. Well, actually, I was just looking for you, and Jane was looking for Liz, but since you're both here—and by the way, why are you both here exactly?"

Before Elizabeth could reply, William cut her off. "She's helping me with the *pas de deux*. What is it you want, Charles?"

"Okay, Jane and I came up with the most amazing idea!" Charles glanced excitedly from William to Elizabeth and back. "We were saying how we both wanted the most important people in our lives to get to know each other a little bit better, and then I mentioned the cabin upstate. What do you say? This weekend, all five of us, in Rhinebeck?"

"Who's 'us'?" William wanted to know.

At the same time, Elizabeth asked, "All five of us?"

"Jane and I, of course. And then Caroline and the both of you! A little friends and family bonding?"

William glanced at Elizabeth, who was clearly attempting to hide her horror under an insincere smile. He didn't blame her. An entire weekend in Caroline's presence didn't exactly sound appealing. Her expression nearly made him smile.

"Sounds fine with me," said William, never taking his eyes off Elizabeth.

"Liz?" Charles asked.

"Um... that's very... I..."

"In fact, Charles, Ms. Bennet was just saying how she didn't do much on weekends," William said. Elizabeth's face went scarlet.

"Perfect! Then, you'll come?"

"I... have some schoolwork that's due by Monday."

Charles laughed. "You can do it there! I promise we won't bother you. Come on, Liz. It will be snowing! We can roast s'mores and go snowshoeing in the woods. Rhinebeck is gorgeous this time of year."

Elizabeth glared at William before looking back at Charles and smiling stiffly. "Okay, sure."

"Awesome! Jane will be thrilled. And we'll all get to know each other better. It's going to be perfect. We'll leave on Friday night."

Elizabeth raised the corner of her lips and nodded. "I'm going to go get showered."

Once she was gone, Charles smiled at William. "This is going to be fun."

"Yep," said William.

"What?"

"Elizabeth didn't seem too thrilled. Maybe she wants to spend the weekend with her boyfriend."

"You were the one that said she didn't have any weekend plans. Jane's never mentioned that Liz has a boyfriend. And as far as I know, she doesn't have one."

William nodded, feeling suddenly lighter.

"And what's the deal with this anyway?" Charles asked gesturing to William, the studio, and the open door through which Elizabeth had just departed.

"With rehearsals?"

"Just wondering if there was a reason you were rehearsing privately with her? You're not one to bother with the *corps de ballet*. That's all."

"I know what you're implying, and it's not that."

"Right. Then why did you care whether she had a boyfriend?"

"I don't really give a crap whether she has one or not. I was just trying to be considerate of her plans." William threw everything into his duffel bag.

Charles laughed. "Yes, because you're so considerate."

William glared at his friend and strode towards the door. "Let's go. I'm getting hungry."

Chapter 5

"Here we are!" Charles announced.

Elizabeth felt a mixture of dread and relief when Charles's BMW pulled into the circular driveway of his "cabin," a gross misnomer for the two-story, sleek chalet sprawling in front of them. Having spent nearly two hours in a car alone with Charles and Jane, Elizabeth needed escape from their constant giggling, their amorous hand-holding, and the general aura of being a third wheel. She noticed with apprehension a sporty red Mini Cooper and a silver Benz in the driveway.

"Oh good, Will and Caroline are already here," Charles said. Elizabeth's stomach fell.

Clutching her overnight bag and her laptop case, she helped Charles and Jane unload their suitcases and some groceries from the trunk. Their constant chatter fueled her anxiety, and she told herself to take deep breaths as she followed them up the driveway. Charles beamed back at Jane and Elizabeth as he opened the door and shouted inside, "We're here!"

A few moments later, Caroline replied from within. "What took you so long?"

"Come on in," Charles said, placing his hand on Jane's back and leading her inside.

At her first glimpse of Charles's country home, Elizabeth suddenly felt very small and very intimidated. The foyer opened into a large living room with high wooden beams and a wall made entirely of windows, which showcased a covered swimming pool and the woods behind it. A fire crackled in a natural stone fireplace. The house exuded that careful haphazardness that only the best and most costly interior decorators knew how to achieve. She knew no one who lived in a house this tastefully decorated.

"Hello!" sang Caroline as she swished in to greet them. She had her arms outstretched, a glass of wine already perched in one hand. She kissed Charles and Jane on the cheek and then smiled saccharinely at Elizabeth behind them. "Will is here. And I invited Louisa, too. We've already started the party. Can I get you a drink?"

Elizabeth swallowed. It suddenly hit her that she would be spending seventy-two hours with some of Ballet Theater's most famous dancers and, clearly, did not belong. Their hostess wore a slinky black dress with enormous diamond studs and a solitaire pendant to match. Her hair was perfectly coifed and her makeup flawless. This wasn't just a weekend in a cabin; this was a soiree.

"You can take some groceries," Charles suggested to his sister.

Caroline made a face and waved him off. "Jane, darling," she said, hooking her arm. "Do you like the place? The decorator just finished before Christmas. It's nice, isn't it? We were going for Indian-chic, and I think she hit just the right note. I picked out the rug."

Elizabeth glanced at the large floor rug, which did not look like a Native American weaving but rather something bright and geometric picked up in a swanky Chelsea furniture gallery.

"Liz, you can just set your bags down, and the maid will take them to your room," Charles said before disappearing through a door.

Overwhelmed, Elizabeth complied silently and stayed in the living room, pretending to listen as Caroline explained the intricacies of throw pillow fabrics to Jane. Occasionally, Caroline graced Elizabeth with a disinterested glance. When Caroline finally finished, she showed her guests to the kitchen where Louisa Hirsch, another principal dancer from the company, sat perched on a bar stool with a glass of wine in front of her. They greeted each other with polite nods and hellos. Darcy stood off in the corner, making small talk with Charles. He glanced her way when she came in but made no effort to greet her. Jane went over to say hello, and Elizabeth remained awkwardly by the kitchen counters.

"Can I offer you a drink?" Caroline asked. Her demeanor was polite though not warm.

"Whatever you're drinking," replied Elizabeth, and in a matter of seconds, she had a glass of white wine in her hands. She took a long sip. Looking over to the corner, she noticed how different Darcy looked in a pair of jeans and a snug sweater.

"We have dinner warming in the oven," Caroline said.

Attempting small talk, Elizabeth replied, "What did you make?"

Caroline and Louisa looked at each other and laughed.

"I didn't make it. That's too funny. The maid did!" Caroline opened the oven and peeked in. "Let's see...we've got some roasted carrots, roasted potatoes, and, ugh, stuffed chicken breasts."

Slamming the over door shut, Caroline rolled her eyes at Louisa. "This one is the worst. I've told her a thousand times, I watch what I eat, and she ruins the chicken by putting cheese in it. We have to get rid of her."

Louisa shook her head in sympathy. Elizabeth decided, Darcy or not, she would join her sister at the opposite end of the room. She headed towards them and met with an apologetic smile from Charles.

"I have to apologize in advance for anything Caroline may or may not say to you," he said.

"I'll forgive you in advance," Elizabeth whispered back and smiled. She looked up at Darcy, who stared severely at her and then at Caroline.

"Lizzy, where'd you get the wine?" Jane asked.

"Caroline's pouring."

"Let's go get some, sweetheart," Charles said and led Jane away by the elbow. That left Elizabeth alone with Darcy.

"Mr. Darcy."

"Hello," he replied.

"How was your drive up?"

"Peaceful. I came alone."

Something in his tone made it seem as if he might be sympathizing with her, but Elizabeth couldn't be sure. She remained silent, and they stood uneasily next to each other.

"It's a beautiful house," remarked Elizabeth finally.

"Very Indian-chic."

And then, in spite of herself, she laughed. "Particularly the rug."

Then Darcy laughed. She took a sip of wine. Darcy took a sip of water from his glass. The awkward silence returned. Elizabeth finished her glass of wine.

"Dinner, everybody," Charles announced.

They were ushered into a dining room, surrounded on two sides by floor-to-ceiling windows. A deer antler chandelier hung above a rustic wood table that was decorated with glowing candelabras.

"Oh, it's beautiful, Charles!" gasped Jane.

Caroline emerged with a stack of plates. She looked annoyed and dropped it on the table with a clank. "I'm sorry, everyone. Charles let the maid go for the evening, so we'll have to serve ourselves."

"Can I help with anything?" Elizabeth offered.

Charles reddened. "No, Liz, you sit. You're our guest."

Caroline huffed, and, amidst the air of awkwardness, everyone sat down. Caroline and Charles raced back and forth from the kitchen to the dining room, carrying hot pans of food with them. Caroline cursed when she burned her finger on the pan of potatoes. Finally, the meal was set, and they began to serve themselves while Caroline preached about the injustice of paying someone to do something improperly. When she offered Elizabeth more wine, Elizabeth did not decline.

For all of his affability, Charles made a terrible host. He spoke and listened to no one but Jane, which, while endearing, also gave Elizabeth no one to talk to. Caroline and Louisa kept making inside jokes that, frankly, Elizabeth didn't want to be any part of, and Darcy was silent at the opposite end of the table.

"And my manicurist keeps telling me to moisturize, but it's the funniest thing, the older I get, the drier my hands get. Which, let me tell you, is not easy on the bank account when you have to use $100-an-ounce moisturizer," complained Caroline with a resigned shake of the head. "And then, of course, Rodrigo tells me they're raising prices at the salon! Forty dollars for a manicure? I told him that he and his little salon were both crazy, and I would just have to take my business elsewhere."

Elizabeth glanced around the table and caught Darcy's eyes. They held no expression except for intense boredom. She'd caught him staring at her like that a few times throughout dinner. What—was he waiting for her to add her thoughts to the conversation? Frankly, Elizabeth didn't know whether she could dumb down enough to participate in Caroline and Louisa's chatter.

It had become a game; she'd catch him starting at her blankly, and she'd stare back blankly until he looked away. This perverse game had become Elizabeth's dinnertime entertainment. His overt disapproval made her want to do things to actually earn it.

She offered a remark then. "Forty dollars for a manicure?"

Surprised, Caroline's face warmed at the outpouring of sympathy. "It's horrible, right?"

"How much were they before?" Elizabeth asked.

"Thirty-five."

"What!"

"I know!" Caroline sighed and smiled across the table to Darcy, who had suddenly lifted his eyes from his fork.

"Thirty-five dollars for a manicure is still pretty outrageous," Elizabeth said.

Caroline's face fell. Elizabeth suddenly wanted to force Caroline to admit what a snob she was. She blurted out, "You know, you should forget Rodrigo and come get your nails done up my way. There's this place on 135th and Amsterdam, Harlem Nailz. That's with a 'z.' They're really cheap, and on Mondays, they have a manicure and pedicure special for twenty bucks. Extra for nail art, of course."

Elizabeth saw Darcy's lips twitch, but she didn't care if he thought she was tacky.

"Ask for Sun-yun. She does great work but doesn't speak much English. If you want, I'll give you her card," Elizabeth said.

Caroline glanced meaningfully at Louisa. "Uh, well, thank you. But, you know, I do tend to exaggerate. I mean, Rodrigo does do a fabulous job. I think I'll be able to spare the extra five dollars every week if I have to."

"Oh, okay. Well, just let me know. Anytime. We can go together," replied Elizabeth, smiling wickedly. The conversation shifted to people Elizabeth didn't know in a deliberate shut-out. She sighed softly and pushed a carrot around on her plate.

"You okay, Lizzy?" Jane asked, noticing her sister deflate.

Attempting a smile, Elizabeth replied that she was. Jane, Charles, and she then got into a short conversation about the surrounding town and its activities—rich-people hobbies: wine tasting, horseback riding, skiing, shopping. Charles relayed a tale from his childhood that involved him falling off a horse. Elizabeth stifled a yawn with the back of her hand.

"Perhaps you ought to change the subject," interjected Darcy suddenly. The sound of his voice silenced everyone at the table. "You're boring Elizabeth."

Caroline cut her eyes over to Elizabeth, who in turn glowered at Darcy.

"Sorry, Liz," Charles apologized.

Elizabeth shook her head. "No, it's okay, really. I'm just—"

"What should we talk about then?" asked Caroline with a pointed raise of her eyebrows.

"Really, I was just tired, not necessarily—"

"So, then let's talk about something that we all know about," Caroline interrupted. With a flirtatious look, she turned to Darcy. "I hope you're choreographing a wonderful *pas de deux* for me."

Elizabeth had a small heart attack.

Darcy folded his arms. "I'm choreographing it. Whether it's wonderful or not has yet to be determined."

Staring at the grain of the wood in the table, Elizabeth didn't dare look up.

"Liz, what do you think?" asked Charles.

Both Elizabeth and Darcy shot him simultaneous looks of death, and Charles started at their gaze. Straightening in her chair, Caroline arched an eyebrow and looked to Elizabeth.

"How would *she* know about it?" she asked, her voice tinged with danger.

"I asked her to stay and work on the *pas de deux* once I'd dismissed you all after Jane's—after Monday's rehearsal." Darcy's voice was emotionless.

"Oh, and is she understudying the part?" Caroline asked, unable to take her eyes off Elizabeth. The quality of her look had changed to cold scrutiny.

"No," Darcy answered.

The energy of the entire table shifted.

"More wine?" Louisa asked after she'd topped off her glass.

"Please," said Elizabeth. Caroline also accepted the refill.

"Why don't we head to the living room for coffee?" Charles suggested. "We've got dessert, too."

Everyone agreed, and Elizabeth polished off her glass of wine in a few nervous gulps. The heat of the room made her head swim and her temple throb. The sweet-smoky scent of the fire, once rustic and cozy, now made her throat twist in nausea. She desperately wanted to escape to the solitude of her bedroom, but without knowing its location, she remained where she was.

Elizabeth followed Charles and Jane into the kitchen to help them make coffee, but they sent her out to the living room with a platter of cheese and chocolates and another bottle of wine. Charles insisted she relax in the living room, the most stressful place in the house at the moment given Caroline and Darcy's presence there. In the living room, Louisa lounged on a leather chair, and Caroline had her legs stretched out on the expensive-looking white sofa. Darcy stood off in a corner, staring out into the darkness of the night. Elizabeth chose a loveseat close to the chocolate, popped a few pieces in her mouth, and drank generously from the glass of Riesling she'd poured herself.

"So," Caroline said, looking at her, "what have you danced before, Elizabeth?"

She sensed that Caroline's conversation was not meant to be friendly. She answered carefully. "Not really anything that memorable. I danced Odile in college and some other contemporary roles overseas."

Caroline glanced towards Darcy in the corner. Elizabeth couldn't see him but could only assume that he'd done something rude like roll his eyes or shake his head.

"College?" she asked. "Where?"

"Well, only for a semester. Butler University. In Indiana."

"And why didn't you finish?"

"I got a job offer from a company in Germany, so I went."

"I see. It's a good thing you did. I can't imagine that very talented dancers come out of college programs." Caroline cast another meaningful look in Darcy's direction. Louisa covered her mouth with her hand and looked away.

Elizabeth inhaled slowly, her insides starting to simmer. The wine had relaxed her inhibitions, and she felt like cursing out Caroline. With torturous self-control, she replied, "I didn't find that to be the case."

"Well, I mean *ballet* dancers. If you want to spend your career in some weird, experimental German company, then I suppose college is fine."

"I'm sure there's nothing wrong with experimental dance companies, Caroline," said Darcy, who'd approached them and leaned his hip against the back of the sofa.

Caroline smiled sweetly at him. "No, *of course* not. What I'm saying is that college isn't really the place for serious professional ballet dancers. Why waste the best years of your career reading stuffy, old books? I'm sure you'd agree with that."

Darcy shrugged.

Then, turning to Elizabeth, Caroline smiled coldly. "Oh, no offense. I'm an avid reader, too, of course. Everyone should read, including dancers."

"Yes," retorted Elizabeth, "there's nothing worse than a dumb ballerina." Darcy cut her a sharp look, which she ignored.

"So, you danced mostly *modern* pieces then?" she asked, trying to rip into Elizabeth from another angle. "A lot of rolling on the floor, that kind of thing?"

"Yes, amongst other things, there was sometimes rolling."

"I've never liked contemporary pieces much. Any savage can flail around on the floor. Wouldn't you agree, Will?"

"I wouldn't go as far as to say that."

"How far would you go?" Elizabeth interjected with a razor's edge of contempt.

Darcy met her eyes and replied in measure. "I would say that many contemporary pieces and most other kinds of modern dance, really, do not require the same kind of technical proficiency required in ballet."

Caroline smiled and turned to her. "There's no use arguing with him. Will's quite firm in his views on dance, aren't you?"

"I have my opinions, yes. But I'm not inflexible."

Elizabeth snorted. "That's not what it sounds like to me."

"Well, I don't think modern dance is just 'rolling around on the floor' as Caroline put it," replied Darcy, "but I do think modern dance has had a decidedly negative influence on ballet."

"Really. How?"

"Technique has been sacrificed for fashion."

"Fashion?"

"Well, rolling, as Caroline put it. Pop music, melodrama."

Elizabeth inhaled to prevent herself from rolling her eyes. "And how are we to prevent the further deterioration of the art form?"

He ignored her sarcasm. "Go back to the basics. More form, more technique, more logic."

"Sounds like every audience's dream. I can see it now: *Robot Lake*," Elizabeth said, miming the unveiling of a marquis.

"Not *Robot Lake*," he countered, the corner of his mouth rising. "Being technical and being robotic are not the same. Right now, there's a lot being sacrificed to please audiences and sell more tickets."

"But don't we dance to please?" asked Elizabeth.

Caroline leaned back on the sofa and smirked at Louisa.

Darcy said, "We dance to express something, not pander to audiences."

"Don't you think we can do both?" countered Elizabeth.

Darcy smiled. "I suppose a true artist can."

Sensing a veiled barb, Elizabeth grew defensive. "I'd love to hear what you think a 'true artist' is."

"Somebody who can do more than just a series of double *fouetté* turns and kick their leg up to their ears. Somebody who understands both music and choreography, who gets human nature, and who feels things keenly. And somebody who hasn't spent her life holed up in a ballet studio. Somebody who has read great books at college and who has seen something of the world."

Elizabeth snorted. "And does this person ride their unicorn to rehearsal?"

"Coffee's ready!" called Charles from the kitchen. "Come and get it!"

Downing the last of her wine, Elizabeth popped up from the sofa. Before she fled to the kitchen, she turned to Darcy and said, "Those seem like pretty impossible standards. I'm surprised you know any 'true' artists at all."

Fifteen minutes later, William walked into the kitchen to see Elizabeth cradling a mug of coffee in both hands. She glanced up at him and then deliberately turned her back and leaned against the kitchen counter.

Charles and Jane stood together next to her, thumbing through a hiking guide.

"Too long for tomorrow?" asked Charles.

"No, it'd be perfect, I think. What do you say, Lizzy?" Jane asked.

"Hm?" Elizabeth took a long distracted sip from her mug.

"Hello, silly! The hike? Is three miles too much?"

"Sorry. Yeah. That's fine."

"Will?" Charles asked.

"Sounds great." The coffee pot was behind Elizabeth on the counter. Darcy grabbed the pot and poured himself a cup. As he replaced it, he brushed Elizabeth's shoulder blade and she flinched.

He stared at her fingers where she held her mug. They were long and delicate, but the nails were bitten to the quick. A smile curved his lips.

"You don't get manicures, do you?" William asked only loud enough for her to hear.

She looked at him strangely.

"Or if you do, Sun-yun doesn't do a very good job."

Elizabeth looked to her fingernails and frowned. "I'm sorry?"

A wicked smirk passed over his face. "There's no Sun-yun, is there?"

He saw recognition light in her eyes. Elizabeth shrugged. "There's no Harlem Nailz."

"And what if she had wanted the business card?"

Cutting him a sideward glance, Elizabeth arched one eyebrow.

"Point taken," he muttered. Caroline hadn't even known what hit her. Although she'd spent the last fifteen minutes gloating over her assumed victory over Elizabeth, Caroline, actually, had been completely bested. He couldn't help but smile.

Just then, Caroline sashayed into the kitchen with her wine glass.

"Coffee, Caroline?" Jane asked.

"Oh, you're sweet. No, I'm here for more vino."

As Caroline selected another bottle from the wine refrigerator, she made sure to bend over in a way that best displayed her ass. William felt a little bad for her then. With her bottle selected, Caroline sidled up to where he was. Having discovered long ago that talking about ballet was the way to get him to open up, Caroline turned the subject of discussion back to dance.

"So, Will, what did you think about my brother's arrangement of *Giselle*?"

William took a sip of coffee before replying. "I think he did a great job. The critics agreed too."

Charles colored and thanked him.

"I made a great Myrna, didn't I?" Caroline popped out the cork of a bottle of pinot noir.

"Ideal," he replied. From the corner of his eye, he noticed Elizabeth smile into her mug. William appreciated that only she had understood his quip.

Caroline glanced over to Elizabeth.

"And what did you think, Elizabeth? It might be nice to hear a perspective from someone on a totally different level than Will and me."

William steeled his face to hide the disgust he felt. Underhanded bullying wasn't his style, but Elizabeth was an adult and could fend for herself. She'd proven it that evening multiple times.

With a graciousness that William never could have mustered, she replied, "I think Charles did an admirable job on a barely tolerable ballet."

"All this flattery," Charles said. "You guys are embarrassing me." Jane beamed up at her boyfriend and rubbed his shoulder.

"Barely tolerable?" William said to Elizabeth. "You're not a fan?"

"*Giselle* isn't my favorite, no."

Caroline gasped melodramatically and shot a look at William. "What?! *Giselle* is one of the great ballets!"

"Lizzy has her opinions," commented Jane, looking heavenwards as if she'd heard this one too many times.

Elizabeth smiled at Jane. "I do love the dancing. And the music. Just not the plot. He's cheating on her. She dies of heartbreak. It's so . . . *melodramatic*. Too many hysterics."

She looked pointedly at William, referring back to their conversation in the living room. *Touché,* he thought. She'd proven her point—that classical ballet wasn't immune to the "hysterics" that he loathed in contemporary pieces—and done it with such finesse, he was more impressed than annoyed.

The corner of his mouth rose. "*Giselle* was never one of my favorites, either."

Caroline paused with the glass of wine halfway to her lips. "And why not?"

William smiled at Elizabeth. "It's every dancer's nightmare: dancing until you die. I can't imagine a worse way to go."

Everyone laughed, including Elizabeth, and he felt something warm in his chest. Caroline turned to Elizabeth. "Isn't he funny?"

Elizabeth said nothing.

"What do you find so distasteful about the ballet?" William asked her.

She considered her answer. "The ending."

"But the ending is beautiful. It's true love," Jane protested.

Elizabeth grimaced. "Albrecht wronged Giselle. He lied to her. He cheated on her. And she let him off the hook? That's not true love! That's battered wife syndrome."

Jane shook her head and hugged her sister. "You're too levelheaded for your own good, Lizzy. It's a story of forgiveness. That's what *makes* it powerful. That Albrecht wronged her, but through the strength of her love, she overcame any hatred and resentment towards him."

"I just don't believe any love can be that powerful."

"Maybe you just don't have any first-hand experience," Caroline said in a way that was both casual and cutting.

Elizabeth reddened from her hairline to where her décolletage disappeared into her sweater. Suppressing his own vicarious embarrassment, William felt the sting of Caroline's remark but itched to know how Elizabeth would respond.

Charles frowned. "Caroline..."

"What? Did I say something?" She muttered a halfhearted apology and then turned the conversation back to her first performance ever as Giselle and her four curtain calls.

The conversation dulled. William realized that, as long as Elizabeth remained sullen and silent, there was really nothing worthwhile to listen to. He tried to follow the thread of their chatter but kept sneaking glances at Elizabeth, who grew more catatonic each minute. She stared blankly at the patterns in the granite countertop, into her coffee cup, and down to the tips of her sneakers. She refused to look at him, at anyone really, and he wondered whether that exciting spark before had been a mere fluke.

"Lizzy, are you okay?" Jane asked suddenly, interrupting Caroline.

"I... I'm fine. I just need a second."

"You sure?"

Elizabeth nodded curtly.

Rolling her eyes, Caroline left the kitchen to return to her friend in the living room. Charles offered to give Jane and Elizabeth a tour of the house. Jane accepted eagerly, and Elizabeth mentioned a headache. Charles began a lengthy explanation of his journey to purchase the property from the previous owners, a story William had heard endless times.

Eyeing Elizabeth again, William noticed her face had paled to a gray-white and wondered why she was so upset about Caroline's comment.

"Ms. Bennet," William said, "the tour is leaving without you."

"I... think I..." she said, waving vaguely in front of her, "I'd rather just not be with anyone at the moment."

He frowned. Was she dismissing him? William straightened, miffed that Elizabeth didn't appreciate his sympathy. His tender feelings melted away like the remains of gray gutter snow. He gave her the liquid nitrogen stare for which he was infamous, and replied, "I've been told to fuck off in nicer ways, but okay, if you need to be alone, I'll—"

Then, she jerked forward, coughed, and then puked all over his fine Italian leather shoes.

Chapter 6

Elizabeth awoke the next morning feeling as if she'd chewed on a bag of cotton balls in her sleep. The room circled around her, her temples pounded, and a powerful wave of nausea sent her head spinning. Luckily, that time, she made it to the bathroom. She gulped down several handfuls of water from the sink and then trudged back to bed.

When she woke up again, she checked the time. It was past noon. She hadn't slept that late since high school. Everything hurt. Her mouth still felt dry, and her stomach lurched. Unfortunately, she had drunk enough wine the night before to have a raging hangover but not enough to have blacked out the humiliation of vomiting on William Darcy's shoes.

Elizabeth groaned. "No."

It was too humiliating. She wanted to cry. Sitting up in bed, the room spun again, and it took her a moment to right her vision. There was a note, a glass of water, and two ibuprofens on the nightstand.

Lizzy,

We went hiking. I figured you'd need to sleep. Take these and get some rest. Charles says help yourself to anything in the kitchen and make yourself some coffee. We'll be back before dinner.

Love,
Jane

Elizabeth swallowed the pills and the entire glass of water. She needed a shower, coffee, and the next train to take her as far away as possible from Charles's cursed Rhinebeck cabin.

The good thing about having his shoes puked on was getting out of hiking and being able to sit inside by a fireplace and read. The bad thing was that William really liked those shoes, but he would just get another pair the next time he was at Barney's.

William hadn't gotten much sleep that night, and it wasn't because of the chaos that had ensued after Elizabeth's accident. He had awakened several times, keenly aware of her presence two doors away. He rolled his eyes. She'd thrown up on his shoes for Christ's sake! Shouldn't he be disgusted with her?

But he wasn't. In fact, at two in the morning, he kept replaying moments of their dinner conversation and smiling to himself when he remembered the funny parts.

What was he doing? It was annoying. Sure, she was pretty, and he was attracted to her as any man would be around a pretty woman, but it was starting to go somewhere that made him nervous. She was too young—the same age as his kid sister. She danced in the *corps de ballet* and was in his piece! His self-imposed hands-off policy forbade him from ever considering a liaison with her.

Yet, in the wee hours of the morning, William had spent a lot of time considering Elizabeth. At three-thirty, he'd gotten up and done a short workout in his room, hoping the exercise would tire him. Then, he started reading his book. By the time the rest of the hiking party was getting dressed, William had been awake for hours, and he refused to go with them. He needed rest. It had nothing to do with the fact that he would be alone in the house with Elizabeth Bennet. Nothing. And to prove that to himself, he hid out in the library, not the kitchen or the living room where he might run into her. Besides, she didn't seem to be awake yet.

At one o'clock in the afternoon, his stomach grumbled, and William took his book to the kitchen to make himself a sandwich. When he got there, however, his heart nearly stopped. With her back turned to him, Elizabeth stood on her tiptoes, reaching for something on a high cabinet shelf. She wore nothing but an oversized sweatshirt that stopped mid-thigh. William tried not to stare, but he couldn't help glimpsing the stretch of bare thighs and lean calves. Her wet hair hung down her back, making a little damp spot at the top of her sweatshirt. When she heard him, Elizabeth whirled around instantly.

"How are you feeling?" William blurted at the same time Elizabeth said,

"I was looking for the coffee."

"Fine," Elizabeth answered at the same time as William said, "Over there."

They both chuckled uncomfortably. William walked over to the right cabinet and took out a canister of coffee. He handed it to her, and she accepted it, unable to make eye contact.

"Thanks," she murmured.

"I'm making myself a sandwich. Want one?"

"No, thanks."

They worked in silence, Elizabeth brewing herself some coffee and William taking out the ingredients for a ham and cheese sandwich from the fridge. With her back facing him, William snuck a look at her legs. He turned around and shook his head.

"Um... I'm really sorry... about your shoes," Elizabeth said suddenly.

"Forget about it. They're just shoes."

A long moment of silence passed between them again.

"I thought you went hiking."

William chuckled. "Someone ruined my shoes."

"You couldn't go hiking in those shoes, could you? They weren't hiking shoes!"

Shrugging, he replied, "I hadn't planned on going hiking anyway. That was Charles's idea, not mine."

"Oh."

Another long silence as Elizabeth spooned coffee into a filter. Once it began brewing, Elizabeth chuckled.

"What?" he asked.

"I was just wondering if I hold the honor of being the only girl to ever barf on you. It's not every day someone like me gets to ruin the shoes of the infallible Mr. Darcy."

She was mocking him again in that way of hers. "Please don't call me Mr. Darcy on a Saturday. And I'm not infallible."

"I was under the impression that you believed yourself one step down from a god." She smirked at him.

"Not one step down. Maybe two or three."

William saw her lips curve faintly. The coffeemaker stopped spurting and gurgling. Grabbing a mug, Elizabeth poured herself coffee and headed his way towards the fridge. She splashed in some milk and took a long sip.

Something about what she just said bothered William. He certainly didn't put on airs in the studio. It was typical *corps de ballet* thinking: *He's strict so it means he's an ass.* He hated that. Elizabeth seemed on the verge of leaving the kitchen, and William didn't want her to go before she understood his point of view.

"I don't admit to being perfect. I just don't think the dance studio is any place to bare all my flaws."

Elizabeth raised an eyebrow and leaned her hip against the counter. "Right. You've *never* demonstrated any insensitivity or self-importance in the studio."

"And what's so wrong with self-importance? What is so wrong with taking pride in yourself, in your work, and holding others to that same standard?"

Elizabeth took a long sip of coffee. "There's nothing wrong with that. But when you take *too* much pride in yourself? Certainly you admit that's a flaw."

"I call it confidence."

"Yes, you're confident that you're better than everyone!" Elizabeth's voice was tinted with an edge that William couldn't fail to catch.

"And you're confident that you're always right without knowing the specifics of a person or a situation."

Elizabeth paused. "Who would have thought you could know me so well in barely a day?"

"My credentials in psychoanalysis are as good as yours."

She shook her head. "Excuse me, Mr. Darcy. I'm not feeling well. I'm heading back to bed."

She breezed past him, leaving William exasperated and titillated at the same time. He sighed in frustration, replaced the sandwich fixings in the refrigerator, and retreated to the library where he spent the remainder of the day until the hikers returned.

Fortunately for both Elizabeth and William, they did not encounter each other anymore that afternoon. Elizabeth remained in her room with her laptop, finishing a paper for the online history course she was taking, and William remained in the library with his book.

The hikers returned exhausted a little before sunset, and they agreed that dinner would be a casual affair. They ordered pizzas and, except for Elizabeth and William, drank wine. As it was the night before, Charles and Caroline led most of the conversation. William glanced over at Elizabeth every so often and noticed that she looked tired. After dinner, she excused herself, saying she wanted to head to sleep early. No one seemed to mind, though her absence disappointed William, who knew he'd have to bear the brunt of Caroline's attention. Jane and Charles, making lover's eyes at each other all night, excused themselves as well, probably so they could have intimate time on their own. That left Caroline and Louisa in the room with him.

Before he could make his escape, Caroline leaned forward and grazed William's hand. "Thank God we don't have to deal with the sister again tonight," she said.

Louisa snorted.

"'The sister' has a name," replied William.

"She was *so* annoying last night. And what she did to your shoes! I would have died."

"Accidents happen."

"I'd be suspect of anyone who showed such little self-control," Caroline continued obliviously. "It's so amateurish."

William repressed an annoyed sigh and said nothing.

"The thing with the German company makes sense though," Louisa offered.

"How so?" asked Caroline.

"The first time I saw her dance, I thought to myself, 'This girl is *so* not Ballet Theater material. How on earth did she get in?'"

Caroline shook her head. "He yells at her at practically every rehearsal, don't you, Will?"

"I don't yell at her. I give her feedback."

"I can't see why you would want to rehearse the *pas de deux* with her. I hope you weren't afraid to ask me, Will. You know I'm always happy to help you."

"I'll keep that in mind."

"I wish Charles hadn't asked her to come. She really brought down the whole weekend."

No longer able to control his anger, William replied, "Actually, it was good getting to know Elizabeth. She's smart and handles herself with grace, which is more than I can say for others I know."

"If you say so, William," replied Louisa with a wrinkle of her nose.

It was all he could take. Sighing, he stood. "I think it's time for me to get some sleep. I'm getting on the road early tomorrow. I need to be back in the city for an engagement." It was a spur-of-the-moment lie. The only engagement he had was reading the Sunday paper with his cat.

Caroline pouted. "Well, if you go, I'm getting out of here early tomorrow, too. No way I'm sticking around with those three. Louisa?"

"Sounds good to me. As long as I don't have to wake up early."

William nodded. "I'll see you in the studio on Tuesday then. Good night."

As he headed back to his room, William felt immense relief. He wanted to go home. He couldn't stand to be under the same roof as Caroline and Louisa anymore. He couldn't stand to feel constantly annoyed by and jealous of the syrupy goings-on between Charles and Jane. And he couldn't stand to feel constantly depraved by the thoughts he was having about Elizabeth. All he wanted was the escape of solitude: somewhere he could sip coffee and read without the need to constantly pantomime interest when he felt none and indifference when he felt anything but.

Chapter 7

Elizabeth noticed him the instant he stepped into the Dance Rhythm studio: chiseled, shirtless, gorgeous. She looked at him in the mirror during warm-ups and as he snaked across the floor in every combination of the Afro-Carribbean dance class. Although she only sporadically attended these classes on Mondays, her day off, she thought she knew all the regulars: Maddie, tall, brash, with cappuccino skin and washboard abs; Keyshia, short, round, with dreads and hips that could tell a novel-length story in the way they swayed and curved; Alexa in her signature tie-dyed head scarf and mismatched sarong. She didn't recognize him though he seemed to know many of them. The man—demigod, really—laughed, hugged, and playfully pinched several of the dancers on his way across the studio.

Then, he noticed her and kept noticing her as their teacher swept in and the drum players began with the slow, low beats of warm-up.

She caught his eyes on her in the mirror. They grazed across her lazily. Elizabeth tried not to stare back, but sometimes she looked, and sometimes he caught her looking. After a combination across the floor that involved a lot of hip-thrusting and shoulder-shaking, she saw him flash a crooked, sexy smile that revealed the dimple in his left cheek. Elizabeth's stomach dropped, and she returned the smile shyly.

Normally, the frenzied drumming swept her up in its rhythm, transporting her out of her head and into the solid presence of her body. That feeling of utter "here-ness" explained her craving for those Afro-Carribbean classes, even though they were exhausting and expensive. That day, however, she felt discombobulated. When the final drums crashed, signaling the end of class, Elizabeth could barely catch her breath. Doubled-over, she panted heavily. Her high-necked leotard was soaked with sweat. Stumbling to the side of the room, she chugged from her water bottle and choked when she heard a melted-chocolate voice from behind.

"You're good... for a ballerina."

Coughing for a few seconds before she could reply, Elizabeth thought she would die from embarrassment as the shirtless hottie smiled at her. Finally, she eked out, "How could you tell I was a ballerina?"

His smile deepened and Elizabeth's pulse pitter-pattered at the sight of that dimple.

"I can spot them a mile away."

"It must take one to know one."

"Busted," he said, laughing. He really was a gorgeous man: green-eyed, corded-shouldered, a hint of dark stubble across his chin and jaw. He toweled sweat off his pecs. "Where do you dance?"

"Ballet Theater of New York."

His eyes widened. "I'm impressed that a ballerina of your caliber would be here gettin' down."

Elizabeth laughed throatily. "Guess I can do a lot more than strut around in a tutu."

The man's smile deepened. "I'll say."

If it were possible, Elizabeth warmed even more. He looked her body up and down, and feeling brazen, she subtly arched her shoulders to improve the view.

"So where do you dance?" she asked.

"A few companies here and there," he replied, seeming less interested in that line of conversation. It took him a few seconds too long to tear his eyes away from her chest. "I just moved back here a few weeks ago and haven't found work yet."

"And where were you before?"

"All over. I do a lot of hip-hop, so L.A. for a bit, Miami for a few years. But New York is home. What about you?"

Swinging her dance bag over her shoulder, Elizabeth replied, "I'm originally from a town in Michigan no one's ever heard of."

"The Midwest, huh? I hear the girls are naughty up there."

"Yes, very. Smoking pot behind the movie theater, buying forties at the gas station with a fake ID. Very, very naughty."

The man smiled, his green eyes on Elizabeth's face in a way that made her cheeks burn.

"What's your name?"

"Elizabeth."

"Elizabeth from Ballet Theater of New York. Are you going to give me a last name, or are you going to make me Google you?"

Laughing, Elizabeth told him her full name and asked for his.

"It's Greg. Greg Wickham," he said, extending a hand. "Very pleased to meet you, Elizabeth Bennet."

"My friends call me Lizzy."

"Are we friends?"

"Seems that way."

"Okay, then, Lizzy. How about a friendly coffee?"

Elizabeth blinked. Was this really happening? A sexy, luscious man asking her for coffee? Things like this didn't happen to her.

"Sure. When do you have in mind?"

"How 'bout now?"

Oh. My. God, thought Elizabeth, as everything in her turned warm and wet. She took a long sip of water. "Give me ten minutes to change."

Greg agreed, and Elizabeth made sure to stride cool and confident from the studio because she knew he was looking.

They sat at a table in a coffee shop, Elizabeth sipping a latté and Greg a chai tea. Too nervous to sustain chitchat, Elizabeth kept running out of things to say. The way Greg looked at her unnerved her. Unless they were flirtatiously bantering or talking about dance, there seemed to be nothing to say. Their conversation dripped with innuendo. Still, who needed to talk when you could stare and drool? Elizabeth couldn't help stealing glances at their reflections in the window. Greg leaned casually back in his chair, his dark hair falling into his eyes, and a tight black t-shirt doing everything for that glorious expanse of chest. *Holy crap,* thought Elizabeth, *every girl in this place is staring.* When he started running the tip of his finger lightly over Elizabeth's knuckles, she thought she would break into a slow pant.

"I have a confession," Greg said suddenly, smiling into his drink.

Elizabeth's eyes widened. Oh, no. This was it. She knew it had been too perfect. What could it be? He was broke and needed to borrow a couple hundred dollars? Or, he was already seeing someone? Or, he was gay?

"I actually danced at Ballet Theater," he said.

Elizabeth exhaled and then smiled in relief. "You did? When?"

"Long time ago. Ten years? Maybe less. I was there when little Carrie Bingley was in the *corps de ballet* and Charlie was a soloist."

"You know Caroline Bingley?"

"Knew her. Real bitch, even then."

Elizabeth threw her head back and laughed.

"Charles was a good guy, though," Greg continued. "Don't know what happened with the DNA of those two."

Elizabeth smiled. "Charles is dating my sister. She's in Ballet Theater, too."

"No kidding?" Greg said. "Who else is there that I would know?"

"William Darcy?" The name came to Elizabeth's head like a bubble popping up to the surface of a lake, and she blurted it out unthinkingly.

Greg inhaled slowly. "Yes, William Darcy was there," he said slowly, his eyes darting down to his lap.

"And was he just as pompous then as he is now?"

Greg looked up, the reservation in his eyes wholly changed. "So, he's still an asshole?"

Elizabeth nodded. "Guess some things don't change much."

"No, they don't. He was already a principal dancer when I got in to the *corps de ballet*. The ego was alive and well then, too. In fact, he—well, maybe I shouldn't say this."

"Trust me, Greg. There will be no love lost between Mr. Darcy and me."

"Okay, Darcy was the reason I stopped dancing at Ballet Theater."

Elizabeth emptied the last of her latté down her throat. "Why?"

"Why? Hm... here's the short version. I was a pretty good dancer. When I got into the company, they were already talking about promoting me to soloist. Of course, you know Darcy's ego. He was the best, and he didn't want anyone beating him. I guess he felt threatened by me, but he made my life in the company a living hell."

Elizabeth frowned. "What'd he do?"

"Oh, petty stuff like bumping into me during exercises. But there were other things... a few incidents. Plus, he knows people—people who donate a lot of money to Webster Lucas and his company. I crossed Darcy, and the next year they didn't renew my contract."

Elizabeth was stunned.

"Well, as you can imagine, once you've been fired from Ballet Theater, it's kinda hard to find work in New York. No one wants to hire you. Word spreads fast. So I had to move out to L.A. to find work."

"Wow," Elizabeth said, finally regaining her voice. "I knew he was a jerk, but I didn't realize he could sink that low."

"He's got powerful allies, Lizzy. His godmother is Catherine Boroughs. Lucas eats out of the palm of Boroughs' hand. Plus the Bingleys, the Netherfields, the Tisches, the Rockefellers—they're all old friends of his family. You think in America we don't have an aristocracy, but you're wrong. William Darcy belongs to a rare breed of New York blue bloods whose heads are still back in nineteenth-century England."

Elizabeth could only shake her head. "Incredible. I never knew."

"Not many people do."

"How do you?"

Greg leaned in to Elizabeth, his green eyes piercing. "I've danced with William Darcy ever since we were kids. We went to the same dance studio. Even though I was four years his junior, I was just as good as he was. He's been jealous of me since I was eight years old."

Elizabeth could scarcely believe this. William Darcy didn't seem like the type to react with jealous wrath. He regarded himself too highly to be envious of others. His narcissism spared him the insecurities that would have led others to jealousy. Apparently, however, she did not know him as well as she believed.

The conversation continued on a separate subject. Elizabeth spent the next hour with Greg until he left for a lunch date with a friend. Before that, he asked for Elizabeth's number, which she happily provided. He promised to call sometime that week and take her to dinner. They parted ways with a kiss on the cheek, Greg walking downtown, Elizabeth walking west to get back on the subway.

She had met a funny, charming, handsome, and—by all outward appearances—straight man in New York City. Plus, he was a dancer. Elizabeth nearly skipped to the subway, her face full up to the tops of the buildings.

Yet, an unidentifiable sensation chewed at her at the same time. On the subway ride back up to Harlem, Elizabeth thought of Greg Wickham and

William Darcy the entire time.

AT REHEARSAL LATER THAT WEEK, William noticed that Elizabeth could hardly focus. He was frustrated at having to explain arm movements that she should have instinctively understood. Only a month stood between then and the piece's debut at the spring world premiere. William hadn't even finished half of it.

"No," he growled, when she once again missed the rhythm for the jump before the lift. "You're going to get dropped if you jump like that."

"*I'm* not going to get dropped," she grumbled. "That'll be Caroline."

"You're the one dancing now!" he said. "Stay focused, Ms. Bennet. I'm not going to be responsible for any injuries."

When Elizabeth only stared at him with silent disdain, he sighed. "Let's try it again."

Standing behind Elizabeth, William placed his hands on the sides of her rib cage and waited for her to perform the jump leading up to a lift that would have her sitting eight feet up in the air balanced only on his palm. Elizabeth concentrated and jumped. William reacted to her rhythm and lifted her off the ground. With his arms, he propelled her upwards, trying to get her over his head. He felt her wobble and jerk to the left suddenly.

"Whoa!" she cried, falling out of his grasp. Luckily, William caught her with ease, seizing her with his left hand and pulling her to his body to break the fall.

Elizabeth buried her face in his chest. He felt her breath rising and falling fast against him. Several seconds later, she pushed herself away, her expression fearful.

"Crap," she whispered, rubbing her eyes with the tips of her fingers.

William simply stood there, not quite sure what to do. The fall had been her fault. She hadn't trusted him and wavered on the lift. Had she gone straight up, she wouldn't have fallen. Any experienced dancer knew this. Yet, as she stood before him trembling, how was he supposed to tell her that?

Elizabeth was shaking. As a choreographer, he felt responsible for pointing out her mistakes. Another part of him, however, a part that went beyond a mere choreographer, wanted to keep her against his chest until she stopped trembling. William swallowed and dismissed that thought swiftly.

"Why didn't you trust me?" he asked her harshly.

Elizabeth exhaled and dropped her hands. She stared at him with flames crackling in her eyes, a look so familiar to him by now.

"So this is my fault?" she asked.

"You have to trust your partner completely."

"*You* dropped me."

"You fell."

Elizabeth's chest rose with the long inhalation of breath she took. Her hands were still trembling. William studied her coolly, wanting to continue but knowing it was fruitless. Something was wrong with Elizabeth today. She wasn't dancing as well as she normally did.

"I think we'd better finish here," he said.

Elizabeth immediately turned away and headed towards the side of the room. Sitting, she began unraveling her pointe shoe ribbons.

William slowly paced towards her. "What's wrong with you today?"

"Nothing." She avoided eye contact.

"Your dancing was off."

She shrugged petulantly. God, he hated it when she did childish things like that.

Spinning on his heel, he stalked away. "Fine, I'll see you tomorrow."

She left the studio quickly, not bothering to say good-bye to him. William watched her in the mirror as she left and then groaned in exasperation. Knots of panic gripped his stomach, and he worried that the piece would never be finished. The first and third movements, thank God, were choreographed and blocked. The fourth movement was nearly all choreographed and just needed to be taught to the dancers. It was the damned *pas de deux* that kept him up at night.

The problem was Elizabeth Bennet. William would go home at night and wring out the steps in the solitude of his studio, but when he brought it to Elizabeth in rehearsal, she changed the quality of the movement so completely that it made everything he had accomplished the previous night dull and inferior. Basically, he was winging his choreography with her, though he would never tell her that, and when she had bad days like this one, it set him further back.

"Damn," he groaned, rubbing his face. Standing, he gathered his things, headed to his office, and packed up. He figured he would stop at La Fiore for an order of the gnocchi to go and then try to finish the rest of the *pas de deux* that evening, so he could finally start teaching it to Caroline and Ben in rehearsals that week.

He pushed open the door to the building, and the frigid air whipped his face. William stepped out, his hands deep in the pockets of his favorite brown suede coat. Then, he stopped. Elizabeth stood outside, too. She turned to see who it was, and William felt his breath catch when those sharp eyes bored into him with an intensity he couldn't quite place.

Her hair was pulled into a high ponytail, her face was made up, and she wore—he was surprised to note—black leather high-heeled boots.

"I thought you would have gone home by now," William said, ignoring the thrum of desire that was coursing through him.

"I'm waiting for someone." She looked down the block.

He made no immediate reply, simply choosing to stare. "Are you going somewhere?" he finally asked.

Elizabeth glanced up at him. "Yes, in fact, I have a date."

"A date," he repeated. "Well, have fun."

He turned and then froze. There in front of him stood Greg Wickham. Stunned, William could only stare dumbly. Greg's eyes met William's for a brief second before he cast them over to Elizabeth.

"Hey, Lizzy." His face broke into a smile.

"Hello to you, too," she responded with a warmth that William rarely heard.

"William," Greg said. A hint of spite lay under his tone, as fine and sharp as a razor's edge.

He felt his stomach turn cold, and his eyesight go red at the tone behind Wickham's words. William straightened and fixed Greg with a look of disgust and rage. Brushing past Elizabeth, he saw her look at him in confusion, but he didn't care. He just needed to get the hell out of there.

William's head swam, flashing back months, years, decades, building fury that pressed against his rib cage. He thought of Upper East Side Dance Academy, of playing hide-and-go-seek in Central Park, of BTNY classes, of a tutu, of Caroline Bingley, of Miami, of his sister, his mother, of lawyers' offices and a courtroom, of that fucking piece of shit, of all the ways he wanted to beat his face in. Why had he been there? What was he doing with Elizabeth?

Elizabeth. His thoughts stopped. He stopped. Looking up, William realized he'd walked nine blocks in the wrong direction. His breathing came fast and shallow. Closing his eyes, he ran his hands over his face and took deep breaths to calm himself. An old woman walking a shih tzu stared at him as if he were dangerous and moved as far away from him on the sidewalk as she could. William stepped to the curb and hailed a cab.

Sitting in the confines of the car, he watched the scenery of a New York City Tuesday night rush by. He thought of the smug look on Greg Wickham's face, and he thought of Elizabeth. His chest hurt as if he'd fallen five floors onto the pavement. William thought Greg had finally disappeared—finally, after years of screwing over William and his family. But for him to reappear so suddenly and to reappear with Elizabeth . . . Someone up there must truly loathe him, William thought, unless Greg had sought her out on purpose to screw with him. But that was impossible. There was nothing to screw with. No one, not even Charles, knew about his feelings for Elizabeth.

He smiled bitterly as he caught his reflection in the window. In a city of eight million, why her? There must have been at least two million lonely, single women in New York City. Why did Greg Wickham have to somehow impossibly find *her*?

Chapter 8

Catherine Boroughs hailed from a *very* rich, *very* respectable, and *very* old Manhattan family. Having no need for the inconvenience of paid work, she did what was expected of an heiress: She bought enough antique art to fill her six homes around the world. She belonged to three country clubs. She had her name on wings in a hospital, museum, and library. She fixed her face, neck, and stomach—twice, actually, but that was her secret. She'd sent her daughter, now thirty years old, to the best private school in Manhattan and hired the best nannies and au pairs to help raise her. And she supported the arts.

"No one in New York City appreciates the arts as much as I," she often said with an affected accent. Catherine was a Platinum Rung benefactor for the Metropolitan Opera, the New York Philharmonic, and the New York City Ballet. She had sat on the board of trustees for all of the major New York arts institutions at least once during the past twenty years of her career as philanthropist. She had a scholarship at the Julliard School named after her.

Arts administrators worshipped and feared her. One misstaged opera, one ill-chosen season line-up, and Catherine could withdraw her favor and her million dollar gifts, sending a company's finances into disarray for years. Artistic directors despised her. Catherine believed her donations were like an investment in a corporation and that her money entitled her to artistic input. The blessing of her wealth and background, she felt, endowed her with artistic sensibility, despite any lack of training.

Charles found himself despising her again that evening. Spinning his chair around to face the window, he sighed and read the memo again.

Big C strikes again. Threatened to pull her gift if A.B. doesn't get promoted. Will she work in any of next season's rep? Let's think about this seriously!! -W.L.

Attached to the memo were two headshots: Jane Bennet and Anne Boroughs, daughter of Catherine and perhaps the most uninspiring ballerina in the company. Two dancers up for one soloist slot.

It was tradition to announce the names of new soloists and principals at the Netherfield Gala, a Ballet Theater tradition that kicked off the company's spring season a little over a month away. At the gala, the company's most generous benefactors hobnobbed at a lavish reception in the Netherfield Hotel, all done in the name of getting New York's wealthiest to open up their checkbooks and donate. If the gala evening weren't enough, the company opened up rehearsals that week to benefactors and provided them a front-row seat at company-only dress rehearsals before the season opening. That week alone raked in millions of dollars in donations for the company, and thus, no expense was spared. This year, William Darcy's piece would premiere, and the guest list already surpassed anything the company had ever seen. Everyone who was anyone in the New York performing arts scene would be there.

As the end of February approached, the dressing rooms had become rife with speculation about promotions. Everyone pinned Jane Bennet for the only soloist role opening up. She was consistently dancing soloist roles in the major ballets and understudied principal dancer roles as well.

Despite Jane's achievements, however, other voices whispered that, of course, she was a shoo-in for soloist since she was screwing the assistant artistic director. Charles knew of these opinions; his sister chided him every night about them, and he figured her voice was chief amongst the gossip.

But Anne Boroughs? Charles could never credibly pass up Jane to promote Anne. Mousy and lethargic, Anne had languished in the *corps de ballet* for nearly eight years. Anne's dancing was acceptable, but had no verve. Indeed, the only reason she had gotten into the company in the first place was due to her mother's money. Anne Boroughs as soloist? No one, neither the dancers nor the audiences, would be able to swallow that one.

Charles rubbed his eyes with his thumb and forefinger. He loathed this part of the job. He just wanted to create ballets for a world-class dance company, but too often, politics and money got in the way. He wanted Jane Bennet promoted, but Lucas would never approve, not when Catherine Boroughs and her donations were at stake.

Never one to deal with conflict well, Charles threw the memo beneath a stack of paperwork. Tomorrow. He would think about it tomorrow.

ELIZABETH FLOATED INTO HER APARTMENT to find Jane lounging on the sofa. The older sister looked up and smiled. "Well, how was it?"

Sighing, Elizabeth threw her bag down with an exaggerated sweep of her hand and then twirled and jumped into the living room. Jane giggled. Finally, Elizabeth turned and finished with an overdone plop into the couch.

"Wonderful, spectacular, marvelous!" she answered.

"Ready to marry him yet?"

Elizabeth wrinkled her nose. "I'm not ready to marry anyone. But I'd definitely like to get him in bed."

"Did he kiss good?" Jane asked, leaning in towards Elizabeth.

"Oh yeah! It should be a crime for a man to kiss that good."

Jane giggled. "Ooh, tell me everything! Where did you go? What did you talk about?"

Kicking off her shoes, Elizabeth tucked her feet under herself. "Well, he took me to an Italian restaurant in TriBeCa where he knew one of the waiters. Real swanky. We talked about everything, Jane! About dance, about you, about... about William Darcy." Elizabeth rolled her eyes.

"About William?"

"Yeah, he told me everything. Darcy's rotten, Jane. You wouldn't believe some of the stuff Greg told me."

Jane frowned, not making any reply.

"Okay, first, he comes from the most conceited family on the East Coast. You should have *heard* the way they treat their maids, the people they've bribed with their money! Greg says Darcy's sister is a royal brat. She got a Louis Vuitton purse for her twelfth birthday and a BMW when she turned sixteen. Who gets a Beemer when they're sixteen? Oh, and— What?"

Jane's face had fallen into an expression halfway between disapproval and disbelief. "I don't mean to contradict you or tell you you're wrong or anything, but it just seems so... unexpected."

"Unexpected? How?"

"William is a little severe, but he doesn't seem cruel. And Charles says the best things about him. He always gushes to me about William. You know what they say: you can judge a person by his friends. Charles is great. Why would he associate with a slimeball?"

Elizabeth sighed. "You've seen Caroline, haven't you?"

"Family's different, Lizzy."

Elizabeth waved Jane's comment away. "Why would Greg lie? From all of my interactions with Mr. Darcy, I don't doubt Greg for one second. Darcy is pretentious, he's rude, and worst of all, he's a horrible person."

Jane shrugged and swiftly changed the subject to plans for a next date. Elizabeth replied that there weren't any, but she was thinking of asking Greg to the Netherfield Gala. All talk of William Darcy, fortunately, died amid a heated debate about the propriety of a woman asking a man out to a black-tie affair. They finally concluded that in the twenty-first century such endeavors could be undertaken, and it was decided that Elizabeth would ask Greg to be her date to the gala.

William stared at himself in the full-length mirror of the studio. He had been trying to choreograph all night, yet the steps would not come. Listening to the music over and over again did nothing to help. He simply ended up thinking about Elizabeth's body, her eyes, her lips. In fact, trying to work on this piece and not think of her was nearly impossible.

How had this happened? William ran both hands through his hair and turned off the stereo. Shutting off the lights in the studio, he walked down the hall of his apartment towards the kitchen. His orange tabby, Austin, lounged on the counter. She stood and stretched her front legs when her master appeared.

"What have I told you about the kitchen counter?" he said, scooping up the cat and placing her on the tile. It mewed in response.

"Don't talk back."

Austin purred and nudged William's ankle with her soft head. Chuckling, William wondered why all women couldn't be as compliant as his little cat. He sighed, thinking of Elizabeth again. Getting himself a glass of water, William leaned on the kitchen counter and let his mind wander to her.

Her eyes, the color of olives, her supple body, nimble movements, her legs poking out from under Charles's sweatshirt, her thighs, what it might be like to run his hands up those thighs. And her voice: rich, throaty, and warm. But not for him—for that cretin, Greg Wickham. William took a long sip of water, quenching the dryness in his mouth.

He felt a tidal wave of anger rip through him again. This June would mark one year since he had last seen Greg Wickham walking out of the courtroom, and his fury had hardly cooled since then. How did a man like that manage to rope in all of the women who mattered to William? First, his mother, then his sister, and now Elizabeth.

William froze and swallowed another mouthful of water.

Does Elizabeth matter to me? he asked himself.

"No," he said out loud, giving Austin pause in the midst of her tongue bath.

The word rang false in his ears even as he spoke it. For weeks, William had been able to admit his physical attraction for Elizabeth. He admired her dancing. He respected her resolve and her sense of humor. Not many dancers her age thought beyond physical steps. She did. She thought about music and expression. Elizabeth had been in the world and wasn't a sheltered bunhead like so many dancers.

But she was so young. She sometimes made poor choices involving too much wine. She had a mouth on her. She was a *corps* dancer. And she was in his piece.

But he wanted her, and that said something. He hadn't cared enough about any woman to want her this badly in a long time. For the past few years, his life had been nothing but dance and choreography. And it still was. The problem was that, every time he tried to dance, every time he tried to choreograph, Elizabeth was there.

William laughed at the absurdity of it. A muse. They only existed in Greek myths and Broadway musicals. He had enough experience, enough talent, and enough passion to choreograph without the help of a twentysomething *corps* girl. Yet, here he was, genuflecting at the altar of Elizabeth Bennet. He got in a studio with her and felt his senses burst alive. He touched her and created minutes of choreography. He watched her dance and wanted to possess her.

William could admit all of that to himself. He could admit that, perhaps, it was the reason for his despair that evening because Greg Wickham had, yet again, gotten something William wanted. It was jealousy and bitterness and past resentments that had very little, really, to do with Elizabeth Bennet.

In fact, to prove to himself that it wasn't really about her, William resolved that he was through with her. The season premiere was fast approaching, and he needed to begin teaching the steps to Caroline and Ben. Starting tomorrow, there would be no more private rehearsals with Elizabeth Bennet.

He was William Darcy. He didn't need a muse.

Chapter 9

The next day William strode into the studio with purpose. He did not seek out Elizabeth Bennet, didn't even care that she was in the room.

He moved to the stereo. "Good afternoon, everyone. Caroline and Ben, we're going to begin the *pas de deux*."

Even then, he refused to scan the room for her. It felt empowering to know that he could do this on his own, just as he had done for years. A wave of relief fueled his manic zest.

William paired up the principal dancers. Off to the side, the *corps de ballet* stretched, sipped on water bottles, whispered quietly amongst themselves, or watched the dance.

Caroline stared at him with cat eyes, alert and calculating, as William talked through the first few steps. Then, he saw her scan the room through the reflection in the mirror. Her eyes stopped in one corner where a few *corps* members sat stretching their legs. She zeroed in on Elizabeth. For the first time in that rehearsal, William glanced at her too and pushed down the squirming in his stomach.

"Okay, let's just try that much," William said, turning back to the principal dancers. Caroline leaned into Ben's arms and repeated the steps Elizabeth had executed so many times. But everything about them seemed wrong —Caroline's timing, her expression, the sterile accuracy of her movements. She danced too literally, without any nuance. William frowned.

"No, there needs to be a lift before you arch back… No, that's too big; it's not a *port de bras*. It's a breath."

Caroline laughed. "What? You're not making any sense."

"It does make sense," he growled, looking at the back of the room. He saw that chatty brunette kneeling next to Elizabeth, whispering. He pushed down his annoyance.

"Try it again, and really *listen* to the music," William said as he turned towards the stereo.

When Darcy started marking out the steps for Caroline and Ben, several sets of eyes darted to Elizabeth. There were Jane's, scandalized. There were Lydia's, teasing. There were Charlotte's, astonished. And there were Caroline's, yellow and slicing.

Now that Elizabeth could see the *pas de deux* from a distance, she understood the looks. Despite Caroline's wooden execution, Ben's preference for men, and the fact that they shared no sexual attraction for each other, the choreography radiated eroticism. Now everyone knew that *this* was what transpired when she'd been alone with Darcy all those afternoons in the studio. It hadn't felt flirtatious when she'd been with him, but that's not how others interpreted it.

Lydia skooched over to Elizabeth and whispered, "Who knew Bach could be this sexy?"

Elizabeth arched an eyebrow at her friend.

"Must have been fun working with him on this," Lydia said.

"A riot," responded Elizabeth.

Caroline and Ben tried the opening bars again. Studying them, Elizabeth sensed that something was off. Caroline tried to get her *arabesque* as high as possible which made her miss the natural breath that the violins took in the first bar. It was an important breath though because it was the moment her partner first reached for her and the push-pull tension between the couple started to build. Without Caroline acknowledging that breath, the remaining steps didn't flow into each other, and the timing became stunted.

Elizabeth instinctually checked for Darcy's reaction. He glanced at her too, his face placid. But she could imagine the frustration he felt because she felt it, too. She looked away and pursed her lips.

Caroline and Ben reached the end of the steps.

"You're still not getting the timing right, Caroline," Darcy said. Pausing, he glanced over at Elizabeth again, considering something. His expression changed. "Ms. Bennet, will you come here, please?"

All of the dancers stared at Elizabeth. The room went silent. Taken off guard, Elizabeth tried to clear the look of surprise from her face. She took a shaky breath, pushed herself off the floor, and walked warily to the center of the studio.

It was an act of desperation. Caroline just didn't understand what he wanted. He saw rehearsal time draining away while he tried to make her understand the musicality of the phrase. Panic gripped him. Despite himself, William needed Elizabeth's help.

She avoided Caroline's glare as she approached, hands twisting, eyes radiating an expression somewhere between fear, confusion, and murder. With a slight nod, William tried to send her a wordless signal of reassurance.

"Will you demonstrate the movement quality in the opening sequence, please?" he asked softly.

William nodded towards Ben, indicating Elizabeth was to perform the steps with him. Raising the corners of his lips, Ben attempted to calm the obviously flustered *corps* dancer. Throwing a last look in William's direction, Elizabeth returned Ben's hesitant smile and then stepped into the *arabesque.*

"Fine. Now, after the *développé* front, you fall back," William said to Caroline, who looked icily at the demonstrating dancers.

Elizabeth complied, and Ben caught her well enough, but she wobbled slightly. His grip was far less stable than William's. They eked out the steps, Caroline's eyes slicing into Elizabeth the whole time. She clearly did not appreciate receiving dance lessons from a member of the *corps de ballet.* William talked Caroline through the steps as Elizabeth and Ben performed them. But even when William turned the *pas de deux* back over to the two principal dancers, their dancing still fell short of the image in William's head. As the opening sequence, this phrase would either capture the audience's attention for the next five minutes or give them an excuse to catch a brief nap. These steps needed to be perfect.

"No," he sighed. He looked to the floor in obvious frustration, and as he looked up, caught Elizabeth's gaze. His breath hitched. For the first time since he'd known her, she looked to him with sympathy, a beautiful, calming look of compassion. She understood his frustration. He raised the corner of his mouth in a resigned smile, visible to no one but her.

"Watch us do it with the music." William gestured from himself to

Elizabeth. "You all watch the dynamics. It's not about the steps, it's about the dynamics."

He started the music and then returned to the center of the room. The speakers crackled. Caroline and Ben fell back, fire radiating from Caroline's eyes. It was so silent in the studio, they could hear laughter from the halls.

The first plucked notes of the violins began. Elizabeth stepped into William's hands and began to dance. She performed the first steps tentatively, still shy in front of her peers. William sensed her nervousness. When she fell back into him, he squeezed her sides and whispered in her ear.

"Relax, Elizabeth."

Elizabeth exhaled slowly, melting into his hands. He felt her acquiesce and forget the room. She danced, and it was perfect. Caught in the momentum of the music, they continued.

The disastrous lift approached, but Elizabeth showed no signs of stopping. When she jumped, he vaulted her up. She wobbled, but then steadied herself. Slowly lowering her to the final pose of what had been choreographed so far, William caught the expression on Elizabeth's face. She bit her lip, concealing a satisfied grin. William's head swam with gratification and pride. And suddenly, he understood what he'd been denying for weeks: *I'm in love with her.*

As if those in the room consented, they applauded lightly.

William studied Elizabeth carefully. She stood in the center of the studio, arms akimbo and panting from exertion. Muse or not, he loved her. He felt giddy, high, strong. Dancing with her felt like the best sex he'd ever had. Even better, actually, because the pleasure wasn't just carnal, it was aesthetic, too.

"Like that," he said brusquely and returned to the stereo to re-cue the music. "Thank you, Ms. Bennet," he added without looking at her. She received more light applause, and he heard her jog back to the side of the room.

Caroline and Ben performed the sequence with far more vigor than before, and while it still wasn't perfect, William found it acceptable enough to end rehearsal. His heart continued to hammer in his chest, and he dismissed them all, craving solitude and calm.

Elizabeth lingered anyway, purposely avoiding Caroline Bingley. Some of the dancers complimented Elizabeth on their way out, but more shot her puzzled or cutting stares. Once the high of her performance wore off, she recognized those looks. The other dancers' jealous stares burned off

Elizabeth's joy. She tried to ignore them, but her stomach twisted inside.

Once everyone had left, Elizabeth went to the door and shut it. Standing at the front of the room, Darcy turned at the sound. She leaned against the door as she spoke.

"I don't think that was such a great idea," she said to him.

Darcy dismissed her concern with a wave of his hand. "Caroline and Ben wouldn't have gotten it unless we'd shown them."

"And will they ever, do you think?"

Darcy furrowed his eyebrows. "I'm not sure."

"Then please don't single me out like that."

Darcy allowed a silence to pass between them. Without anger to shield her, she found she could not look at him directly. Elizabeth stared down at her feet.

Then, he said, "I'm curious to know why you don't want to be singled out. Any other *corps de ballet* dancer would claw her way through half the company to be in your shoes."

There it was—that arrogance. And suddenly, like a gust of cool wind, anger inflated Elizabeth's sails. "What does *that* mean?"

"It means it's not everyday that—"

"Someone like *you* would even consider someone like me?"

Darcy opened his mouth and then quickly shut it, apparently censoring himself before making his reply. "I'm not going to lie to you, Ms. Bennet. Someone in my position typically doesn't give someone in your position the treatment I've given—"

"I knew—"

"But you're a good dancer," he insisted before she could say anything else, "and so I don't see what the problem is."

He had never complimented her before. The curses died on her lips. Shaking her head, she tried to show restraint.

"Mr. Darcy, I'm sure *you* would be the first to admit that dance companies are full of petty jealousies—full of politics." She thought of Greg Wickham as she spoke.

"Yes, that's true."

"And that some dancers, motivated by jealousy, will do anything to cut down a younger, upcoming dancer?"

"What are you getting at?"

"Caroline Bingley is a viper, and there are others in this room who aren't much better. I'm sure *you* realize the kinds of things they would do to me." She again referred subtly to the way Darcy had sabotaged Greg's career.

"They won't do anything to you because, if they did, they'd find themselves out of a job."

Elizabeth could only think of Greg, who'd found himself out of a job because of Darcy's prejudice and pettiness. William Darcy wielded the power to fire people, and he used it indiscriminately. Incensed, she spat, "Do you really think..."

He stood without warning and strode to her with such intent that the words faded in her mouth.

"Let's not do this right now," he said. "I know Caroline. She won't do anything because she knows I'm standing behind you."

Bewildered, Elizabeth could only stare up at him. Was he standing behind her? With the way he constantly criticized and demeaned her, it didn't seem like it.

"You saw what it looked like today, Elizabeth. You have to— I need you to show them."

His voice took on a plaintive timber that she'd never heard before. It was low and soft. He had said her name, Elizabeth—not Ms. Bennet—and she became frightened because he took one step closer to her. Kissing distance. Darcy stared at her mouth. Instinctively, Elizabeth licked her lips and pursed them. His eyes were smoldering like gray, long-burning coals, the same way they did when he choreographed. She swallowed, trying to moisten her parchment-dry mouth and throat. He was going to kiss her.

She knew he was a bastard, that she should recoil or at least not encourage him, but those sensuous, bowed lips did nothing for her resolve. He was going to kiss her, and as if passing a roadside collision, she couldn't look away. His hand reached out to her, and as Elizabeth wondered what his lips would feel like over her own, he did something she never expected.

He patted her shoulder.

He *patted* her *shoulder*? Twice, in fact. Like a T-ball coach would pat his pitcher before the other team's star hitter went up to bat. Startled, Elizabeth looked down at his hand and back up to his face.

"Ms. Bennet?"

"Uh... I'm sorry... What?" she stammered.

"Don't quit," he said. "Not yet."

She shook her head and swallowed again. It took her a moment to answer, and when she did, it came out caustically. "Okay, fine. Whatever."

"Thanks," he said, the light in his eyes disappearing like a burst light bulb. He nodded, business-like. "Then I'll see you Friday."

Elizabeth nodded, wetting her lips again. She fumbled for the doorknob and stumbled from the room, nearly tripping herself as she burst into the stairwell. Leaning against the cold, metal banister, she cradled her face in her hands, and cursed her utter, utter stupidity.

Charles heard the humming from down the hallway. It grew louder and then William breezed by Charles's office on the way to his own.

"Will!" Charles called out.

The humming ceased and the choreographer's figure appeared in the doorway.

"What's wrong?" Charles asked.

Leaning against the door frame, William looked puzzled. "Wrong? Nothing."

"You're humming... Bach?"

"Yes, and your point is?"

"Didn't you once say whistlers, hummers, and knuckle-crackers deserved a special place in hell?"

William chuckled. "Your memory's too sharp for your own good. Rehearsal went well. I have some good direction for the *pas de deux*."

"So the dancers are picking it up, then?"

"Actually, no. I don't think they get it at all."

Charles frowned. "Oh. Then why was rehearsal so good?"

"Uh, just... like I said. I got some good direction. That's all."

"Right. Speaking of direction, I need yours. Can you close the door?"

William stepped in and shut the door behind him. "What is it?"

Reaching across his desk, Charles handed William Sir Webster Lucas's note about the upcoming soloist promotion. William skimmed it and handed it back.

"What do you think?" Charles asked.

"It seems you have no other choice."

"I wanted to promote Jane."

William sucked in his breath slowly. He resisted the urge to shake his head. His friend could be so daft about business matters sometimes. "I don't think that's a good idea."

"Why not?"

"Look, Charles. There are some people who think Jane's with you for this very reason." Granted, those people were Caroline and Louisa, but William wasn't going to say that. He had his doubts about Jane Bennet, too, sometimes. Nobody could be that good.

"What!?" Charles cried. "Jane isn't like that."

"Maybe not, but you realize how that will make her look, don't you? To the rest of the company?"

"I don't care what the rest of the company thinks."

"Yes, but what about Jane? She hasn't been around long enough to be able to defend herself credibly from that kind of criticism. They'll think she's with you just to further her career."

Charles hesitated. "But she's a good dancer."

"You also have a reputation to maintain, and so does this company. How do you think everyone's going to react when the girlfriend of the artistic director gets promoted?"

"She deserves it, though. She's a good dancer."

"Regardless."

Charles stared at his friend sourly. William returned the look.

"Okay, let's forget about all that for a minute," reasoned William. "Last year, Boroughs donated how much money to the company?"

"Two million."

"Fine. And how many people did you still have to lay off last year?"

"Three."

"Okay. And how many ballets needed to be cut from the repertoire this season?"

"We couldn't produce *Don Q* because it would have been too expensive to refurbish the costumes."

"Exactly."

"She won't *not* donate," Charles said sharply. "She's on the board."

"Yes, but how much can the company afford to lose?" William replied with the same edge in his voice.

Charles sighed, rubbed his eyes, and groaned. "But... Anne?"

William nodded in agreement. "You lose the battle. You win the war.

She won't be a fabulous soloist, but she'll keep her mother's money where it should be and keep the company's finances healthy."

Charles shook his head. "I don't understand how you and Lucas think. I just don't think I'm cut out for this job sometimes. Jane deserves this."

"You aren't thinking practically, Charles. Just promote Anne. Jane Bennet can wait another season. She's young."

Charles made no reply. William took this as a sign of assent. Turning, he opened the door again, but before he left the room, he looked over his shoulder and smiled sadly at his friend.

"The reason I declined that position in San Francisco was because I like making my own decisions. I don't envy you."

Charles returned the weary smile and watched William leave. He leaned back in his chair, closed his eyes, and made a silent apology to Jane. He would promote her next season, he promised himself.

Chapter 10

"Tell me what you know about Anne Boroughs," Elizabeth said, taking a sip of her beer.

"Anne Boroughs?" Greg repeated. They sat at a darkened booth in the back corner of an East Village dive bar. "Not much. She's Catherine Boroughs' daughter. She's been lusting after William Darcy since she was sixteen."

Elizabeth guffawed. "Anne Boroughs doesn't seem like the *lusting* type."

"She does have the whole unsmiling, gray, Communist Russia look going on, doesn't she? That must be the only kind of woman who could tolerate old Darce. Last I heard, there was something going on between them. Not sure if those rumors are true, though." Greg shuddered theatrically.

Elizabeth laughed, but the comment gave her pause. Darcy and Anne? She'd never even seen them together in the same room.

Greg continued. "Why do you ask? What's little Annie doing now?"

Elizabeth grew thoughtful. "She's been promoted to soloist."

"She must have become a better dancer over the years."

Shaking her head, Elizabeth added, "My sister was up for that promotion."

Greg clucked sympathetically. "That sucks. Mommy's doing, no doubt. Money rules everything in this business. Money, connections, and of course" —Greg swigged his beer—"sex."

Elizabeth's mouth went dry, and she, too, took a long sip of her beer. Greg gently continued to rub his thumb against the sensitive skin at the inside of her wrist.

"How's your sister taking it?" he asked.

Elizabeth thought back to her sister's behavior that past week—listless and unsmiling in dance class, pensive at home, prone to staring out windows, and crying in her room. Jane would never confess it, but she had been expecting that promotion.

Seeing her sister like that made Elizabeth feel helpless. Jane had never known disappointment's swift kick to the gut. Elizabeth had. She was acquainted with the demons of self-doubt that plagued a dancer after rejection. She knew Jane was probably second-guessing herself every time she stepped into a dance studio—wondering whether her arms hung like wet noodles, her feet flapped during jumps, or she did something awkward with her neck when she moved—and when her microscopic self-examination provided no revelation, sinking into despair and just wondering *why*.

Elizabeth replied, "She's disappointed. She's really trying to hide it, but she's been mopey ever since it was announced a week ago."

"That's too bad. Money, sex, and connections—I'm telling you, that's what it's about."

"If it were all about sex, she'd have gotten the promotion."

Greg's eyes flew up. "Don't tell me your sister's *that girl*."

"What do you mean by *that girl*?" Elizabeth asked.

"You know, the girl who'd do anything for a part."

Elizabeth frowned. "Jane isn't like that. I mean, she's dating Charles. So if it really were about sex, shouldn't she have been promoted?"

"I dunno, Lizzy. Guess it's all about who you know and how much you have."

Shrugging, Elizabeth grew pensive for a few moments and forced herself to move on to a happier subject. "My sister wants to meet you. Lord knows, I've spoken so much about you."

A feline smile spread across Greg's gorgeous mouth. "Do you? What kinds of things do you tell her?"

"You know, the whole thing about you and Darcy. That kind of stuff. You should come over for dinner one day and meet her."

Greg leaned forward in the booth. "I'd like to meet your sister. And I'd love to come over. Preferably, though, when your sister isn't there."

Elizabeth leaned her cheek on her palm. "Oh? And why is that?"

"You know as well as I do that there are certain *activities* that were made for only two people," Greg teased, his tone full of innuendo.

She laughed and, taking a final sip of her beer, replied with a shake of her head. Greg met her admonition with a single, arched brow and took his own sip. He continued to stare at her in a way that felt like he was stripping her out of her clothes.

Elizabeth changed the subject. "When you were in the company, did you go to the Netherfield Gala?"

It took him a moment to reply. "The Netherfield Zoo?"

"Why do you call it that?"

"It was the chance for us to perform like monkeys for all the rich folk."

"Oh," Elizabeth said, her stomach dropping in disappointment. Her face must have fallen with it because Greg asked her why she wanted to know.

"I was actually going to ask if you'd like to go with me," Elizabeth began. "It's in two weeks, and I don't have a date, so . . . "

Greg grinned. "Are you going to wear something sexy?"

Elizabeth reddened to her hairline. "Possibly."

"Then I guess I'll have to go," Greg said.

"Really?" asked Elizabeth.

Greg deliberately scanned his gaze over Elizabeth's face, down to her breasts, and back up again. "I wouldn't miss it."

Suddenly, he stood from the booth, switched sides to where Elizabeth sat, and squeezed in next to her. For the next ten minutes, they made out in the back corner of the bar. It took all of Elizabeth's self-control to resist Greg's invitation back to his apartment, where she was sure things would progress to a point she desperately wanted and was strangely afraid to go.

Although it would have been moronic to ask Elizabeth to be his date to the Netherfield Gala, William had thought about it more than a few times. In quiet moments, his thoughts clouded with visions of whisking Elizabeth into the Netherfield Hotel and then taking her back to his apartment afterwards.

Sir Webster Lucas quickly killed that vision when he begged William to be seen in public with his "fiancée," Anne Boroughs.

"Just think of the PR, William. The PR! The benefactors will love it," the artistic director chirped. "The star choreographer with the newly promoted soloist! PR gold!"

William had nothing against Anne Boroughs and, at times, rather enjoyed her company. She was morose and plain, but William found her lack of duplicity a welcome change from the simpering likes of Caroline Bingley. He and Anne had been friends since childhood—quiet friends. The kind of friend he wouldn't speak to for months, but who would fly to his side if he ever needed her. They understood each other, each in their own severe and detached way. He regretted ever getting "engaged" to her, but she wasn't the worst woman with whom to spend an evening.

Besides, Anne would take his mind off things—and people—that he should not be thinking of. He struggled to resist the lure of Elizabeth Bennet. With each *pas de deux* rehearsal, his staunch self-control slipped further from his hands like dry sand. At least in the studio, he had dance to cover his blatant desire. As unethical as it was, William allowed himself some release in touching Elizabeth's waist, feeling her breath on his neck, having her watch him intently as he demonstrated a step. He dreaded, almost feared, her outside of those walls, though. He couldn't credibly explain away his desire then.

"I'll take Anne if she'll go with me," William answered.

Opening his mouth to protest, Sir Webster snapped it shut and then eyed the choreographer. "You will?"

"That's what I said."

"Oh. Okay. And you'll both actually mingle?"

William replied dryly, "I'll do anything for a check."

"Because you both have rather—how do I put this—*unsociable* personalities."

"Lucas, you're all compliments today."

"But it would be so good for PR."

William stood abruptly from the cushy leather chair in Sir Webster's office. "I said I'd do it. No more."

"Thank you, William. You know I love you," Lucas simpered.

In spite of himself, William smiled, too. The old man should have been locked up in a mental institution or retired on a beach somewhere in Fiji with his pool boy, but it was that quirkiness in the artistic director that had sustained William through his dancing career and after its demise. He couldn't fault the man his eccentricities now. William was satisfied. Left with no choice but to go to the gala with Anne, he no longer had to worry about his mouth countering all reason and asking Elizabeth Bennet to go instead.

Chapter 11

"Let's begin," Darcy said, dropping his notebook down on the chair and walking towards Elizabeth. "I need to get this thing finished today."

Standing alone in the center of Studio B, Elizabeth responded with a small nod. She'd known it would be their last rehearsal together; there only remained a few more seconds of empty music, after all. Darcy stopped in front of her and half-smiled. "I'll bet you're relieved."

Elizabeth shrugged. Truth be told, she had mixed feelings. Yes, she was relieved. She wouldn't miss the scrutiny from the other dancers. She wouldn't miss their burning eyes as they left her behind in Studio B after rehearsals. She was tired of the inquiries, thinly veiled with jealousy, about what *exactly* she and Darcy did in those rehearsals. She just wanted her career to go back to normal.

Kind of. Regret lay beneath the relief. She would miss the rush that dancing with William Darcy gave her. Yes, he made her nervous, angry, and uncomfortable to be sure. But when she was alone in that studio with him, she became the kind of dancer she wanted to be all of the time. She got to pretend like she mattered in the company.

Darcy began explaining the final steps of the piece. In contrast to the sedate fade of violins, the movement quickened, became more urgent. Elizabeth couldn't grasp the phrasing, and in a moment of frustration, cursed.

"*Plié* more before the turn," Darcy told her.

Elizabeth tried, but it didn't help. He repeated his correction. She tried the step again, feeling a self-defeating satisfaction when, again, she stumbled out of the turn. She didn't want to prove him right, no matter how bad her dancing looked. Darcy frowned.

"Take a break," he said, returning to the chair at the front and opening his notebook.

Elizabeth remained still, feeling disappointed. Her face grew hot. She went for her water and took a long gulp. Swallowing, she saw Darcy looking at her.

"Are you going to the gala?" he asked suddenly.

"I am," she replied.

"With someone?" he asked, the tone of his voice making her burn. Anyone, he seemed to imply, could go to the gala. It only mattered *who* you went *with*.

"I *am* going with someone, in fact. Greg Wickham."

She saw Darcy's eyes frost over. He seemed to retreat into himself, but she wanted him to say something; she'd just dared him. Instead, he rubbed his mouth and continued to frown at nothing. Then he turned sharply and went to the stereo.

"From the beginning," he mumbled, his back towards her as he cued the music. "Let's try the timing of that sequence again."

Elizabeth looked to the tips of her pointe shoes and muttered a curse under her breath. She closed her eyes, trying to suppress the weird feeling gnawing at her. Somehow, she'd hoped to guilt-trip Darcy about Greg, let him know that she knew about his dirty tricks. But he'd burrowed inside, which made her uneasy because she didn't know how to deal with a William Darcy who was anything but cocky and conceited.

He avoided eye contact as he made his way back to the center of the room. Once the music began, Elizabeth tried to focus on the steps. However, she found it difficult when her partner refused to respond to her. His touch was hesitant, his eyes vacant. The steps felt dead. To compensate, Elizabeth exaggerated hers even more. She became someone else: the temptress of Darcy's *pas de deux* and not some unsophisticated *corps* girl. Elizabeth looked at him with eyes not her own. She was sultry and provocative.

It seemed to work. About a minute into the *pas de deux*, his eyes rested on hers. They brewed with an intensity that unsettled her. Yet, he still danced weakly. When she attempted a *pirouette*, she could barely feel his supporting hands on her back, and she sighed.

"Can you hold me a little tighter?" asked Elizabeth.

That seemed to wake him from his stupor. Elizabeth felt his grasp tighten against her back.

She started to dance the final sequence of steps when she unexpectedly felt pulled in the opposite direction. She frowned at Darcy. He never forgot his own choreography.

"New choreography: *échappé*, then *sous-sus*," he barked.

"But—"

"Can you just do it?"

Startled, Elizabeth complied as well as she could with the impromptu instructions. On the tips of her pointe shoes, her eyes were even with his. He seized her wrists and twisted them around his neck. The final phrases of the music filled the room, but Darcy did nothing.

And then his mouth came down angrily on hers. Elizabeth gasped and tried to pull away, but he held fast to her hands.

The track changed to the darker *Fugue in G*. Suddenly, Darcy yanked himself away and brushed past her to stop the music.

"That's it," he said, returning. "Just *échappé*, *sous-sus*, and the kiss."

Elizabeth could think of no retort, no reproof, no anything. Nodding, she felt her throat become as dry as paper.

The second time they tried the ending, it stunned her just as much as it had the first time. Except that time, she noted the feeling of his lips on her own, hard but warm.

The music stopped. Darcy breathed hard and looked at her with what seemed like contempt.

"I'll finish here today. Thanks for your help." He walked away from her without another word.

Elizabeth tripped on her feet as she gathered her things and stumbled out of the studio. On the landing of the stairwell, she clutched onto the rail and stared at her trembling fingers.

"What the hell?" she whispered—just to hear her voice, just to make sure what had happened had not been a hallucination.

The final bars of Bach played on a loop in her head. She still felt the pressure of his lips on hers. Her thoughts raced. Even if it *had* been his choreography, he could have warned her. A dance step and a kiss were in two different leagues, after all. She should have been livid.

Why, then, did she want to tear back up the stairs and have him do it again?

It was a sick thought. She disgusted herself. Back in the locker room, she threw on clothes over her dancewear, and ran out of the building to get some fresh air.

That evening, Jane wondered about the thudding and crinkling sounds coming from her sister's room. Even over the blare of the television, she heard Elizabeth tearing things apart. During the commercial break, Jane rose from the sofa and went to her sister's closed bedroom door. She knocked softly and let herself in.

Elizabeth sat in the middle of several boxes, their contents—papers, old trophies, and stuffed animals—sprawled across her bedroom floor. Jane raised an eyebrow. "Should I even ask?"

Elizabeth shook her head. "Jane, I promise I'll explain all of this tomorrow. Right now, I just need you to leave me alone, okay?"

Nodding, she made no reply and closed the door.

After nearly an hour of going through two boxes of old stuff, Elizabeth finally hit upon the thin manila folder she had been looking for. Her frenzy died, and she pulled it from the large cardboard box in front of her with as much reverence and anticipation as an archeologist digging up a priceless urn. Opening it, she gingerly went through a stack of magazine clippings: Mikhail Baryshnikov, Darci Kistler of New York City Ballet, some nameless dancer in a gorgeous leap, the Bolshoi ballerinas lined up perfectly in the second act of *Swan Lake*, and then what she was looking for: Perfection, by Hermes.

It was a black and white photo of William Darcy, naked, his leg straightened behind him in a rigid *tendu*. Shadows sheathed half of his body. His muscles rippled everywhere. A sculpted calf rose to a bulge of thigh muscles, which rose even further to the indentation of his gluteus. Half of his abdominals hid in darkness. His head was thrown back, eyes closed in either a look of fierce concentration or of lust. He was male perfection—just like the name of the Hermes cologne.

She hadn't seen the photograph in years. When the ad came out, she'd been a prepubescent eleven-year-old, but now she could appreciate the picture through a woman's eyes. Her breathing stopped. Finally, Elizabeth understood the commotion it had caused. Suddenly, she understood why flocks of teenage girls had, at the time, swarmed to Ballet Theater performances like groupies at a boy-band concert.

William Darcy, Principal Dancer, Ballet Theater of New York, said the fine print running up the left edge of the advertisement. She touched her lips.

For a minute, for an hour—Elizabeth couldn't be sure which—she stared at the photograph. A cacophony of emotions careened through her. Such a beautiful, rotten man—sometimes funny, sometimes tender, though usually obnoxious and arrogant. But those lips . . . those lips.

Primal impulses lapped inside of her.

"Elizabeth, are you crazy?" she whispered sharply to herself.

She groaned and closed the manila folder. Setting the Hermes ad aside, she cleaned up the mess, shoving papers and memorabilia back into the boxes. She reappeared in the living room just in time to catch a fashion design show with Jane. Her sister, fortunately, asked no questions. The two girls argued over who would be voted off the runway that evening. In the end, it was the designer neither of them expected.

The next day, Jane went to retrieve a leotard from Elizabeth's room that she wanted to borrow. Unfolded on Elizabeth's dresser was the photo of William Darcy that her sister had taped to her bedroom wall years ago. Jane picked it up and stared at it for a moment. She wondered what possibly could have prompted Elizabeth to tear her room apart looking for this photo. A smile curved Jane's lips, and she left the room quietly, replacing the advertisement of Perfection by Hermes exactly where she found it.

ON AN UNSEASONABLY WARM MONDAY afternoon when Jane was meeting Charles and his parents for lunch downtown, Elizabeth decided to take the subway down to the East Village. She emerged at Astor Place to the sounds of a bluegrass band playing for change on the corner. She sauntered through the streets and avenues, window-shopping. Stopping at Veniero's, Elizabeth purchased a cannoli to go and a coffee from the deli next door; she ate her snack on the stoop of a red brick building.

During her wanderings, a belt displayed in the window of a vintage clothing boutique caught her eye. She paused and, though she didn't have the money to afford such luxuries, decided a peek wouldn't cost her anything. A tattooed shopgirl greeted her. Elizabeth eyed the belt, but then a sparkling strap hanging from a clothes rack grabbed her attention. She reached her hand into the rack and pushed aside the clothes, revealing a long, black ball gown with beaded straps and neckline.

"That's a great piece," the shop lady offered. "Just came in a couple days ago. Authentic 1940s. Exquisite beadwork."

Elizabeth plucked it from the rack and sighed. The immaculate black silk did not reveal the dress's age; it looked as if it had never been worn.

"It's gorgeous," she sighed, fingering the glimmering, black beads at the collar. Her fingers edged inside the dress and plucked out the price tag: $275. Sighing again, this time in resignation, Elizabeth tucked the tag back in. Sensing her customer's interest, the saleslady emerged from behind the register.

"This dress was handmade. All of the beads were stitched on by hand. They don't make dresses like this anymore. Really, for this price, the dress is a steal. It will last you another sixty years."

Elizabeth frowned. "I wish I could agree with you. It's a bit out of my price range."

Shaking her head, the saleslady smiled. "You won't say that once you try it on." She took the dress from Elizabeth's hand and whisked her to a small dressing room in the back of the store. "Let me know if you need any help."

Once alone, Elizabeth shrugged. Trying it on didn't cost anything either, after all. She slipped out of her coat and clothes and zipped up the gown. Her eyes widened. The dress fit her as if it had been tailored for her. Meant to be worn with a corset, it cinched at the waist and had a gracefully scooped neckline. It hugged her hips and thighs, flaring out under her knees. Granted, because of her height, the dress trailed on the floor more than it should, but it was nothing a pair of four-inch heels wouldn't fix. Elizabeth twirled in the mirror, imagining the look on Greg's face when he saw her in a dress like this—and a corset and four-inch heels. She smiled wickedly. He *had* wanted sexy after all. The saleslady was right; for $275, a dress that fit her like this was a bargain.

"How's it going in there?" the saleslady called.

Elizabeth opened the door to the dressing room. "I'm taking it."

Caroline Bingley's eyes radiated anger like a spotlight. William had just demonstrated the last steps of the *pas de deux,* and she clearly did not like what she saw. The choreography itself did not bother her—rather, how and with whom the steps had been choreographed incensed the prima ballerina.

"And after the kiss, the lights fade," William said nonchalantly.

The entire *pas de deux* was five minutes of foreplay set to classical music. Elizabeth Bennet must have clearly wielded a heavy influence over William. How had she done it? Caroline had been trying to seduce William back to her bed for the last few months. Elizabeth was plain, had an ugly body, and fought with William all the time. Didn't William always tell her that getting involved with his dancers would "compromise the integrity of his work"? Well, William Darcy had been compromised. That was clear. Caroline refused to make out on stage as if she was in a burlesque freak show.

Crossing her arms over her chest, she asked, "Is this really appropriate?"

Her partner, Ben, laughed. "Don't worry, hun. I won't be thinking about you."

William glared at her. "I'll be the judge of what's proper for my choreography."

Caroline glanced over to Elizabeth, who was doing an excellent job of avoiding everyone's gaze. Ben tore a hangnail off his pinky with his teeth.

"Oh, it's your decision, after all," Caroline spat to William. "I would just hate to see *our* artistic integrity compromised just because you and some *corps de ballet* girl went a little overboard in one of your private rehearsals. That's all."

She saw William's lips narrow to a thin line. "Ms. Bingley, let me make you an offer. Since you're so worried about your artistic integrity, I invite you to get the hell out of my rehearsal until you feel you're ready to work like a professional."

"You have no right to tell *me* what's professional when *you're* the one going at it with Elizabeth!" she retorted.

"There's the door." William nodded to the opposite end of the room with his chin.

The prima ballerina paused, glaring at William. She wasn't sloppy seconds to *anybody*, much less *corps* dancers. Caroline huffed and whirled on the ball of her toe, storming from the room. She made sure to cast Elizabeth the most dangerous expression she could manage. The younger dancer's face had lost all color, Caroline was pleased to note.

The last thing she heard before the door slamming behind her was William's immovable voice saying, "Let's try that section from the beginning."

After rehearsal, Elizabeth sat trembling on a bench in the locker room as she changed clothes. She couldn't tell why her body shook—perhaps from fear, perhaps from fury.

Darcy hadn't defended her from Caroline's accusation. He'd defended *his* choreography, *his* integrity, *his* professionalism. But when Caroline had spat Elizabeth's name in that studio for the other dancers to hear, what had Darcy done? Nothing.

And all of them had looked at *Elizabeth* with accusing eyes. Not Caroline. Not Darcy. Elizabeth, who hadn't much of a choice in Darcy's arrangement.

Tears leaked from the corners of her eyes. Elizabeth smeared them away so that no one would see.

At home at last, William cradled a mug of chamomile tea in his hands and sat watching the traffic stream up Central Park West. That day's rehearsal had been a disaster. After Caroline stormed out in a huff, he had worked with her understudy, Louisa Hirsch, who was an even less capable dancer than Caroline. He'd had to block out the *pas de deux* all over again. It looked so very, very wrong. William hadn't the nerve to ask for Elizabeth's assistance in rehearsal that day. She had looked too stricken and brittle after Caroline's scene. So he'd let her be.

The gala was next week and the premiere after that. William began to panic. Louisa could never perform this role. She had been a talented dancer during his time at the company, but she was nearing forty now. Rumors circulated that this would be her last season at Ballet Theater and not necessarily by her choosing. He respected Louisa—had partnered her on many occasions—but it was clear today by her belabored extensions that her hips just weren't what they used to be. He did not want her dancing this *pas de deux*.

He wanted Elizabeth Bennet to do it.

Fuck Caroline and fuck Louisa and, most of all, fuck Sir Webster and Charles, who would probably fight him hard on it. He was the choreographer. He got the ultimate say in casting decisions. Sure, Caroline had already been announced in the role, but shit happened in dance companies all the time. The audience would be disappointed, but they were used to last-minute casting changes.

And he wanted Elizabeth to dance it. The *pas de deux* was hers, and though other dancers in other stagings would eventually take on the role, for the world premiere, William wanted to see the *pas de deux* exactly the way he envisioned it. And that meant he would be making some changes, despite what Charles or Lucas or Caroline or anyone else thought.

"I'm sorry, what?" Elizabeth said, her mouth halfway to her coffee cup.

"Colin is picking me up at seven thirty," Charlotte repeated.

"Colin *Williams*?"

"Yes." Charlotte stirred a third packet of sugar into her coffee.

Elizabeth blinked twice and looked across the table at her friend. Colin Williams was the controller of Ballet Theater of New York. While the dancers didn't typically associate with the administrative staff in the finance office, Colin was infamous for two reasons.

First, he was known to be under the thumb of the company's largest donor, Catherine Boroughs. In fact, nearly everyone at Ballet Theater knew that Catherine had gotten Colin his job with the directive to keep tabs on the company's goings-on. They laughed at the picture he kept in his cubicle: Colin and Catherine at a gala several years back, Colin beaming widely, spit encrusted at the right corner of his mouth, and Catherine looking off to the side, cross with boredom or annoyance—probably both.

Second, he hit on nearly every *corps de ballet* member in the company. Unfortunately, genetics had not been kind to Colin Williams, who was short, round, and prematurely bald. On top of that, Colin also vibed "creepy uncle," offering new dancers, many of whom were still in their teens, inappropriate shoulder rubs. He could often be found on the rehearsal floors, despite no need to be there, peeking into rehearsals and attempting to flirt with the dancers.

At first, Elizabeth though Charlotte was joking when she said she was going to the gala with him. She laughed. "Okay, Charlotte. Good one."

Charlotte didn't smile. "No, Liz. I'm not kidding. He asked me the other day, and we're going together."

"Okay," Elizabeth said, attempting to rein in her shock and disgust. "Wow. I didn't know you were into him."

"I'm not really. But it's not a requirement to be in love with a guy before you go out on a date, is it?"

"All right, but you should be able to stand him."

Charlotte exhaled sharply and looked past her friend's shoulder. "Why is it so hard for you to believe I'd want to give him a chance? Just because *you* can't stand him? He's not a bad guy, Liz."

Elizabeth made no reply. She was sure Charlotte wasn't going to the gala with Colin Williams so she could get to know him better. Rather, it had more to do with getting to know the people Colin knew—the person, rather. Charlotte was mildly obsessed with Catherine Boroughs and was convinced that knowing the *grande dame* would get her better parts, maybe even promotions. She talked about Boroughs constantly. Some of the girls in the company had even started making fun of her behind her back for it.

"Speaking of which," Charlotte asked, "have you heard from Greg? Did you ask him about the limo?"

Elizabeth's annoyance melted away as she thought about her date to the gala. Although he had been out of town for the past week filming a hip-hop video in Jamaica, they had still spoken twice over Skype. Each time, Greg mentioned how excited he was to see Elizabeth's "hot body" in her dress—and hopefully out of it. Comments like that made her gooey inside. He would be away until Saturday and take a morning red-eye back to New York just to go to the gala with her.

"I have heard from him, but I keep forgetting to mention the limo," said Elizabeth.

"Liz, we have to book this thing," Charlotte insisted.

Elizabeth downed a long sip of cappuccino. "How much did you say it was?"

"Eighty bucks an hour, two hour minimum."

Elizabeth swallowed. "That's a lot of money."

"It's supposedly a good deal. It's a friend of one of Colin's friends."

"I don't know. That's almost twice as much as a cab."

"It'll be better if we split it four ways. Plus, how cool would it be to roll up in a limo? Come on, Liz. It'll be like prom all over again." Charlotte shook Elizabeth's shoulders.

Elizabeth smiled sheepishly. "I never went to my prom. We had a dance performance that night."

Charlotte clapped her hands together. "Even better. Now you'll get to see what it's like."

Perhaps it would be easier to ignore Colin Williams while sipping on champagne in their own limousine, Elizabeth reasoned. Plus, Greg would be there to help buffer Colin's buffoonery. "Okay, I'm in. I'll mention it to Greg."

Charlotte beamed and told her they would swing by her place around eight.

Elizabeth let herself into the apartment. "Jane?"

"In my room!" her sister called.

Grinning, Elizabeth checked her reflection in the hallway mirror and then tiptoed to Jane's room. Sitting on her bed, Jane was thumbing through that month's *Cosmo.*

"Hey, where've you been? You're— Holy crap!" she said, looking up at her younger sister in the doorway. Elizabeth burst into giggles and bounded into her sister's room.

"Do you like it?"

"Your hair!" Jane cried, touching the now chocolate strands falling over her sister's shoulders. "It's so dark! You look amazing," Jane smiled. "What made you do it?"

"Oh, I don't know. It was time for a change, and I thought I'd make a terrible redhead. You think Greg will like it?"

"He'd be a fool not to."

"And look," Elizabeth said, opening her purse and picking out a small, flat parcel. "I went downtown and found these on sale." Opening the bag, Elizabeth dumped a pair of dangly silver earrings and matching bracelet onto the bed.

"Very nice," Jane said, picking up the bracelet and trying it on. "And how much did all of this cost?"

"A trim, the dye job, and the jewelry cost exactly $185.95. Plus the $360 for the dress, shoes, and corset. I'll be eating ramen for the rest of the month."

Jane smiled. "But it will be worth it once Greg sees you tomorrow. He'll drop dead. Especially with that dress."

"I know. I already called him and told him that he was going to have the hottest girlfriend at the gala!" giggled Elizabeth.

"What did he say?"

"He just kind of laughed and said he couldn't wait. Ohmigosh, *I* can't wait! I feel like I'm in middle school," Elizabeth exclaimed.

"Well, relax," laughed Jane, "we've still got a full twenty-four hours to go."

"I know! There's so much left to do yet. I have to do my nails."

Elizabeth bounded off her sister's bed and headed to her room to do just that with the new cherry red nail polish she had also purchased during that afternoon's shopping spree.

Chapter 12

With only thirty minutes left separating her from Greg and the Netherfield Gala, Elizabeth began to panic. She paced the length of her living room, fraught with anxiety. Although Greg had told her he would call when his flight got in at seven that morning, she hadn't heard from him. Elizabeth had tried his cell three times. Finally, she checked the airline's website to confirm that his flight had not been cancelled or delayed. It had actually landed fourteen minutes early.

Saturday inched along, Elizabeth's stomach dissolving to butterflies the later it got. She meant to dress leisurely, but she was so nervous that doing her hair and makeup and getting dressed had taken her less than an hour. Jane had gone to Charles's apartment to get ready, sip champagne, eat canapés, and relax in the lap of luxury with the Bingleys before the gala, leaving Elizabeth alone to gnaw at her fingernails.

Succumbing to her anxiety, Elizabeth called Greg's cell phone again. This time, it rang. Elizabeth's heart leapt, but then sank when, after three rings, the call went to voice mail. She tried again: voice mail. Elizabeth threw her cell phone onto her bed, a sob stuck in her throat.

"Mascara," she said, fanning her eyes, willing herself not to cry. He would come. Greg wouldn't just stand her up like that.

To calm her nerves, Elizabeth scoured the refrigerator for the open jug of wine. She poured a large mug full and winced through the acidity. She paced around her apartment. The clock read 7:42. Instinctively, Elizabeth knew he wasn't coming. Her chin trembled.

She'd spent so much money! Elizabeth did the math and nearly started to cry again. She might not be able to make rent, and Jane would be annoyed if she had to lend her the money. Elizabeth stared at herself in the full-length mirror. Damn, she looked good! More than good, she looked stunning. Even she didn't recognize herself. But who cared? There'd be no one to appreciate it.

The door buzzed. Charlotte, probably, with the limo.

"I'll be right down!" Elizabeth called into the buzzer. Steeling herself with a deep breath, she took once last glance in the mirror, grabbed her clutch, and headed down. It wasn't easy teetering around in four-inch stilettos, particularly cheap and not very well-made stilettos. She clung to the bannister in the narrow staircase so she wouldn't go tumbling down the stairs, feeling the indignity of it.

Elizabeth flung open the door. Charlotte stood outside in a ruffled red cocktail dress. Eyes widening, she took in Elizabeth and told her how fantastic she looked. Then, Charlotte asked about Greg. Elizabeth's chin wobbled, and she relayed that evening's tragedy. Charlotte was furious and offered one of Colin's friends as a last-minute escort.

The limo driver honked the horn, and it was only then that Elizabeth noticed the chariot that waited to take them to the ball. She almost choked. Gaudy and white, the limo was a relic from the 1980s. A long scratch marred the left side of the car. One of the back windows sputtered down.

"Charlotte, we should really go. Catherine frowns upon those who show up later than she does," yelled Colin out of the window.

Charlotte tittered and cast Elizabeth an apologetic glance. "Let's make the best of it, Liz."

Nodding, Elizabeth was grateful when her friend threaded her arm through the crook of her elbow and escorted her down the stoop.

The interior of the limousine looked even worse than the exterior. A crystal chandelier dangled from the roof of the car and cigarettes had burned little holes in the burgundy velour seats here and there. A curtain was missing from the purple-tinted windows.

"Good evening, Elizabeth," Colin said, ogling Elizabeth's breasts. "Where's your beau?"

Thankfully, Charlotte interjected a trite comment about the weather, which navigated the topic of conversation to safer waters. Elizabeth spent the limo ride avoiding the lascivious eyes of Colin Williams. As she gazed out of the window, her mind settled on only one thought: *Wouldn't Mr. Darcy love this?* Her face burned with humiliation.

The limo pulled into the driveway of the Netherfield Hotel. Fortunately, no one arrived along with them to witness their horrible carriage. Elizabeth scrambled out of the beat-up limo; Charlotte and Colin soon followed.

"You can give me your and Greg's share of the limo fare on Monday, Elizabeth," Colin said to Elizabeth's cleavage.

Biting down on the inside of her lip, she merely nodded and strode up the steps, figuring acquiescence was a small price to pay to get the hell out of Colin Williams's company. She wondered why she just hadn't stayed home with a pint of ice cream instead of subjecting herself to this clusterfuck of an evening.

By nine o'clock, the Netherfield Gala was in full swing with couples moving across the dance floor to snappy renditions of Sinatra songs. William hated the din at events like these. He couldn't think straight through the noise, the clinking, the raucous laughter, and the bad music.

He stood off to the side of the room, sipping a glass of ginger ale. Next to him, Anne remained silent, her gaze intent on the opposite side of the room. They had barely spoken the entire evening, but he didn't mind her silence. Anne didn't want to be with him anymore than he wanted to be with her. She was distracted by the bleach-blonde in the sequined peach gown on the far side of the ballroom. Mariah Lucia, Anne's longtime girlfriend.

An hour into the gala, Elizabeth still hadn't arrived. Her sister was there, stunning in a strapless white number that offset her bronze skin and light hair. Jane looked wholesome, healthy, and blonde, and William smirked when he saw the self-satisfied smile plastered across Charles's face. He caught his friend's eye, and Charles made his way through the crowd to join William on the sideline.

"Having fun?" William asked dryly, when his friend reached him.

"I am. Hello, Anne," Charles said, nodding to the mousy woman at William's left. She smiled weakly and then shirked away.

"You don't seem to be having fun," Charles said, frowning.

"Compared to you, no."

Beaming, Charles glanced back to Jane. "I'm so drop-dead in love, Will. I'm tempted to kidnap her, take her to Vegas, and just get married right now."

"And what would Mr. and Mrs. Bingley say about that?" William replied.

"They love Jane."

"But I'm sure they wouldn't love an elopement." William laughed. "They want a wedding where they can show off their money to five hundred of their closest friends."

Charles rolled his eyes but smiled.

"Where's Elizabeth?" William asked casually.

Scanning the room, Charles shrugged. "She's here, apparently. Jane got a text from her."

"You know, she's coming with Wickham," spat William.

Charles's face grew serious, "I don't know about that. Jane mentioned something about him not coming,"

"Really?" William took a long sip of ginger ale. "Hm."

Anne then returned with a plate of caviar-laden crackers and began to crunch on them. Charles looked at her and smiled, and then he turned to William.

"I'd better get back to Jane before my parents find her again."

"I thought you said they liked her."

"They do. I'm afraid my dad will start giving her stock market tips, and once you get him started, he never shuts up," Charles joked before waving and then walking away.

William smiled and then looked back down to Anne.

"Cracker?" she offered.

William held up his hand. "No thanks. You don't have to stick around on my account, Anne."

Anne shrugged and licked a stray fish egg off her finger. "It's not like I can talk to her anyway. Mother's here. We have to pretend like we don't know each other."

Shaking his head, William took another sip of ginger ale, looked over to Mariah at the far end of the room, and then did a double take.

He wouldn't have recognized Elizabeth if she hadn't made a beeline for Jane Bennet. Her hair was no longer a sun-kissed straw color. Now the shade and sheen of polished mahogany, her hair fell down her back and shoulders in lush waves. In a simple black dress that did amazing things for the natural curves of her body, she was classic, sophisticated, and mesmerizingly beautiful.

"Huh?" Anne asked, eyeing him queerly.

"Huh?" he replied, unable to peel his eyes away from Elizabeth at the far end of the ballroom.

"You said, 'Shit.'" Anne's eyes followed the line of William's gaze.

"Oh." He downed the last of his ginger ale. "I'll be back."

He made his way casually, swerving through the bejeweled throng, accepting words of congratulations and yet never taking his eyes off of Elizabeth Bennet. His heart thumped louder in his ears the closer he got to Elizabeth. She whispered furiously with Jane, her forehead creased in anger. William swallowed, feeling jittery and thrilled at the same time. He approached close enough to hear Jane ask, "How much have you had to drink?" before the words died on the older sister's lips. Both Bennets looked up to him with equally surprised and expectant faces.

They could not have looked any different. Jane was luminescent with her blonde hair, bronzed skin, and white gown. William briefly complimented her, but then turned towards the darker sister and lost all ability to speak. Jane smiled and then slipped away.

Elizabeth's face flushed, and she reached for a ringlet, slowly twirling it in her fingers. In that gown, with her lips painted burgundy, her dark hair curled in soft waves, and her bright eyes bare except for heavy mascara, she looked like someone straight out of a George Hurrell photograph, dark and luscious. Elizabeth parted her lips, but William spoke first.

"Your hair."

She paused. "I dyed it."

He considered her new face. "I like you better this way."

Elizabeth smirked softly, the apples of her cheeks plumping and her eyes narrowing seductively. "I appreciate the compliment, but I didn't do it for you." Her voice was heady and sweet.

William arched an eyebrow. "For Wickham then?"

He saw the flame in her eyes waver.

"No, for myself."

A sadistic urge seized him. "Nevertheless, Greg's a lucky guy. He's with the most beautiful woman in the room. Where is he? I didn't see him come in."

He watched as the fire in her eyes died, leaving only embers of melancholy in its place. Averting her gaze, she murmured to the floor, "He, uh, actually didn't—"

"Wait, he didn't break up with you before the gala, did he?"

Elizabeth lifted her chin in that haughty, defiant way that drove him nuts. "He stood me up, actually." She said it, almost as if she were proud of it.

The expression on William's face curdled. "I'm sorry to hear it."

The defiance left her features, revealing troubled eyes. "Thanks. I'm going to..." Elizabeth pointed to nothing and then brushed past him, unable to meet his eyes.

William suddenly hated Greg only a little more than he hated himself. Did he really have to bring up Wickham? He sighed and rubbed his mouth. Cursing under his breath, he turned and headed back to the same wall where Anne Boroughs sat nursing the same glass of champagne she had when he left.

Elizabeth watched Charles sway with her sister on the dance floor, his eyes closed blissfully. She snorted when Colin plunked his foot down on Charlotte's toes, causing her to limp off the dance floor. Downing her fourth glass of bubbly, Elizabeth contemplated checking her voice mail again, but she couldn't bear to hear the electronic voice tell her that she had no new messages.

A waiter came by with a tray of champagne flutes. He stopped in front of her, and Elizabeth picked up another one. With each successive drink, the room grew dimmer, the music more melodious. Around the third glass of champagne, she became able to laugh when people asked her where that handsome date was she'd been bragging about so much.

She dragged her eyes over to William Darcy, standing in a throng of old women who dripped with sequins and jewels. He smiled politely and nodded at something one old biddy said. Elizabeth hadn't seen him with Anne Boroughs once that evening. What a crappy date Darcy made. At least Greg had the courtesy not to show up. Elizabeth slowly prowled the perimeter of the room, unable to take her eyes off William's tuxedoed back.

Elizabeth came upon Sir Webster Lucas deep in conversation with a tall, regal-looking woman. Elizabeth pulled into the crowd, not wanting to be accosted by the artistic director and banal small talk. She wasn't in the mood to fake being jolly. The woman standing next to Lucas looked about sixty, with a sculpted face and proud, upturned nose. A heavy Harry Winston choker hinted at her high net worth.

"...I don't like what I'm hearing about this new piece, Webster," the woman said, faint traces of an upper-class Manhattan accent in her speech.

"Anne's not even in it."

"I can talk to him about that," Lucas said in the most deferential tone Elizabeth had ever heard him use. The woman folded her arms across her chest.

"I don't like my money wasted on nonsense," she continued, her tone harsh.

"Catherine, some concessions must be made. We did promote Anne and will begin to cast her in more appropriate roles."

Elizabeth swallowed, positive she shouldn't be listening in on this conversation. The woman—Catherine Boroughs, no doubt—craned her neck and eyed Sir Webster with disgust on her face.

"I have it on good authority that Charles didn't want to promote her."

Sir Webster tittered uncomfortably. "Well, his girlfriend was a candidate for promotion as well, you know."

Despite the alcohol, Elizabeth's head suddenly zeroed into focus. She straightened her spine and turned away, her breath growing ragged.

"Well, I'm glad to know there's someone with some *sense* in your company. How vulgar to think that the girlfriend would have been promoted over a dancer with far more accomplishments and years of experience."

Lucas chuckled nervously again.

"It's a good thing that Anne's fiancé looks out for her," Catherine continued, nodding her bony chin towards the group where William stood. "If it weren't for William Darcy, she'd be going on her eighth year as a *corps* girl."

The woman would have kept talking, but their conversation was interrupted by several other socialites, coming over to say hello to Lucas. It was just as well since Elizabeth could no longer hear anything but the building pulse in her ears.

First of all, Darcy and Anne were *engaged*?! Why hadn't Darcy ever said anything? Why didn't he ever acknowledge Anne's presence at work? Why had he *kissed* Elizabeth if he was engaged? Her head swam with shock and anger.

Elizabeth strode to a deserted corner of the ballroom where several waiters ambled about. Her mind raced, but the champagne weighed down her rational thoughts like mud. Something about that conversation hadn't been right—something about Catherine Boroughs, her daughter, a donation, Charles Bingley, and William Darcy. Elizabeth tried to recall the particulars again, trying to piece together the situation. The waltz in the background didn't help.

"Ms. Bennet," came a voice, interrupting her thoughts. She jerked her head up. Darcy stood before her, his face taut. "Well, will you?" he asked.

Elizabeth glowered. "Will I *what*?"

He sighed and looked away momentarily. "Will you dance with me?"

Confusion flickered across Elizabeth's face. She stared at him, her head light. Quite frankly, he was the last person she wanted to see at the moment. But she was startled by him, and his metallic eyes drew her in like tractor beams; it would have cost her too much mental energy to refuse, so she didn't.

"Fine!"

Darcy extended his arm to her. Elizabeth eyed it before weaving her hand through, resting her palm against the soft wool of his jacket. As they approached the dance floor, the upbeat waltz ended, and the crooning notes of a "Music of the Night" rendition began.

Unthinkingly, Elizabeth wrapped her arms around Darcy. From somewhere beyond her buzz, she knew half the room was watching her and the man of the hour dance. Yet, she had been there—dancing in his arms—too many times to be nervous. She swayed in annoyed silence, resentful of Darcy's intrusion and now his reticence. Casting her eyes up from his lapel, Elizabeth caught him staring down at her. His placid expression further soured her mood.

"Is my company that unbearable?" she spat.

He blinked. "Your company?"

"Well, you haven't said anything to me since you asked me to dance."

Darcy smirked. "I thought that dancing was typically done silently."

"We're not in the studio," Elizabeth replied.

"Okay, so what would you like to talk about?"

Elizabeth rolled her eyes. "Forget it."

With mischief in his eyes, Darcy teased, "Is there something you need to get off your chest, Ms. Bennet? We've always been pretty honest with each other."

Elizabeth studied the choreographer's face. If he was going to mock her, she would be brutally honest with him. "I think it's pretty crappy that you've ignored your fiancée all evening."

"I'm sorry?" Darcy looked shocked.

"Your fiancée. Anne. You *do* remember her, don't you?"

Darcy chuckled once. "Ah, right. My fiancée."

"You forget her a lot, it seems," spat Elizabeth.

Darcy frowned, but amusement twinkled in his eyes. "You're not jealous, are you?"

Elizabeth turned her face away. "N-no! How much have you had to drink?"

"I'm perfectly sober," he said, smiling playfully. "Rest assured—first impressions are not always what they seem to be."

Elizabeth snorted. "Perhaps you would care to enlighten me then?"

He laughed, and the sound made her tingly. "You see that woman over there? Bleach blonde, peach dress."

Elizabeth craned her head to the right, wondering why Darcy was suddenly pointing out the woman in the loud gown. She nodded.

"That's Mariah Lucia. She's a painter. Have you ever seen her work?"

Elizabeth shook her head, even more puzzled.

"She does mostly abstract stuff. Had a few shows in some galleries downtown. Anne dragged me to one three years ago. That's where they met. They've been seeing each other ever since, but Anne's never told her mother since the old bitch wouldn't approve."

It took a few moments for understanding to flicker through Elizabeth's eyes. When it did, she lowered them, only the crown of her head visible to William. "Oh."

"I trust you won't say anything. I'm one of the only people Anne's told, and the fiancé ruse keeps her mother off her back."

"Of course. I won't say anything."

THE CONVERSATION DIED. CONTENT WITH the silence, William let "The Music of the Night" be the only sound between them. He looked down at the woman in his arms, feeling smug. She was interested in his relationship with Anne, and William suspected she was jealous. Why else would she be so concerned? Her eyes gleamed like amber under the dim lights of the ballroom's chandelier, but she refused to look at him. A troubled frown marred her face. Every so often, her eyebrows flinched, reflecting the storm of thoughts that must be brewing.

He desperately wanted to know what she was thinking, what insecurities about him and Anne were running through her head. He wanted to tell her that Anne, Caroline, and any other woman meant as much to him as his doorman, that it was Elizabeth he wanted to be near the whole night. He allowed the hand on the small of her back to pull her into him. Elizabeth looked up then, and he saw confusion and something else entirely flashing in her eyes. She inhaled softly and again looked away.

William had seen *Phantom of the Opera* enough to know that the last notes of the song were upon them. He didn't want it to end. He wanted to iron out the wrinkle in her brow. He wanted to keep touching her. He wanted the communion they shared in the dance studio.

Suddenly, she looked up at him. "I have another question. Something I can't figure out at all. Why was Anne promoted and not Jane?"

William flinched and went speechless.

"You were involved somehow, weren't you?" Elizabeth said accusingly.

Trying to answer, William stammered, "That's not—"

Just then, the music ended, and the orchestra received their applause from the room. Sir Webster Lucas's voice boomed from the speakers: *"Ladies and gentlemen—"* The screech of the microphone cut him off and made the room cringe.

William glanced down at Elizabeth.

"Was it for the same reason you got Greg Wickham fired?" she snapped, trying to pull out of his embrace. He started. Wickham again? Scanning her face in bewilderment, he grabbed her elbow and led her to the edge of the dance floor.

"What are you doing?" Elizabeth hissed.

"Thank you for coming tonight and supporting Ballet Theater of New York. I hope you're all having a wonderful time at our annual Netherfield Gala. The party's just getting started, so I invite you to eat, drink, dance, and of course, donate, to your heart's content."

"What did Wickham tell you?" His eyes were fierce. Elizabeth instinctively shirked back but then caught herself. *He* was to blame. *He* had ruined Greg's career, and judging by the look of fear on his face, he probably also knew Elizabeth had caught him pulling the same tricks with Jane.

"There are three company members here tonight who I would like to call to your attention. They represent the very best and very brightest of our company's future. If they could come up here when I call their names. The first is Melissa

Dawson, who has just been promoted from soloist to principal dancer."

As the room politely applauded, William froze. He looked up to the stage, realization dawning over his face.

"Dammit," he muttered.

"Anne Boroughs, who has just been promoted from the corps de ballet to soloist."

"Don't go away," he commanded before straightening his tie and righting his posture.

"And, of course, the fabulous William Darcy, who has come back home to choreograph for us."

He turned and cast Elizabeth a meaningful look before plastering on a fake smile and heading towards the stage.

Applause thundered through the ballroom, the noise making Elizabeth's head spin. She suddenly felt exhausted. She was so tired of William Darcy. She hated him. She hated Anne and Catherine Boroughs. And Charles Bingley. And Sir Webster Lucas. And while she was at it, Greg Wickham and everyone in that damn ballroom.

Elizabeth swallowed. The champagne had caught up with her. She needed to use the bathroom, and then she needed to leave. Backing into the crowd, Elizabeth edged along the perimeter of the ballroom, making for the door. She burst into the empty hallway and stumbled on the carpet. Righting herself, she scolded her fuzzy head and then made her way to the restroom. A few *corps* girls were returning from that direction. They complimented Elizabeth on her hair as they passed her. Smiling in reply, she walked into the restroom and first ran her hands under the faucet. Elizabeth pressed her cool fingers onto her face, reining in the fire on her cheeks.

She stared at her reflection. Rotating her head from one side to the other, she smiled sadly.

"What a waste!" she muttered, turning away from the mirror and into one of the stalls.

Her reflection reemerged when she opened the door once again. She looked so unlike herself with her hair now dark. Propping both hands on the counter, she leaned into the mirror and stared hard at her reflection. She opened her bag and went to take out her lipstick but decided against reapplying. She popped two mints in her mouth instead to take away its stale, sticky feeling.

Snapping the bag shut, Elizabeth decided she'd had enough of the Netherfield Gala. She would grab a taxi, stop off at the bodega on the way home, grab a pint of ice cream, and still make it back in time to watch late-night television. With the decision made, Elizabeth felt a resigned calm wash over her. This disaster of a night was finally over. She left the powder room and headed back inside to say goodbye to Jane.

As she neared the ballroom, she almost plowed into Darcy, who had just stepped panther-like from the entrance. Elizabeth started and stared, her reflexes dulled by the alcohol.

"Why did you leave?" he asked brusquely.

"I went to the restroom. Or did I need your permission for that?"

His features softened. "I thought you'd left for good."

"Well, I'm about to. Excuse me; I'm going to say goodbye to my sister."

"Why?"

"Why? Well, she would worry if I just disappeared." Elizabeth again tried to brush past him, but he grabbed her upper arms to stop her.

"Why are you leaving?"

"Why do you care?"

Darcy said nothing but continued to stare. She felt the bile rise in her throat. Before she allowed it to overwhelm her, she attempted to wrest her arms from him.

"You need to tell me what Wickham told you." His voice was glacial.

"Listen," she growled, shoving her pointer finger at his nose, "I don't need to do anything. You can boss me around in the studio, but don't try that shit here."

Elizabeth's heartbeat had skyrocketed. She felt dizzy and hot. Rubbing her eyes, she lowered her face and tried to rein in her fury. Darcy still stood in front of her, his breathing deep but labored. She looked up at him.

"I'm leaving," she repeated but with less determination than before.

His eyes were so intense that Elizabeth couldn't move. Like Medusa, his horrible stare had turned her to stone. The music and ruckus of the ballroom filtered out into the deserted hallway. Laughter and the clinking of plates in the background contrasted with Darcy's ragged breath. His jaw was set resolutely, his eyes glinting like sheet metal in the sun and his lips pursed.

Her breath hitched. Elizabeth felt an awful pressure at her throat. She could only stare, hypnotized. Her mind rippled with one, abrupt thought:

My God, he's beautiful.

Who moved first, Elizabeth could not be sure. It was immediate and reactive. Suddenly, her mouth and Darcy's were moving over each other's. He clasped her face between his hands. She tangled her fingers into the hair at the nape of his neck. They kissed, frenzied against each other.

Elizabeth's shoulder blades suddenly scraped against rough wallpaper. Letting her weight fall back on the wall, she pulled him down and opened her lips to him. Her head swam, and she felt liquid under the soft purposefulness of his mouth, the spice of his cologne, and the roughness of his jacket on her bare arms. He pressed himself down on her, rubbing her waist roughly with his thumbs. Closing her eyes, Elizabeth allowed herself to be pulled under by the sensations.

Suddenly, he pulled away.

Elizabeth's vision swam. She blinked twice. Darcy's face was taut and his jaw rigid, but his eyes darted up the length of her chest and face. After a few seconds, he took her hand.

"Let's go," he said hoarsely, pulling her down the hall.

"But Jane—" Elizabeth protested feebly.

"You can call her when we get home."

They stopped only at the cloakroom to retrieve their coats before bursting into the frigid March night and stepping into the first taxi waiting in the driveway of the hotel.

Chapter 13

Elizabeth groaned. Opening her eyes, she panicked momentarily at the unfamiliar bedroom. Then, she remembered the previous night.

"Oh my God," she muttered, pressing her fingers over her closed eyelids. Her stomach churned, her mouth felt cottony and dry, and her head throbbed. Sitting up in the king-sized bed, Elizabeth was alone amidst the rumpled sheets. Light peeked in through the gap in the curtains. She looked around: white sheets, beige carpet, mahogany poster bed with matching dresser and armoire, and a tasteful landscape painting on the far wall.

She hung her head in her hands, murmuring a choice four-letter word. Elizabeth stayed in that position for several minutes, contemplating how to proceed and how last night had happened. Her gown, along with her corset, hose, and panties, rested on a plush antique chair in the corner of the room.

How in the world had last night happened? She had been furious with him—something about Anne and Catherine Boroughs, Sir Webster Lucas, and her sister. She could only recall the night in flashes—like photographs in a slide show:

Banging her knee against an iron bistro chair as they scurried, mid-kiss, back into the bedroom... The touch of his fingertips as they brushed against the nape of her neck... The feel of his abdomen under her fingers, ridged yet soft when she'd peeled off his shirt. She didn't even recall how the first time proceeded or ended.

She remembered napping. They'd awakened afterwards and tripped into the bathroom. She remembered the cold tile under her bare feet. Her memory grew clearer, thanks to the invigorating effect of the shower. She recalled taking him in her soapy hands, his groans reverberating in the huge, tiled shower. Her own cries and gasps punctuated the steady sound of the water beating down. Her hand splayed before her on the navy tiles, bracing herself against the shower wall as he sank into her from behind, his bronze fingers kneading the white flesh of her breast. And she remembered climaxing so hard that she banged her head on the wall.

Elizabeth touched her forehead. A piece of skin was gone. She swallowed down the urge to cry. It got worse.

Sometime in the middle of the night, she remembered waking. She had lain on her side, her legs curled into a loose fetal position. Her head ached a bit then, but her thoughts had been clear. William was awake. He faced her, propped up on an elbow, his torso naked, his lower half outlined by the graceful fall of the sheets. He ran his hand lightly over the swell of her hipbone. Elizabeth had stared at him until her eyes adjusted to the darkness.

Both gazed at each other for a small eternity. She recalled the look in his eyes: tenderness and an unspoken question. Elizabeth had smiled sleepily and reached up for his face, bringing it down to hers for a deep, deliberate kiss.

"Elizabeth," he had whispered into the flesh under her ear, "you screamed 'Mr. Darcy' when you came in the shower."

Elizabeth chuckled.

"You might want to fix that."

"Are you ordering me around again?"

He'd answered with an unhurried kiss.

The third and last time they made love had been languid and exploring. He had murmured things to her, words that now sent her face burning. The back of his fingers grazing her neck, her throat, her cheek, Elizabeth was tugged back to their rehearsals, marveling at how very similar his hands felt on her naked skin. She remembered that time in rehearsal when they'd improvised the *pas de deux*, and it had felt so right, she hadn't been able to stop. Their lovemaking had felt like that.

And in that final climax, she buried her face into the warm crook of his neck and gasped the word he wanted to hear: William.

"William?" she called. The word felt strange on her lips. There was no reply.

Elizabeth swung her legs off the bed, pulling the sheet with her. Her head pounded as the blood rushed up to it. Wrapping the sheet around her body, she tiptoed to the bathroom—no William. She swallowed down a quake of annoyance and a small aftershock of fear. The bedroom door was cracked open. Pulling it back, she stepped into the hallway. Several doors lined both sides of the cream-carpeted hall. At the far end was a staircase. Elizabeth padded to it and got halfway down before her jaw dropped.

Under her, sprawled a massive, high-ceilinged living room, the far wall lined by glass windows that ran the entire height. The hardwood floors gleamed, and she saw a marble fireplace on another wall. Elizabeth never knew apartments in New York could have more than one floor, not to mention their own fireplaces.

Being careful not to trip on the sheet, she made it down the stairs and then called out his name again. This time she received a sweet "mew" in reply. An orange cat appeared from around the staircase, its tail swaying.

"Hello there," Elizabeth cooed. She was surprised that he had a pet. He didn't seem like the nurturing type. She knelt down to stroke the cat, and it purred. "Where's your master?"

The cat rubbed the top of its head against Elizabeth's hand.

"You know—the big, scary guy with the bad temper?"

Elizabeth again received a loud purr. Sighing, she stood and gazed around the enormous living room. Two hallways led off to either side. Looking right, she saw the breakfast bar and the chair she had run into the night before. She chose left, down another hallway, and finally heard the soft strains of classical music.

A door at the end of the hallway was ajar. Elizabeth approached silently and peeked into a small dance studio. She saw Darcy in the center, clad in sweatpants. He was shirtless, his chest glistening with sweat. Elizabeth swallowed hard, staring at his abdominals moving in and out as he panted from exertion. She admired the muscles of his shoulders rippling down to unyielding triceps. Forearms flexed gracefully and ridges of muscle flanked his hipbones.

The rush of desire slowly trickled out to irritation. True to character, Darcy played the role of ungracious lover immaculately. Damn, couldn't he have stayed in bed with her? He was sending quite a message that he was ready to move on from whatever had happened last night. Backing away from the door, she tiptoed down the hall and back into the palatial living room. She was humiliated.

Treading to the huge windows, Elizabeth leaned her forehead against the cool glass, gazed out at Central Park beneath her, and absentmindedly chewed on a fingernail. For a few seconds, she watched taxis whiz by dozens of stories below. The sky was a vibrant, cloudless blue. Elizabeth cursed herself. Closing her eyes, she winced in a simple remembrance of the previous night.

She was so absorbed in her remonstrations that she missed Darcy's soft footsteps on the carpet.

William paused, watching her, a slow smile warming his face. He couldn't believe it. Elizabeth was here, and they'd spent an entire night having amazing sex that puckered his skin when he remembered it.

Women, he thought—so predictable.

Although he had to admit her transformation had astounded him, maybe it shouldn't have. Elizabeth's angry snarls all evening had just come from pent-up desire. No matter how much she had protested otherwise, when it came down to it, Elizabeth had probably wanted him as much as he wanted her.

God, what a night! William felt high—the way he'd felt during the curtain call following an amazing performance. Even after that ghastly gala, three lovemaking sessions, and a sleepless night thereafter, he had the energy to sneak out of bed sometime around six in the morning and choreograph for two hours straight. He grinned like a milk-satiated cat. Every nerve in his body hummed. In his bed slept a gorgeous and eager twenty-three-year-old. Not only that, but a gorgeous and eager twenty-three-year-old he'd made love to three times and probably given twice as many orgasms.

He still had it! He felt invincible. That morning, he had begun the choreography for what was sure to be his next piece.

He gazed at her silently as she stood in the far end of his living room, draped in his sheet. Her dark hair fell over the white linen and those elegant shoulders. Elizabeth sighed, the sound reminiscent of her soft gasps in his ear the night before. William's desire began to simmer slowly. He cleared his throat, making her jump.

"Sorry," he said, approaching her.

Her lips fell open, a momentary rebelliousness bubbling up in her eyes, before a pink flush spread across her cheeks. He saw her eyes trail down his torso briefly before she forced them back to his face.

"Have you been awake long?" he asked.

"No." Elizabeth avoided looking at him.

William grinned lopsidedly. "The toga look suits you."

"I didn't..."

He looked at her forehead, a small pink wound marring the skin next to her hairline. Elizabeth flinched when he ran his thumb across it.

"We have to be more careful next time," he murmured, brushing the hair off her shoulders and exposing her neck. William grasped the nape and brought his lips down to nibble at the skin under her jawbone. She stiffened and inhaled sharply. Moments later, a stifled moan escaped from her throat.

His lips moved to her mouth, and he kissed her slowly. Elizabeth hesitated. William pressed her against him and deepened the pressure of his mouth to encourage her. She responded, but without the same intensity from the night before. After a few more moments, however, Elizabeth began to melt. William trailed his hands lower to cup and knead her breasts. He moved to undo the dastardly sheet when Elizabeth groaned into his mouth and then pushed him away.

She stood several feet from him, panting. Elizabeth refused to meet his gaze. She was so ashamed and angry with herself. Damn! How could he make her feel those things again? She would *not* succumb to them this time! Darcy looked puzzled. As he breathed raggedly, she wondered what was going through his mind. Was he angry? Did he think her a complete tease?

Staring up at him, Elizabeth bit her lower lip. Suddenly, her hungry stomach piped in with a protest of its own. Darcy heard it growl, and the expression on his face changed.

"Ah, I see." He smiled. "What do you want to eat?"

"Um... really, that's okay. I can get something after I go."

Darcy frowned.

"I—I just want to take a shower." She saw his eyes smolder, and so she added, "Alone."

The frown deepened. Reluctantly, he turned and motioned for her to follow him upstairs. As she trailed behind him, Elizabeth gawked at a bead of sweat running down the channel of William's spine. Cords of muscles ran parallel to it, rising up to two ridges under his shoulder blades. She was shaken, ashamed, and angry, yet all she wanted to do was reach out and caress that powerful back.

They climbed the stairs, William pausing at the top. "You can use the shower in my bathroom. Call me if you need anything."

Nodding, Elizabeth lowered her eyes as she swept past him through the master bedroom and into his enormous bathroom. Closing the door, Elizabeth sighed, her shoulders slumping. She stared at herself in the mirror, fingering her now dark brown hair. She didn't look like herself. Hell, she didn't feel like herself.

"Elizabeth," came a muffled voice from the bedroom, "I need the sheet to make the bed."

Removing it, she saw a deep, berry-colored mark on her right breast, undeniable proof that last night had been no dream. She pushed open the bathroom door to pass Darcy the sheet. Through the crack, Darcy ran his eyes down her nude body.

"That's not fair," she said, crossing her arms over her chest.

A wicked grin curved his lips. "You didn't seem to mind last night."

Elizabeth's nostrils flared. "I'm closing the door."

Darcy raised an eyebrow and swept his eyes up Elizabeth's trembling body one last time before she shut him out.

Once he left, she quickly stepped into the shower and turned on the water. She rubbed her face, hoping the soothing stream of hot water would settle her frazzled senses. It had the opposite effect. The navy blue tiles on the wall only reminded her of Sex Romp Number Two. She immediately picked up a bottle of shampoo and began to wash her hair.

How could she have done what she did last night? Her eyes watered. Elizabeth wished she could rewind time to change the decisions she'd made. Darcy was hot; that had never been in doubt. She was powerfully attracted to him. That, too, had never been in doubt. But every interaction she had with him made her feel clumsy, insecure, and angry. And now she'd gone and slept with him! She and Darcy never had a record of cordiality towards one another. Their one-night stand would probably make their interactions that much more awkward and painful for Elizabeth. Staring vacantly, she shivered.

Finally, Elizabeth finished washing, stepped from the shower, and dried herself off with a lush white towel. She looked around the bathroom, elegantly decorated with navy tiles and white touches all around. She felt like she was staying at the Ritz-Carlton—or what she imagined staying at the Ritz-Carlton would feel like. Just then, she realized she had nothing to change into but her evening gown.

She laughed at herself bitterly. Oh, but wouldn't her walk of shame that morning be grand? She rubbed a tear from the corner of her eye.

Elizabeth tentatively opened the bathroom door and stepped out onto the soft beige carpet of Darcy's bedroom. He'd made the bed and opened the curtains. Everything looked pristine and bright. Her gown was no longer on the chair in the bedroom. In fact, it was nowhere in sight. In a neat pile on his bed were some folded clothes and a note.

Hope some of these fit. I'll be back in 10. —W

Under the note was a selection of sweaters, t-shirts, sweatpants, and leggings. Elizabeth briefly wondered why William had a collection of women's clothing. Was this some kind of morning-after courtesy that he extended to all of his one-night stands? Still, it was better than wearing an evening gown home on the subway.

Elizabeth chose a pair of leggings and a sweater. They fit a bit too snugly, but she couldn't be particular at this point.

Then, she had a realization. "Oh, my God! Jane!"

She bolted to her clutch, fished out her cell phone, and saw that she had eleven missed calls, five texts, and four voice mails. She called Jane immediately.

"Hello?" answered a groggy voice.

"Jane?"

"Oh, God! Elizabeth Bennet! Where did you go last night? I was frantic."

"Sorry," Elizabeth whispered.

"Sorry! That's it? Sorry? Where are you? Why are you whispering?"

"I was a bit drunk last night."

"Oh, my God. Are you in jail? What did you do, Elizabeth?"

Elizabeth rolled her eyes. "No, Jane! I'm fine. I'll be home later this afternoon."

"Where are you?"

Elizabeth paused, wondering whether to lie or not. Then she realized that there was no point in lying. The whole story would come out later when Elizabeth got home. She would need to tell someone.

"I'm at... William Darcy's place."

No reply came from the other end of the line.

"Hello?" Elizabeth asked.

"William Darcy?" This time, Elizabeth did not reply. Jane chuckled low on the other end. *"Oh, boy, Lizzy!"*

"You have to promise me not to say anything to Charles."

"What happened?"

Elizabeth heard a door slam shut downstairs.

"I'm leaving soon, and I'll tell you everything when I get home. Gotta go now. Bye!" She ended the call and shoved her phone back into her clutch.

Elizabeth's heart began pounding wildly, and she didn't know why. She was having another out-of-body experience, still unable to believe that she was in Darcy's apartment. Taking several deep breaths, she walked out of the bedroom.

"Hello?" she called.

"In the kitchen!"

She went downstairs to find Darcy setting down a bowl of cat food. Sucking in her breath, Elizabeth tried hard not to stare but thought it extremely cruel of him to look so damn good. His hair was mussed, his chin dusted with stubble. The clothes he wore—trim jeans and a hooded zip-up sweatshirt—gave him an edgy urban look. William caught the look in her eyes and smirked.

"Good, the clothes fit," he said.

"The sweater's a bit tight," replied Elizabeth, running her hands over her waist.

His eyes caressed her in the same place. "My sister must be slightly smaller than you."

"You have a sister?" Now that Darcy mentioned it, she remembered Greg had spoken of a sister.

"Why else would I have women's clothing in the house?"

Elizabeth shrugged. "Old girlfriend? I don't know."

Again, Darcy smirked. "How inconsiderate do you think I am?"

Elizabeth didn't reply.

Suddenly, Darcy turned around, grabbed a plastic bag off the granite countertop, and produced two palm-sized bundles from it. "Roasted vegetables with goat cheese, or prosciutto and arugula?"

"Huh?"

"I picked up some sandwiches. Which one do you want?"

Elizabeth stared at him. "You didn't have to do that. I told you I could pick something up on my way home."

His smile soured. "What kind of man do you think I am? First, I give you an old girlfriend's clothes, and then I send you home starving? I try to be a little more gentlemanly than that. Veggies or prosciutto?"

Pursing her lips, Elizabeth looked away. "Veggies, please."

She accepted the sandwich from Darcy and unwrapped it, salivating. Pulling a plastic bottle of orange juice from the bag, he got two glasses down from a cabinet and poured her some. Elizabeth accepted the glass with a polite smile and took a sip.

"Mm, fresh squeezed," she said.

Darcy only smiled in response and walked around the kitchen counter to join Elizabeth at the breakfast bar. They ate in awkward silence for a few minutes. Elizabeth complimented the sandwiches, and they chatted about the deli around the corner. That conversation soon sputtered to an end.

Darcy ate with his eyes riveted on her, which made Elizabeth nervous. A roasted pepper fell out of her sandwich and landed on her borrowed leggings. Cursing, she picked it up quickly and apologized to him. He just shrugged.

"My sister never wears them anyway."

Sensing an opportunity for conversation, Elizabeth picked up the cue. "Is your sister home?"

"She doesn't live in New York anymore," he answered curtly.

Elizabeth dropped the subject, and the conversation once again lapsed into silence. She chewed monotonously, not tasting a thing. Placing her sandwich down, she glanced around the apartment, desperate to hit upon a topic of conversation until she could flee.

"This is a really nice apartment."

Darcy smiled. "Thanks."

"It's beautiful. It could be in a magazine."

"It was, a few years back. Right after I'd gotten it done."

Elizabeth paused to let that one sink in. "It's so clean."

"One man living in an apartment this big doesn't really do much damage."

"Yeah, how does one man live in an apartment this big? It's a little excessive, isn't it?"

"It's been in the family a long time. I'm lucky that I inherited it when my dad died."

"Oh." Elizabeth was so used to living in poverty, and all of her friends and coworkers living in poverty, that it shocked her to learn that some ballet dancers came from money—lots of money, apparently.

"Yeah, I guess it's one of the perks of being the son, grandson, and great-grandson of New York City real estate tycoons." There was an edge in his voice.

"Now you're just bragging. I'm sure that there are many more perks."

"I'm sure there are," he said bitterly.

Finishing her sandwich in silence, Elizabeth avoided prying too deeply. She didn't want any more altercations, and she didn't want him to turn around and ask her about her nutty family. She just wanted to go home, take two ibuprofens, talk to Jane, and attempt to forget this entire mistake. Darcy probably wanted the same. Swallowing the last bite of bread and washing it down with the orange juice, she turned to him and smiled weakly.

"Thanks for breakfast."

"Like I said, it was the least I could do."

"So," Elizabeth said nervously.

"So."

"So what do we do tomorrow?"

Darcy answered, "This won't change anything about the way we interact in the studio, so you know."

Elizabeth swallowed down a tightness in her throat. "I hadn't expected it to."

Darcy nodded.

"I'd better get going then. I'm sure you want your Sunday back."

"You don't have to run out," he replied.

"No, I... have things to do."

Darcy nodded again.

"I'll go get my stuff," Elizabeth said finally.

When she came back downstairs, she looked puzzled. "What happened to my gown?"

Darcy was in the middle of clearing the breakfast bar of their sandwich wrappers. It felt weird to see him with a paper towel in his hand wiping his counters. Elizabeth had never imagined the choreographer engaged in such mundane things.

"I dropped it off at the dry cleaners when I went to get the sandwiches."

For some reason, the gesture stunned her. She cocked her head to the side. "Oh . . . thank you. You didn't have to do that."

Darcy waved her off.

Digging in her purse, Elizabeth added, "Well, let me know how much it cost. I'll pay you back."

"Don't worry about it."

"No, please, I'm—"

"Elizabeth," Darcy interrupted in a warning tone, "I got it. Don't worry about it."

She opened her mouth to protest, but he quickly spun around and walked in the direction of the foyer. Fearing she would get lost if she didn't follow, Elizabeth skirted after him. He stood next to the front door, his hand already on the handle.

Elizabeth recognized the customary coldness in his eyes. William Darcy, the choreographer, had returned. There had been glimpses of a different William Darcy, but perhaps it had just been the sex.

Elizabeth buttoned up her coat quickly, feeling his eyes on her the entire time. When she fastened the last button at her neck, she glanced up at him.

"Be careful getting home." His voice was wooden.

"It's broad daylight. I think I'll be okay."

He opened the door for Elizabeth.

"See you Tuesday."

He nodded perfunctorily. She thought she detected wistfulness in his eyes, but she breezed by him so fast she could not be sure. She pressed the elevator button. His door was the only one in the hall. The elevator dinged, announcing its arrival. Still, he waited in the doorway. The doors slid open.

"Bye," Elizabeth said, turning her head slightly to look at him. He made no reply. Instead, he retreated silently into the confines of his apartment and closed the door with a sharp, resounding thud. Elizabeth frowned.

"Asshole," she muttered, before stepping into the elevator's blissful emptiness.

Chapter 14

Elizabeth stepped into the studio on Tuesday, her fingers trembling. Her heart beat heavily throughout company class and not from exertion. Feeling disconnected from her body, Elizabeth received a verbal lashing from the ballet mistress when she forgot a step in the waltz, nearly crashing into another dancer. In the *adagio*, the teacher once again yelled at her about her hip alignment. Elizabeth repressed a scowl, but once the exercise was over, she rushed off to the back of the room to lick her wounds. Stretching out her calves over the *barre*, she caught Caroline Bingley's eyes fixed on her. They narrowed and the prima turned away with a prickly glare. Elizabeth's stomach clenched. She scanned the room, feeling as though everyone's eyes were on her. From across the room, Louisa seemed to be glowering too—and Robert, and Laurie, and Anne, and even Katherine.

Moving towards her sister, Elizabeth muttered, "Why is everyone looking at me?"

Jane frowned. "No one's looking at you."

Elizabeth bit her lip and watched the rest of the exercise feeling unbearably scrutinized.

After that, she hadn't been able to eat lunch. And then it was time for Darcy's rehearsal. She felt afraid of what would happen in that studio. Would everyone be able to tell she'd slept with him? How could they not? Elizabeth prayed that Darcy would not betray their secret. She prayed that she wouldn't either.

When Darcy walked into the studio, however, he didn't even glance at her. Elizabeth's heart pounded, and she avoided looking directly at him. He scanned the room quickly, but not for her.

"No Caroline?" he asked.

Everyone shrugged. She hadn't shown up to rehearsals since her tantrum the week prior.

"Ms. Bennet, can you fill in for her?" he asked nonchalantly.

Perhaps Elizabeth would have felt more nervous about stepping in for Caroline if she hadn't been so tense about appearing unconcerned. As it was, however, it required all of her attention to control the blush that threatened to overtake her cheeks, neck, and chest whenever Darcy glanced at her.

He was cleaning the third movement that day, making sure all of the *corps de ballet's* arms stretched into the exact same angle, smoothing out a rough transition between formations. As rehearsal passed, Elizabeth calmed. Darcy focused only on his choreography. Why had she expected it to be any different? That was the one thing Elizabeth should have known for certain. Darcy would never reveal anything, not the slightest look or the slightest gesture, in his rehearsals.

The *corps* ran through the movement twice. Fortunately, the principal dancer incorporated herself quite often into the *corps de ballet's* dancing in the final movement, so the steps came naturally to Elizabeth. Darcy reminded her patiently when she didn't know them. When the music died and the dancers were in their final poses, Darcy nodded. His lips curved upwards.

"I think we're ready for the stage."

The dancers looked at each other in relief and broke into smiles. A few applauded and cheered softly. They were blocking on stage Wednesday and Thursday. Friday was dress rehearsal, and Saturday evening was the piece's world premier.

Elizabeth exhaled as she turned with the other dancers and walked away. Darcy had not called after her. He hadn't said or done anything in rehearsal that revealed the awful mistake they'd made after the gala. Perhaps he would be just as willing as she was to simply let it go.

She felt oddly disoriented. There was relief there, to be sure. And there was something else underneath, tickling at her insides, something that felt like discontent, which she didn't understand.

She went to the locker room to change before making the walk uptown to stage rehearsal at the theater for another ballet. Brushing out her sweaty hair, Elizabeth chatted with some of the other dancers, her friends. They talked about getting back into the musty smelling dressing rooms behind the Met, about the cute stage manager, and about their various aches and pains.

Elizabeth grabbed her dance bag and walked out with Jane and two soloists. She stopped at her mailbox in the office before leaving. She found a memo about the floors being waxed, a flyer for an upcoming Alvin Ailey performance, and a blue envelope, sealed, with nothing written on the front or back. Glancing into the other dancers' mailboxes, she noticed no such envelope in any of them. Her heart began racing.

Ripping the envelope open, she pulled out a sheet of lined paper, folded in precise thirds. Her fingers trembled when she read the small, neat writing.

I'll meet you outside of the stage door after your rehearsal. —WD

She didn't like it. What if someone saw them together? Balling up the note, she shoved it deep in her bag and headed outside.

Elizabeth deliberately took longer backstage to pack up her shoes, warmers, and tights. She wanted everyone else to be gone before she met up with him so they wouldn't be spotted together. Whatever Darcy wanted to say to Elizabeth was sure to be awkward for both of them. Elizabeth had already rehearsed her apology for the other night. She would say she was sorry, he would too, and they would agree never to talk about it again.

Elizabeth just needed a way to stop thinking about it. For two days, her every thought had been of Saturday night. The humiliation cut freshly each time—her fury at Greg and at Darcy, and the inexplicable desire she felt when she relived the words, touches, and movements she remembered. Despite her best efforts, a hefty chunk of her memory from that night had been swept away in the aftermath of champagne.

Elizabeth looked at herself in the mirror of the empty dressing room and practiced what she would say to Darcy. She needed to practice it because she felt that same desire for him again and would not let herself—*could not* let herself—act upon it.

She pushed open the backstage door, and there he was, several yards away, pacing back and forth, his hands shoved deeply into the pockets of his leather coat. He saw her, stopped, and slowly walked towards her. How could he look so calm when she felt so frazzled?

"Ready?" he asked, his voice low and melting.

It took a moment before Elizabeth trusted her voice to reply. "Ready for what?"

"I thought we'd go to dinner."

Elizabeth crammed down any nervousness she felt under a veneer of anger. "You didn't even ask me if I had plans. I might have plans, you know."

"Okay. Do you have plans?"

"No."

Darcy looked at her curiously. "Then let's go." Without waiting for her, he turned and began walking uptown.

Elizabeth's chest heaved in anger. If they were going to have this awkward conversation, did it really need to be over dinner? Couldn't they just let bygones be bygones right there?

"Hold on!" she cried, rushing to catch up. He stared down at her again with that patronizing look. "You don't have to take me to dinner, you know."

Then, he cracked a grin. "Let me take you to dinner. It's the least I can do. Come on. We have an eight o'clock reservation, and we've got nine minutes to make it."

Bewildered, Elizabeth followed in silence. It was *the least* he could do? For what? For dumping her? Well, not really dumping her, per se, since they weren't officially anything, and Elizabeth didn't really want to be associated with him anyway.

Nothing else was said until they reached the restaurant, which allowed Elizabeth to stew in confusion, anger, and anxiety. Once inside, Darcy removed his coat, revealing a gray cashmere sweater and perfectly tailored wool pants that were far nicer than the jeans and sneakers she had on. Elizabeth swore she saw the hostess wrinkle her nose.

"You could have warned me," Elizabeth whispered sharply once they were seated across a candle-lit table.

"Of—?" She gestured to her sweatshirt. Darcy shrugged. "You look fine."

"The hostess doesn't seem to think so."

"Don't worry about her. You don't look any worse than some of the tourists that come through here."

Elizabeth bristled and scanned the drink menu. Skimming the list, her eyes widened at the prices. Six dollars for a soda? A sharply dressed waiter came to take their drink order.

"Iced tea," William ordered.

"Just water, please," Elizabeth said.

"Sparkling or still?"

"Uh... just tap water will be fine."

The waiter paused, then nodded and headed back to the kitchen. Elizabeth let a small sigh escape her lungs, which seemed unnoticed by William as he looked over the menu.

"The gnocchi here is outstanding. But so is the roast pork loin," he commented.

Elizabeth opened up her menu. The cheapest entrée, goat cheese ravioli in a sage-butter sauce, was twenty-nine dollars. She sat in silence, running her eyes up the page, desperation wracking at her chest. Swallowing, she closed the menu and tried to smile.

"I'll let you recommend something."

Glancing up at her, Darcy went back to his menu. The waiter returned with their drinks. Elizabeth shifted in her chair, making a mental tally as William ordered, and then realized she wasn't hungry at all. She was too on-edge to eat. After the waiter departed, William stirred his tea casually with a straw and stared at her. Elizabeth felt her heartbeat trip in anxiety.

"So," she said, "What's up?"

Darcy smiled lopsidedly. "Nothing's up."

"Okay... then why did you want to talk to me?"

"I didn't want to talk to you. I mean, I do. Want to talk to you. But I had nothing specific in mind."

Elizabeth frowned and adjusted the napkin in her lap. "I just thought... because of the note and all... that you wanted to talk about—"

"No. I had no agenda in taking you out, Elizabeth." A ghost of a smile played on his lips, and his eyes danced as if keeping a funny secret.

The way he said *Elizabeth* made the hairs on her arm stand on end. She shifted again. "You don't want to talk about Saturday night?"

"Do *you* want to talk about Saturday night?"

Elizabeth shrugged, feeling her face warm. Suddenly, her resolve drained away. If he had no particular agenda, why had he brought her here? It had all of the trappings of a date: a man and a woman, a fancy restaurant, a candlelit table. But the idea of a date with William Darcy was ludicrous.

She knew she must have had a deer-in-the-headlights look on her face.

Taking a deep breath, she struggled to regain her composure. Elizabeth looked up and smiled nervously. Then, looking away, she made a trite comment on the décor of the restaurant.

William propped up his cheek with his hand. Light from the small candle on their table flickered over Elizabeth's face, deepening the color of her skin and lips. He saw the flame's reflection bouncing in her bright eyes and felt a deep satisfaction warm him. It felt good to finally be with her like this. He had wrestled with his emotions for so long, been haunted by her in the studio and in his bed before sleep. Now, he was simply relieved. At Saturday's gala, she had made the decision for him with her sudden, zealous kiss. That was the hard part, wasn't it? Acting. And he hadn't even had to. Now, he simply needed to proceed as usual. The hard part was over.

He didn't mind the lapses in their conversation. It gave him the opportunity to observe her—her adorably freckled nose, her small, heart-shaped lips, her intelligent eyes, and that hair, straight and glossy and aching for his fingers. William felt his body respond and pushed those thoughts away until he could lose himself in her again tonight.

The soup arrived, and William smiled smugly as Elizabeth blathered her way through it, making nervous comments about what was in the broth and the designs on the bowls. He was struck again by how young she was. Maybe the guys she dated only wanted to get her in bed, and that's why she had been surprised by the dinner date. William found it a welcome change from the sophistication of the women he normally dated, who wanted to be wined and dined and given a whole resume of his life before dessert. Elizabeth wasn't like that. He liked her girlish nervousness. She was twenty-three, beautiful, bright, a miracle lover, and she was with him. William leaned back in his chair and grinned. Yes, he still had it.

Elizabeth had nearly had it. For twenty minutes, she had sustained a monologue about the goddamned tablecloths, soup broth, filigree on the bowls, Florence, and Leonardo da *friggin'* Vinci, and she was through. If Darcy wanted to keep smiling his patronizing little smiles, then he could do it in silence. She didn't know why he had brought her here if he simply meant to stare condescendingly the entire evening. Elizabeth wondered what Jane was doing and inwardly scowled when she imagined her sister with her perfect, affable, unpatronizing boyfriend.

The pasta came. Elizabeth hated cream sauces. She hated sharing a plate of pasta with William Darcy even more. If he liked the gnocchi so damn much, she would let him at it.

"You're not going to eat any more?" he asked.

"I'm watching my figure," she lied. "Some recent feedback."

Darcy frowned and let his eyes rake down her torso. Clearly, her quip hadn't registered.

Tapping her foot against the floor, she cringed when she made contact with Darcy's leg. "Sorry."

"Are you nervous?" he asked.

Elizabeth arched an eyebrow. "Yes."

"Because of me?"

"Good guess, Sherlock." Looking away, Elizabeth felt like she would explode with ire. How could such a man, so smooth and handsome, be such a schmuck?

The evening crawled along. Little meaningful conversation was to be had, and she nearly cried with happiness when the check came. Darcy slipped his platinum Amex into the leather folder and handed it back to the waiter. Although Elizabeth offered to pay, he waved her off.

She couldn't wait to get outside when they could just agree never to talk about what happened Saturday night and she could leave. She just wanted to get home, change into her PJs, and join Jane on the sofa for sitcom reruns.

At the coat check, Darcy held her jacket for her as she awkwardly twisted herself into it. He opened the door for her, and she squeezed past him. The night was unseasonably cold for March. Elizabeth shivered, and Darcy grabbed her hand. Her heart stopped beating. Darcy entwined his fingers in hers and pulled her to him. Wordlessly, he ran his thumb over her mouth and then replaced it with his own.

She loathed him; she really, really did. But she had to give it to him. He could kiss. She was about to melt into the movements of his lips when Elizabeth suddenly realized what the kiss was all about—Darcy didn't *want* it to end! He had planned for an encore of Saturday's performance! Suddenly the awkward pretensions of dinner made sense; it was just a prelude to what he really wanted.

Elizabeth pushed herself off of him. "I . . . I'm going home." She felt dazed.

"What?"

"There's class tomorrow at ten o'clock. I have to go home."

"You can go to class from my place."

Biting the inside of her cheek, Elizabeth glowered. She backed away, unable to control the quiver of anger in her voice.

"No, I'm going home. Good night."

Before he had the chance to reply, she spun on her heel and began walking in the direction of the subway station. Several long moments later, she heard a car door slam and a taxi speed off uptown.

William had lived in his apartment for twenty years—seventeen when he'd been growing up and a little over three since his father died. Yet, Elizabeth had been there for only a night—several hours, really—and suddenly the whole place reminded him of her. He glanced at his bed, perfectly made, but could remember what it had looked like when she'd been curled in his sheets. He disrobed absentmindedly and stepped into the shower.

William stood under the jet spray, letting the water soothe him. He was pissed. He had taken her to a meal at one of his favorite restaurants, smiled at her the whole night, listened to her talk. Isn't that what women claimed they wanted? A man who listened? Yet, she'd blown him off.

Turning off the water, William quickly reached for a towel and patted himself dry. He wrapped the towel around his waist and stepped out of the shower, padding over to the bathroom counter. Leaning into it, he inspected himself in the mirror. Sure, there were a few tiny wrinkles by the corners of his eyes, but he looked better than most men his age who were stuck in some nine-to-five desk job. He stepped back and rubbed his biceps. Rotating to profile, he flexed his triceps and nodded in approval. He looked good. He'd always known it. Women thought so. So what was Elizabeth's problem? It just made him all the more frustrated.

He paced back into his bedroom. While his body was not burning with need anymore, his thoughts were still racked with confusion. William stopped, looked around, and grew livid. She hadn't even thanked him for dinner.

Here he was, banging his head against the wall over some ungrateful *corps de ballet* dancer. He dated lawyers, socialites, wannabe actresses—*women*. Not silly, ungracious girls. Resuming his pacing, he glanced at his bed and could only remember how pleasantly disheveled and sheetless it had been a few mornings ago. His anger collapsed.

He had been so happy on Saturday night—happy like he hadn't felt in months, maybe years. Light, giddy, satisfied. Like good things stretched before him for miles *finally.* Like years of gray had ended on Saturday night. And now he felt like they were back with a vengeance. All because of some ungrateful, disrespectful, simple *corps de ballet* dancer.

William had been in love once, years ago. It had been frustrating and painful, and he remembered those feelings again now. He didn't understand why Elizabeth was playing hard to get. Annoyed, he sighed and sank onto his bed. What did she want? Did she want him to go down to her level? Maybe he had been insensitive? Maybe he should have asked Elizabeth what she wanted to do rather than presume she liked posh Italian meals. Maybe she preferred fluorescent-lit pizza parlors.

He imagined himself spending the night in her Harlem apartment, being dragged to clubs in Brooklyn warehouses or to Soho to shop or whatever normal twenty-three-year-old girls did for fun. He sighed and supposed there was nothing he could do. He would have to apologize to her on Friday and learn how to accommodate her lifestyle if he wanted this to work. That was what love was about, right?

Chapter 15

On Wednesday when Elizabeth stepped onto the stage, she immediately saw William Darcy standing in the empty house. He held his arms akimbo, frowning. The sea of red seats engulfed him, but not his presence. Elizabeth could feel his command despite the distance between them. She remembered their date from the night before and swallowed down a cocktail of anger and anxiety. Looking away sourly, she did a few *relevés* to soften her pointe shoes.

"Can we get it a bit warmer?" Darcy called out into the void. Suddenly, the red gels above them lit up, and the stage brightened. Many of the dancers took no notice and continued to stretch out in the wings and on stage.

Darcy then called out to the *corps de ballet.* "Dancers, I need you in your places."

They complied, although Elizabeth looked nervously around for the one dancer she hadn't seen in a long time, Caroline Bingley. The diva still had not showed up to rehearsal. Shockingly, Darcy had made no mention of it and had continued to ask Elizabeth to stand in for Caroline. The piece premiered on Friday evening. The highest-level benefactors would be watching tomorrow's dress rehearsal. It seemed uncharacteristically laid-back for him, and it made Elizabeth nervous.

"Still no Caroline?" Darcy asked.

The dancers shrugged and looked at each other.

"Fine," Darcy said evenly. "Ms. Bennet, you'll fill in again."

She nodded and swallowed heavily, hoping to moisten her parched mouth. The sound of nearly a dozen pairs of pointe shoes clopping on the wooden floor heightened the chaos in Elizabeth's head. She couldn't explain it, but she was terrified. Yes, she knew the *pas de deux* better than anyone. Dancing it felt like second nature. And she knew Caroline's part in the first and third movements well enough. But there was Louisa Hirsch, Caroline's understudy. Why didn't Darcy just ask her to fill in?

Her hands were freezing. Shaking them vigorously, Elizabeth hoped to return some warmth to her fingertips. She jumped up and down a few times to do the same for her feet. Panic pushed up in her throat, and she swallowed it down.

"I really wish Caroline would start showing up to rehearsal," she muttered to her partner, Ben.

"Not me," he replied. "So, are you really dancing this?"

"No," Elizabeth replied.

"Well," he said, patting her hip, "seems like you are, honey. Be ready."

Elizabeth stared at him in bewilderment.

"Let's go!" Darcy snapped loudly.

She looked out to the house where he stood like a sentinel in the expanse of the theater, his arms folded over his chest, his face stern. Elizabeth prepared the opening pose.

"And . . . " he cued, and she stepped on to the tip of her pointe shoe and into the waiting hand of her partner.

Blocking for the *pas de deux* was relatively easy, since there were only two people on stage. Every now and again, a correction from the choreographer would boom into the empty space—"Ms. Bennet, cover a wider area in that *glissade*" or "A little further upstage"—but the rehearsal proceeded quickly.

About two-thirds of the way through the *pas de deux*, another voice echoed backstage.

"Sorry I'm late!" Caroline sang, as she strode on stage. She cast Elizabeth a nasty glance and turned to Darcy. "What did I miss?"

Darcy replied evenly, "Over a week's worth of rehearsals."

"You know how nervous I get during Gala Week," said Caroline.

Ben snorted under his breath and muttered something indecipherable. If there was one thing everyone knew, it was that Caroline Bingley never got nervous, especially during Gala Week when she had a daily opportunity to strut in front of New York's wealthiest. Elizabeth's heartbeat picked up when she saw Darcy make no reaction.

Still smiling, Caroline sashayed to center stage. "Thanks, sweetie, I can take it from here," she said to Elizabeth.

"Ms. Bingley, there have been some casting changes since you were last here," Darcy said brusquely.

"Oh? I've heard nothing about any casting changes."

"They were last minute. You've been cut."

Elizabeth felt her insides squeeze together, understanding immediately the implications of Darcy's casting changes: he intended for her to perform the role! Her face going white with anger, Caroline clearly understood that, too. She began sputtering. "I'm sorry? Does Lucas know about this?"

"You walked out of rehearsal last week and have missed three rehearsals since. You can tell Lucas whatever you like, but you don't know the choreography, and you're not dancing in my piece." Darcy turned his focus back to the dancers. "Let's go from that section again."

Caroline seethed. "You can't just kick me out! Or have you forgotten who's dancing the lead role in the premiere?"

Darcy smirked at her. "I haven't forgotten at all. Thank you, Ms. Bingley."

Laughing, Caroline turned her sharp nose from Darcy to Elizabeth, who inhaled slowly, squaring her shoulders against Caroline's bared canines.

"Oh no, William. Have you gone mad? *Her*? Oh, my God. This is too hysterical. Wait until I tell Lucas."

"Ms. Bennet is dancing the *pas de deux*," the choreographer replied calmly, "in spite of what you or Lucas want."

Everyone on stage gaped at her. Panic gave Elizabeth the courage she needed to speak.

"Mr. Darcy, I think you've proven your point—"

"Elizabeth, *we'll* talk about this later," he growled.

"Oh, no"—Caroline laughed, a touch of hysteria in her voice—"I'm dancing the *pas de deux*. And I'm sure both Charles and Lucas will back me up on this one."

Darcy breathed deeply. Looking at his dancers, he snapped, "From that section again."

Caroline's nostrils flared. "I won't be ignored, William!" She whirled around and stormed into the wings. Elizabeth stood mute and trembling in the center of the stage, feeling the eyes of the dancers and stagehands on her as if she were the one to blame for bringing on the sudden burst of chaos.

"Ms. Bennet, let's go," Darcy clipped.

Elizabeth glared out at him, her hands shaking in rage. Her throat constricted painfully as she willed herself not to cry. With barely a day of preparation, there was no way she would be able to dance this role tomorrow. Then she felt Ben's comforting hand on her waist.

"Come on, Liz," he whispered. "You're ready. This is how stars are made."

She looked up into his sympathetic eyes. Nodding, she took a few deep breaths to compose herself.

"Can we cue the music back to the beginning?" Darcy called out into the empty theater. "Dancers, places."

And then his cell phone rang. He sighed in frustration and answered it in a clipped tone. The conversation lasted no longer than a minute because Darcy hung up abruptly.

Somehow, Elizabeth managed to dance through the terror she felt. With every movement, she pictured herself flailing, tripping, or wobbling, disappointing a theater full of patrons and critics—disappointing Darcy. She wasn't ready for this. She hadn't even been fitted for the lead's costume. She didn't know the part in the third movement as well as she should. Her breath came in pants towards the end of the *pas de deux*. Elizabeth danced just to get through it so that, when it was over, she could go backstage and cry.

But that wouldn't be possible.

Because, midway through a lift, she saw three familiar figures slip in towards the back of the theater: Caroline, Charles, and Sir Webster. They began speaking to Darcy. And although the music drowned out their conversation, Elizabeth could tell from the cutting and wild hand gestures they made that it was not a happy interaction. The music ended, and their angry whispers could be heard echoing through the empty theater.

Then, Sir Webster spoke. "Dancers, take ten. Elizabeth, can we speak to you in the dressing room, please?"

The artistic director sounded as serious as Elizabeth had ever heard him. Ignoring the eyes around her, she pressed down her mounting panic and rushed to the fluorescent-lit halls of the backstage area.

Charles met her there with an apologetic look on his face.

"What's going on?" asked Elizabeth.

He sighed deeply. "I don't know. I'm sorry, Liz. I'm not sure what Will was thinking with this one."

Although Charles probably hadn't meant to offend, Elizabeth bristled at the comment. Did he have to seem so incredulous that Darcy would have wanted her to dance the role? It made no sense to be furious both at Darcy for thrusting her into the spotlight and at Charles for thinking the choreographer was crazy to have done so.

"Anyway, they're waiting for us in there," he said, gesturing to one of the stars' dressing rooms. "I think Lucas just wants to know what's going on."

Elizabeth replied, "I don't know much, Charles."

He looked resigned. "I'm sorry. Would you mind just giving your side of things?"

She nodded and Charles thanked her. When she opened the door, Elizabeth felt the feral atmosphere of the dressing room. Caroline glowered at her and muttered something under her breath. Darcy wore an expression of stone, and although he at least made eye contact with her when she entered, his eyes reflected no feeling.

The artistic director, at least, smiled at Elizabeth. He had his arms crossed over his generous stomach. "I'm sorry about this, honey. Don't worry; I just need to hear your side of the story."

"Okay," began Elizabeth. "If you could tell me what you'd like to—"

"We're trying to understand what's going on here." Sir Webster gestured from Caroline to Darcy to herself.

Elizabeth took a deep breath and willed her voice not to tremble. "I've been filling in for the role since Caroline... left. I assumed when she returned to rehearsals, that things would proceed as usual."

"As usual?"

"That Caroline would dance the part."

"I see." Sir Webster nodded. "And had you been understudying the part?"

"No."

Caroline snorted. "She's been dancing the thing all along."

"She wasn't—" interjected Darcy.

"When I ask for your opinion, you'll give it to me," the artistic director snapped. Looking away, Darcy paced to the opposite side of the room and stood with his back towards them. Caroline simply arched an eyebrow and inspected a cuticle.

"I hadn't been *dancing* the part necessarily. I helped Mr. Darcy choreograph it. I was his guinea pig, so to speak." Elizabeth looked to the back of

Darcy's head and felt her temper flaring. *Thanks for all your help,* she thought bitterly as the choreographer remained silent.

"So, you weren't understudying it?" Sir Webster asked.

"No, sir. At least, if I were, I didn't know about it."

Caroline suddenly took a step towards Elizabeth, her eyes ablaze. "You left out the part about fucking Darcy! How convenient."

Darcy snapped his head around, a snarl on his lips.

Charles broke in first. "Caroline, out!" He flung open the door and gestured for her to leave. The prima glared at Elizabeth before walking out in a huff.

Recovering his composure, Sir Webster managed a reassuring smile at Elizabeth. "I'm so sorry about this, love. Thank you for your help. Last minute casting changes, as you know, are quite the norm for us. But they're never under such... special circumstances. Why don't you wait outside for a few moments while I talk to Darcy?"

Nodding mutely, Elizabeth scurried out of the dressing room. She cast one last look in Darcy's direction before she left. He didn't look back at her.

Once she was in the hallway, Elizabeth threw her back against the wall and, shutting her eyes, sighed. Her hands trembled uncontrollably. Rubbing her eyes with them, she contemplated her fate. Would she be fired? Her heartbeat began racing again. No, she reasoned, attempting to calm herself. The artistic director hadn't seemed angry with her at all. He had just called her in to more fairly assess the situation.

Then her fear turned to fury towards William Darcy. What a selfish idiot! When was he planning to announce that minor casting change? Couldn't he have given her the courtesy of letting her know what she would be dancing at least a few days before she was expected to dance it? He had no consideration for her feelings! Sudden, muffled shouts filtered from behind the door. She recognized Darcy and Sir Webster's voices.

Elizabeth felt no pity for the choreographer. It was typical of him. Ever the self-serving egomaniac, Darcy thought of himself before he thought of anyone else. As long as he knew what he wanted for his piece, everyone else be damned!

With anger coursing through her blood, Elizabeth hurried away from the dressing room and nearly crashed into Caroline who had just rounded a corner, a bottle of water in her hands. Elizabeth started. Caroline smiled dangerously and leaned her bony shoulder against the wall.

When Elizabeth tried to skirt past her, Caroline said, "Would you like to know the irony of this situation?"

"Not really." Elizabeth steeled her expression, feigning bravery she didn't feel.

"William gave you a better part because you put out, but he told Charles not to promote Jane because it would look bad. A bit hypocritical, don't you think?"

Shock registered on Elizabeth's face before she could help it.

Caroline smirked. "William didn't tell you? My brother wanted to promote Jane. William wanted Anne. And, well," Caroline casually plucked a piece of lint off her sweatpants and flicked it to the floor, "we all know how it turned out. It's sad because Jane's a far better dancer than you. Frankly, I don't know what William was thinking. Unless . . . you do great things in bed."

Too stunned to reply, Elizabeth simply stared at the prima ballerina. She felt that she should say something and heard herself stuttering a reply, but the only thing she was cognizant of was Caroline's smug expression.

Suddenly, the door swung open, and Darcy charged out with a black expression on his face. He paused, glaring at Caroline, before storming wordlessly down the hall and through the doorway that led to the stage area. Caroline grinned and slithered back into the dressing room. Elizabeth heard her sing, "I knew he'd come around."

Charles came outside. Smiling sadly to Elizabeth, he shrugged. "I'm sorry, Liz. Caroline's going to be dancing the part."

She held her hand up and lowered it when she saw her fingers shaking. "You don't have to apologize, Charles."

Charles sighed, half in relief, half in resignation. "I think Will still wants to finish blocking."

Elizabeth glanced towards the stage. Her face flushed. She didn't think she could face the other dancers. Demoted so quickly. She smiled wobbly at Charles, thanked him, and slowly made her way to the stage area.

When she stepped into the wings, a group of *corps* dancers that included Lydia and Charlotte stopped their chattering. Everyone eyed her. Inhaling, Elizabeth quickly skirted them and concentrated hard on ignoring their stares.

Charlotte approached her friend. "Are you okay?"

Elizabeth nodded.

"What happened?" Charlotte asked.

"I'll tell you later," whispered Elizabeth, not really wanting to say anything at all. Jane approached and hugged her sister's shoulders. Inwardly, Elizabeth cringed. She heard Caroline's voice in her head. *The irony is that William gave you a better part because you put out, but he told Charles not to promote Jane because it would look bad.* She looked at Jane, stricken.

"Lizzy?" Jane asked worriedly.

"Places!" she heard Darcy yell.

"Lizzy, what's wrong?" her sister asked with tenderness and concern in her voice. Her gentle and good sister, who always did everything right. Who was kind to everyone. Who'd had her career damaged by William Darcy's meddling.

"I'm—nothing. Let's talk later," Elizabeth said, her voice cracking.

Unconvinced, Jane squeezed Elizabeth's shoulders in support. Elizabeth stepped onto the stage and took her place with all of the other *corps de ballet* in the back, where she belonged.

Wallet in hand, Elizabeth stepped out of the stage door onto Columbus Avenue. A breeze cooled her face. She paused and collected herself, hoping to exorcise the thoughts that still haunted her. Caroline's voice echoed in her head: *"Frankly, I don't know what William was thinking. Unless... you do great things in bed."*

Elizabeth exhaled sharply in frustration and turned onto Columbus Avenue. Regardless of the afternoon's excitement, she needed to get food before getting dressed for that night's performance.

She suddenly heard her name. Without looking, Elizabeth recognized the deep timbre instantly, and her stomach clenched. She looked over her shoulder and saw Darcy approach.

"What?" she snapped.

"I know you're upset," he said.

"I am." Acid rose into her voice.

"I fought for you, but Lucas can see nothing but dollar signs in his head."

Elizabeth hardened her expression. "Yeah, it really looked like it."

"What?"

"I need to grab something to eat." She turned to leave, and he seized her arm.

"The least you could do is give me a minute," Darcy said.

"The least *I* could do?" She was so furious that tears sprang into her eyes.

Darcy either didn't notice or didn't care because he continued. "I wanted you in the *pas de deux*. It doesn't look right without you."

"If that were the case," Elizabeth spat, "didn't you think it would be important for me to *know* I would be dancing the part? Why wouldn't you tell me?"

Darcy looked nervously back to the stage door and, with her arm still in his grasp, pulled her halfway down the block where prying ears would be less likely to overhear. Elizabeth huffed as she walked.

Almost yanking her to face him, Darcy replied in a low voice, "Do you want to know why I didn't tell you sooner? Because I knew you'd react like *this!*"

"Can you stop?" Elizabeth pulled her arm away and glared. "You knew I'd react like what?"

"Like... like it was the hugest insult to cast you in the leading role in the piece. I do you a favor, and you resent me for it. Damn it, Elizabeth, I've never met a dancer as... as ..."

"As what?"

"As self-sabotaging as you are!"

Elizabeth felt the tears come back. Her voice shook. "I do *not* sabotage myself! I bust my ass every day in this company."

"You *do* sabotage yourself. Because here you go, your first principal role in an original work by *me,* no less, and all you can do is stand there screaming at me about how I ruined your life!"

"You don't get it. You act like I'm supposed to kneel and kiss your feet, and you blame me when I don't want to!" Elizabeth retorted. "And besides, you're good at ruining people's lives."

Darcy rubbed his face in frustration. "What the hell does that mean?"

"You ruined Greg Wickham's life."

Shock jolted Darcy's expression before it darkened into hatred. "Greg Wickham? That asshole stood you up, and you're still defending him?"

"You ruined his career just like you screwed my—"

"Ruined his career! Yes, I've wanted to hear you explain that gem since the gala. Exactly how did *I* ruin Greg Wickham's career?"

Two young women passed them on the street, staring curiously at their argument. Elizabeth suddenly felt like kicking them.

"You got him booted out of the company."

"Did I? And how did I manage that?"

"He... he didn't say."

Darcy snorted. "Yes, of course. Of course, he didn't say! But you believed him anyway. Because it's so easy to believe someone who simpers and flatters and lies as easily as most people breathe!" The veins on his neck bulged. At the outburst, Elizabeth stepped back, feeling momentarily intimidated by his rage.

Then she remembered Jane and found her voice again. "And what about my sister?"

"What about your sister?"

"Caroline told me everything. Are you going to deny that you told Charles to promote Anne Boroughs over Jane because her mother sits on the board and donates a ton of money?"

Darcy paused, looking momentarily humbled. "I'm not going to deny it, no. Your sister is a fine dancer, but it would have been horrible for the company if Anne wasn't promoted this season."

"Charles wanted to promote Jane. Jane deserved it over Anne. Everyone knows that!"

"Not *everyone*, Elizabeth! You don't get how ballet companies work, do you? Sometimes it isn't just about making dance. Sometimes people need to be practical and make rational decisions." Almost as an aside, he added, "If only *I'd* been as rational as I advised him to be." He rubbed his face again in frustration.

"What?" challenged Elizabeth.

Darcy's face turned to stone. He repeated frigidly, "We should have kept our feelings for each other completely separate from my choreography. Then maybe this whole thing wouldn't have become the clusterfuck it is."

She took a step back. *Our feelings for each other,* she kept hearing. She went quiet with confusion. What feelings?

Misinterpreting her silence for appeasement, Darcy took a moment to collect himself and then softened his expression. "Elizabeth, I didn't want this to happen tonight. I wanted you to know that I fought for you, and I won't bring this into the studio anymore."

"What *feelings* are you talking about?" Elizabeth asked. Her voice shook.

Darcy looked at her quizzically. "Yours and mine."

Perhaps he truly couldn't read the shock on her face as shock. Or perhaps he thought her voice trembled with happiness. Or perhaps he was simply that clueless.

For whatever reason, Darcy continued. "Look, I get it. You're young. You're in the *corps*. I'm fairly accomplished in my career. But things like this have worked out before between two people. I've learned my lesson. I'll keep our relationship out of the studio."

An ambulance screamed past them. Elizabeth could only stare at him in dumb astonishment as if he'd just spoken in tongues.

"Elizabeth?"

"I'm sorry," she replied, shaking her head. "I didn't think we *had* a relationship."

Darcy frowned momentarily, and then his eyes lightened with a mistaken explanation. "Elizabeth, I'm way past the age when I just sleep with women meaninglessly. I thought you knew that. Of course, I have feelings for you." Elizabeth's eyes widened. "I'm in love with you."

Everything in Elizabeth's brain went white and molten. He *loved* her? She could only think of one thing, and so she blurted it out.

"*This* is the way you treat people you love?"

Darcy blinked.

Her throat constricted, but she continued in a grave whisper. "Do you expect me to believe that? After the way you've treated me today? After the way you always treat me?"

"I'm sorry?" he asked angrily.

"You order me around. You treat me like some kind of doll—"

"What are you talking about? I brought you back to my house, I cast you in my *pas de deux*—"

They were shouting over each other.

"—and not a person with *feelings*. Not even someone who deserves common courtesy or kindness!"

"I don't do those things, and you know it."

"No, you do. You treat everyone like that: me, Charles, even Caroline, whose face I want to badly mangle right now but who deserves better than your arrogant contempt! You're not in love with me. You're in love with yourself—or rather, with your choreography."

"I've never given you anything but preferential treatment," he protested.

Now that the floodgates were opened, Elizabeth continued. "Yeah, I've always been the one you preferred to insult!"

"Insult?! That's called *feedback*, Elizabeth. It's what *professional* dancers in professional dance companies get in case you needed to know," he said with the aim to injure.

Closing her eyes briefly, she shook her head. "There. Right there. When you say stuff like that. *That* is what I'm talking about," she said quietly. "I'm almost insulted that a man like you would fall in love with me."

Nostrils flaring, Darcy answered her with a deadly calm. "Hold on. Then why did you sleep with me?"

"That was a mistake."

"A mistake you made three times?"

"You've never fucked someone just for the hell of it?"

Opening his mouth, Darcy tried to respond but shut it suddenly. He reminded Elizabeth of a fish gasping for its last breath, but she couldn't savor her victory. His storm-cloud eyes were drained of everything. She tried to care, but his words stung too much. Only in the awful silence did she realize her face was wet with tears. Her voice broke into a sob. He fished out a pack of tissues from his jacket pocket and handed her one.

"All right. I see. I misunderstood. Clearly." He chuckled emptily. He cleared his throat. "I'm sorry if I've offended you. *Merde* tonight."

He cast her a look she couldn't read and then strode past her, leaving Elizabeth with the tissue and the sounds of Manhattan's streets surrounding her.

Chapter 16

Jane watched her sister listlessly push a piece of fried tofu around the take-out tray with a chopstick. Elizabeth turned the cube on its side, then pushed it back over. More suspicious yet, she had only eaten a bite of her egg roll before tossing it back into its waxed paper bag. Elizabeth loved egg rolls and always begged Jane for hers.

It was close to midnight. That evening's performance over, Jane and Elizabeth were finally back in their apartment eating Chinese take-out.

"Are you sure you don't want to talk about it?" Jane asked again.

Elizabeth looked up with dead eyes, shook her head, and went back to skewering the piece of tofu.

"I know you're embarrassed about what happened today, but no one blames you. Everyone thinks it was Caroline's fault."

Making no reply, Elizabeth set her chopstick down and looked at her sister. Elizabeth's heart lurched as she remembered what Caroline had told her in the backstage hallway. Elizabeth felt angry all over again—at Caroline, at Darcy, even at Charles. She felt like she'd been betrayed by them all and felt guilty because she was betraying Jane. Elizabeth could never, not for anyone or anything, ever admit to Jane how she'd come so close this season to a promotion and that Charles, her boyfriend, the man she loved, had been complicit in denying it to her. It would shatter Jane. Elizabeth buried her face in her palms.

"Elizabeth, what?"

"I can't talk about it!" she cried. "I'm so goddamned angry at him, I can't even think straight."

"Why? Just tell me!"

But she couldn't. Standing from the sofa, Elizabeth dropped her box of Chinese food onto the coffee table. She wiped at her eyes. "I'm sorry, Jane. I need some time alone."

She walked into her room and shut the door with a cold thud. Elizabeth collapsed onto her bed, burying her face in the pillow. She could not cry. She had nothing left in her for that. After William Darcy had left her on the sidewalk, she'd sobbed uncontrollably in the middle of the street. Pedestrians had graciously skirted around her and avoided eye contact, and she thanked God then for New Yorkers and their self-absorbed bubbles. She'd been so racked with volatile feelings that she didn't want to interact with anyone.

Unfortunately, Elizabeth had to force herself to recoup fast; she had to perform that night, after all. Taking gulps of air, she'd blown her nose with Darcy's tissue, shoved it into her jacket pocket, and gone into a deli to buy dinner. By the time she returned to the theater, her nose and eyes were still red, but at least she was calm.

Once the curtain had come down on the night's show, however, Elizabeth had burrowed back into her head, reliving the horrible argument over and over again. She heard Darcy's scornful voice. Her skin tingled again at all of the ways he had insulted her.

And he claimed to be in love with her? It was unfathomable. He'd confessed his feelings with shame and dismay. Judging by all of the horrible things he said about her—that she was self-sabotaging, amateurish, naïve—there was little wonder he detested having feelings for her. Elizabeth wouldn't be happy to love someone like that either. He loved her, and he hated himself for it.

She thought they had an understanding: They turned each other on physically and turned each other off personally. She hated him, and she thought it was the same for Darcy—that he hated her. Elizabeth thought he'd made his attraction to her so obvious as a way to intimidate her.

The thought made her angry all over again. What did Darcy expect? For her to melt into his arms just because he said he loved her? Did he expect her to forgive his arrogance, his underhanded machinations with her sister, the inequity with which he treated her, the fact that they'd never shared a meaningful or respectful conversation throughout their entire acquaintance? Whatever Darcy thought he felt, it wasn't love. It wasn't even close to love. It was desire and control. He probably just said he loved her as a way of getting the upper hand again. The whole thing just disgusted her.

Elizabeth sat up in bed and looked across to the mirror hanging on her wall. She looked puffy and pink and five years older. Her eyes refocused and darkened when she saw the magazine cutout of Perfection by Hermes. She did not want William Darcy, even an image of the man, anywhere near her. Bounding off her bed, she yanked it from her mirror, crumpled it, and threw it towards the garbage. She missed, but it was fine.

Backstage before dress rehearsal, the dancers were finishing their makeup. Elizabeth tapped the corner of her eyelid, setting the false eyelash in place. Frowning, she turned to Jane and asked, "Are these even?"

Jane studied Elizabeth's eyes and replied that it was close enough; then she reached into her sister's makeup bag to borrow an eyebrow pencil.

Several dozen of the company's most generous patrons sat in the audience, eagerly anticipating their first glimpse of William Darcy's new piece. After company class that day, Sir Webster Lucas had spoken to them all, encouraging the dancers to treat the dress rehearsal as if it were a real show. These people were important to the company's future, after all.

The dancers buzzed with nervous excitement backstage.

"These costumes are god-awful," Charlotte whined, gazing at her butt in the mirror. "Unitards? What was the man thinking? I look like a pole."

Cracking a weak smile, Elizabeth looked at Charlotte. "You look fine."

"Dancers in William Darcy's piece. Places in ten," the stage manager announced over the intercom.

Jane and Charlotte stood. "Lizzy, hurry up and get your shoes on," Jane said.

"Yup, I got it. It'll take me two minutes." Rummaging through her bag, Elizabeth pulled out a brand new pointe shoe, the pink satin shimmering under the bright dressing room lights. She pushed aside leg warmers trying to find the other one.

"Jane, do you have my other shoe?"

Jane inspected the inside of her bag. "Nope, not in here."

Narrowing her eyes in concentration, Elizabeth went through her bag again, opening every zipper and looking through every pocket. She turned the bag over and dumped the contents on the floor.

"It's not here!" she cried. Jane's eyes widened and she began searching through the mess of makeup and leg warmers on the counter.

"Has anyone here seen my pointe shoe?" Elizabeth asked the dressing room. A few dancers shook their heads, looking at her with concern.

"Charlotte, go tell Roger we'll be up," Jane said. Charlotte nodded and jogged out of the dressing room to tell the stage manager.

"Are you sure you put it in your bag?" Jane asked.

"Yes!" Elizabeth exclaimed, unable to suppress her panic. "You saw me. I picked them up from Mindy before we came down here. They were wrapped up in each other. I put them both in my bag!"

"Did you take them out?"

"Jane, you saw me. I put my bag down, got out my warmers, and then went to class."

Jane chewed on her lip.

"Dancers in "Pygmalion and Galatea" must come backstage. You're on in five."

"Damn!" Elizabeth cried, throwing her hands up in frustration.

"Lizzy, just wear the shoes you wore in class."

"They're filthy!"

"At this point, it doesn't matter. Come on, get them on, and let's go."

Elizabeth pulled the dirty, worn shoes from her bag and threw them on in record speed. She laced the ribbons, tucking them in securely, and then jumped up and ran backstage. She and Jane made it just as they heard light applause from the small but important audience. William Darcy, wearing a gray-collared shirt and black slacks, walked offstage and into the wings.

Elizabeth was shaken, and seeing him shook her even more. She hadn't even begun dancing, and she was already breathing hard. The music began, and she jumped out into formation. But her mind tripped over itself. Panicking, she blanked on the upcoming phrase. Luckily, she copied Lydia, who was in front of her. Willing herself to concentrate, Elizabeth made it through the opening sequence and ran offstage, her chest heaving harder than it should have been for only one minute of dancing.

She felt tears well in her eyes. Fanning her face, Elizabeth commanded herself to stop the histrionics. She knew Darcy would explode if she made a careless mistake, and frankly, she wanted nothing more to do with him. Taking three deep breaths, she let the music take her, and she calmly waltzed back on stage.

Only the first three rows in the orchestra section were full, but their occupants were millionaires and billionaires who had given heaps of money to the company. If they liked what they saw tonight, they might give more. Elizabeth knew that Catherine Boroughs was amongst them, but the lights prevented her from picking out the woman's face.

The music ended. Elizabeth's chest heaved in the final pose before the lights went dark, and she scrambled off-stage.

The lights went up on stage again, a deep lavender. *Air in G* began. In her white unitard, Caroline stood center stage, regal and lithe. She stepped into the first *piqué arabesque* of the *pas de deux*. Elizabeth looked away and walked deeper into the backstage area. She did not want to watch.

As the familiar music played, Elizabeth tried to recall what she had done with her new pair of pointe shoes after she had picked them up from the pointe shoe room. She had definitely placed them in her bag and hadn't removed them. There had been two, of that she was positive. She looked down at her dirty pointe shoes and thanked God that it was just a dress rehearsal. Feeling calmer than before, Elizabeth danced the remaining third and fourth movements with more presence of mind. The piece ended, and the dancers bowed.

Back in the dressing room, Elizabeth checked her dance bag again. The shoe was not there. She morosely removed her earrings and costume and headed towards the costume mistress.

"Mindy, you gave me both pointe shoes, right?" she asked, handing over the deep blue unitard.

The costume mistress nodded. "I'm nearly certain. What happened? You had on old shoes out there."

Elizabeth shook her head and smiled plastically. "I... I must have misplaced one of the shoes. I couldn't find it."

Mindy frowned. "Be careful next time. You know if this were a real performance, Lucas would have docked your pay."

Elizabeth nodded mutely and left the costume room. As she walked down the hall, Darcy emerged from the stage and walked intently in her direction. She froze. The look in his eyes changed when he recognized her, and his pace slowed.

"Ms. Bennet," he said in a clipped tone, "what happened out there?"

Coloring, she could not maintain eye contact. "What do you mean?"

"Your shoes. Didn't you get new ones before the performance?"

Elizabeth exhaled loudly. He must have thought that she was truly stupid. "Of course, I did. I . . . I couldn't find one of them. I came back from warm up, and it was just . . . gone. I had to use my old ones."

She expected him to bark a reprimand. Instead, he remained silent. Looking up at him, Elizabeth was surprised to see him frowning.

"What do you mean you couldn't find one? Did you lose it?"

"I got them from Mindy, put them in my bag before warm up, and didn't touch them afterwards. I don't know. Maybe one fell out."

The choreographer looked away, his forehead creased in a frown. He rubbed his mouth, nodded at Elizabeth, and then strode past her. Standing alone in the hall, Elizabeth sank against the wall. She stared at the pattern in the linoleum tile, everything in her heavy and gray. It had been a terrible rehearsal. The premiere was that evening. They still had to listen to notes from Darcy. Elizabeth had no energy left. She didn't want to dance tonight. It was the first time she'd felt that way since joining Ballet Theater.

"Paige," William said, finding the old ballet mistress backstage. She turned and looked up at him suspiciously. She had never liked the man when he was a conceited principal dancer, and now, as a conceited choreographer, she hated him even more.

"Were all of the dancers in warm up today?"

The old woman looked him up and down before replying. "Why?"

"Just were they?"

Folding her arms over her chest, she glared up at William. "They were."

"All of them?"

"Yes."

"Did any of them leave early? Or come in late?"

"Caroline Bingley came in after *frappés*. But she's always late."

William nodded tightly and brushed past the ballet mistress without thanking her. She muttered something under her breath, which he ignored.

William stalked through the backstage halls, his thoughts racing. A few technicians stared at him oddly as he rummaged through garbage cans. Finding nothing, William walked to the emergency exit that led into the back alley of the theater. His heart pumped crazily in his chest. Deactivating the alarm, he pushed open the door and wrinkled his nose at the awful smells coming from the alley. There was a rusting dumpster there. William eyed it for a long moment, wondering if it were the same one from all those years ago. Holding his breath, he lifted up the metal cover and peered in.

There it was. On top of a heap of garbage bags was a flash of satin: a brand new pointe shoe, just like years ago.

The performance went beautifully. Elizabeth was now wearing two new pointe shoes. The audience's reception was warm. Caroline and Ben received three curtain calls.

As the dancers scampered off stage, Caroline swept past Elizabeth. She turned her head and smirked.

Elizabeth was unable to get the bitter taste out of her mouth for the rest of the evening.

William threw down the newspaper, leaned back in his leather recliner, and cursed. Closing his eyes, he breathed deeply, letting a wave of self-pity break over him before he opened his eyelids again to the sunlight of a Manhattan Saturday morning. The height and insulation of his apartment shielded William from any street noise, but he felt it. On weekends, the city awoke slower. The air calmed and settled.

He bounded up from his chair, deciding then to enjoy the spring air with a walk in Central Park. Leaving everything else, William brought the Arts section of The New York Times with him.

It had been cold for the past week, but that morning was unseasonably cloudless and crisp. He hoped the air would relieve the gnawing in his stomach. Sitting on a bench in an uncrowded section of the park, William once again opened to page three and read. He had always known he possessed a resentful nature but never knew how deep its roots went. Rereading the awful review, William's only consolation was that there would be someone in the city who would feel worse than he did after reading it: Caroline.

The review had called him a choreographic genius, compared him again to Balanchine. They said his first endeavor for Ballet Theater had been an "ambitious work of dance that explored the nurturing and parasitic relationship between artist and muse." The *corps de ballet*, the review lauded, danced crisply. Like Balanchine before him, William Darcy choreographed for the *corps de ballet*, using structure and syncopation to best showcase their talent. However, Caroline Bingley and Benjamin Boyne in the *pas de deux* had "seemed like two junior high school kids, flustered and awkward after a vigorous session of heavy petting, rather than artist and muse exploring their relationship, muddled with both sexual desire and artistic inspiration."

The only part of the review that had made William smile was this: "Ms. Bingley, while a spectacular classical dancer, simply does not possess the range or depth to triumph in such an expressively demanding role. She danced Galatea as she would Odile—all seduction with little nuance. Mr. Boyne's portrayal of Pygmalion was heartbreaking, not so much for the desperation and melancholy he brought to his fine portrayal, but rather because the audience had to endure watching him maneuver through six minutes of a smirking, slinking Ms. Bingley."

The final kicker was the last sentence of the review. "For a ballet about an artist and his muse, ironically, this work is undoubtedly Mr. Darcy's most uninspired."

For what could have been three minutes or thirty, William sat on that park bench staring vacantly at the pigeons lumbering around him. He began to feel cold but still could not move. It had been a week of firsts: his first scathing review and his first scathing rejection by a woman. He rewound through his argument with Elizabeth for what felt like the thousandth time. With each remembrance, his fury grew more acute until his chest felt tight. William just couldn't understand. He had singled her out countless times —in the studio, at the gala. He had brought her back to his apartment, taken her to his favorite restaurant. How could there be any misunderstanding on her part?

"I'm almost insulted that a man like you would fall in love with me," Elizabeth had said. To be hated liked that—how could there have been any misunderstanding on his part?

A man like *you*? What kind of man was that? An honest one? A dedicated one? Loyal to his family, someone who would do anything to help the people he loved when they needed him? Maybe William had given Elizabeth too much credit. He thought it could have worked between them, but maybe she wasn't as clever or insightful as he thought. Elizabeth Bennet didn't know anything about him! All she knew were the lies Greg Wickham had fed her. God, he *hated* that dickwad! And he was so angry, he felt close to hating Elizabeth, too. But every time he tried, it just hurt too much.

He was an idiot.

And then there was that thing with the pointe shoe, probably hers, though he would have to do some digging with Mindy. He didn't want to feel angry *for* Elizabeth; he wanted to feel angry *at* her. But every time he remembered the sight of that pointe shoe in a back alley dumpster, every time he saw its brand-new satin gleam on the table in his foyer, he wanted to throttle Caroline Bingley over the head with it.

Thank God, he would be leaving in a few weeks. Seattle Ballet had commissioned a work, and he couldn't wait to get the hell out of New York and the hell away from Elizabeth.

William felt like a balloon was pressing against the walls of his throat. He had to get out of there. Standing, he dumped his newspaper in the nearest trash can and strode out of Central Park before he did something really stupid, like cry in public.

And now, he wasn't even showing up to his own rehearsals. And he hadn't showed at that night's performance either. Even though it was normal for choreographers to create a work and then leave to choreograph at their next company without even seeing the work performed, the dancers knew Darcy should have been there. There were whispers that he was pouting or that he had quit. Elizabeth was grateful. It would have been too much to have to deal with him and her coworkers. She didn't want to see him ever again.

Anne Boroughs typically preferred to keep out of notice, much less controversy. So she didn't know how she found herself in the elevator of the Pemberley Building, gliding up to Darcy's penthouse. Lately, he and his dancers were tornados of controversy, charging through everyone in their path as if the rest of the Ballet Theater *corps* didn't have other ballets to dance and their own lives to worry about. She hated these kinds of things, but Webster had practically begged her, so here she was.

Growing nervous, Anne hoped he hadn't drunk himself into a stupor and done something stupid. Luckily, Pemberley's doorman recognized her, and she still had the spare key Darcy had given her years back. She let herself in and steeled her nerves.

"William?" she called, stepping into his living room. There was no answer. She called his name as she toured the apartment. It was the first time she had been inside in years, but the apartment looked the same as it had since

Darcy remodeled after his dad died. Austin, the cat, poked her head out from around a corner and mewed. Crouching to pet her, Anne checked the bowl of food and water in the kitchen, newly replenished. At least Darcy wasn't dead.

As she walked further into the apartment, she heard the strains of angry piano music: Beethoven.

Relieved, Anne sighed and walked toward the sound. She opened the door to Darcy's home studio and found it occupied by the owner. He sat on the floor, his back against the mirror, glaring at her as she peeked her head in. Anne paused, looked Darcy up and down, and wrinkled her nose. He hadn't shaved. There were dark shadows under his eyes.

"What, Anne?" he snapped. "I'm choreographing."

"Doesn't look like that to me," she replied. Walking over to where he was, Anne slid her back down the mirror and sat next to him. She said nothing for a long moment, instead tracing her fingernail over the pattern in the wood floor.

Darcy sighed heavily. "Why are you here?"

"You haven't been coming to the shows."

"I'm sure no one misses me."

"The audiences do. They wanted to applaud the prodigal son returned home."

Darcy snorted and continued to stare acridly at the floor.

"People kind of miss you. Although I guess *miss* isn't the right word. I guess *feel your absence* would be a better way of saying it," Anne said.

Again, Darcy made no reply.

"When do you leave?" asked Anne.

"The day after tomorrow."

Anne nodded. "And how's the new work coming?"

Only then did Darcy betray any emotion. He suddenly flew into a fury, shoving his fingers through his hair and shouting, "It's not! Okay?"

Staring at Darcy, she allowed him to feel guilty for his outburst. Only when Anne sensed his self-reproach, did she speak. "Been to any meetings lately?"

Rolling his eyes, Darcy snapped, "I'm not drinking again."

"But you're not sober."

"Is that why you came here? To criticize me?"

"I came here, William, to see if you were alive because no one's been able to get hold of you for thirty-six hours."

They sat together in silence, Darcy staring across the room, sighing every few minutes, Anne picking lint off her skirt. Ten minutes passed. Finally, Darcy turned his head to her.

"I'm sorry."

"There. That wasn't so bad, was it?"

Finally, Darcy's face cracked into a small smile.

"What happened?" Anne asked.

"I don't want to talk about it."

"Is it about that girl from the gala?"

Darcy's eyes widened. Anne smirked. When he realized she had his number, he didn't bother denying it. "Yes. Her name's Elizabeth. You could at least bother to learn your coworkers' names."

"Now *that's* the pot calling the kettle black," snorted Anne. "You're upset because *Elizabeth's* not dancing the *pas de deux?*"

"How do you know about that?"

"It's Ballet Theater. Everyone knew about that ten minutes after it happened."

Darcy cursed. "I'm upset for a lot of reasons."

Waiting for his reply, Anne gestured for him to continue. He grew angry again.

"Because I put her in my *pas de deux,* and she got pissed at me. Pissed at *me*! Then, she says that I've ruined her sister's career, and oh, I've ruined Greg Wickham's career, too."

"Wickham? How does she know him?"

"She was dating him."

Anne frowned. "She sounds grossly misinformed. And what about her sister?"

Darcy groaned and rubbed his face with his hands. "Anne, please. You already know what your mother did."

"Oh, that." The donation her mother had given for Anne's promotion still made Anne queasy.

"I was the one who convinced Charles to take your mom's money over promoting Jane."

"Yeah, so glad that worked out." Anne said sourly. "Lucas would have forced Charles to promote me anyway, with or without your convincing." She hadn't exactly been aching for the promotion. Anne didn't crave the fame and didn't need the money. She'd been hoping to retire next season to pursue an art project with Mariah.

Again, he ran his hands down his face and settled his fingertips at his eyes. "She hates me," he muttered.

And then Anne understood the situation and the meaning of Darcy's exaggerated interest in Elizabeth the night of the Netherfield Gala. "And you like her."

Dropping his hands, William cast Anne a serious look. She started and frowned. "You more than like her?"

"Something like that."

Anne considered that. "Whoa! That's so . . . unexpected."

"Yeah, she thought so, too."

Leaning his head back against the mirror, Darcy stared at the ceiling mournfully. It seemed as if he were going to say something, so Anne waited.

"She said," he croaked finally, "that she felt insulted that a man like me could be in love with her."

Now Anne became angry. "She said *what*? Who is this girl, anyway? She sounds like a jerk."

Darcy's face blackened. "What?"

"She sounds stupid. How could she say that about you? And get upset with *you* for giving her a good part. And she was dating Wickham, trusting his word over yours."

"Hey," he warned, "Wickham's taken in some smart women before."

Anne held up her hands defensively. "All I'm saying is you don't need her. You're going to Seattle soon, right?"

"On Sunday."

"So you'll probably forget all about her when you're there. And good riddance."

William stared at her for a few moments then shook his head. He didn't seem comforted. Anne didn't get it. Throughout their long friendship, she'd seen William at his worst: when his mother died, after his knee blew, last year when his sister was going through her divorce. But she hadn't seen him get this way over a girl.

"Maybe you need to go on antidepressants," she suggested.

"Anne," he warned.

"Are you still seeing that therapist?"

"That guy was an idiot."

"Maybe…" Anne thought, "maybe, you should write her one of those angry letters."

Darcy stared at Anne quizzically.

"You know, the kind where you say everything you want to say to the person, and you curse them out, and then you rip it up and throw it away," she said. "It's very cathartic, supposedly."

He mumbled, "Maybe."

They sat together in heavy silence for several more minutes. Finally, Anne put her hand on her friend's shoulder and stood. "Get some sleep, William. And shave."

When Darcy cursed at her under his breath, Anne knew he would be okay.

Chapter 17

Elizabeth didn't want to seem paranoid, but everyone was gossiping about her. Whenever she walked into the dressing room, conversation stopped, and dancers she'd been friendly with looked at her funny. That day in rehearsal, a soloist referred to Elizabeth as "the girl who steals people's parts." Dancers watched her during class, particularly Caroline Bingley. Someone almost kicked her in *grande battements*. Another *corps de ballet* dancer spat, "Can you move up and stop hogging the floor?" during the *grande allegro*.

Elizabeth's pointe shoe was still missing. Certainly, she could have simply misplaced it. She'd been so tired and disoriented from the stress of dealing with Darcy that she couldn't rule that out. But the more she felt targeted by poisonous stares and whispers, the more she wondered if it had been stolen.

No one else noticed the bad vibes. She told Lydia and Charlotte, who listened seriously to Elizabeth and threatened to kick the ass of anyone harassing her, but they hadn't seen anything. To Elizabeth's chagrin, Jane couldn't believe that anyone in the company would stoop so low and wondered whether she was just stressed out and tired from the season opening.

Sometimes Elizabeth wondered that, too. Maybe it *was* all in her head. She hadn't slept well in over a week, since the day of Darcy's stage rehearsal. Fear kept her awake. When she joined Ballet Theater last year, Elizabeth wanted to build her repertoire in the company and eventually work her way up. She envisioned a long career at BTNY, one where the company would reward her perseverance and talent by making her a principal dancer. Younger dancers would admire her.

Now, everyone reviled her as the kind of dancer who slept with choreographers to get parts. She hated herself, too. And she hated Darcy because he'd created this storm and then plunked her in the middle of it.

Thoughts of Darcy also plagued her in the early morning darkness. She would lie in her bed fuming as she relived Darcy's arrogance, disbelieving that he actually harbored tender feelings for her.

Regret kept her up, too. She wallowed in the "what-might-have-beens," wondering what her life would be like if she had performed the *pas de deux* as Darcy had wanted. She wondered whether the *Times* review would have been different if she had been in the principal role and not Caroline. Those thoughts frustrated her most, and she quickly squelched them.

Every morning, Elizabeth awoke, groggy and unfocused. She stepped into the studio, and rather than the rush of excitement and energy she'd felt months ago, she felt drained and afraid. The season had just begun; weeks more of performances sprawled in front of her. She didn't know how she was going to make it, and worse than that, Elizabeth suddenly had no inclination to care.

That week, after a studio rehearsal for *La Bayadere*, Elizabeth plodded downstairs, dance bag slung over her shoulder, to make the walk a few blocks uptown to the theater where she had a stage rehearsal for *Coppelia*, a ballet she despised, in which she would be performing the next evening.

She stopped on her way down to check her mailbox in the administrative offices and spied a bulging manila envelope tucked in it. Suspicious, she removed it and turned it over in her hands. It was unmarked, and she wondered momentarily if it was really meant for her. A few *corps de ballet* dancers walked over to the mailboxes. One smiled tersely at Elizabeth, and the other glared. Elizabeth shoved the envelope in her dance bag and skirted past them.

The package weighed down her bag as she walked the few blocks to Lincoln Center. She wondered what was inside: A prank like a dead rat? A surprise gift from a repentant friend? She debated waiting until she got home to open the package, but curiosity overwhelmed her. Fishing it out of her bag, she hurried past the stage door and into the plaza of Lincoln Center. She had a few minutes before rehearsals began. She couldn't wait until her long day of rehearsals, makeup, hair, and performing was over. She had to know now.

Feeling the cool spray of the fountain against her face, Elizabeth pulled out the envelope. She tore it open and inside saw a neatly folded letter and something wrapped in tissue paper. Her heart plummeted. She recognized the fine blue grain of the paper and knew instantly that William Darcy was responsible for this.

It made her wary. She didn't want gifts from him. She didn't know why he would get her anything after their brutal exchange on Columbus Avenue. Reaching into the envelope, she pulled out the tissue-wrapped object and sucked in her breath when she saw that it was the pointe shoe she'd lost at rehearsal. Had he stolen it from her? Now desperate to know why he'd given her this thing, she snapped the notepaper from the envelope and saw that it was several sheets thick.

She began to read.

Elizabeth,

I'm sure you're wondering why I have your shoe. Given how much you hate me, I'm sure you're thinking the worst. No, I was not the one who took it the day of rehearsal, but I was the one who found it. I hope it will serve as sufficient proof for what I'm about to write and to correct your wild misconceptions of me.

Elizabeth quickly lowered the letter and tried to calm her racing heart. He had written to her. He'd had her shoe. Her head swam. She continued reading.

You accused me of three things: of ruining your sister's career, of ruining Greg Wickham's, and of ruining yours.

I stand by what I said to you the other afternoon. I did convince Charles to promote Anne over your sister. I won't apologize for this. I would do it again.

Your sister is a beautiful dancer, but Ballet Theater is a business. Promoting Anne and not Jane was not a personal decision, but rather a professional one. Catherine Boroughs threatened to withdraw her patronage of Ballet Theater if Anne wasn't promoted. It was as simple as that.

Last year, Catherine donated several million dollars to the company. This company wouldn't be able to support itself without that money. Would it have been right for Charles to make a bad business decision because of his feelings for your sister? Would it have been right to lose that money and lose a few dancers in the process? Charles is an excellent man and a great friend, but he isn't practical. This company is my home, and I don't want to see it in dire financial straits. I want dancers to have jobs, and I want this company to stage ballets. Many others do, too. Catherine Boroughs' money makes that happen.

Elizabeth looked up from the letter, troubled and confused. She checked her watch. Five minutes had passed. She needed to be at rehearsal in ten minutes. But she couldn't put down the letter.

As to your second accusation concerning Greg Wickham, I believe I can more credibly defend myself on this point.

Greg and I met in a dance studio. I was twelve, and he was eight. Even then, he was a great dancer and was automatically placed in a higher level —my class. We were the only boys in a class of almost twenty-five girls, so naturally, we bonded although we couldn't have been more different. I went to expensive Manhattan private schools; he went to run-down public schools in Brooklyn.

Greg was a troublemaker, though, and he did something—I can't even remember what at this point—that caused the studio to take away his scholarship. He was distraught. I was, too. Greg came from a rough family, and ballet was the only thing that made him happy. I begged my parents to help him, and my mother, being softhearted, agreed to pay for his dance tuition. Eventually, the two of them developed a close bond. Mom even once told me she considered him to be a second son.

As we got older, Greg and I drifted apart. I started high school and began competing pre-professionally. At eighteen, I began dancing at BTNY. Greg was still at the studio, but his interest in ballet waned. Even though my mother still paid for his dance class, he skipped most of the time to go smoke pot with his friends from high school. I never told my mom. It would have crushed her. She had always been a delicate woman, too trusting and naïve to how the world worked.

I was twenty-two when my mother passed away. I'd been in the company for four years and a principal dancer for a little over a year. Greg was eighteen, about to graduate from high school (barely), and in need of a job.

His dancing was rusty, but he begged me to put in a good word for him at BTNY. I did. Despite my resentment towards him, I thought it was what my mom would have wanted.

Everything went great for a while, but that changed when Caroline Bingley joined the company. They became great friends and possibly more. Surprisingly, Caroline has mellowed considerably since her early days in the company when she and Greg would go clubbing and get coked up after performances. With Caroline as his ally, Greg started to revert to his old ways: skipping rehearsal, doing drugs. I was angry with him because I had pushed Lucas hard to accept a mediocre dancer into the company, and now Greg was pissing all over my kindness just as he had my mother's.

So what does this have to do with your pointe shoe?

The similarities between then and now are striking. The February after Caroline entered the company, there was only one corps-to-soloist promotion as there was this year. Everyone pinned either a dancer named Harriet James or Caroline for the promotion. Harriet was promoted.

It was opening night of the spring season. We were performing an all Tchaikovsky program. Thirty minutes before curtains-up, Harriet couldn't find her tutu—one minute it was in her dressing room, the next it wasn't. She was a tall girl, so it would have been difficult to find her a replacement costume in such a short period of time. Everyone looked frantically. The whole company was in a panic.

As you will be the first to attest, I didn't (and probably, according to you, still don't) care about corps de ballet girls. I went to the alley of the theater to have a cigarette. On my way out, I ran into Greg, who had just come in. He smiled and laughed. I asked him what he had been up to. He just winked and said, "Mischief." Greg was always up to no good, so I didn't think anything of it. But midway through my cigarette, I noticed a corner of tulle sticking out of a dumpster: Harriet's tutu, stolen by Greg at Caroline's bidding. She was understudying Harriet's role that night.

Lucas never disclosed who had found the tutu, but Greg knew. How could he not? I was in the right place at the right time. Greg was fired the next day. I wasn't sorry to see him go.

The story could end there. It doesn't. If I stopped at this point, I don't think you'd understand the kind of asshole Greg Wickham really is.

Greg's coke habit required money, of course. He'd traveled around the country for years, getting jobs here and there. One of them was in Miami. I mentioned to you that my sister lives there. She's exactly your age, twenty-three, and similar to you in many ways. We've always been close, and Greg doted on her as if she were his little sister, too.

This part is hard for me to write. A year after I retired from Ballet Theater, my father passed away. Almost a year after that, Greg ran off with my sister, and they got married in Las Vegas. She was nineteen. To this day, I don't know why she did it. She knew what kind of man he was. She knew about his drug habit and philandering. She didn't know what he'd done to get kicked out of Ballet Theater, but even if she had, I'm not sure it would have mattered. But my sister is, in many ways, a carbon copy of my mother. Perhaps she thought she could change him or save him. Perhaps he lied to her.

Elizabeth was three minutes late to rehearsal at this point, but she couldn't stop reading.

The marriage was, of course, a horrible and brief one. When my sister told me, I was livid. I'm ashamed to say that I cut her off. Fortunately and unfortunately, our silence didn't last long. Months later, she called me, hysterically crying. Greg was cheating on her. Greg was out of his mind on cocaine. She wanted a divorce. He refused. He'd already blown a good part of her money on drugs and partying. Why would he cut himself off from the source?

There has only been one time in my life that I've thanked God my family has the wealth it does. It was then. We hired the best divorce lawyer in the city. Greg dragged the case out for over a year, trying to get his hands on my sister's trust fund. My sister doesn't know this, but finally, I paid him a disgusting sum of money just to walk away. He was so desperate at that point that he did.

During that whole time, I traveled back and forth between Miami and wherever I was creating choreography. My sister was completely alone. She dropped out of school. I was an irresponsible guardian and brother.

No doubt, Greg left all of this out when he told you about me. He's a brilliant con.

Elizabeth swallowed down the feeling of dread in her stomach. Nearly half a page remained. She continued reading.

Let's get back to the third issue: your career. I apologize if I hurt you in the process of creating my choreography. I only thought of myself. I wanted to use your talents in my choreography, but you were right. I used you. Perhaps I confused that with love. I'm still not sure. I do know that I have created many, many ballets and worked with countless dancers, and none of them affected me as you did. You are still a young dancer, and you're rough in a few places, Elizabeth. I suppose I hoped to polish the edges. But I know that when you dance, I feel things. Your audience does, too. You don't look like a typical ballerina, but Charles and Webster saw past that because they recognize your tremendous talent. Do you?

That was what I meant when I called you self-sabotaging. It was a thoughtless remark, but those were the feelings behind it. Your career will not be ruined because of this setback if you choose not to let it be ruined.

Thank you for sharing your time and talent with me. I wish you the very best this season and in your career.

WD

Scarcely believing what she'd read and a full ten minutes late to rehearsal, Elizabeth stuffed the letter into her bag and ran across the Lincoln Center plaza to the theater.

Chapter 18

Elizabeth reread the letter after rehearsal in a private corner of the dressing room. Feeling self-righteous and still in shock, she fought Darcy's words. She felt both vindicated and infuriated at his admission that he'd used her. She nearly crumpled the letter up and threw it away.

On the subway back to Harlem, she reread the letter again, convinced Darcy was lying. It was too convoluted, too fabricated to be real. Certainly, she could believe Wickham for the liar and bastard that he was. But a thief? A gold digger? A con? She read the letter, picking apart every detail as she went.

That night, she turned over the details of the letter in her mind as she tried —but failed—to sleep. She realized that Darcy's story matched everything she knew about Wickham, everything he'd told her about his dealings with Darcy. Darcy *had* gotten Wickham fired. Only, Greg left out the part about his theft and sabotage. Greg *had* mentioned Darcy's spoiled sister but neglected to mention she'd been his ex-wife. Elizabeth might doubt it as being too farfetched, but she also knew Greg clearly cared nothing for the feelings of others as evidenced by his no-show the night of the gala. Panic overtook her. Suddenly, Darcy's story didn't seem so farfetched.

What did she really know about Greg Wickham? She knew he was the hottest man who'd ever paid her a shred of attention. Elizabeth had been so willing to believe Greg Wickham because he was handsome and she wanted to have sex with him.

Elizabeth read Darcy's letter twice the next day, digesting the part about Jane's promotion. Pausing to consider Darcy's argument that promoting Jane would have cost the company dearly, Elizabeth realized that, if she had been faced with the same choice, she might have promoted Anne, too. She felt ashamed.

In fact, reading the letter became a nightly mortification. Before bed, Elizabeth unearthed it from her nightstand and read over Darcy's careful script. She relived their argument on the corner of Columbus and Sixty-Fourth Street, rewinding through the ignorant and self-righteous things she'd said about how he'd ruined Wickham and her sister. Elizabeth's insides sank, and her face colored with humiliation, even when she was alone. If only she hadn't been so furious. If only she hadn't spat secondhand insults in his face. If only she'd been more rational.

Certainly, Darcy wasn't blameless. His demeanor in the studio abraded like sandpaper. But hadn't he been a little right? All of those times she'd thought he was picking on her, hadn't he just been giving her feedback on her dancing? He spoke callously, to be sure, but so did many ballet teachers. Their harshness had never bothered her before.

With Darcy, it had. Elizabeth remembered that first, wounding comment she'd overheard him say to Charles: *You never would have considered this girl if it hadn't been for your little affair... She's short, she's got tits, and she'll have full-blown tendonitis in a few years if she doesn't already.*

The memory still smarted. Still, had she let that one comment overcome all other rational thought? Had she sabotaged herself? She'd refused everything Darcy had ever offered her because she thought it would punish *him*? It was lunacy!

She clearly knew nothing. Nothing about Greg Wickham. Nothing about ballet companies, nothing about their finances, and nothing about how company promotions worked. And she knew—or had known—nothing about William Darcy.

But now that she knew, Elizabeth wished she didn't. It was easier to hate him.

Now, she just hated herself.

Elizabeth was in a mood again. She'd been sullen for weeks since the premier of Darcy's piece. Jane had initially thought her sister was suffering from the disappointment of being cast out of the *pas de deux*, but Elizabeth's listlessness persisted.

It was May. They'd had a beautiful spring, days of warm weather, blue skies, and packed, grateful theaters of enthusiastic balletomanes. None of it moved Elizabeth. She had pulled inside of herself like a turtle. Elizabeth usually emoted passion. Delight, rage, and despair were highlights in her repertoire; Elizabeth didn't do gray. But Jane could see that something had sucked the intensity from her sister, leaving a hologram that looked and sounded like Elizabeth but lacked matter.

That evening after their performance, Jane invited Elizabeth to dinner along with Charlotte and Lydia. She'd shaken her head no. She wanted to go home. She was tired. She wasn't sleeping well.

Jane knew that was the truth. For the last few weeks, Elizabeth's bedroom light had remained on even after she wished Jane good night. Jane had no idea what she was doing in there. Reading, perhaps. Elizabeth had always been an avid reader. But in the mornings, she appeared from her bedroom, puffy-eyed, groggy, and distant.

Lydia and Charlotte were worried, too. That night, Jane promised that she would speak to her younger sister.

It was past midnight, but the light in Elizabeth's bedroom was on. Jane rapped on the door.

"Come in," Elizabeth said.

Peeking in, Jane saw her sister lying on the bed, folding up several sheets of notepaper and tucking them under her leg. She looked heartsick.

"Lizzy, what's wrong?"

"I'm just tired, Jane. Don't worry about me."

Jane frowned. "What's that?"

Elizabeth slipped the note further beneath her leg. "Just a note from someone."

"From who?"

"What's gotten into you, Jane? You're being awfully nosy," Elizabeth teased, feigning a lightness Jane knew she didn't feel.

"I should ask what's gotten into *you*. I can tell something's wrong. Something's been wrong for weeks. I'm worried. Charlotte and Lydia are, too."

The pretense of lightness fell from Elizabeth's face, and her forehead creased. Joining her on the bed, Jane brushed Elizabeth's hair from her face.

"Tell me."

It felt good having Jane stroke her hair. Elizabeth set her head down on

Jane's shoulder. "Don't tell Charlotte or Lydia, okay?"

Jane promised she wouldn't, crossing her heart with crossed fingers as she had when they were girls. She smiled kindly.

"Mr. Darcy... the other day... he told me he was in love with me."

Jane nodded. "I see."

A blush spread over Elizabeth's face.

"Oh, Lizzy." Jane pulled her sister into a tight hug.

Pressed up against her sister's shoulder, Elizabeth mumbled, "I thought you'd be more surprised."

"Well, you did sleep with him."

"That's not a prerequisite for being in love with someone," Elizabeth said. "I didn't think it meant anything."

Jane frowned and looked at her sympathetically. Elizabeth knew her sister and knew there must have been so much she wanted to say. Jane just asked, "What happened to bring this all out?"

"We got in a huge fight the day of his dress rehearsal. I said some pretty horrible things to him."

"What things?"

Elizabeth chewed on her lip, considering her words carefully before answering. She knew she didn't have the heart to tell Jane everything.

"I accused him of ruining Greg Wickham. Turns out Mr. Darcy had his own side of the story."

She relayed the details of the note hidden under her thigh, about Greg and Darcy's childhood friendship, their animosity at BTNY, Greg and Caroline's relationship, and the incident with the tutu. Elizabeth left out any mention of Jane and of Darcy's sister, figuring that it wasn't her secret to share.

Jane shook her head incredulously. "It all seems so unbelievable," she said.

"I believe him," replied Elizabeth. "And I feel like the dumbest person on the planet."

"Why?"

"Because I said some awful things to Mr. Darcy. Because I thought I was utterly right when I said them. Because I must seem like such an idiot to him."

"Poor William," frowned Jane. When Elizabeth didn't reply, Jane added, "And you don't want to seem like an idiot to him."

"Of course not!"

"Because you want him to think well of you."

"I'm not in love with him, Jane."

"That's not what I was implying. I was just wondering why you cared. You said a while ago that you didn't really concern yourself with his opinions or anyone else's."

Elizabeth wondered why she did care so much, why it wrung out her insides to know she'd acted the fool with Darcy.

"Am I pigheaded, Jane?" she blurted out.

"Pigheaded? No! Why?"

Elizabeth wasn't laughing. "Am I self-righteous?"

"No."

"Are you just saying that because you're my sister?"

"Lizzy, what is this? You're a wonderful person."

"You probably think the same thing about Caroline."

Jane scrunched up her nose.

Elizabeth was quiet. She wasn't so sure she agreed with her sister. Was she a wonderful person? Did wonderful people treat others with contempt based on gossip and assumptions?

"Earth to Lizzy," Jane said.

Refocusing her gaze, Elizabeth apologized.

Jane held her shoulders. "You're a good person. You're passionate, and you stand by what you think is right. You're funny and smart and—"

"And too opinionated and judgmental and self-righteous."

"Everyone has flaws, Lizzy."

Elizabeth traced her finger along the swirling pattern of her bedspread. She looked up at Jane, who gazed back at her with tenderness. Underneath Jane's sympathetic gaze, Elizabeth felt even worse because she felt she didn't deserve it.

It was, of course, true. Everyone had flaws. It didn't make it any easier to stomach hers, however.

In a different dance studio in a different city, a different set of dancers stood around with the same expression of anticipation in their eyes. And William felt the same sense of trepidation that he always did before he began to choreograph a new work. It was the same fear that it would be a failure and the same fear that he didn't really care. He steeled his face in his practiced way and began to place the dancers around the room.

They reflected the same rapt attention and silent deference, and he scanned the room for a pair of eyes that held a different look. Then he remembered what he was doing and stopped.

Fortunately, he had the first full minute of the music choreographed—Beethoven, this time. It was just a matter of showing it to these new dancers. William marked the steps. The two soloists and their partners mimicked him, though one of the female dancers twirled her wrist in a distasteful flourish.

"Not like that," he said. Her eyes went wide in the same way a young dancer's always did.

And something inside of William deflated. The dancer tried the *pirouette* and *port de bras* again, but the motion of her arms still annoyed him.

Pursing his lips, William remembered Elizabeth's accusations and then said, in a way that felt very different to him, "That's a little better, but try using your wrist less and your back more. Like this."

He thought of Elizabeth Bennet when he said it.

Chapter 19

Only two weeks remained in the performance season. Elizabeth was body-and-soul-exhausted. As much as she hated admitting it, the last time she could recall feeling any excitement in a dance studio was in Darcy's rehearsals. She wanted to feel something again, not just the purposelessness that had plagued her since being demoted out of Darcy's *pas de deux*.

On Monday, Elizabeth awoke feeling restless. Afraid of running into Greg again, Elizabeth had stopped attending the Afro-Caribbean dance classes she'd loved so much. However, that morning, her stomach churned and her heart pounded. She needed release. She wanted to sweat, jump, stomp, and shake her head around. She decided to risk running into Greg and return to Afro-Caribbean class.

When Elizabeth stepped into the locker room of the studio to store her things before class, she was greeted with smiles and a few calls of "hey" and "long time, no see." It felt good to be recognized as a familiar face and not as the dancer who stole other people's roles. Even better, when Elizabeth stepped into the studio, she noticed Greg wasn't there. The teacher called the dancers together and the drums began. As she hoped, the energy soon swept Elizabeth in. The drums pounded, her feet stomped, and her lungs burned.

After class, she collapsed against the wall of the studio, her senses alive. A dancer with caramel skin and spiked black hair plopped down next to her, knocked her shoulder against Elizabeth's, and smiled. Like herself, the dancer, Madeleine Garcia, danced professionally, but in various modern-dance companies around the city. She and Madeleine had been friends from Elizabeth's first days in New York City due to Madeleine's insistence on talking to, hugging, and offering advice to anyone she came into contact with. Thanks to an inborn loquaciousness that Elizabeth secretly envied, Madeleine had initiated several conversations with Elizabeth in Afro-Caribbean dance classes, and they had developed a friendly rapport. Madeleine offered unsolicited but good-natured advice on the stomping and rolling steps that couldn't have been more different from the rigid and polished ballet movements Elizabeth was used to. Elizabeth accepted the older dancer's advice and her good-natured teasing. In turn, Madeleine joked that she was the "auntie" Elizabeth had never asked for who couldn't keep her nose out of anybody's business.

So that day after class, when Madeleine asked Elizabeth how the season was going, Elizabeth felt comfortable divulging her troubles to her.

Madeleine listened with genuine sympathy. "I get it. Dancing professionally takes it out of you. By the end of the season, I feel like I have nothing left to give."

"It's been a rough time for me personally, too," Elizabeth admitted. "I just feel . . . lost. I don't know."

"Stress can do that to you. And you're how old?"

"Almost twenty-four."

"You're still a baby!" cried Madeleine, squeezing Elizabeth's shoulder. "You're just figuring it all out. Go easy on yourself, sweetie. What are you doing during your break?"

"I'm not sure." Elizabeth frowned. "Probably trying to find a part-time job somewhere so I can earn a little money."

Again, Madeleine nodded. "I get that. You gotta pay the bills. But you gotta feed your soul, too, Lizzy."

The corner of Elizabeth's lip rose. "Rent and electricity and gas are hungry little bastards, though."

Madeleine laughed. "Yeah, look at me talking all this smack. I'm the biggest workaholic of them all. Touring Canada. Off to Cali after that. Man!"

"So no break for you?"

"Oh, I get a break. A few weeks in July. And what am I doing? Dancing, of course. There's this African dance festival that's happening in Miami, and it's gonna be wild! I can't wait."

Elizabeth's eyes lit up. "Oh, wow!"

"Yeah, I went last year when they started it, and it was the best time I'd ever had at a dance festival. It's pretty small, but a couple of really well-known teachers and companies are going to be there."

"That sounds incredible."

"You should come!" Madeleine said. "It'll be just the thing for you. I've seen how you move in this class. You would love it!"

Elizabeth shook her head. "I don't think I could afford it."

"It won't be that expensive. The festival is cheap because it's still so small. And the tickets down to Miami are cheap because it's summer. There are a bunch of girls getting together and renting a house on Miami Beach for a week. We still have room, so you could stay with us!"

Elizabeth's heart began to pound in a rhythm of excitement. "Really?"

"Yeah! It'd be good for you, little bunhead! This festival—it's some soul-feeding stuff! Trust your auntie, Lizzy."

Laughing, Elizabeth replied that she would think about it. Madeleine gave Elizabeth her telephone number without prompting and made Elizabeth promise to text if she decided to come. Then Madeleine patted Elizabeth on the shoulder twice and bounded up. They bid each other goodbye, and Elizabeth finished her stretches. As she changed in the locker room, she turned over Madeleine's suggestion.

After class, Elizabeth stepped out into the radiant midday sun, blinked, and looked around. Union Square was loud with cars, idling trucks, screaming children in the playground, and the faint beat of hip-hop from the south end of the park. Curious customers crowded under the white canopies of farmers' market stalls. Elizabeth ambled over and purchased an expensive box of strawberries that glimmered like rubies between her fingers. They tasted like tart sunshine. She walked to the subway entrance, astonished that, suddenly, the trees above her had burst into the most verdant greens. It was almost summer, she realized. End of May. The city had somehow come alive.

Elizabeth inhaled deeply and knew. She needed sunshine and drumbeats. She was going to Miami.

The season ended with little fanfare. Exhausted from their grueling schedules, the dancers of Ballet Theater couldn't wait to scatter off to other endeavors. To pay the bills, many would dance with other companies as guest artists for a few weeks. Some would pursue their "other lives" as mothers or bicyclists or readers or normal people. Many just planned on hanging around in New York City although none were too happy about it. Summers in the city were steamy and miserable.

Jane, along with Charles, took off to the cabin in Rhinebeck for most of the week. One weekend early into their break, Elizabeth accompanied them upstate. They hiked, swam in the pool, and made vegetable sautés with produce from the farmers' market. With Caroline and Darcy absent this time, she should have enjoyed the trip. Yet, the cabin reminded Elizabeth of Darcy. She sat on the sofa in the living room and pictured him by the windows as they sparred over aesthetics. In the kitchen, she remembered puking on his shoes, which always made her wilt a little.

Back in the city, Elizabeth took ballet class every few days at a large Midtown dance studio, but rather than taking the advanced classes with every other off-season ballerina, she opted for a lower level, filled with ballet hobbyists. Amidst the imperfect bodies—young, old, tall, short—Elizabeth felt more at ease. She worked on her alignment, sacrificing ear-high extensions and light speed *petit allegros* for dancing that demanded just as much from her because it was fundamentally correct. She felt as though she was slogging through damp sand, but she accepted that this new kind of dancing would be better for her in the long run.

Elizabeth and Jane made arrangements to sublet their apartment for a week to a family of German tourists for an ungodly sum of money. Some of that money would offset the costs of Elizabeth's dance festival, and Jane decided to go out to California to visit friends. Without the chaos of rehearsals and performances, the days inched by.

Finally, in the middle of July, during one of the worst heat waves that year, Elizabeth lugged her bags onto a crosstown bus and made her way to LaGuardia Airport. She could barely contain the wild punching of her heart as she boarded the plane to Miami and actually squealed in delight when the aircraft made its first turn over South Florida, revealing through the portal of the airplane window, turquoise waters and condominiums stretching endlessly along the coastline.

The taxi dropped her off at a little pink and white bungalow on a palm tree-lined street. Madeleine and another dancer she didn't know were already there, sitting on the porch in rocking chairs, sipping wine coolers. After paying the cab driver, Elizabeth rolled her suitcase up the walk, grinning.

Madeleine tipped up her wine cooler at her younger friend in greeting, introduced the woman sitting next to her as Rielle, and pointed to the house. "Welcome to paradise, Lizzy. Put that suitcase in there, grab a drink, and get your butt out here. We need to get your soul back in shape."

Elizabeth complied without delay.

THE NEXT DAY, ELIZABETH TOASTED herself like a marshmallow on the beach. The day after that, the dance festival began, and Elizabeth wondered whether she'd been crazy to come. If she thought walking twelve New York City blocks in the scorching summer heat was bad, she'd clearly never attempted the feat in Miami. Although not even ten o'clock in the morning, she and the rest of her housemates arrived at the dance studio drenched in sweat. One African dance class later, Elizabeth's temples throbbed with exertion. She was undoubtedly the worst dancer in the room. The other festival participants came from professional Afro-Caribbean and modern dance companies. They shook, swirled, and thrust effortlessly. Elizabeth, however, looked like she was having a seizure.

Madeleine teased her good-naturedly. "Too much for the Bunhead, huh?"

The nickname stuck immediately, and from that moment on, the rest of the festival dancers referred to Elizabeth as Bunhead.

In the afternoon, the dancers began rehearsals for an original choreography. The choreographer, a tall and regal Trinidadian man with skin the color of thick espresso, saw past Elizabeth's erratic dancing and cast her in this piece.

"Bunhead," he called, sending the rest of the dancers in paroxysms of laughter, "I like how you move softly. We can use that somehow."

Rehearsal lasted several hours. Fortunately for Elizabeth, the choreographer, Mr. Bates, had little use for her in the beginning of his piece, so she sat on the sidelines, stretching out her already spent legs.

The trek back to her little bungalow again coated her in sweat. Once home, she threw off her sweaty leotard, donned her blue and white polka-dot bikini, and walked to the beach. The warm Atlantic waters revived her.

Over the next few days, that became her routine: sweaty walk to the studio, sweaty morning dance classes, exhausting three-hour rehearsals, followed by a solitary dip in the ocean.

On the third day of the festival, in rehearsal for Mr. Bates' work, the choreographer called out to her in his resonant voice, "Okay, Little Miss

Bunhead, time for you to stand up. You come out like this."

Elizabeth popped up from the side of the room. The soreness that had debilitated her legs the whole day subsided as Mr. Bates demonstrated the roll of her shoulders and hips as she strutted on stage. She tried it, and was met with cries of encouragement from the sidelines: "Go on, Bunhead," "All right now!"

The moves were curvy and languid. Mr. Bates was clearly playing to her strengths. The choreography mixed everything sensuous about ballet and Afro-Caribbean dancing together. Elizabeth twirled her hips and extended her legs. An *entrechat quatre* ended in a body roll.

"Got to use some of that ballet, hm?" teased Mr. Bates.

"Sure," Elizabeth laughed.

She wasn't sure how it happened, but despite being the worst dancer there, Elizabeth found herself with a small solo.

As she walked home with Madeleine, her friend said, "You looked great out there, Lizzy. You sure you don't want to give up ballet and come dance with me?"

"I'm tempted. It'll take me another decade to land a soloist spot where I am."

Madeleine looked at Elizabeth in disbelief. "No way. You'll make soloist in a year."

"Yeah, right. The same time pigs fly."

"No. You got something when you dance, honey. Something... I don't know—spicy. Hasn't anyone ever told you that before?"

Elizabeth pursed her lips and thought of William Darcy. She didn't want to because she'd been having such a blissful time in Miami so far, and thoughts of Darcy confused her. She answered carefully. "Some people have said that before, yes."

"You need to listen to those people. They know what they're talking about," said Madeleine, who continued to look at Elizabeth intensely. "You don't dance like a lot of people. And a lot of people don't know what to do with that. Fortunately, Mr. Bates is one of the best choreographers I've worked with, and he spotted what you've got immediately. Good thing he's letting you show it off."

Although Madeleine didn't mean to do it, Elizabeth felt immediately chastised. She couldn't help but think of another choreographer, one who had also apparently spotted what she had immediately. She felt the familiar clench of regret and pushed it down.

As she walked along with Madeleine and the other dancers in the house, Elizabeth talked about the cute drummer who kept staring at Madeleine and dissected what it meant. When they returned to the bungalow, they decided to order pizza for dinner. Elizabeth, per her routine, grabbed her swimsuit and headed east to the ocean. Although still light out, the sun had set enough to be obscured behind the condominium tower. The beach glowed yellow with the warm evening light, and the water was a muted aqua. Dunking her head into the ocean, Elizabeth came up for air and then floated on her back. She stared up at the peachy clouds and thought of William Darcy.

She wasn't sure whether she would ever see him again. He might never come back to Ballet Theater to choreograph, particularly since the critics had mauled his piece. While Elizabeth knew it was probably better for the two of them never to meet again given their contentious relationship, she wondered whether things could have been different. What if he had never said that hurtful thing about her the first day after rehearsal? Or, at least, what if she'd never overheard it? He might have choreographed the *pas de deux* on her, and it might have thrilled Elizabeth in the same way her solo in Mr. Bates' choreography thrilled her now.

It had been months since she'd seen Mr. Darcy, and her opinion of him had softened. There were still certain parts of him—sharp, cutting parts—that she couldn't approve of, but overall, Elizabeth felt she understood him better. She could appreciate the enormous honor he'd bestowed on her and the risk he'd taken by giving her a chance in his piece. Elizabeth still wasn't sure how to understand his feelings for her. She strongly suspected he'd mixed up his admiration of her dancing with his admiration of her as a woman. Still, she was now able to accept that compliment, too. She wondered whether their relationship might also have gone differently if she hadn't been so eager to cast him as a villain.

The sky darkened to a deeper blue, and Elizabeth knew she needed to go back. The pizza would certainly be cold.

When she returned, Elizabeth discovered the pizza was gone. Her housemates apologized profusely; they'd been hungry and weren't sure whether she would be home for dinner. Not that it mattered to Elizabeth. Pizza was fattening anyway, and she wanted some time alone for reflection. She told her housemates she would go for a walk to find dinner.

Donning shorts, an old t-shirt, and a pair of sneakers, Elizabeth took off along the side streets of Miami Beach. There weren't many pedestrians around, nor were there restaurants. Her stomach rumbling, Elizabeth decided to stop at the next place she saw and grab anything, even if it was just a granola bar. As if God-sent, she spotted a small restaurant on the corner of the next block. The lettering on the window was all in Spanish, but Elizabeth recognized the word "café."

When she entered, bells clanked against the glass. The interior was white and fluorescent-lit, but clean. An older man behind the counter conversed in rapid-fire Spanish with a young woman sitting alone at a table, the only patron in the café. Studying the menu, Elizabeth discovered she'd walked into a small Cuban restaurant with only heavy-sounding meat dishes complete with rice, beans, and fried things.

"Excuse me," Elizabeth said, approaching the counter, "do you have salads?"

The man stopped speaking and stared strangely at her, making no reply.

"Do you have salads?" Elizabeth repeated.

"*Ensalada? No.* No salad." The man spoke with a heavy Spanish accent.

"Oh. Okay. Do you have anything that isn't fried?"

He looked blankly at Elizabeth. She returned the look.

"Anything. Not. Fried?" Elizabeth asked slowly, hoping he would understand.

The man's face twisted with annoyance. Again, he said something in Spanish. Elizabeth stood in mute confusion. Helplessly, she looked to the fashionable woman sitting behind her. The young woman stared back.

"Help?" Elizabeth pleaded.

The woman's lips twitched. "It's Cuban food, so it's kinda hard to find anything healthy."

Elizabeth frowned and would have left, but her stomach protested in a pleading gurgle. "Okay, can you recommend anything?

In Spanish, the woman said something to the older gentleman. He nodded in approval and went about the work of preparing Elizabeth's dinner.

"What am I having?" Elizabeth asked the young woman.

"A *medianoche*. It's a sandwich. It has pickles, which are technically vegetables."

Elizabeth shrugged. "Sounds good to me. Thanks."

The woman said no more, but she stared in a way that made Elizabeth uncomfortable. She didn't sense judgment or condescension in the look, but Elizabeth did feel a little like a scientific specimen. To divert her attention, Elizabeth fished her wallet out of her bag.

She studied the young woman from the corner of her eye. She seemed completely out of place in this small, plain diner. She was young, maybe Elizabeth's age, and gorgeous. Her hefty Louis Vuitton bag sat on the plastic tabletop under which she crossed her legs daintily. Four-inch strappy sandals graced her perfectly pedicured feet, Chanel sunglasses perched on the crown of her head, and a silver Tiffany bracelet encircled her wrist. She fulfilled every stereotype that Elizabeth had about Miami women: tanned, dark, raven-haired, and in the shortest shorts Elizabeth had ever seen.

"Are you a tourist?" asked Miss Louis Vuitton.

Elizabeth chuckled. "What gave it away?"

"People from Miami don't wear sneakers in July."

Elizabeth looked down at her feet.

"How long are you in Miami for?"

Elizabeth plucked a ten-dollar bill from her wallet. "Just a few days."

"Planning on going to the beach?"

"I did already. A few times."

"Just a few times?"

"I'm here for a dance festival, so I haven't really had much leisure time yet."

"A dance festival!" The woman smiled then. "That's cool! So you're a dancer?"

Elizabeth nodded.

"Have you ever eaten Cuban food before?" the woman asked. "You should definitely have a pastry! Pepe makes *the* best *pastelitos.* Here, try the guava and cheese one. It's on me." Then, the woman said something in Spanish to the man, possibly Pepe, who turned and walked over to a heat lamp, plucking two pastries from underneath.

"Really," protested Elizabeth, "I probably shouldn't. I need to get going anyway."

"I swear, just try this. They're the best in Miami. You have to just try this."

Shrugging and smiling in resignation, Elizabeth let the woman buy her a pastry. She motioned for Elizabeth to sit, her heavy Tiffany bracelet jingling as she removed the designer bag from the tabletop.

"Thanks, you really didn't have to," said Elizabeth.

"It's totally okay. You're so going to die when you eat that," Miss Vuitton said.

"Shouldn't I wait for my sandwich?"

The woman poo-pooed her. "Life's short. Eat dessert first. In high school, I had a throw pillow that said that."

Elizabeth laughed. "Okay, then. Here's to dessert." Elizabeth clinked pastries with her benefactor. A large blot of grease remained in its place on the paper plate. The woman held her treat in between long, French-manicured nails and chomped down happily.

Closing her eyes, she smiled and sighed, "Yum."

Elizabeth took a tentative bite of her own pastry and then another. On the third bite, she struck gold; guava paste and warm melted cream cheese oozed out of the sides. "Ummm," moaned Elizabeth.

The two women looked at each other and then burst into giggles.

"I told you it was good!"

Elizabeth hungrily scarfed down the pastry.

"So, what do you do in Miami?" Elizabeth asked her.

"College. I go to UM."

Elizabeth furrowed her eyebrows, and then understood. She laughed. "Oh. I'm originally from Michigan, and we call the University of Michigan 'UM,' too. That's where I thought you meant."

Miss Vuitton giggled. "Oh, no way. I meant Miami, silly."

"What's your major?"

"Econ and international politics."

"Wow, that's pretty heavy-duty." She'd expected the woman across from her to say tanning or underwater basket weaving.

"Well," the woman shrugged, "I really like it. I'm pretty dumb when it comes to books and reading and stuff, but, like, I totally get numbers and logic and all that boring junk. Oh, gross. I have guava all in my fingernails. I'm, like, super nasty."

Elizabeth laughed. She hadn't expected the woman in front of her to giggle or lick guava paste off her finger or tend to say "like" like a valley girl.

Just then, the door swung open, and a portly older woman with maroon hair walked in.

"Oh, hey, Reynalda," Miss Vuitton called.

"*Hola, mija*," Reynalda answered, "Where's Pepe?"

Pepe grunted from under the counter. Reynalda walked to the counter and began talking to the man in Spanish. Elizabeth recognized a few English words thrown in.

"They're married," whispered Miss Vuitton.

Just then, Reynalda, who had grabbed a croquette from under the heat lamp, came to their table and sat without invitation. She smiled politely at Elizabeth.

"Are you Georgiana's friend from school?" Her English, while still tinged with a Spanish accent, was far better than her husband's.

Shaking her head, Elizabeth opened her mouth to reply but was cut off. "No, she's from out of town," answered the woman, who Elizabeth now knew was called Georgiana.

"Oh, yeah?" asked Reynalda. "From where?"

"New York," Elizabeth answered.

Georgiana slapped the table so suddenly, Elizabeth jumped. "You're *kidding. I'm* from New York!"

"Oh wow. Small world," Elizabeth said.

"Where in New York? New York City?"

Elizabeth nodded. Georgiana pounded the table again. "This is too crazy. Me, *too.* Where in the city?"

"Harlem."

Leaning forward, Georgiana sucked in a breath. "We. Are. Practically. *Neighbors!* I live on Central Park West. Is it scary up there in Harlem?" Georgiana asked.

"No. It's fine," said Elizabeth.

"You were born in New York?" Reynalda asked.

"I'm from Michigan originally."

Reynalda made a face. "From Michigan? It's so cold there, no? When I first came over from Cuba, I lived in Chicago for a few months with my cousin. I thought I was gonna freeze to death. I can't even stand New York, but at least it's better than Chicago."

Elizabeth laughed, feeling a little overwhelmed with the sudden inquisition. Pepe shuffled out from behind the counter then and brought her sandwich. He asked her something in Spanish, which Georgiana translated. "Want another pastry?"

Elizabeth said maybe she'd get one later. Pepe shrugged and shuffled off.

Reynalda and Georgiana watched Elizabeth eat for a few moments and then began chatting in a strange mixture of English and Spanish. The older woman asked Elizabeth how she liked Miami, and as Elizabeth had only been in town for a few days, she replied that it was extremely humid but pretty. Reynalda seemed satisfied by that answer and mentioned again how cold Chicago was. Then, a shrill rendition of *Ode to Joy* came from the Louis Vuitton bag. Fumbling through it, Georgiana plucked out a thin, rhinestone-encrusted cell phone and answered it. Her eyes lit up.

"Yo, Dub! Where are you? … No way! … No *way*! … I thought you weren't coming 'til tomorrow. … Cool! … At Reynalda's. Oh, crap, who's picking you up? … Oh, good. … Oh, crap, he was supposed to pick *me* up. I didn't bring the car. … Dub, you know I hate driving. … Can you? … Aww, you're so sweet. … Fifteen minutes. … I'm so excited to see you, too! … Oh, man! Why is *she* coming? … Yeah, yeah. If I have to, I guess I'll put up with her. … Okay, so fifteen minutes? … Great! … Love you! I'm so excited to see you. … Okay, love you. Bye."

The woman looked at Reynalda with dancing eyes. "He's already here!"

"You're kidding! He said he was coming tomorrow."

"He wanted to surprise us."

The woman laughed, clapped her hands, and then yelled something in Spanish to Pepe, who only smiled in response. Georgiana turned to Elizabeth and explained. "My brother's coming in from New York. He was supposed to come tomorrow, though."

"That's a nice surprise."

"Her brother," Reynalda interrupted, "he always does stuff like that. He's so good to her. He's so good to all of us."

Georgiana shook her head. "Reynalda, you always say the exact same thing."

"Because it's true, *mija*! Her brother is the—"

"She does this to, like, almost everyone," explained Georgiana. Reynalda lightly slapped the girl's arm and told her to be quiet.

"You know, I worked for his family for years. I took care of him since he was this big. I was like his grandmother, you know? And their parents," Reynalda pointed at Georgiana, "may God rest their souls, they were the best people, too. When you were about how old, Georgianita?"

"I don't know, like five, or something."

"When she was five, my sister, they helped her come over from Cuba. You know, she had nothing. Just the clothes on her back. And her kids. Her husband couldn't come over. And you know what their parents did?"

Georgiana rolled her eyes with a good-natured smile on her face. Elizabeth raised her eyebrows, awaiting the response.

"Her parents, they gave my sister and her kids an apartment for a year. My sister couldn't even speak English. They got her a job. They fed her and her kids 'til she got on her feet. The best family. The best! I'm telling you. It didn't matter if I was the housekeeper, they treated me with respect, you know. Respect. Now, that's something you don't see a lot of lately."

"No, indeed," agreed Elizabeth. Georgiana smiled softly and simply shrugged.

"And her brother, he's the same way, you know. Let me tell you, a couple years ago, I started getting back problems, and the doctor told me to take it easy. You know, from years of dusting and vacuuming and taking care of these ones. My back just couldn't take it anymore. And Pepe, he'd been working for years in the factory, but how's an old fart supposed to work day after day on the same line with kids two times younger than him? So, I told her brother, 'I'm sorry, but the doctor says I have to take it easy, and I can't work anymore.' I had been working for this family for nearly thirty years, you know?"

At this point, Reynalda paused in her account to dab away the moisture from the corners of her eyes.

"And let me tell you what her brother did. When I retired, her brother bought me and Pepe a house. And not some filthy, run-down place in Hialeah. No, a nice little house in Kendall, close to my sister and her husband and her kids."

Elizabeth nodded in approval. "That's very generous of him."

"But that's not all. He buys me a house, and he gives me a retirement bonus bigger than what most businessmen get. Can you believe it? I nearly died of shock when I saw that check. Pepe here, he just burst into tears. And I told him, I said, 'I can't accept this.' But he wouldn't hear it. He told me, 'Reynalda, you're like family.' Isn't that something? So, what are we going to do with all that money? Pepe, he always made the best *pastelitos*, so we said, why not open a *cafetería*? So we bought this place."

Elizabeth was impressed, not only by the display of goodwill, but also by the vast amounts of money being thrown around by Georgiana's brother. No wonder the girl had more designer brands on her than a duty-free store.

"I'm warning you," Georgiana joked, "this woman exaggerates, like, everything."

"*Oye*, hush. You know your brother's the best man in the world."

Georgiana giggled and winked at Elizabeth. "He is. He'll drop whatever he's doing and help me if I'm in trouble."

Elizabeth replied, "He sounds like an ideal brother. I've always wanted a brother."

"You don't have any siblings?"

"I do. A perfect older sister."

"Hey," Reynalda said, leaning into Elizabeth, "give me your sister's number. We could set them up. I keep telling him to get married and give me grandbabies, but you know, he's all over the place. He won't settle down."

Picking up half of her sandwich, Elizabeth was about to bite into the corner when Reynalda bolted up and shrieked. Elizabeth jumped, her sandwich falling from her hands and landing on the tile. Running to the door, Reynalda laughed, screeched, and clapped like someone possessed. Suddenly, Georgiana joined in the pandemonium, leaving Elizabeth alone and picking up pickles and ham from the floor.

Looking over the table, Elizabeth plucked a napkin off it and then froze. Her mouth plunked open. There, at the door—strangled in a vice-like embrace by both Reynalda and Georgiana—stood William Darcy, his baritone laughter resounding through the small cafeteria like a roll of thunder.

"Shit!" Elizabeth panicked, ducking back under the table. Her heartbeat exploded in her chest. Then, realizing what she would look like to Darcy, hiding under the table, she shut her eyes and knew she would have to stand and reveal herself. A shiver rippled over her skin. She stood and looked awkwardly.

The reunion lasted for a long minute, but finally Reynalda calmed enough to stop screaming and crying. Darcy answered all of her questions: how he was, how his flight was. When her interrogation ended, he turned to his little sister.

"What have you done to your hair, G?" he asked.

"You like it? I got it cut!"

"I see that. You look like Audrey Hep—"

The words died on his mouth as he finally glanced beyond his sister and noticed Elizabeth standing in the background. He started, paled, and then blushed a shade of red to match Elizabeth. Georgiana stared at him strangely. "Dub, it's Hepburn."

Elizabeth saw his jaw stiffen. She didn't have to imagine his thoughts because his face reflected the same raw disbelief that she, too, felt.

Georgiana followed his gaze to Elizabeth and then understood. "Oh, we were making a new friend. Dub, this is— Oh, crap; I'm such an airhead. I totally didn't even ask you your name."

"Elizabeth," Darcy murmured. Elizabeth felt her heart stop and then stumble into a frantic rhythm. She had no words, and so she simply stared dumb and wide-eyed, which was fine since Darcy could only do the same.

Chapter 20

"Oh, my God, this is super creepy. You both know each other?" Georgiana asked, looking from her brother to Elizabeth.

Elizabeth opened her mouth to reply but only stammered a few syllables.

Darcy summoned his voice before she could. "Yes, Elizabeth dances at Ballet Theater."

"*Qué mundo tan pequeño!*" exclaimed Reynalda, clapping her hands together and looking in delight at Darcy.

"For real!" Georgiana cried.

"*Mijo*, you sit. Pepe will make you a *café con leche,* and we'll get you something to eat." Reynalda pushed him towards the table and then retreated to the counter to help her husband fix Darcy a snack. He gave Elizabeth an embarrassed look.

How was this even possible? It was the most preposterous coincidence that he now stood right in front of her in some hole-in-the-wall restaurant in Miami after she'd been thinking of him no less than an hour ago!

"How are you, Elizabeth?" he asked.

Elizabeth started. His voice was so unexpectedly soft. Not knowing how to respond, Elizabeth stuttered her answer. "G-good, and you?"

"Good. I'm good." He nodded. "I... it's a surprise to see you here."

"I... we..." stammered Elizabeth, gesturing back and forth between herself and Georgiana.

"Elizabeth just came in to get dinner, and we became friends," explained Georgiana.

Darcy looked surprised but only nodded. She saw him swallow. He asked her again how she was.

Finally, Elizabeth smiled. "I'm much the same as I was fifteen seconds ago. Doing well, thanks."

It was Darcy's turn to laugh. He ran a hand through his hair and smiled. "Right. Sorry."

Reynalda yelled at them to sit, and they complied. Darcy took a seat next to his sister and across from Elizabeth. She took the opportunity to stare at him, her stomach fluttering. Although rumpled from his travels and sporting a five-o'-clock shadow, Darcy still looked as handsome as she remembered. He caught her eye then. Elizabeth quickly looked down at her hands.

"Wait, so," Georgiana asked Elizabeth, "is that dance festival with Ballet Theater?"

"No, we're on our summer break right now," Elizabeth explained. "It's another festival."

"Which one?" asked Darcy, leaning his forearms onto the table.

"The New World Dance Festival. It's an—"

"The Afro-Caribbean festival?"

"Yes," answered Elizabeth, astonished that Darcy would know of it.

"Archibald Bates is choreographing something for that festival, isn't he?" Darcy asked.

Elizabeth nodded. "I'm in his piece, actually."

"That's fantastic. Archie's a visionary. And how are you enjoying the festival?"

"I'm liking it. It's so different dancing here than it is at Ballet Theater. It's a nice change."

"When are you performing?"

"On Saturday night."

Darcy turned to his sister. "Do you want to go see some really incredible dance?"

Georgiana's eyes lit up. "I'd *love* to, Dub!"

"That is," Darcy said again to Elizabeth, "if there are still tickets?"

"There are. But I'll give you my comps," said Elizabeth.

Georgiana cheered and hugged her brother. Darcy laughed, glanced at Elizabeth, and then blushed for the second time that night. She was incredulous. William Darcy, engaging in conversation? Asking how she was (twice)? Smiling and *blushing*?

"Hey, G, that reminds me," Darcy added, "we should invite Elizabeth to the barbecue we're having tomorrow."

Georgiana's smile took on a tinge of puzzlement. Opening her mouth to reply, she quickly closed it and simply nodded.

Darcy turned towards Elizabeth. "We're having a barbecue tomorrow. Come. Please. I mean, if you want to."

Elizabeth's expression mimicked Georgiana's. Who was this man? He looked like William Darcy, but he didn't act anything like the gruff and unsociable choreographer she'd known. She didn't understand this congeniality.

"Charles will be there," Darcy added as if that was more convincing.

"Oh, please, Elizabeth, *please* come," begged Georgiana. "It'll be super fun, and we can go in the pool and, oh my God, Dub makes the *best* steak in the entire universe. You have to come."

Elizabeth reddened. "I, um, don't have a car."

"That's okay!" Georgiana gushed. "Our driver, Miguel, can pick you up—"

"G..." Darcy said, in a warning tone.

Georgiana made a face. "Or I could pick you up. Dub wants me to drive more, but I hate it."

"Or I wouldn't mind picking you up. We're only about ten minutes from here," Darcy explained.

Elizabeth blinked. "I wouldn't want to impose on your family reunion."

Georgiana opened her mouth to reply, but her brother answered first. "No. You wouldn't be imposing. I want... *we* want you to come." Georgiana nodded in agreement.

Elizabeth stared from one sibling to the other. Finally, she consented in a voice barely above a whisper.

"Yay!" Georgiana cried. Then, she turned to Reynalda and Pepe and told them about the barbecue. Reynalda shuffled over to them, a Styrofoam cup of coffee in one hand and a paper plate with a greasy croquette in the other. Frowning, she said that this was the first she'd heard of any barbecue, and how was she supposed to cook something with so little preparation? She set both the cup and plate down in front of Darcy and chided him in Spanish.

Then, Darcy replied to her in perfect Spanish—or what sounded like perfect Spanish since Elizabeth couldn't be sure. Elizabeth stared. She'd thought she'd known him. But here was this other side, this gentle, smiling,

Spanish-speaking other side. Looking at her, he caught her staring and raised his eyebrow in question.

"I didn't know you spoke Spanish," she said.

Reynalda took the liberty of explaining. "I practically raised this boy. He'd better speak some Spanish."

"There you have it," said Darcy.

After that, Reynalda began asking Darcy another string of questions. How was New York? How was the weather there? Was he eating properly? Was he getting enough sleep? Did he have a girlfriend yet? Elizabeth quickly lowered her eyes to her lap when he answered "no" to that one. She left them there for the remainder of the conversation.

Burrowing inside of her thoughts, Elizabeth wondered again how something like this could have happened. More pressing, she wondered at Darcy's acting so differently here than he had in New York. Although her head whispered that perhaps he was altered for her sake, reason told her it was likely for his sister and former nanny. Still, it was surprising to see such a difference in his personality.

When one of Reynalda's monologues came to an end, Darcy interrupted Elizabeth's thoughts. "Where are you staying, Elizabeth?"

"Um, up the way a bit. On Lambton Street."

"Oh, that's on our way back home. We'll drop you off."

Elizabeth shook her head. "No, no. I can walk. It's only a short way away, really. I'll be fine." She said it with more embarrassment than defiance.

"If it's only a short way away, then it'll be no problem for us to drop you off," Darcy said, looking to his sister who nodded vigorously.

Elizabeth flashed a self-deprecating half smile. "I guess you got me there. Thank you."

Georgiana stood and, kissing Reynalda on the cheek, went outside to find Miguel, their driver. Darcy also pecked the older woman on the cheek and wished her good night. Elizabeth thanked Reynalda and Pepe for dinner, and stepped out of the restaurant silently with Darcy following behind her. Georgiana was nowhere to be seen. Standing awkwardly, Elizabeth shifted back on her heels and stared at her toes. She wished she'd dressed in something a little nicer than sneakers and a t-shirt. She felt Darcy's eyes on her, but she said nothing. Hazarding a glance, she caught the look in his eyes—mysterious and searching but certainly not cold.

"So, what time should I pick you up tomorrow?" he asked.

"We finish rehearsals at five."

"I'll come for you at five, then. Where are you rehearsing?"

She gave Darcy the cross streets. He nodded and then winced a little. "I feel like I owe you a bit of an apology."

Elizabeth's heart thudded. Was he going to apologize for what had passed between them all those months ago?

"I forgot to tell you that we have other guests besides Charles. Caroline will be there."

Elizabeth pursed her lips, hiding her disappointment. Was fate conspiring to bring all of her Ballet Theater nemeses together? "Oh."

"I hope you don't reconsider our invitation?" There was plaintiveness in his voice, and something inside of her fluttered again.

"No," she answered. "I'll still come." Then, her lips twitched. "I need to test out this claim that you make the best steaks in the world."

He kept his poker face when he replied, "It's the universe, actually." Then he grinned. "But Georgiana has a tendency to exaggerate."

They laughed together, and for the third time that evening, Elizabeth felt that light and nervous feeling in her stomach.

William glanced at Elizabeth again, her features warmed by laughter. He was tempted again to shake his head hard, still wondering whether he weren't dreaming or at least the butt of a reality television show prank.

In Seattle, not a day had gone by when he hadn't thought of her, but the real-life version of Elizabeth paled to all of those fantasies. The apples of her cheeks, the freckles on her nose, and those eyes, bright and sparkling even in the darkness were more appealing when lit up with warmth than cold with frost as they'd been too often in his presence.

Finally, the car pulled around the corner. It slowed to a stop at the curb, and William darted to the door, opening it wide for Elizabeth to enter first. She stared up at him in surprise and then nodded her thanks

"Sorry," Georgiana said, twisting around in the front seat, "we had to drive around. The parking meter ran out, and there was a cop totally staring us down."

William said nothing as he slipped next to Elizabeth and closed the door. The car started smoothly and turned the corner.

"Dub, what time's this party start tomorrow?" Georgiana asked.

Turning to Elizabeth, William answered, "I'm picking Elizabeth up at five. So after that, I suppose."

Elizabeth stared oddly at them. Then she asked, "Can I bring anything?"

"No, just yourself."

"Oh, that's me, right up ahead." She pointed to the cute pink and white house on the corner. The drive hadn't lasted longer than a minute, which disappointed William.

"Well, thank you for the ride." Elizabeth opened the door when the car stopped in front of the house.

"No problem. I'll meet you outside tomorrow at five," he said.

"Okay, I'll see you tomorrow, then. Nice meeting you, Georgiana."

"It was fate!" Georgiana chirped.

Georgiana didn't know how right she was, William mused. Closing the car door, Elizabeth practically skipped to the front door. She opened it and, before disappearing inside, looked over her shoulder and waved. William was struck again by how rarely he had ever seen Elizabeth smile at him like that.

After Elizabeth disappeared into the house and Miguel slowly pulled out of the driveway, Georgiana turned around and looked at William.

"Am I a total airhead?" she asked. "Did I forget we were having a party?"

"No, you didn't forget anything."

"Oh, that's what I thought. So it was, like, a spur-of-the-moment kinda thing?"

"You could say I was spurred," William said mysteriously.

"Oh. Cool." Satisfied, Georgiana sat back in the seat and hummed along with the radio. Then she stopped, her eyes growing wide, and she turned around again. Both siblings stared, one with a placid, but satisfied, expression, the other with a look of dawning realization. Georgiana grinned.

"I figured it out," she sang.

"Did you?" William returned playfully.

"That was so her, wasn't it? The girl you told me about."

"Yes, that was 'so' her."

"Oh my God! This is way weird! It *is* like, fate. Dub! She didn't hate your guts."

"Not now, no."

"She's chill. I like her."

William just smiled.

"She likes you, too."

"No." He shook his head.

"She does. I can so tell. Don't you think she liked him, Miguel?"

"Don't ask me. You know I'm pretty bad with the ladies," answered their driver.

"Well, she's into you."

"G, I think I can safely say that Elizabeth is most definitely not into me."

"Hello! I'm a girl, and we girls can read other girls. We're like dolphins, you know? We have a sixth sense."

William laughed and playfully rolled his eyes at his sister. He sat back in the seat, gazing out of the window as hotels and condos slipped by. A breeze made the palm fronds dance. They would take the causeway and be home in less than ten minutes. The thought made William smile in the darkness.

Tomorrow, by some bizarre but providential stroke of chance, Elizabeth would be there with him. William suddenly grew nervous. He remembered, with stunning clarity, everything spoken between them the last time they'd been together. Something in Elizabeth's eyes did seem softer and more open to him, but maybe it hadn't been like that at all. Maybe she had just been embarrassed or wanted to escape. The smile slipped from his face. He had imagined so much before; William wondered whether he weren't doing it again.

"Don't worry, Dub," came Georgiana's voice from the silent darkness. "She'll totally love you. She has to."

"I haven't told you half of the things I said to her."

"Like what?"

"I really don't want to repeat them," William said, rubbing the bridge of his nose. "Just things that I'm not proud of."

Georgiana was silent for a long moment. Sitting back in her seat, she stared out of the window. William wondered when she would respond, and finally, when nearly a minute had passed, he gave up hoping for an answer. Just then, she did reply in a low voice.

"We all do dumb things, Dub. That's what second chances are for."

William paused and stared at his sister in the side mirror. Her profile was outlined by the streetlights, obscuring a full view of her face, but he knew from the melancholy in her voice exactly what she was feeling. Georgiana was thinking of love or the loss of it.

"Second chances, huh?" William repeated.

Georgiana turned again and stared at her brother with a look of quiet empathy. Then she grinned, and William laughed, shaking his head in silence, and turned his face to look at the rush of cars on the other side of the causeway.

Deep in the early morning darkness, Elizabeth still could not sleep. She knew she would pay dearly for her insomnia tomorrow when she would be sluggish in Mr. Bates' rehearsal, but she just couldn't stop the merry-go-round of thoughts.

She couldn't believe the coincidence of running in to Darcy. She couldn't believe the difference in his demeanor. Elizabeth had never seen him so open and pleasant. He'd invited her to a family barbecue at his home! And he'd seemed so willing, so eager to please—dropping Elizabeth off at her bungalow even though it was only a few blocks away, offering to pick her up the next day and chauffeur her to his home.

She lay in the dark, analyzing what it could mean. Sometimes, she believed he was merely acting nice for the sake of his sister, but in the next moment, she would remember the warmth in his eyes or the tone of his voice and sense instinctively that the only person it had been for was her.

Chiding herself, she wondered why it mattered so much. This was a man who, two months ago, made her tear up in rage whenever she thought about him. Elizabeth thought very differently now. For the past few months, she had punished herself on his behalf, calling herself stupid, wallowing in guilt and humiliation. But even if his amiable behavior had been an act that evening, it had been an act of kindness. He could have been cold, accusing, or reproving. Despite the horrible things she'd said and done to him, Darcy had shown her nothing but politeness and courtesy. He was, clearly, a much better person than she'd ever given him credit for.

Underneath her gratitude, there were whisperings of something else —something she didn't understand and didn't want to name. It was a quickening and fluttering thing in her stomach, a nervousness that felt new.

It was the feeling that kept her up until three in the morning and the feeling that powered her like jet-fuel the next day during rehearsal in anticipation of seeing him again that evening.

With the piece nearing completion, Mr. Bates had the dancers running through much of what had been accomplished over the past few days. They would spend the next day cleaning the piece and perform it in two days. The process moved at lightning speed, and although Elizabeth still wanted to work slowly through the musical timing in her solo, there simply wasn't the time in rehearsals when the drummers were present.

"From the second break," called Mr. Bates. The drummers began pounding on their instruments, and the dozen dancers in the piece swirled and thumped in the circular formation that preceded Elizabeth's solo. Then, it was Elizabeth's turn in the center of the studio. She dipped and swirled as the choreography dictated, but she still felt half a beat off the music after the side extension.

"You're too slow, Bunhead!" Mr. Bates yelled over the drums.

Exhaling in frustration, Elizabeth rejoined the other dancers and continued to the choreography's completion.

The dancers panted and braced their hands on their knees as they received their feedback from the choreographer. While Mr. Bates was working with one of the lead dancers on an impossible jump sequence, he suddenly paused and looked over to the windows that faced Lincoln Road on the studio's furthermost wall. He broke into a grin, held up his hand to the dancer he'd been speaking to, and went over to the windows. This aroused most of the dancers' attention, and Elizabeth craned her head to see the passerby who so interested Mr. Bates. It was William Darcy.

Mr. Bates gestured for him to come into the studio. Darcy caught Elizabeth's eye for a millisecond and then complied. Shaking hands, the two men chatted inaudibly; then Mr. Bates turned and looked at Elizabeth. At the same time, the dancers looked at each other in puzzlement.

"Do you know who that is?" Madeleine whispered.

Elizabeth whispered back. "Yeah. It's William Darcy. He choreographed for—"

"Oh, wow! I know the name," she said, eyeing Darcy. "Didn't know it came with that face. Or that body."

The choreographers finished their conversation, and Mr. Bates returned to his dancers. He finished his feedback, during which time Elizabeth struggled to keep her focus on him and not the other choreographer leaning on the far wall of the dance studio. Finally, Mr. Bates thanked the dancers and wished them a good evening. Applauding, the dancers dispersed to the sides of the room to collect water bottles, sweats, and bags.

Nervously, Elizabeth smiled at Darcy, who glimpsed at her during his conversation with Mr. Bates.

Ever observant, Madeleine asked, "Does he know you?"

"Yeah, we worked together at Ballet Theater," answered Elizabeth, trying to appear casual.

"He sure keeps looking over here. And you keep looking over there." Madeleine raised an eyebrow. "You guys just worked together?"

The more Elizabeth attempted indifference, the more forced she sounded. "We're friends. Kinda. I'm . . . he invited me to a party at his house."

"Oh, *friends.* Uh-huh. When's this party?"

"Now. He came to get me."

Madeleine cackled and patted Elizabeth's shoulder. "Just text me if you're not coming home."

"Will you stop!" chided Elizabeth, swatting at her friend's hand.

Madeleine swung her dance bag over her shoulder, sashayed across the floor, and paused in from of William Darcy before giving him a flirtatious once-over. Then she strutted out the door and to the dressing rooms to change.

Elizabeth made her way cautiously to Darcy and saw his smile deepen as she approached.

"Sorry," she apologized.

"What for?" He frowned.

Elizabeth didn't know what for, but she thought maybe for the meaningful way Madeleine had checked him out. She chose not to answer.

"Thanks for waiting," said Elizabeth.

Darcy shrugged. "I came early. I wanted a sneak peek. Hope you don't mind."

"You've seen me make a fool of myself in a dance studio before, so I guess I shouldn't mind."

He chuckled. "You didn't make a fool of yourself. You look great."

Elizabeth hid her embarrassment under a self-deprecating joke. "I'm not sure this kind of dancing is my *forte.*"

Studying her face, he wore an uncertain expression on his, as if he wanted to speak but was restraining himself. "Can I give you some feedback?"

She was surprised that he asked. She nodded her assent. Holding her gaze, he walked past her a little into the studio. "Your rhythm after the jumps is slightly off the beat."

Elizabeth nodded. "I can feel that, but it's like I just can't catch the rhythm."

"What are the steps before that sequence?"

Elizabeth performed them, not full out, but close enough that Darcy could get the gist of the steps. He asked her to repeat the sequence, and she did. She noticed the look on his face transform. His features hardened into that stony expression. Resting his hand over his mouth, Darcy studied her body.

"You're reaching too far over before your body has to collapse. It's throwing off your momentum."

Elizabeth tried it again.

"That looks weak now. Perhaps the reach is mostly with the arms, and you hold your torso in place a little more," he suggested. "Try that."

Inhaling slowly, she did, and the sequence, for the first time, seemed to work. Elizabeth didn't feel like she was scrambling towards the jumps and fumbling through the steps after them. He had a crooked smile on his face that lit up his eyes and made them look like clouds with rays of sun breaking through.

"That looked great," he said.

"Yes, that makes sense. Thanks."

When nothing more was said between them, Elizabeth said, "I guess I'll go grab my things and change. I don't want to keep people waiting."

Darcy nodded, saying he would meet her outside.

Most of the dancers had finished changing by the time Elizabeth hit the dressing room. She decided on a quick shower just to rinse of the sweat and grime of the studio. As she toweled herself off, she thought back to the way Darcy's face and the tone of his voice hardened as he gave her feedback. Then, she thought back to Darcy's face, cracked open in a smile. He changed in the dance studio, the warmth and humor in his demeanor replaced by a hard-edged intensity.

Sweeping a coat of mascara across her eyelashes, Elizabeth thought she looked quite becoming in her post-rehearsal flush and then wondered why that really mattered anyway. She grabbed her bag and pushed herself out of the building.

Once in the brightness of late afternoon, she glanced around for Darcy. She heard a car horn and looked straight ahead at a black BMW. The door opened, and Darcy stepped from the driver's side.

"Holy crap," she whispered through a smile and strode towards his car. By the time she reached it, he was holding the passenger door open for her. Elizabeth entered the car and, in the ten seconds that she was alone in the BMW, commanded herself to look less awestruck. When Darcy slid in beside her, however, she knew it was a lost cause and covered by pretending to search for something in her bag.

"Do you have everything?" he asked.

"Yes," she said, pulling out her sunglasses in a moment of improvisational brilliance.

On the drive down South Beach, they discussed the weather, the buildings, and the people. While not verbose, Darcy carried his share of the conversation. Elizabeth cringed at the obvious nervousness in her voice. As they slipped onto the causeway, the conversation trickled into silence. Elizabeth smoothed the legs of her jeans and looked out the window at the turquoise ocean.

"I can understand why your sister would want to go to college here," Elizabeth said in an attempt to re-ignite their small talk.

"Why is that?"

"It's beautiful! I'd go to the beach every day if I lived here."

Darcy smiled. "Once you've lived here long enough, Miami just becomes your average semi-tropical sauna. Not much to do except the beach. And the clubs. But I've outgrown that."

Elizabeth chuckled. "Does your sister go?"

"She used to. I think she was on a first name basis with all of the bouncers on the Beach. She doesn't go clubbing so much anymore."

"Has she outgrown them, too?"

"No," Darcy said, his voice stiffening, "she stopped after she got married."

"Oh." Elizabeth slumped in the black leather. Glancing out of the corner of her eye at Darcy, she saw him boring at the highway ahead.

Elizabeth let out a soft sigh and closed her eyes. Knowing their talent for always saying the wrong thing to each other, she wondered whether it had really been a good idea for her to go to this barbecue. So much between them remained unsaid, unfinished, and misunderstood, although things between them now seemed friendly enough. But it was tenuous. Elizabeth felt like they were teetering along the top a very narrow fence and that anything could push them off into rancor again. She didn't want that.

They drove the rest of the way in silence. Elizabeth's embarrassment gave way to stupefaction when Darcy turned the car onto a smaller road lined with palm trees and blooming tropical hedges. He slowed at a guard gate then smiled and waved at the guard who returned the greeting with equal cheer. As they drove, Elizabeth's jaw dropped lower and lower. The neighborhood—a small island, actually, set in the middle of the bay—was a haven of palm tree-lined driveways, wrought iron gates, and sprawling mansions beyond.

"Madonna used to live there," Darcy said as they zipped by an enormous mansion.

Elizabeth craned her head backwards to catch a glimpse of yet another gate, fading in the distance.

"And here we are," he said, slowing the BMW and making a right turn into a tree-covered, gateless entryway.

Chapter 21

Elizabeth sucked in a breath as she stepped from the car. She gazed in wonder at the Eden of tropical foliage—birds-of-paradise, hibiscus, and bougainvillea—blooming in front of her. Tall palm, cypress, and tamarind trees towered over a Spanish mission style house, the terra-cotta tiles of the roof vivid amongst the greenery. Limestone columns and arches fell back into a courtyard that sheltered the front door.

"Wow," she breathed, "it's just amazing."

Closing the door of the car, Darcy smiled as if he already knew it and pushed his sunglasses onto the top of his head. He gestured for her to follow, which Elizabeth did.

The interior of the house was everything Elizabeth expected. Understated and classic, just like Darcy's Manhattan apartment, the furnishings were neutrally colored—beige sofas, dark woods, and white walls. But something about this home jumped out at Elizabeth more than the New York City penthouse. Splashes of color popped through in every room like a cheery hello—a large, red lacquer bowl on the coffee table; a modern painting in yellows and oranges on the wall; white, turquoise, and navy pillows on the sofa in the living room.

"Don't tell me this house has also been in Architectural Digest," she said, as Darcy led her through the terra-cotta tiled kitchen.

"May, 2006," he answered.

Elizabeth shook her head and caught her first glimpse of the backyard through the large window in the kitchen.

"Holy crap! Ocean view! You're on the freaking ocean!"

"It's a bay, really."

Still shaking her head, Elizabeth grinned. "Can we go in?"

"There's no beach here. The pool's a lot nicer, anyway."

Just then, a blonde in a tiny, white bikini strutted into view: Caroline. Panic reverberated through Elizabeth. She'd forgotten the prima ballerina would be there.

As if he could sense her discomfort, Darcy put his hand on her back. "Come on in," he said and led her inside. His touch awakened every nerve receptor in Elizabeth's body, and she forgot her fear of Caroline.

"Elizabeth!" Georgiana bounded into the kitchen and threw her arms around her new friend. Darcy's sister wore a skimpy bikini with a sarong. "Thank God you're here!" She cast her brother a knowing look.

"Have you had fun entertaining our guests?" Darcy asked saccharinely.

Georgiana scrunched her nose. "Um, no. But now Elizabeth's here, and she can save me. Did you bring your bathing suit?"

Elizabeth said it was in her bag, and Georgiana offered her bedroom as a changing space. Darcy's sister tugged at Elizabeth's hand and led her there. It made Elizabeth feel as if she were eight years old again and on a play date with a new friend. She giggled.

"I hope I didn't offend you," Georgiana said once they were in private, "but I'm *so* not a fan of Caroline."

"No, I'm not either."

"Ooh, good! So now we can spend the whole time laughing at her behind her back and being really bitchy." Georgiana twisted her hands together. "So, do you like my room?"

Elizabeth laughed and looked around at what seemed like the annex to the Rock and Roll Hall of Fame. She had framed posters, photographs, and post cards of musicians from nearly every imaginable genre: Mozart, Run DMC, Blondie, Dusty Springfield, Taylor Swift. A signed electric guitar decorated the wall space above Georgiana's bed, and in a corner of the room were a stereo, mixer, and turntable that seemed as if they belonged to a music producer instead of a young woman in her early twenties.

"You like music, I take it."

"I *love* music," Georgiana said, her voice light but her face reverent. "You can change in there." She pointed to a connecting bathroom.

The bathroom continued the music theme with framed LP covers of some of the most famous albums in rock history.

As Elizabeth slipped out of her clothes, Georgiana asked about her rehearsal, and they made small talk. When that died out, Elizabeth said, "Hey, so, I was wondering something."

"Sure."

"Why do you call your brother Dub?"

Georgiana giggled. "It's kind of an inside joke. Because my name's so freaking long, he always used to call me G, which was okay when I was nine, but then when I entered middle school I was on this *Georgiana* kick. I wanted to be called Georgiana, but Dub refused. He said it'd take him all day. But, I *totally* hated G, so for revenge, I started calling him W. But try saying W."

Elizabeth did.

"It takes forever, right? What's the point of a nickname if it takes a million years to say? So, I shortened it to Dub."

Elizabeth laughed. "Ah, I see. But by that logic, didn't it make sense for him to call you G?"

Georgiana considered the remark. "Oh. I'd never thought of that. Duh!"

Meanwhile, Elizabeth stepped out wearing her polka-dot bikini.

"Wow! I love that bikini!" Georgiana cried. "It's, like, *so* 1950s pin-up girl! Do you have red lipstick? You *need* some red lipstick!"

"But we're going swimming!"

Georgiana clucked, as she swept past Elizabeth and into her bathroom. "Well, yeah, but you need to make an entrance."

Elizabeth heard shuffling through a cabinet. Georgiana cried, "Found it!" and re-emerged with a tube of lipstick already unsheathed. Elizabeth allowed her to apply it, and then struck a sultry pose befitting a pin-up wannabe. Laughing, the two women walked from Georgiana's room through the terra-cotta halls of the Darcys' home. They stepped onto a porch, and Elizabeth exhaled in delight.

To all sides sprawled a tropical garden very much like the one in the front driveway. Immediately in front of her was a pool lined with limestone, and in the distance stretched the turquoise waters of the bay. In between the pool and the bay, Caroline Bingley lounged on a deck chair. Her eyes were closed and covered by large sunglasses.

"Liz!" she heard from behind her. Turning around, she saw Charles walking towards her, a broad grin on his face.

"Hey!" Elizabeth replied. "Fancy meeting you here!"

"I was thinking the same thing," Charles exclaimed. "Will told me the story of how he ran into you yesterday. Small world, huh?"

In the middle of Elizabeth's chat with Charles, Georgiana had disappeared, leaving Elizabeth alone with the Bingley siblings. By this time, Caroline was glaring over the edge of her sunglasses at Elizabeth.

When Elizabeth accidentally made eye contact, she was forced to say, "Hey, Caroline."

"Elizabeth," Caroline returned.

"How are you?"

"I'm fine. Surprised to see you here."

"Likewise."

And that was the extent of their conversation. Fortunately, Darcy appeared holding a bag of charcoal, and Georgiana trailed behind him with a heaping platter of steaks, salmon, and vegetable skewers.

With his back to her, she took the opportunity to stare at Darcy. He wore a well-fitting white polo and khaki shorts, looking classic and understated in a way only millionaires can. His calves were muscular, sculpted from years of dancing, and sexy as hell. As if reading her licentious thoughts, Darcy turned then. His eyes caught Elizabeth's, and his lips curved up in an acknowledging smile. Georgiana said something to him—Elizabeth was too far away to hear what—and he nodded, glancing back at Elizabeth. She wondered whether the same kinds of thoughts were running through his head.

With just the five of them, the barbecue began as an awkward affair. Darcy spent most of the time at the grill, getting the charcoals started. Georgiana ran back and forth from the patio to the kitchen in her attempt to be a good assistant. Caroline lay mutely on the chaise lounge, focusing on her tan and ignoring Elizabeth.

That left Charles. Dipping her feet in the water, Elizabeth sat on the edge of the pool chatting with him. She'd seen Charles over a week ago, but given the new context of their meeting, their conversation felt awkward. She wished Jane were here and not halfway across the country visiting her friends in California. Charles and Elizabeth chatted about Jane, Miami, and the dance festival, but Darcy was always on the edge of Elizabeth's thoughts. She stared across the patio where he stood peering into the grill, a pair of tongs in his hand.

"Jane would want to be here," Charles said suddenly.

"Yeah," said Elizabeth.

"She'll be disappointed when she finds out we were all here without her. Although it's no fault of mine if Will decides to throw spontaneous house parties."

"You didn't know about this?"

"No," Charles snorted, "Will doesn't throw parties. I'm shocked that he'd bother with a welcome party for Caroline and me. There's never been so much ceremony for the other times we've come to visit."

Suddenly, from across the patio, Caroline chimed in. "Charles, you're being ungenerous. Will has always been quite hospitable with *me*. Remember that time in Tahoe when . . ."

Elizabeth ignored her, her thoughts churning. Apparently, Georgiana hadn't been the only one taken off guard. Elizabeth wondered whether the spontaneous and uncharacteristic gathering had anything to do with her. Just then, Darcy slowly turned his head and eyed the three of them sitting by the edge of the pool.

"What?" he asked.

"They're being mean to you, Will," flirted Caroline, standing to reveal her long, toned legs.

Darcy cocked an eyebrow and glanced from Caroline to where Charles and Elizabeth were sitting.

"Yes, Liz and I are gossiping about you," Charles said with uncharacteristic sarcasm.

"And have I done anything to deserve this gossip?" Darcy asked, more towards Elizabeth than anyone.

"Oh, Will! Ignore them. You've done nothing. You've been so generous having us here and throwing this little party in our honor," praised Caroline.

"You're sucking up, Caroline," said Charles, nudging Elizabeth in the side. "Right, Liz?"

Elizabeth replied, "I agree with Caroline, actually." And then to Darcy she said, "You've been very generous."

Charles and Caroline paused at the comment, unused to hearing pleasantries between Elizabeth and Darcy. Then, as if to reclaim her reputation, Elizabeth replied, "Besides, you shouldn't gossip. It's really unflattering."

She looked right at Caroline when she said it.

A few minutes later, Reynalda and Pepe showed up, bearing a huge aluminum tray of rice and beans and just as large a platter of pastries. Pepe joined William at the grill, and as they chatted about the grilling plan of attack, he felt her eyes on him. He'd been having trouble keeping his breathing steady since he'd stepped onto the patio, knowing she was there. He couldn't believe it. She was here in that bikini, looking like a bombshell from another time, smiling, happy, and checking him out. The warm timbre of her voice trickled to his ears and made the skin on his arms tingle. He replayed her remark to Caroline and couldn't help but smile.

"Why don't you let me take over here?" offered Pepe in Spanish, knowing most men didn't grin like fools at a salmon steak.

Smiling in appreciation, William handed over the barbecue tongs and patted Pepe on the shoulder. He strolled to where Elizabeth stood at the edge of the deck admiring a bird-of-paradise flower.

"Your backyard makes me feel like I'm on some gorgeous, tropical island," she said. "Probably because I am."

"Would you like a tour of the gardens?" offered William.

"They're that big that I would need a tour?"

"Well, no, not really. But they're much more interesting that way."

Elizabeth gestured for William to lead the way. As they walked through the grass, William began by pointing out the various flora, but he sensed Elizabeth didn't want a lecture on botany. He decided to lead her in silence, sneaking glances at the calm expression on her face as her eyes skimmed over the garden.

"Do you come down here often?" Elizabeth asked, breaking the silence.

"No, not as often as I'd like. Especially not in the past few years."

"Oh, that's a shame. I wouldn't be able to stay away."

As the grass swished quietly under their feet, William recalled winter and spring vacations spent in this house with his parents.

"I don't have the greatest memories of this place," he explained. "I just remember being bored here a lot."

"Really?" asked Elizabeth.

"This place was more of a show house for my parents. They'd come here every winter, throw their lavish cocktail parties, go boating with their rich friends, play tennis. And Reynalda took care of me. And that was it. At least until Georgiana came along."

Elizabeth's eyes searched him. "I see," she said. "I can't say I relate, but I get it."

"Why's that?"

"I was never bored at home because it was always chaos!" She laughed, but the spark in her eyes faded. William didn't know whether he should ask her more, but she supplied her own clarification. "My mother has a flair for the dramatic, you could say."

"How so?

"She was your typical stage mother—nosy, gossipy. She was always harping on about something. She and my dad fought a lot. She and I fought even more. I was a horrible teenager. Very temperamental. Some things don't change, I guess." She shot William a wry smile, and he would have returned with a quip of his own, but he sensed that it wouldn't have been appropriate. She turned away from him to glance out to the bay and commented on the color of the water.

William wanted to know more. Elizabeth had been right that day on Columbus Avenue. He hadn't known her at all. He didn't know whether she had any other siblings besides Jane. He didn't know whether her parents were still married or even living. He didn't know what she did on weekends, what kind of books she liked, even whether she had any food allergies. How could he have thought that was love? Standing there next to her, he felt humbled by his own foolishness.

They reached the edge of the garden.

"Well, that's the tour," William said.

"Oh." If he hadn't known better, William would have said she looked disappointed. "It was lovely."

Both made their way back to the patio. William noticed Caroline's pointed glare as they returned.

"Elizabeth!" Georgiana exclaimed. "There you are! I've been looking everywhere for you."

His sister practically skipped over to the two of them and grabbed Elizabeth's arm.

"Don't hog her all for yourself," Georgiana said to him. "Elizabeth, what kind of music do you like? Help me pick some out."

"Okay," laughed Elizabeth, and as Georgiana pulled her away, she looked over her shoulder at William and gave him a shy smile. He felt a warmth bloom inside of him.

Glancing around, William took in his small party. Charles was over by the grill with Pepe. They couldn't speak each other's language, but somehow they communicated through the universal male language of grilling meat. Reynalda zipped in and out of the kitchen, each time with a new dish in her hands, muttering to herself in Spanish. Caroline, fortunately, had remained silent and out of the way since Elizabeth put her in her place. And across the patio, hovering over an iPod, were his sister and Elizabeth, both looking happy.

William watched Georgiana. Although he hadn't realized how tense and worried he'd been, a heaviness in the pit of his stomach suddenly dissipated. He felt peace. This was the Georgiana he remembered before Greg Wickham had slithered back into their lives—the silly, blithe girl who smiled. He had seen too many glimpses of himself in her over the past year, too many moments of darkness, of introspection, of melancholy. He saw Elizabeth saying something to her and Georgiana giggling. He'd never even considered how Georgiana and Elizabeth would get along in all of the fantasies he'd had about Elizabeth. So their blossoming friendship was a surprise that made him profoundly grateful and relieved, even though that, too, was pointless.

"Georgiana's really hit it off with your friend," observed Reynalda in Spanish, sneaking up on William.

William nodded slowly. "Yeah, I think so. Although I'm not sure you could call Elizabeth and me friends, really," he replied in English.

"Girlfriend?" Reynalda asked.

William shook his head and chuckled. "No."

Just then, Elizabeth glanced up at him, caught his eye briefly, and then looked back down at the iPod.

Reynalda sighed and patted William's arm. "You should give her a chance, *mijo.* She's a nice girl, very pretty. And she hasn't been able to stop looking at you all evening. Don't be so picky." Sauntering away, Reynalda left William alone and light-headed on the patio.

Soon afterwards, the meat finished cooking, and they all gathered around the patio table to heap food on their plates. As they ate, the sunset dazzled them with a neon light show. In an ironic role-reversal, William found himself carrying the conversation among his guests while Elizabeth remained very quiet. Once, he caught her studying him, her eyes questioning, the corners of her mouth pulled down in an imperceptible frown. He didn't like that expression, and he looked away first.

The sun sank into the bay, and a half-moon rose in the sky. Empty plates lay before them, as conversation around the table drifted off. A salsa song came on the speakers. Reynalda stood and thrust her hand at William.

"*Venga, mi amor*," she said. "Let's dance."

William chuckled, stood, and accepted her offer. It was their thing. She'd taught him long ago, when he was an awkward and bored twelve-year-old, how to dance all of the Latin dances. And his old nanny still insisted that he amuse her with a dance. Georgiana shrieked, clapped in delight, and grabbed the first male hand she could find, which happened to be Charles's. He protested fiercely that he didn't know how to dance the salsa, and Georgiana teased him by asking, "Weren't you a *professional* dancer? Come on! *Venga!*"

Elizabeth, of course, knew that Darcy was a good dancer, but she couldn't believe he danced salsa well, too. He glided Reynalda across the floor with natural grace. It was yet another side of William Darcy that she hadn't known existed, an appealing and surprising side. It had been an evening of amazements, a humbling reminder of how she'd judged him as indifferent to human emotion.

Suddenly, Pepe came over to her and, in Spanish, asked Elizabeth to dance.

"I don't know how," she protested.

He just waved her off and said something to her in Spanish. Helplessly, she looked to Georgiana to translate.

"He said, 'A good partner allows herself to be led.'"

Glancing over to where Darcy was dancing with Reynalda, she saw he'd heard. He arched an eyebrow playfully at her.

Pepe was a patient teacher. Once Elizabeth had the basic salsa step down, she let the older man glide her around the patio and spin her. She laughed and swayed her hips and apologized when she crashed into Georgiana behind her. Somehow, the barbecue turned into a dance party. When the song changed, so did the partners, and Elizabeth found herself with Charles.

After the second time he accidentally kicked her in the shin, Darcy laughed. "Don't take down one of your own dancers, Charles."

"I can do ballet, but this is beyond me!" he cried.

"Can we switch?" Darcy asked Reynalda. She nodded and pushed him towards Elizabeth.

Elizabeth's stomach tightened, and she laughed nervously.

"We're off the clock, so I'll go easy on you," Darcy joked. When he smiled, his eyes crinkled at the corners.

He wrapped his hand around her waist, and Elizabeth reached up to set her hand on his shoulder. They hadn't touched like this in months, and his body felt both new and familiar. She laughed as she stumbled through the salsa steps.

"Just let me lead you," Darcy said.

Once Elizabeth let go of trying to figure out which way they were going and whether she would be turned, the movement flowed much better. She was getting into the dancing—circling her hips, letting Darcy press her hip into his as they turned—when the song ended. Everyone clapped.

The next song began with a lazy guitar strum. The tempo slowed.

"Ay, me encanta esta canción," sighed Reynalda. "*Venga, papi.*" She held out her hand to her husband, who had been dancing with Georgiana. Pepe gave his wife a secret smile, and they began to sway, cheek-to-cheek.

Elizabeth and Darcy slowed their pace as well. She stared over her shoulder at Pepe and Reynalda. "They're cute."

"They celebrated their fifty-fifth wedding anniversary a few months ago," explained Darcy.

"Wow! I can't imagine being married that long."

"Me, either. It's a pretty rare thing these days."

Elizabeth agreed. They swayed wordlessly together after that. Elizabeth let the Spanish guitar, soft maracas, and easy percussions of the song wash over her. It should have relaxed her, but she knew it was a love song even though the lyrics were in Spanish. The music spoke of easy companionship rather than passion. She breathed in, smelling Darcy's shirt, clean like aftershave and smoky like charcoal, and felt her heart throb with regret.

Elizabeth pressed her eyelids shut, her chest clenching with unnameable feelings. She'd always been attracted to him physically; when he'd touched her, it had always sent a little thrill through her. But now, there was something else she was feeling towards Darcy beyond a physical magnetism—something close to longing. Not like sex longing but a longing to know more about him, a longing for the song not to end.

But, it did, and a rowdy merengue song replaced it.

Elizabeth hazarded a glance up at him, and *his* face seemed serious, too. To dispel the tension, she made a joke. "I don't know if anyone's ever told you this, but you're a good dancer, Mr. Darcy."

"I've heard that once or twice, yes. You did really well. And I'm not just saying that because I went easy on you," he replied.

She reddened.

"And, Elizabeth," he added, "enough with *Mr. Darcy.*"

The corner of Elizabeth's mouth popped up. "Then thank you, William, for going easy on me."

Back in his car, they turned onto the causeway. The bay spread around them on all sides, the water dark. They'd both been very quiet since their dance, and somehow he felt that, if he spoke, the memory of his name on her lips would vanish. As they crossed the causeway onto Miami Beach, William felt a rising panic. He didn't want Elizabeth to go. He felt like something between them was shifting, and he didn't want to leave things between them unsettled.

Finally, he spoke. "I hope you enjoyed yourself tonight."

She turned her face to him and smiled. "I had a blast. Thanks again for inviting me."

William should have felt relieved, but anxiety still gnawed at him. "Are you nervous about your performance?"

"No. I'm excited. I'm glad I'll know someone in the audience."

"I'm looking forward to it." Then, he just asked the thing he wanted to ask. "What are you doing tomorrow?"

"We have dress rehearsal. And then some of the dancers were going out for drinks."

"Oh," William said, trying to hide his disappointment. "And on Saturday you'll be gearing up for the performance, I suppose."

Elizabeth paused before answering. "Yes. When do you go back to Seattle?"

"Sunday." William felt his heart sink. He'd wanted to see Elizabeth again, there in Miami, where none of the old baggage lived.

Then, Elizabeth added, "No one's mentioned any plans for after the show."

And suddenly he hoped again. "Then let Georgiana and me take you out."

He hazarded a look at Elizabeth's face and saw satisfaction there although she replied with hesitation. "Please don't feel like you need to entertain me while I'm here. I'm sure that a few people will end up doing something, and I don't want to take away from your time with your sister."

William paused. Her face said one thing, and then her words said another. He didn't know what to think or to say, so he just said the truth. "I'd like to see you again, and I know Georgiana would, too. Let us take you out."

A crooked smile again. "Okay," she said.

His heart hoped a little more as William turned onto Lambton Street. Elizabeth's bungalow was just a few blocks away. He pulled up next to it and put the car in park.

"I had fun tonight," said Elizabeth, pushing her hair behind her ears.

"Me, too," he said, drawing his eyes away from it. "We'll see you after tomorrow's performance."

"Okay." Elizabeth slipped out of the BMW, closed the door gently, and walked up the driveway. William watched her retreating figure with a mixture of satisfaction and loneliness.

William heard Caroline's high-pitched laughter all the way from the foyer when he stepped through the door. He steeled himself with the mental armor he would need to deal with a night of Caroline Bingley. As he neared the living room, her voice grew clearer.

"And really, that bathing suit! It was so unattractive." Then, she laughed again, making William wince.

He stepped into the room to find his sister sitting on the couch, arms folded across her chest, glaring up at Caroline, and Charles burying his nose in an old copy of *National Geographic.*

"I thought it was cute," Georgiana responded.

"It was okay, but between you and me, I think she needs to go on a diet."

Georgiana flashed William a poisonous look that told everything. His face went dark as he stood in the doorway with his arms crossed over his chest in a stance mirroring his sister's. Noticing William, Caroling turned around and smiled.

"What do you think, Will?"

William glared at her. "I didn't notice any remarkable difference."

"Well, no one will cast her. She'll bust out of her tutu if she gets any wider!"

William saw Charles hide his nose further into the pages of the magazine, and it made him angry that his friend said nothing while Caroline made fun of Elizabeth.

"Fortunately, you're not the one doing any casting," William retorted. The ice in his voice was unmistakable.

Caroline smirked at him and gave him a look of defiance. "Hm, it didn't seem like that before," she said.

William's nostrils flared, and a retort was on his tongue. But before it could pass from his lips, he glanced over at Charles, whose face was so red that he looked sunburned.

"Shut up!" Charles said. His voice quivered with anger.

Caroline started. Charles roughly tossed the magazine down next to him and stared at her with such fury, that she, William, and Georgiana were speechless.

"You're rude, Caroline! Will invites us here, and you act like . . . that!"

"Oh, please, Charles. Don't talk to me as if I were a child."

"You act like a child!" Charles shot up.

In all the years William had known him, Charles had never confronted Caroline on her behavior. This was new and unexpected. Charles paced for several seconds, his face twisted in turmoil, and then stopped.

Unable to face his sister, he said in a small voice, "I know what you did to Elizabeth."

Georgiana looked in shock and confusion at her brother. He shook his head imperceptibly as if to say *"Later."*

"What are you on? I was just tanning," Caroline protested.

"No, not today—before."

"What?"

"I knew something was going on. I just didn't know what. It didn't take long for some *friends* of yours to confess once they'd been asked." Charles's voice took on a hint of bitterness.

"What?" Caroline whispered.

"If something like that ever happens again, you're fired. And you're not dancing in the fall season."

"What?"

"And Lucas agrees."

"What? You told Lucas?" Caroline's voice cracked.

"Yes."

Caroline's eyes bugged out in fear. "Charles!"

"And you can go back to New York tomorrow." Charles merely raised his hands for her to stop. He gave her a last look filled with anger, sadness, and betrayal. Caroline's chin trembled. But Charles only turned away from her, glanced at the Darcy siblings, and muttered, "I'm sorry." Then he walked down the hallway to his room.

"Come on, G," William said, extending his hand towards his sister. She was more than happy to bound off the sofa and be escorted back to her room, leaving Caroline alone.

The next day dawned sunny and warm, a perfect day for a flight back to New York.

Chapter 22

Elizabeth frowned at her reflection. Backstage at the small theater on Lincoln Road, she and the other dancers in the festival had just finished their performance of Archibald Bates' piece. A full house of dance aficionados had given the dancers and the choreographer a standing ovation. At the moment, however, none of it mattered since Elizabeth couldn't figure out how to get off the piece of eyelash glue stuck to her eyelids or the hair spray flakes dusting her hairline.

"Can you see the glue?" she asked Madeleine, who was touching up her makeup for the South Beach nightclubs.

Glancing at her friend in the mirror, Madeleine grinned. "Yeah, but don't worry. It only looks like eye crud."

"Oh, wonderful." Elizabeth rubbed at the corner of her eye.

"You sure you don't want to come with us?" she asked again. "Your *friends* can come, too. I'll make sure Darcy has a good time." Madeleine cackled and clapped at her own joke.

Patting on lip gloss, Elizabeth arched an eyebrow and replied, "As will I."

The other dancers in the room broke into laughter. "Watch out! Bunhead's letting her hair down."

"Ooh!"

"Get it, girl!"

Elizabeth playfully tossed her hair around as if she were in a shampoo commercial. Grasping her friend's wrist, Madeleine said, "Just a word of advice: If you kiss him, make sure it's dark so he can't see your hair spray dandruff." Elizabeth joined in the raucous laughter from the other dancers.

Pouting her lower lip, she brushed out her hair again with her fingers and shrugged. "Occupational hazard. Besides, there won't be any making out because it's not like that. And also, his sister's coming."

"Mm-hmm," Madeleine said in that voice that said she didn't believe a word coming out of Elizabeth's mouth.

Elizabeth grabbed her dance bag and purse and gave Madeleine a quick squeeze on the shoulders. "Have fun tonight."

"You, too, my love," her friend said.

Elizabeth bid everyone good-bye and hurried out of the dressing room. She opened the stage door. Fans lingered with programs in their hands, waiting for their favorite dancers to appear and sign autographs. They paid Elizabeth no mind.

She didn't see William at first. It had rained that afternoon, and the light drizzle meant that when she finally did spy him, he was behind a huge golf umbrella. There was no Georgiana.

"Hi," she said, approaching him tentatively.

William turned, his face lighting up. "Hey. Great performance." He held a bunch of white lilies, which he handed over without ceremony. "From Georgiana and me."

Elizabeth inhaled their scent. "Thank you."

William moved the umbrella over Elizabeth's head.

"Oh, thanks," she said, looking up. Then, she joked, "Not that it matters much. My hair's pretty hopeless tonight between the humidity and the bottle of hair spray I had to put in it."

William looked at her hair and then down to her face. By his expression, Elizabeth could tell he appreciated what he saw.

"Where's Georgiana?" she asked.

"She's had a terrible migraine all day. She left just after your performance. She said to tell you—I hope I get this right—'I'm totally sorry for being the biggest jerk in the world.' And she wants me to give you her phone number and tell you to text her."

Elizabeth looked everywhere but his face. She couldn't. She didn't know whether to be excited or scared by Georgiana's absence. Her mouth felt dry.

As if reading her thoughts, William suddenly asked, "Are you still feeling up for a celebration?"

Huddled together under his umbrella, she suddenly felt very warm, though not unpleasantly so, and when she breathed out her assent, her heart leapt a little.

William directed her to his car in a parking lot across the street, grabbed her dance bag from her hands, and shut it in the trunk. He let her into the passenger's side and closed the door for her. His manners were old-fashioned, Elizabeth mused, but they were consistent with the thoughtful gestures she remembered from before: taking her dress to the dry cleaners after the gala, picking up breakfast the morning after, and making reservations for their one supremely awkward dinner date several days after that. Prejudice had blinded her to those gestures before. She appreciated them now.

Once they had cleared the parking lot, William spoke. "My sister made reservations for us at a restaurant called Estrella. It's New American-Caribbean type food. Will that be okay?"

"I have no clue what that even means," teased Elizabeth, "but I'm sure I'll find something to eat."

"Do you have any food allergies?"

"Kiwis make my mouth itch, but other than that, no."

She saw him stare at her mouth for a little longer than was proper. "Hm," he contemplated. "Well, when you go out to eat, what do you normally like?"

"You shouldn't trust my taste," Elizabeth said. "I go wherever's cheap."

"Do you like Japanese food?"

"I *love* Japanese food."

A smile bloomed on William's mouth. "Then I know where we'll go. It's not authentic at all, but they've got crazy sushi rolls and no kiwi."

"Are you sure? We can go to that other place."

He shrugged. "It's your celebration. You should get something you know you'll like to eat."

The gesture struck Elizabeth, and she experienced that same, strange longing feeling that she had the other night. They drove for a few minutes, getting stuck in traffic in the busier parts of South Beach. While they waited, William commented on the performance and Mr. Bates' choreography. Elizabeth listened, offering her own perspective occasionally, but she felt content just listening to him speak about the piece. He talked about the play with rhythms and synchronization, the talent of the dancers, herself included, for finding and playing with the drumbeats.

Finally, they snaked past the congestion, and William nabbed a parking space on a crowded street. Before he could sweep around to the other side of the car, Elizabeth let herself out. He pursed his lips in consternation but said nothing.

As William led Elizabeth down the block, she realized how close to a date this actually was. She wondered about Georgiana's migraine. Was that just a ruse? And if it were, did she even mind? Her pulse rushed, sharpening her senses to every neon sign, the sparks of conversation and laughter around her, and the rain misting her bare arms.

Elizabeth stood in the entry of the Japanese restaurant, inches from William Darcy, feeling strange. Nearly two months ago, they had been screaming at each other on a crowded street. Now, they were going out to dinner like two friends—or something akin to friends. As the hostess showed them to their table, William cast her a small smile.

"Georgiana wants to treat you to dinner," William said, as he settled himself into his chair.

"Oh, no, I couldn't let her."

"It's your celebration. She told me under no circumstances was I to allow you to pay."

Elizabeth smiled in resignation. "In that case, tell her thank you."

Scanning the menu, Elizabeth began to salivate at all of the choices. Looking up, she asked, "So what's good here? Recommend something."

William raised his eyes, and Elizabeth had a difficult time keeping her gaze. He just looked so damn handsome, particularly when he looked at her like that: light and hopeful.

He asked her if she wanted sushi, and when she replied that she did, he made some suggestions. Elizabeth decided to take him up on one of them, a mango, jalapeno, and snapper roll.

Closing her menu, Elizabeth looked out of the window at the activity on the street. She felt William's eyes on her and grew warm. Thankfully, a waitress came to take their drink orders.

"Sake?" the waitress asked.

Elizabeth looked at William. "Would you like to split some?"

He shook his head. "Just an iced tea for me."

"Oh. I'll have the same," replied Elizabeth, although she knew the alcohol would calm her nerves.

Once the waitress left, William frowned. "You could get some if you want."

"No, sorry, I know you're the designated driver."

He smiled down at the table and said, "I never drink, actually."

Elizabeth stared at him, rewinding through her memory of the times she'd been with him at social functions. Come to think of it, she'd never seen him drink. An awkward mood descended over the table, and in her eagerness to dispel it, she added, "I probably shouldn't either. I have a tendency to do dumb things under the influence."

The second the words left her mouth, she wished she could have stuffed them back in. Recognition flashed across William's eyes, and his expression grew serious. The last dumb thing she'd done under the influence of too much champagne, she remembered then, was sleep with him. She stared down at her lap, thinking of the thousand ways she hated herself. An oppressive silence hung between them, in which time, Elizabeth studied her menu as if it were a textbook. At one point, she hazarded a glance at William, who sat with his arms folded tightly across his chest, staring out of the windows. Something inside of Elizabeth wilted.

Finally, the waitress returned with their drinks to take their orders. Once she went away, William lifted his glass.

"A toast."

Elizabeth fumbled for her glass and raised it as well. She locked eyes with William, whose expression lightened.

"To stupidity," he said, "and hopefully learning from our mistakes."

Elizabeth broke into a relieved smile, feeling all of the tension inside of her come undone. "Here, here."

They clinked glasses and brought their straws to their lips at the same time.

From that point on, William and Elizabeth made pleasant but superficial conversation. They discussed the weather, current events in the dance world, and the fall season at Ballet Theater.

Finally, the food came. Elizabeth picked up her chopsticks and plucked up a piece of sushi. Chewing on it, she closed her eyes and smiled. "Good choice."

"Thanks."

"This reminds me of a place we used to go in Berlin," she reminisced. "Weirdest Japanese place ever, but one of the dancers in the company I was with swore by them. They put mayonnaise on everything."

William grimaced, but enjoyed watching her eyes glint with secret relived pleasures.

"Yeah, that's what I thought, too," she said in response to his expression, "until I became addicted to the stuff."

"Would you like to ask the waitress for a side of mayo to go with your sushi?" he joked.

Laughing, Elizabeth refused the offer.

William leaned forward on his elbows. He knew nothing about her life when she lived in Europe. She rarely talked about it. There had been that one time at Charles's house upstate, but she hadn't elaborated on her time with the German company although William had been interested to hear her experiences. He took advantage of it now. "What did you think about Berlin?"

Elizabeth sighed and her face took on a dreamy quality. "It was everything."

"Really?"

Nodding, she replied, "I miss it sometimes. It was only a year ago, but it feels like a dream."

"What about it did you like so much?"

"The art, the foreignness of it. Everyone was so fashionable and cool. It was an escape that I desperately needed."

"An escape from . . . ?"

Elizabeth sighed and some of the happiness left her eyes. "From college. From my parents' divorce. From the constant rejections of ballet companies."

William frowned, and surprisingly, Elizabeth cocked a crooked smile.

"Rejections," she repeated. "You know, it's what happens when people don't want you."

"I know what they are."

"Your face," she chuckled. "It looked like you didn't know the meaning of the word. And you are *William Darcy*, after all."

Although he didn't mind being on the receiving end of her good-natured teasing, something pulled at him. Elizabeth still continued to joke that he was somehow beyond the mundane struggles of artists everywhere—that he'd never had to strive or prove himself or pick up the shards of his dignity after it had been shattered by a careless ballet mistress, choreographer, artistic director, or dance critic.

"I'm not sure what that means," he said, his voice losing some of its merriment.

"I read the article in *Dance Magazine* about you. You had the perfect career. It's probably hard for you to understand how constant rejection feels."

William was struck then by their age difference, that she talked about his career as if it were over—for the record books. "I got where I am somehow. I know what disappointment is."

She studied him warily. William sighed and counted on his fingers. "My dad *hated* that I became a dancer. He never supported my career choice, and it was a point of contention between us until the day he passed away four years ago. And there was Greg Wickham."

Elizabeth glanced away for a second.

"Would you like to know why I got to principal dancer as fast as I did?" continued William. "Good luck on my part and bad financial decisions on Ballet Theater's. At the time I was hired, the company's finances were crap. It had no creative direction until Lucas came along. They were desperate. And I was young, good-looking, came from the right family— Yes, I do realize how arrogant it sounds, but that's why the company was so interested in me. Because I was good for publicity posters. There were better dancers. I shouldn't have been a principal.

"The worst disappointment, though, was my injury. Having to retire earlier than I'd wanted to. It felt like such a failure. I like choreographing dance, don't get me wrong. But there are days when I hate the job. When I'd rather be on stage dancing than behind the scenes creating dance."

Elizabeth looked shocked. It took her a moment to mutter a reply. "I didn't realize that."

William shrugged. "I don't dwell on it."

She said nothing, but she studied him seriously. He didn't know why he'd just blabbed his whole life story to this woman again, but several moments ago, he'd wanted Elizabeth to know and understand him and where he'd come from. William didn't want her to think he'd coasted by, always on the surface, as if he had no deep feelings, as if he had no heart.

Elizabeth asked, "What kept you with it? What keeps you with it?"

He thought about it and then replied, "I love dance."

Elizabeth frowned. "Sometimes it's hard to."

"That's not what it looks like."

"What do you mean?"

He smiled at her. "You look like you love it."

"How can you tell *that?*" she laughed uneasily.

"I don't know. It's just something in your eyes."

She took a sip of her iced tea. "I love to dance. Sometimes, I hate the grind. I hate the gossip."

"I hated it, too," said William. "Why do you think I never associated with the *corps de ballet*?" He laughed, but Elizabeth stared at him with disapproving eyes. "We're in a competitive profession where everyone wants to be the best. Don't let the gossip get to you."

"I can't just tune out the other dancers in the *corps*. I'm one of them. They're my friends. Some of them, anyway. It's hard to just ignore the gossip."

William sighed in exasperation. He hated it when Elizabeth copped the self-effacing, martyr routine. "Fuck them. Let them talk. You concentrate on becoming the best."

She looked wary. "And how would you suggest I do that?"

"Work the hardest. Learn every role in the ballets you're in, especially the roles you want. Take every correction given as if it's for you. Stay ten minutes after rehearsal when you've got the studio to yourself and keep walking through the steps on your own. Those who become the best have the raw talent and work the hardest to refine it. They don't let anyone or anything hold them back. You have the raw talent, Elizabeth. That's more than many can say."

Elizabeth blinked. Wordlessly, she picked up her chopsticks and ate another piece of sushi. She chewed slowly, and William wondered whether he'd inadvertently made her angry. He had a talent for it, it seemed. He'd wanted to make Elizabeth feel good tonight, and there he went, shooting his mouth off with more of his sage wisdom. No wonder she hated him.

Then a smile emerged on her mouth and made his thoughts go still.

"Okay, William Darcy," she said. "I'll try it. Only because you told me to, though."

"Good." He smiled back. Elizabeth held his gaze, something playful and seductive gleaming in her eyes. She'd never looked at him as if she didn't want him to look away. It made William nervous, and he blurted out the news he'd been wanting to tell her all weekend but couldn't, as the contract wasn't yet signed.

"So... Webster Lucas asked me to choreograph something for the fall season."

Elizabeth's face lit up. "He did! That's exciting. Congratulations!"

"Thanks. I'm glad they're giving me another chance."

"Of course, they would. You're the prodigal son. They have to welcome you home."

"And hopefully it's because I'm a good choreographer."

Elizabeth stammered. "Of course. Sorry, that's not what I meant." She looked cute with her foot in her mouth.

William laughed and said, "I'm just teasing you, Elizabeth."

She narrowed her eyes. "You're giving me a taste of my own medicine?"

"Yup."

"I don't like it. I'm supposed to be the impertinent one in this relationship, Darcy."

"And so who do *I* get to be in this relationship?"

Elizabeth leaned back in her chair in mock-contemplation, but her eyes glinted with the jab that he knew was forthcoming. "You're supposed to be the gruff and serious and tease-able one."

"You're making us sound like Laurel and Hardy."

He only got a blank look.

"What!?" he said. "You don't know who Laurel and Hardy are?"

William and Elizabeth spent the rest of dinner trading banter.

AFTER DINNER, THEY RETURNED TO his car. Once they were back onto the congested Saturday night streets, Darcy suggested they listen to some music. He grabbed his iPod from the cup holder in his car and handed it to Elizabeth.

"Pick something for us to listen to."

She accepted it and opened up to William Darcy's music collection, feeling almost as if he'd handed her a secret part of himself. He had an extraordinary compilation: classical musicians from Bach to Stravinsky, classic rock, folk singers from the sixties, hair bands, soul, African gospel music, new age, and a few indie artists. There was little pop music. Scrolling through his music felt strangely intimate.

"Find anything?" he asked.

She stopped when she came upon an artist with a familiar name: Georgiana Darcy.

"Your sister has some songs on here."

Darcy nodded, and Elizabeth played them. What came through the speakers was a mixture of hip-hop, deep house, and Latin music the likes of which Elizabeth had never heard. She sat entranced, listening to the complicated beats.

"Your sister produced this?"

"She started mixing her own music in high school."

"She's incredible!"

Leaning back into the leather seat, Elizabeth inhaled and let the music course through her. She thought of how perfect the evening had been, how perfect this week had been. She would leave on Sunday for New York, and the idea did not fill her with dread. It made her hope.

William would be back there with her. They were friendly now, and perhaps, if things felt the same as they had that night, they could evolve into more. The music pulled her deeper into her thoughts. She remembered their one night together and the way he'd looked into her eyes when he'd made love to her. She wondered whether there was some chance they could build their way back to that.

"Tired?" he asked.

"No," she replied slowly. "Just spellbound. This music... It's ethereal."

"G will be happy to know you like it."

Lazily, Elizabeth said the first thing that popped into her head. "You have to choreograph something to this music. It just speaks to the soul."

They were stopped at a red light, and Elizabeth turned to look at him and saw that same look of intensity on his face.

"What?" she asked.

"Choreograph something? To this?"

Something in his voice made Elizabeth sit up straighter. "Sure."

"Hm, I don't know."

"Why not? Don't you think Georgiana would let you? She'd be thrilled."

"This isn't exactly... balletic."

Elizabeth could tell William had chosen his words politically. "Oh, I forgot. William Darcy doesn't do anything but"—Elizabeth dropped her voice an octave to sound serious—"*neoclassical ballet.*"

"That's right," he said.

Elizabeth shook her head and turned in the BMW's leather seat. "You know, Tchaikovsky was *en vogue* during his time. He was like a pop star in the nineteenth century."

"I've never heard him described like that."

"He was a pretty successful composer. All the stuff we think of as 'high art' now, at one point or another, it was pop culture. Pop music *is* relevant, you know."

"Hm," said William in a non-reply.

"And this music… How can you listen to this and *not* be affected? It's complicated and deep and gorgeous."

"Mm-hm."

Elizabeth frowned. "Oh, stop that! It's not a bad idea. Maybe that's why you get artist's block sometimes."

"Really?" William said, suddenly interested in responding back.

"Yeah, because you choose music that's just… I'm sorry; you choose boring music."

He guffawed. "Bach and Beethoven aren't *boring!*"

"Okay, they're not. Sort of. But listen to this. This is just interesting and *new*. You could do so much with rhythm and syncopation with this music."

Elizabeth glanced at him to gauge his reaction. He had his lips pressed together, looking either disinterested or displeased.

He responded with a noncommittal, "I'll think about it." His tone said: *This conversation is over.*

The song changed to a jazz tune Elizabeth didn't recognize. A long silence extended between them, which felt even more awkward, given how much fun their conversations had been that evening.

She closed her eyes and sank dejectedly into the seat. How did she always manage to say the wrong thing to him? To sound self-righteous on things she knew nothing about? If there was one thing she knew about him, it was that he didn't respond well to unsolicited suggestions for his choreography.

The silence between them suffocated her like tar, and while this might have been the part in the past where she'd filled the discomfort with a sarcastic barb, Elizabeth swallowed down the urge and just stared at the road ahead. The drizzle from earlier in the evening had returned, misting the colors of the headlights and streetlights above.

As they crossed over the causeway and onto Miami Beach, William slowed the car at a red light and spoke. "I hope I'll get to see you when we're in New York."

That was the last thing she'd expected. Thrown off guard, Elizabeth replied, "I'm sure we will since you'll be back in the studio."

He nodded slowly. "Right. Of course."

"When will you get back to the city?"

"We'll start rehearsals in early November, I think."

They chatted about superficial matters until William slowed the car onto Lambton Street. When they finally pulled up to Elizabeth's bungalow, William told her to hold on while he opened his door and stepped out of the car. Grabbing an umbrella and her dance bag and lilies from the trunk, he jogged around to the other side of the car and popped the umbrella open above her as he helped her out of the front seat. Elizabeth's heart quickened.

"Thanks," she whispered, unable to make eye contact. His body was so close that his shirt brushed her chest when he breathed. "And thank Georgiana for tonight. And tell her I was sorry she couldn't come."

"I will," he answered. His voice was low and sensual. She hazarded a glance up at him even though she knew the dangers. His face had that intensity again, freezing and melting her insides at the same time. He parted his lips as if he were either going to say something or kiss her. Elizabeth leaned her face up.

He spoke. "Good night."

No, not that, she thought. "See you in New York," she said.

He smiled. She waved. He got back into his BMW. She sleepwalked to the door. He drove away and she watched the taillights disappear. She let herself in.

William slipped in through the garage door, hung up his keys, and then went looking for Georgiana. He heard the faint strains of Miles Davis coming from the den and figured he would find her there.

She was reclined on the couch, flipping through *Vogue*, and drinking from a plastic bottle of Diet Coke.

"Knock, knock," he said.

Georgiana looked up and grinned. "Hey, I didn't hear you."

Eyeing her posture, he raised a suspicious eyebrow. "How's the headache?"

"Oh, much, much better. I think I just needed some time to chill out. It's been a busy few days. How was your date with Elizabeth?"

Striding slowly towards the couch, William folded his arms over his chest. "Yes, see, that's the thing. It wasn't supposed to be a date."

Georgiana widened her eyes innocently. "Huh?"

"Don't try that trick with me. It won't work."

"Aw, come on, Dub. You know you didn't want me there anyway."

"Well, no."

Georgiana tsked. "Oh, thanks!"

William sat down on the section of sofa not occupied by his sister's legs.

"Well, how was it?" asked Georgiana. "What did you guys talk about? What did she wear? Did she like the flowers?"

"Too many questions," laughed William, holding his hands up for Georgiana to stop.

She frowned at her brother's reticence and stared at him with a pout for a long minute. "You're not going to give me anything?"

"No. I'll tell you that we had a nice time. We talked about, well, a lot. I can't really remember everything now. She wore a skirt. She liked the flowers. She says thank you."

Georgiana sat back, contented. "I really like her, Dub."

"Good. So do I."

"So... are you going to ask her out when you get back to New York?"

William sighed. "G, I've told you, the whole thing is complicated."

Georgiana frowned.

"What?" asked William.

"No, nothing."

"G."

"It's just that you seem really unhappy up there. And I feel like it's my fault somehow."

"How are my moods your fault?"

"I know you wouldn't be like this if it weren't for me being the dumbest girl on the face of the planet," Georgiana said, picking at her socks. "I'm afraid that my mistake has made you, I don't know, jaded."

"I was jaded before your marriage, G."

She looked up at him with an expression that was a cross between anger and sadness. "But I don't want you to be like that! And you weren't like that when Elizabeth was here. You seemed happy. And she did, too, and—"

"No," William interrupted. "It's one-sided."

"What do you mean? She was *into you*. She couldn't take her eyes off of you for, like, the entire party."

William shook his head, but he felt his heart trip at his sister's observation.

"You're imagining things." But he recalled the way she had smiled at him that night across the table, her eyes luminescent, and felt that maybe there was a sliver of a possibility that Georgiana could be right. William, however, quickly dismissed the thought.

Georgiana huffed. "I will bet you . . . " She picked up her magazine and thrust it in his face. "I'll bet you this Prada shoulder bag that if you asked her out again, she would accept."

"Don't you have enough Prada already?"

"Dub! A girl can never have too much Prada!"

Laughing, William stood and ruffled his sister's hair. "Good night, Georgiana Inez."

"Good night, William Fitzpatrick."

Chapter 23

With the remaining weeks of summer, Elizabeth indulged in hazy, sepia-toned memories of Miami. She daydreamed of guava pastries, of a tropical garden and a turquoise bay, of the neon lights of Lincoln Road, and of the soft scent of leather seats. Georgiana Darcy's music supplied the soundtrack. She daydreamed of William Darcy.

It was odd. She had hated him so vehemently, and now, no matter how hard she tried, no matter how many insults or cold looks she remembered, in spite of what he had done to Jane, Elizabeth simply could not feel the same way about him that she once had. In unassuming moments on the subway or waiting in line at the ATM, her mind wandered, and she smiled to herself in secret. She started to hope for something that still felt too amorphous to be expressed.

Elizabeth rediscovered dancing. Rather than the beginner classes she'd settled for earlier in the summer, she opted now for advanced classes that the other off-season professional ballerinas attended. In every class, she imagined William's eyes on her. She not only made sure to set her heels down and right her hip alignment but also to reach for an invisible audience. She nailed triple *pirouettes* with ease, bounced across the floor like a butterfly in *petit allegro*, and soared in *tour jetés* during the *grand allegro.*

She was more excited for the performance season to begin than she had ever been. On the eve of the dancers' return to work, when Elizabeth and Jane sat in their apartment, Jane peered queerly at her sister, whose eyes seemed too bright as she folded a load of leotards and tights. Her body seemed tense and eager, like a bird about to jump into the sky.

When Jane asked her about it, Elizabeth captured her bottom lip under her teeth and smiled her secret smile.

"I'm ready for things to be different this season, that's all."

Judging by the laughter and screeching from the locker room, one never would have guessed it was a Tuesday morning at Ballet Theater of New York. But it was a morning of reunions—friends and colleagues brought back together after their summer hiatus.

When Elizabeth stepped into the studio, Lydia pounced on her in an enormous hug, and when Charlotte came in a few minutes later, together they practically strangled her. Elizabeth laughed, answering their questions about Miami and her summer and asking ones of her own. Mid-conversation, out of the corner of her eye, Elizabeth noticed Caroline Bingley breeze by. The prima, of course, did not stop to acknowledge her, but Elizabeth felt her skin prickle at Caroline's presence.

Throughout class, Elizabeth watched Caroline, searching for signs of malice. Caroline's eyes were often on her as well, but to Elizabeth's surprise, when she stared for longer than a moment, it was the principal dancer who turned her gaze away first. Elizabeth still detected danger in her looks, but Caroline looked like a satiated tiger—still dangerous but bored. Elizabeth wondered at the change; she'd been so sure that she was the principal dancer's prey nearly two months prior.

Company class seemed to stretch on endlessly. Elizabeth had borne the wait for fall season casting throughout the remainder of the summer weeks, but now that the cast lists were only minutes from being posted, she felt light-headed with adrenaline. Her heart raced at the possibility of seeing her name on William Darcy's cast list.

Finally, class ended at noon. A line of sweaty dancers filed out of the studio, Elizabeth sandwiched between Jane and Lydia. Down the hall, a crowd had amassed in front of the boards, dancers investigating the cast lists and rehearsal schedules. Elizabeth joined the fray. To her disappointment, there was neither a cast list for William Darcy's new piece nor any sign of the choreographer himself.

There was one bright spot that day. Elizabeth realized that taking summer classes gave her an edge over many of the other dancers who'd lazed through the off-season. Rehearsals were still exhausting, but mid-way through them, Elizabeth wasn't ready to dry-heave like some of the other dancers. She remembered William's advice: Dance for the part you want, take every correction as yours, and stay later than everyone. That week, she chose tucked away corners where she could mimic the steps of the soloists and principals learning the larger roles. The ballet masters and rehearsal directors said nothing about it, but Elizabeth hadn't expected them to notice.

Her rehearsal schedule got busier, her toes bloodier, and her body more spent. As she enjoyed the camaraderie of her friends in Ballet Theater and constantly scanned dance studios to avoid Caroline's cold glares, Elizabeth felt less consumed with thoughts of William. She still experienced twinges of nervous anticipation when she thought of him, but there was less time for her mind to wander, and her mind wandered less to him.

That was why his sudden appearance in the hallway, a week prior to the opening of the fall season, hit Elizabeth with such force that it left her without breath or speech.

"*Psst*," nudged Lydia, with a sly grin on her face, "it's your favorite person, Lizzy."

Looking up from a lazy stretch on the floor, Elizabeth audibly sucked in her breath. Lydia burst out laughing.

"Be nice," she warned.

William looked tan and tall. He strode with grace and purpose, a notebook in one hand, a pen in the other. Elizabeth tried to keep her expression neutral, but she felt heat spread over her face and neck. He smiled and nodded politely at a group of *corps* dancers passing him, Elizabeth noted with surprise. Since when did William Darcy acknowledge *corps* girls? Then, Elizabeth saw recognition light his eyes as he caught her gaze.

William smiled, not broadly, but wider than he had at the last group. "Ladies," he said. And then keeping his gaze on Elizabeth, he added, "Hi, Elizabeth. How was the rest of your summer?"

Lydia's mouth plunked open.

Elizabeth offered a small smile. "Pretty boring. How was Seattle?"

"The same. It's good to be back." He hesitated and glanced at Lydia. "I'm off to a meeting with Lucas. I'll see you later?"

"Yep." Elizabeth surprised herself with how casual she was able to make her voice sound. He nodded and disappeared around the hallway.

Lydia looked pointedly at Elizabeth. "Um . . . what was that?"

"I don't know what has you so surprised."

"Only, like, who the hell are you? And who the hell was he? And what happened to the real Elizabeth Bennet and William Darcy?"

Elizabeth only giggled and shrugged but said nothing else. She spent the rest of the afternoon remembering the gray in William's eyes that had warmed when he'd spotted her; he seemed different and open, and she wondered if it was for her. That afternoon in rehearsal, her body moved like dandelion fluff. She couldn't wait to see him again.

The feeling was short-lived, though. The next day there was a cast list for William Darcy's piece. Elizabeth stood frozen in front of it for what felt like ten minutes.

Her name wasn't on it. Lydia's was, in a *corps* role. And so was Jane's. At the top, in fact, in the lead role.

How could that be? There must have been some mistake. It should have been *Elizabeth* Bennet. Not Jane Bennet. She was his inspiration. That's what he'd said.

Around her, astonished cries went up. Several dancers congratulated Jane, who wept with genuine shock and joy. Lydia and Charlotte hugged her.

And Elizabeth stared at the cast list, disbelieving.

Her name wasn't on it.

Even with the start of William's rehearsals, Elizabeth still could not believe he hadn't cast her. She got out the mortifying letter and reread the ending again, just to be sure.

It said: *I do know that I have created many, many ballets and worked with countless dancers, and none of them affected me as you did.*

It also said: *But I know that when you dance, I feel things. Your audience does, too.*

If that were the case, then what the hell? What the friggin', bloody hell?

Jane gushed to her sister about each rehearsal: William's brilliance, the difference between this work and his last one, the complicated steps, the speed, the fun. Jane's excitement grew more intolerable each night on the subway ride home. Elizabeth tried to be enthusiastic, but she could only spackle on a smile for so long before the plaster started to crumble.

She couldn't listen without trying to one-up her sister with an anecdote about her own rehearsals with William. Realizing how petty her bragging sounded, Elizabeth resorted to reacting with tense smiles, then one-syllable mutterings, then just terse nods. After a few days, Jane caught on; Elizabeth didn't want to hear about William's rehearsals, so she stopped discussing them.

Another thing irked Elizabeth. When she'd shot to the top of the Ballet Theater hierarchy, Caroline and the other Ballet Theater bullies had nipped at her heels. But when Jane was given a principal role that many thought she didn't deserve, no one turned on her. If anything, Caroline became even more ingratiating, going so far as to kiss Jane hello every morning and give her pointers after company class. Of course, Elizabeth didn't want Jane to be bullied, but if Elizabeth had been subject to their persecution, wasn't it only fair that Jane be as well?

Then again, Jane didn't walk around apologizing for the role. She didn't feel guilty or scared by William Darcy's casting. Jane didn't resent him for bypassing the company's hierarchy. Jane didn't think it was a practical joke. Jane didn't hide it from her friends and coworkers. She accepted the role with equal parts glee and humility. So why hadn't Elizabeth been able to do that?

Guilt ate at her. No one seemed to begrudge Jane except the one person who should have been unconditionally happy for her. Elizabeth tried to celebrate Jane's success, but she couldn't forget her jealousy and her feelings of betrayal. Why in hell had he cast Jane as the lead in his piece?

Occasionally, Elizabeth encountered William in the halls. He nodded hello, and she nodded back. Sometimes he smiled, but they rarely spoke. William didn't come to the studio before noon, and Elizabeth, not wanting to catch a glimpse of his rehearsals with Jane, bolted after she finished her own. More disconcerting, he now behaved pleasantly with everyone. While William would never grin, joke, and call dancers by their nicknames —he wasn't Charles, after all—he now acknowledged their presence in the hallways and even laughed in rehearsals, according to Jane. If he were being nice only with her, Elizabeth could have hope. Now that he was pleasant with everyone, she had none.

Even in their most vitriolic moments, Elizabeth believed she and William had shared a special repartee. She liked his sense of humor, dry and understated. William was only out to impress those clever enough to be impressed. He was unapologetically himself—honest and self-assured—but they were traits that, Elizabeth had discovered, were more rare than diamonds.

One night, when Jane was out with Charles, Elizabeth lay alone on her bed, staring at her crumpled Perfection by Hermes ad. It hardly looked like William Darcy anymore. She no longer saw the chiseled Adonis when she thought of him. She saw instead his letter, his sister, his face in Reynalda Cafeteria, his iPod playlists, the purple-spotted bougainvillea that climbed the walls of his house in Miami, the turquoise of the bay, his face as he sat across from her, and his eyes when he laughed. It fueled the betrayal she felt. Just as her feelings had softened, it seemed that his, too, had changed.

Whereas William and Elizabeth had been unable to avoid each other during his first choreography stint at Ballet Theater, on this second one, William couldn't figure out how to be near Elizabeth even when he tried. Sometimes, if he lucked out, they passed in the halls, trading sterile smiles. But that dissatisfied him more than not seeing her at all because she spurred memories, desire, and hope. He'd come to Ballet Theater this time with so much hope: a renewed excitement in choreography, a cast that would make up for past misdeeds, and the possibility, faint but there, that Elizabeth's feelings has changed.

William thought they'd changed. In Miami, he'd felt the shift. He was still chastising himself for not kissing her in their final moment together. Reflecting on it during the flight back to Seattle, he'd been certain that, had he done so, she would have kissed him back. Now, he was glad he hadn't. It was almost as if she were avoiding him. There were times when he saw her in the halls and tried to talk to her. But Elizabeth's eyes were frozen to him again, crushing hopes of sun and bloom like an April frost. He didn't understand it, and it made him feel so damn vulnerable.

Being a man of action, William never liked sitting in his own helplessness. He hated it. Many times after his rehearsals, he thought of staking out Elizabeth and asking her to dinner the second she stepped out of the studio. Then William remembered their first and last date at his favorite Italian place. He wasn't sure he could stomach the humiliation again.

He needed a sign from her, and it didn't have to be neon: a smile that reached her eyes, a longing look, a touch of her hand. He'd even settle for a "hello" on her part, for God's sake.

Resigned, he and Charles made dinner plans for a certain Thursday evening a week before the start of the fall season. Apparently, Charles wanted to discuss something important. William met his friend in the lobby of the building, and as they stepped outside, they discussed where to eat. Charles wanted Thai, but William wasn't in the mood for spice. As they contemplated their restaurant options, the door swung open behind them. They looked up to see Jane and Elizabeth Bennet. William's heart stopped. This seemed like a sign.

"Hey, Bennets," said Charles.

"Hey, you," Jane answered, pecking him on the lips. "Are you two off to dinner?"

Elizabeth looked at William. She smiled but not with her eyes.

"Yes, if we can only figure out where," said Charles.

"Oh, we know a good place, right, Lizzy? Remember? That little Indian place up the street."

"Right," Elizabeth replied.

"Oh, I love Indian," Charles asserted. "Why don't you both come along? You wouldn't mind, Will, would you?"

William could endure anything, even Indian food, if it meant finally getting to talk with Elizabeth. When he glanced at her, however, she seemed more interested in watching two taxis engage in a honking match on Columbus Avenue. Elizabeth seemed almost reluctant to disengage from it and join their group. They began walking north. Jane and Charles naturally paired off. Several paces behind them, William and Elizabeth strolled side-by-side, saying nothing to each other.

"So," William began, still hoping for his sign, "how are rehearsals?"

Elizabeth paused and then said, "Not bad."

They walked together in silence for another few blocks, until they reached a generic restaurant with white tablecloths and red napkins decorating each table. Other than a lone patron reading The *Times* with his dinner, they were the only ones there. They sat at a corner four-top, Charles and Jane on one side, he and Elizabeth on the other.

"Well, this is nice and intimate," Charles said smiling. Jane brightly returned his grin. William nodded to be polite. Elizabeth fingered the edge of her glass.

"Lizzy, when you and I came here, what did we get? It had those chickpeas," Jane said.

"Chana masala."

"Oh, right! That was good. I'm getting that. You want to split it?"

"Sure."

"And naan? And some samosas?"

"Sure."

William didn't like this lifeless version of Elizabeth, so when the quip popped into his head, he said it.

"And a side of mayo?"

Charles and Jane frowned. But cheesy as the joke was, it worked. The corner of Elizabeth's mouth popped up.

"That's only for sushi," she said.

"What?" laughed Charles. "Mayo on *sushi*?"

"Forget it," Elizabeth said. "It's an inside joke." A moment of delight made her eyes glimmer.

Just then, Jane turned to her sister and giggled. "Oh, Lizzy, I forgot to tell you about this really funny thing that happened in William's rehearsal the other day. Remember, Will? The Dying Pigeon?"

In his peripheral vision, William saw the spark snuff out on Elizabeth's face. A stiff smile replaced it as she listened to Jane retell a story from his rehearsal the day before.

The food came. Elizabeth inspected each spoonful of her chickpeas with the intensity of either a hypochondriac obsessed with food-borne diseases or someone trying to escape dinner conversation. He remembered this version of Elizabeth too well. This had been the Elizabeth at Charles's Rhinebeck home, detached and disinterested. Recalling that night, William had found her disinterest interesting. Now, with more insight into her personality, he wondered whether something was bothering Elizabeth. He wondered whether that something was him.

Since Elizabeth had accused him of disregarding the feelings of others that day on Columbus Avenue, William had become more aware of just how often he let others—Charles, his sister, his dancers, or other strangers—carry the weight of their interactions. He'd never realized that about himself, and it shamed him. So, as conversation at the table died, William wanted to show Elizabeth that he could take the onus of making others comfortable.

He turned to Jane, the person he knew Elizabeth loved most. "How are you feeling about the season so far?"

"Good!" she exclaimed. "Excited. Especially for your piece. I haven't been able to tell you this, but I'm really grateful for the part, Will."

Next to him, William felt Elizabeth shift in her chair. He smiled at Jane. "You were the dancer best suited to the part, Jane. You deserved it. You don't have to thank me."

Hazarding a glance in Elizabeth's direction, William nearly started at the haunted look on her face. She licked her lips, pursed them, and then went back to the tablecloth. William smiled uncomfortably. This was not the reaction he wanted from Elizabeth. She stood abruptly, her chair shrieking against the floor. Everyone looked up to Elizabeth, her napkin balled in her fist.

"Excuse me," she said, "I'm going to the restroom."

She returned her napkin to the table with a sharp toss of her arm. They all watched her go. Jane colored.

"Is she okay?" Charles asked.

Sighing, Jane shrugged. "I'm sorry about her. She's going through this weird phase. I think this season has been a lot for her to handle. She's dancing a lot more, and she says it's wearing her out."

"The season hasn't even begun." Charles frowned.

William simply stared to where Elizabeth had disappeared, a contemplative frown creasing his forehead. He knew this was neither a weird phase nor exhaustion. William marveled that her sister couldn't recognize Elizabeth's mood for what it was. Elizabeth was livid.

Looking down at his lap, William attempted to control his disappointment. How had he managed to anger her this time? The mayo comment? No matter how hard he tried, he pissed her off. William massaged his forehead, wondering whether things would ever be right with them. He was trying and still failing.

Just then, Elizabeth re-emerged from the bathroom. She approached the table, eyes lowered, but as she neared them, she looked up. William saw hurt and anger in her expression, only it was directed at Jane and not him. He started inwardly and looked from sister to sister.

"I'm sorry," Elizabeth said woodenly, returning to her seat. For the remainder of the meal, she continued to give off a "don't talk to me" aura, so no one did. Jane and Charles chattered happily about the intricacies of sequins on tutus, and William sat enveloped in the same cloud of silence hanging over Elizabeth. Every few minutes, he stole a glimpse at her. Her eyes and lips were set in stone. Once, however, he caught Elizabeth staring at him with a look he could only pinpoint as soulful. She quickly looked away.

"Are you okay?" he murmured to her.

She blinked, and her expression changed as she answered, "Sorry. No. I'm tired."

He raised an eyebrow in disbelief. "Well, don't go overboard. You don't seem like yourself."

Elizabeth's eyes widened. Then, with a reassuring smile and a pat of his arm, she leaned towards him. "I'm okay, Dad. I promise."

William smiled, but a hard, cold stone thudded into the pit of his stomach. Sure, he'd gotten his smile, his teasing look, the intimate touch. But... *Dad*? That most certainly wasn't the sign he was looking for. He couldn't say anything else.

The walk back to the subway station was silent. Jane and Charles were still on the subject of tutus. William wondered how two people could talk about the most insipid subject for such a lengthy span of time. With his hands in his pockets, he walked next to Elizabeth, his pace unbearably slow just to match hers.

They rounded the corner and saw the green street-lamp of the Columbus Circle subway entrance. William and Elizabeth tried not to watch as Jane and Charles said their gooey good-byes.

When he heard Elizabeth whisper "good night," it stung.

His hope had shriveled in on itself. *Dad?* William realized then that he'd have to figure out some way to make Elizabeth just his best friend's girlfriend's sister and nothing more.

He and Charles watched the girls descend into the subway. When they were gone, Charles smiled and then rocked back on his heels uncomfortably. "Do you still have some time?" he asked.

"Why?" William just wanted to hail a cab for home.

"There's still something I wanted to discuss with you." Charles refused to make eye contact. It had to be bad news—a perfect ending to a perfect night. With everything that had passed between William and Sir Webster lately, William figured he knew what Charles was going to tell him.

"Let's grab a coffee," said William grimly.

That week Madeleine texted Elizabeth. *Where r u? Don't make me get mad at u.*

Lounging in full costume in a dressing room backstage, Elizabeth smiled as she replied: *Sorry. Been busy with performances. I'm gonna try to go to class on Monday. Will you be there?*

Madeleine texted that she would be in Afro-Caribbean class next Monday and made Elizabeth promise to go out for a coffee with her afterwards. Elizabeth put her phone away and shucked off her leg warmers when she heard the stage manager announce that it was ten minutes to curtain.

On Monday, when she walked into the Union Square dance studio, Elizabeth felt immediately warmed. One of her Miami housemates was there. Elizabeth hugged her and caught her up on life at Ballet Theater.

When Elizabeth heard Madeleine shout "Bunhead!" across the room, she looked over her shoulder and grinned. Madeleine kissed another dancer hello before strolling over to Elizabeth and squeezing her into a hug. Like a protective mother, Madeleine cupped Elizabeth's face and frowned.

"You got dark circles under your eyes, girl. What? Aren't you sleeping?"

Elizabeth shrugged and smiled guiltily. "It's kind of complicated. I'll tell you . . . "

The words dried in her mouth as she saw Greg Wickham walk into the studio. Elizabeth went ashen. After Greg set a bottle of water down in the corner, he rolled his broad shoulders and scanned the room. His eyes landed on her. He paused, surprise flashing across his face before he suppressed it in a suave grin. She snapped her head away. Weaving around stretching dancers, he made for an empty floor space right next to her. Madeleine put her hands on her hips and narrowed her eyes. Greg ignored her.

"Hey, gorgeous," he said when he reached Elizabeth. "Long time, no see."

She could think of nothing to say in reply. She opted for, "Hi."

"How have you been?"

"Fine."

"Okay, ladies and gentlemen," boomed a large, round man at the front, "let's begin."

Spared the humiliation of talking to him, Elizabeth spent all her warm-up time feeling oppressed by the rekindling of his interest. She caught him out of the corner of her eye, smiling at her and watching her body move.

After warm-up, as they prepared for an across-the-floor combination, Greg leaned into her and whispered, "You look great, Liz."

Elizabeth shuddered at the feeling of his hot breath on her neck. She watched him dance across the floor, his movements big and powerful. There was something in the rhythm of it, the wild pelvic movements, arched backs, and neck rolls that murmured hot, wet sex. He was hot as hell, and he knew how to make women pant. She suddenly felt furious with him.

Greg Wickham shouldn't be able to get away with it. He shouldn't get to be as calculating and immoral as he'd been with the Darcy family and strut around without shame afterwards. He shouldn't get to walk into that dance studio with a crocodile grin on his face. It made Elizabeth's ears burn. Why did *she* feel so embarrassed by his presence? Shouldn't it be the other way around? She decided then that Greg Wickham shouldn't be allowed his bravado. He preyed on the weak and, right then, Elizabeth was.

When it was her turn to go across the floor, she let the frenzy of drums carry her. It was like a war dance, and she glared at him in the mirror as she reached the other side of the room.

Class ended. As Elizabeth toweled off her face, Greg sidled up to her and whispered in her ear. "I've been waiting all class to talk to you."

Elizabeth bristled. She twisted to look up at him; he was sexy when he smiled like that, but he was a cretin. Elizabeth nearly pushed him out of her way.

"Is there anything to talk about?" she clipped.

Greg frowned, and his eyes reflected a soapy, insincere pain. "Hey, I hope you're not upset about the gala thing. It's just that scene wasn't really my thing, you know?"

She was about to snap that he could have told her that when she'd asked him out, but Madeleine came up to her, throwing her arm around Elizabeth's neck. "We're going to grab a bite, yeah?"

"Sure," Elizabeth replied.

Madeleine eyed Greg. "Who's this?"

Greg beamed and extended his hand. "Greg Wickham."

Shaking it, Madeleine looked him up and down. "Liz, you gotta tell me where you're meeting so many fine men."

Elizabeth wanted to shout at her friend that Greg was the worst kind of bad apple, shiny on the outside and mealy within.

Greg responded before she could, however. Arching an eyebrow, he looked at Elizabeth. "Were there others?"

The nerve of him, she thought. As if she couldn't attract the attention of other good-looking men besides Greg Wickham!

"Madeleine met William Darcy in Miami," Elizabeth explained. Although she hadn't intended the comment to be a poison dart, alarm flickered on Greg's face. A slow smirk curved Elizabeth's lips.

Greg tried to play it off with a cool roll of his eyes. To Madeleine, he said, "Ugh, I'm sorry."

The remark incensed Elizabeth. How in the world had he duped her? He was all insincerity.

Madeleine frowned, as if she knew what he was about. "I'll see you in a few, Liz?"

Elizabeth nodded.

"How'd you end up in Miami with Darcy?" Greg asked when Madeleine was gone.

"It's a funny story. I ran into his sister completely by coincidence."

Greg tittered. "I haven't seen Gigi Darcy in a while. How's she doing?"

"She was lovely. Friendly. Cheerful."

"Oh, that's a change. I wonder if they changed her meds. She was a huge downer when I saw her last."

"Yeah, well," Elizabeth said, "getting divorced will do that to a person."

Greg's handsome features dropped this time in palpable shock. "I didn't realize you were *that* friendly with her." Although he tried to make his voice light, it shook at the edges. "Yeah, it was too bad about Gigi and me. I really wanted it to work."

Elizabeth just stared.

"Her brother made it difficult for us," Greg explained. "Will lorded over her, told her crazy shit about me. He always stuck his nose where it didn't belong. The strain became too much for us eventually."

Was Greg really divulging his marital troubles to someone he hadn't spoken to in months? How had Elizabeth been blinded by this before? Had she been that desperate to hate William Darcy?

"I saw Darcy and Georgiana together," Elizabeth said. "It didn't seem anything like you're describing."

"Wow," Greg chuckled bitterly, "look at you. *Your* opinion has changed. Darcy didn't buy you off, did he?"

Elizabeth folded her arms across her chest. "Unlike some, I'm not easily compromised by a check."

The expression in Greg's eyes hardened as his charm fell away. He seemed finally to understand that Elizabeth had changed allegiances, and he no longer had hers. "I don't know what lies you've heard, but Darcy's a dickhead, and he's always had it in for me."

Inside, Elizabeth savored the malicious pleasure of pissing him off. She feigned innocence. "I don't know what you mean. What kind of lies?"

Greg flushed. "It's just . . . well, you . . . forget it, Liz. He's a dickhead, and that's all you need to know."

"I can't say I agree with you," she said. "And this conversation isn't really interesting anymore."

His face, so handsome, was splotchy and veined. Clearly, Greg didn't enjoy being dismissed as much as he enjoyed dismissing.

Elizabeth replied, "Nice seeing you today, Greg. Bye."

She breezed past him, throwing her towel around her neck. Pushing her fingers through her hair, Elizabeth blew a long breath out of her cheeks, trying to re-center herself.

She was not the Darcys' knight champion, come to defend their honor. She hadn't avenged William or Georgiana. She had not toppled Greg Wickham, had not made him pay for his sins. He'd probably learned no sort of lesson, and he would go on to seduce and break others. Could anything humble a guy like that, really, except for maybe an ass-kicking that mangled his cherubic face?

Yet, as Elizabeth made her way out of the studio, she skipped a little and felt like punching the air. Like a cat batting around a backyard conquest, she'd enjoyed toying with Greg and watching him squirm. More than that, it felt good to be in the world with a clear head: to finally see things for what they were, to know who was who, to know what to say and just say it. It had felt good to tell Greg, the miserable bastard, to shove it.

There was someone, however, who didn't deserve her unkindness and dishonesty. Someone Elizabeth loved but who also unleashed scaly, writhing feelings in her. They made her daily life a torture. At home, they gnawed at her from within.

She made a decision then. She needed to be honest with Jane.

Chapter 24

Elizabeth spent that night in trepidation. Knowing she should apologize and actually apologizing to Jane were two different things. She avoided her sister more than usual, bypassing their usual Monday night dinner of Chinese takeout in front of the TV. Too jittery to eat, Elizabeth spent most of the evening holed up in her room, reading gossip magazines, and working up the nerve to talk to Jane.

Finally, too thirsty to sequester herself any longer, Elizabeth snuck out past the living room into the kitchen. Jane offered her a cheery "hey" from her place on the couch. Elizabeth grunted a response. She could almost feel Jane deflate. She chugged a glass of water in the kitchen and decided she couldn't live with this "victim" version of herself any longer.

Elizabeth reappeared in the living room and leaned in the doorway. Jane's eyebrows rose in an unasked question.

"I'm jealous," said Elizabeth.

Jane frowned. "What was that?"

"I'm jealous. Of you. That's why I'm acting like this."

Jane didn't ask for specifics. Pursing her lips, she stared at her sister and waited for further elaboration.

"I'm sorry, Jane," was all Elizabeth could say.

"Well, why are you jealous of me?"

"You got the part I wanted in Darcy's piece."

Elizabeth braced herself for Jane's reproach. Instead, Jane smiled faintly. "Ah," she said.

Somehow, Jane's lack of reaction carved out a well of feeling in Elizabeth.

She felt suddenly overwhelmed by exhaustion, and she teared up. "I've been jealous of you a long time, Jane, but I don't want to be anymore."

"Oh, Lizzy," Jane began, opening her arms to her sister. The magnanimous display nearly derailed Elizabeth, but she shook her head.

"No. I mean, things have to be different. I love you, and I hope you know that I say this with love, but it's not enough anymore for me to be the little sister who's your understudy in everything in life. I know you helped get me into Ballet Theater—no, Jane, you did—but I'm going to be the one who moves myself up through this company. No more jealousy. I'm sorry for it, Jane."

As Jane studied her, Elizabeth could see the questions in her eyes. Jane opened her mouth and then closed it. Finally, she said, "I understand what you're saying. I don't blame you for it. You don't need to tiptoe around me."

Elizabeth wiped her eyes with the back of her hand. "Thanks, Jane."

"Can I still tell you when you're acting like a brat?"

Elizabeth burst into laughter "I'm shocked you haven't already."

Jane smiled. "That's 'cause you're always a little bratty."

"I am not!"

"You can be. Sometimes."

"It's part of my charm." Her body felt light with relief and gratitude for a sister like Jane. She also felt a new sense of determination. Even though she would no longer settle for a place in Jane's shadow, breaking free from it wouldn't be easy. Before she turned to go to her bedroom, Elizabeth paused. "I'm going to head out a few minutes early tomorrow. I want to get to the studio early."

Jane nodded as if she'd been expecting it.

The next morning, Elizabeth stepped into the studio with a purpose. With fifteen minutes until company class began, the room belonged to her. Swallowing, Elizabeth hiked up a heavy *barre* and dragged it to the center of the room. She began to warm up, her pulse fluttering in her throat.

Dancers trickled in to the studio. A principal dancer came to stand behind Elizabeth, offering the *corps* girl a simple nod and smile before beginning her own warm-up. Charlotte walked in a few minutes later. She paused when she saw Elizabeth in the center of the room, far from their usual place along the back wall. Charlotte cast her a puzzled look. Shrugging, Elizabeth simply nodded in the mirror and went back to stretching.

Class began as it always did, but the experience felt foreign from Elizabeth's new spot in the room. The ballet mistress eyed her during the first exercise and even asked her to mark *rond de jambes*. Once exercises were over, Elizabeth lugged the *barre* away, her leotard drenched in sweat, half congratulating herself, half kicking herself. She still had center exercises and a full day of rehearsals ahead of her, after all. Plus, she felt watched again by the other dancers, mostly those in the *corps de ballet*. She could practically hear their thoughts. *There goes the brown-noser again!*

Elizabeth contemplated returning to her rightful place behind the more senior dancers. *Forget them.* That's what William would say, though with a different "f-word." The phrase had become her mantra: *forget them, forget them, forget them.* Swallowing down her timidity, she wedged into the crowd of dancers to stand as far forward as she could. The ballet mistress demonstrated the exercise, *tendus*. Elizabeth concentrated only on committing the steps to memory. Eventually, everything else faded against the rhythm of her legs and the sway of her arms. She marked the exercise with the other dancers. The ballet mistress asked for places, and the pianist played the first trill of an *allegro*. Posed in the second row, Elizabeth prepared with a small breath of her hands and then began to dance.

She was doing it again. Sir Webster Lucas glanced to the back of the room where that *corps* girl, Elizabeth Bennet, was mimicking every step that he was teaching the soloist in the center of the studio. She wasn't understudying the role; he'd checked his *Sleeping Beauty* cast list two days before to make sure. When most dancers relished the opportunity to give their aching toes a break, why was she always there in the back, committing the roles to memory? It was odd, but ambition made many a striving dancer do much worse, he supposed.

In one of the Fairy variations, the *corps* girl stumbled through a particular series of hops *en pointe*. Webster spotted the problem: Elizabeth's arms jerked and bobbled in reaction to her bouncing feet. Meant to look bouncy and light, it looked rather like she was stomping out a nest of stinging fire ants underneath her.

In the middle of working with his soloist, Webster paused and called out to Elizabeth, "No, darling. The arm comes up a bit more slowly than that.

And it's *one*-two-three-four, *one*-two-three-four."

Elizabeth looked to him with wide eyes then nodded and tried again. This time, she looked a bit more like a fairy than a victim of a fire ant attack although she still needed to work on the fluidity of her arms. He told her as much, and she thanked him with a nod and smile.

Strange behavior indeed for a *corps* girl, but then again, she knew the part and danced it well. And it eased Sir Webster's mind that one more person knew every Fairy variation in *The Sleeping Beauty.* Who knew when an unanticipated injury or a family emergency would make it impossible for a dancer to perform at the last minute?

At the front of a different studio, William sat watching the dancers run through his piece. A rehearsal director sat next to him, scribbling notes on a pad of paper. It was good that she was there because William could only watch in stupefaction. It was the best thing he'd choreographed in a long time, possibly ever.

I did this, he thought, more a reminder than a boast. *This came from me.*

It was almost true. The choreography was his. The inspiration wasn't. The dancers weren't. Still, William gazed in wonder at the bodies twirling and arching before him. Turning to his rehearsal director, a woman who'd been there during his time at the company, he raised his eyebrows. She smiled in response, patted his arm, and wrote another note about a dancer's arm placement.

The music swelled and then each instrument faded until only a soft, synthesized beat remained. Panting, the dancers looked to William, seeking his approval. He gave it with a wide smile and unencumbered applause. In turn, the dancers broke into their own applause. Jane's *pas de deux* partner, a principal dancer, squeezed her shoulder, and high-fives went all around the room. Everyone there sensed that this piece was special, that it meant something bigger than they could articulate.

William stood to speak. "I've done all I can here. Thank you, everyone. It's been an honor for me to work with you. This piece of choreography has been different from anything I've ever attempted. It's been freeing. I'm grateful to you all for your hard work and for allowing me to use your talents to see it through.

"I'm off to Philadelphia tomorrow to put together something for them, but

I'll be back for the premiere. Until then, you'll be in good hands with Susan."

Whooping and applauding at the end of his speech, many of them came up to William to shake his hand and thank him, too. Jane approached with tears in her eyes and hugged him.

"You'll be great," he told her.

"Thank you for giving me this chance."

As the dancers filed out of the studio to prepare for their next rehearsals and that night's performance, William stayed to clarify some details of the choreography with Susan, who would be in charge of his rehearsals after he left. He showed her the lighting and costume sketches, assuring her that he'd already spoken to the wardrobe department about the billowing pants he wanted the dancers to wear. Susan took thorough notes, and when they were done speaking, she peered up at him as if she wanted to say something.

"You know," she began, "I remember what you were like when you danced here."

William replied, "I wish you didn't."

"And I was a little worried when Webster asked me to take on this ballet, but you've pleasantly surprised me."

He thanked her and found himself blushing, not just for the compliment but also for the reminder of his reputation as a hard-ass. She patted his arm again, gathered her things, and let him know she would keep in touch.

Alone in the studio, William unhooked his iPod from the stereo and contemplated Susan's words. He felt angry with himself again, wishing he'd realized sooner that his totalitarian ways hadn't made him more respected or accomplished, at least not in the eyes of those he worked with. He wished he'd asked Elizabeth to be in his piece. He wanted her to know he'd taken her words to heart.

Charles appeared in the doorway then. "Hey."

"Hey." Things between them had been tense over the last week or so since Charles had told William that the company wouldn't ask for his choreography services again.

"Jane came to tell me that you were finished in here, and I thought I should come by."

William nodded. Charles awkwardly stepped into the studio and approached his friend. He held out his hand, and William shook it.

"Are you still pissed off?" asked Charles.

"Nah. Not at you. Webster's another story, and I doubt I'll have much to say to him for a long time."

"I'm sorry, Will."

William shrugged and slapped his friend on the shoulder. "You've already apologized."

Charles ran his hand through his hair. "I guess I never thanked you as a friend for casting Jane."

His face turning stony, William replied, "I didn't cast Jane because you're my friend or because she's your girlfriend, so you don't have to thank me."

Charles laughed. "Easy there! That wasn't what I meant. I know you didn't cast her because of that. But I wanted to thank you anyway because she's been happy. She never stops gushing about it. Or about you. And I'm happy because she's happy. And I'm grateful to you because you're the reason she's happy." Charles stopped. Even this degree of effusiveness was rare for him.

William had cast Jane to right his karma, because she was a respectable dancer, and losing her soloist promotion had been his fault. He'd also cast her, admittedly, to win a bit of favor with her sister. His choice was a success. She'd worked hard to give William what he'd wanted from the piece. She deserved to feel happy. As for her sister, William had failed in that regard, but that didn't seem to be the point anymore.

"You're welcome" William cleared his throat to cover his own embarrassment. "Are you up for dinner?"

"I can't. Jane and I have dinner plans with Caroline. Unless . . . you want to come?"

"No," said William immediately.

Charles and William laughed together, and it looked as if Charles still wanted to say something. "I'm going to miss having you here," he said finally.

"You're being gushy today," joked William.

Charles shrugged. "Hey, a guy can express his feelings, right?"

Glancing around the studio, William sighed. "I'm going to miss being here. And being in New York."

"I'll work on Webster. You know how he is. Give him a few months; maybe he'll change his mind."

"No. No, this is the right thing. I was sick of what I'd been producing, and that's the stuff Ballet Theater wants."

"Will they want it in Philadelphia? Or Seattle? Or San Francisco?"

"Probably not." Hesitating, William said, "I thought about going back to Miami."

"Miami City Ballet?"

"No. Maybe trying to start up something there."

"Your own company?" Charles broke into a grin. "Will, that's fantastic!"

"I don't know yet. I've just been thinking about it. We both know I like having ultimate artistic control."

Charles smiled. "That's really great. Well, keep me updated. Let's all grab a bite before you leave. That was fun the other night with you, me, Jane, and Liz."

Mumbling a half-hearted assent, William gathered his things and walked out of the studio with his friend. He didn't bother looking back.

"Technically, if I licked my hand, couldn't it be like I made out with Mr. Darcy?" Lydia inspected her palm. She'd just given her friends, Elizabeth included, a play-by-play of William's effusive, meaningful farewell speech. Elizabeth didn't want to hear about it.

Charlotte hit Lydia over the head with a leg warmer.

"What? It's a valid question!" Lydia protested.

"I think, if you're talking technicalities, it would be more like you licked Mr. Darcy's hand," said Charlotte.

Lydia's eyes glowed. "I'll take that, too."

From the other side of the lockers, Elizabeth glowered. "You guys are weird."

"Oh, look!" laughed Lydia. "Lizzy's jealous! Aw, Lizzy, don't cry. Just because you didn't get to touch Mr. Darcy, doesn't mean that you're any less special." Lydia roughly hugged Elizabeth's shoulders. Patting Lydia's hand in mock annoyance, Elizabeth insisted that she needed to change and get to the theater.

"Don't be like that, Lizzy." Lydia frowned.

"She's too good for our jokes now, Lyd," Charlotte said with an edge in her voice.

Elizabeth looked at her friend and asked, "What does that mean?"

"It means you never stand next to us in class anymore, and you never want to hang out in rehearsals," Charlotte explained.

"We miss you," said Lydia.

Elizabeth laughed in disbelief. "You guys are still my friends. But we're at work, and I'm just working."

They frowned as if they didn't believe her. Inside, she sank because, just once, Elizabeth wanted Lydia and Charlotte to applaud her newfound determination. She pushed the disappointment aside and assured them she still loved them. And with that, she bid them goodbye, hefted her dance bag over her shoulder, and went to prepare for that night's performance of *Sleeping Beauty.*

She trudged up the stairs, weary from nearly a full week of rehearsals and from her conversation with her friends. It wasn't just that they were unsupportive; it was also Lydia's comment about William's rehearsal. He seemed changed, and she wished it were for her. With a farewell speech like that, though, he clearly meant it towards everyone. At least now that he was leaving, Elizabeth wouldn't have to hear about him any more from Lydia or Jane. She wouldn't have to run into William and participate in the charade of friendship. The season would be easier. Slowly, the teachers, rehearsal directors, and even Sir Webster were starting to pay attention to her increased efforts.

Why, then, did it feel like an axe had fallen, permanently severing hope from possibility? She would never see William again, and the thought depressed her.

Nudging the front door of the building open with her shoulder, Elizabeth stepped outside. A breath of cool evening air made her shiver, and she turned north towards the theater.

"Ms. Bennet," called a deep voice.

Halting, Elizabeth looked up in surprise to see a tree-trunk of a man standing against a black Bentley. He wore dark aviator sunglasses.

"Ms. Elizabeth Bennet?" he asked.

"Yes?" She frowned. How did this stranger know her name? As far as she knew, the mafia didn't have any grudges against her.

"Ms. Bennet, Ms. Boroughs would like a moment of your time."

"I'm sorry?"

"Ms. Catherine Boroughs."

"Catherine Boroughs wants to speak to *me?*" asked Elizabeth.

Saying nothing else, the man, whom she now understood to be a chauffeur, opened the back door of the car. Elizabeth peered inside, remembering the childhood warning about getting into cars with strangers. Most strangers, however, did not approach their victims in sleek, dark-tinted Bentleys accompanied by sunglassed chauffeurs. They also weren't one of the wealthiest and most public women in the city. Forcing down her dread, Elizabeth ducked into the car and found herself sitting across from the infamous Catherine Boroughs.

She was the product of talented dermatologists and stylists. In her immaculate gray pantsuit and Ferragamo heels, she looked to be nearing sixty, but her skin glowed, and the blonde lowlights in her hair shone. Her jewelry—large diamond studs, a Tiffany choker, and a hunk of sapphire on her ring finger—exuded wealth. She looked at Elizabeth with a raised eyebrow and then smiled. The gesture only reached her lips.

"You probably don't know who I am," Catherine began.

Elizabeth bristled at her tone and raised her chin. "You're Anne's mother," replied Elizabeth.

Catherine's smile wilted. "Yes, I'm that, too. I'm also a very important person to this company."

"Okay…" Elizabeth frowned, unsure what Catherine was implying.

The older woman narrowed her eyes and appraised the young dancer—an intimidation tactic.

"May I help you with something?" Elizabeth asked. "Is there a reason you wanted to speak to me? Anne and I aren't really close, so I'm not sure if that's what this is about."

Refusing to be anywhere but at the helm of the conversation, Catherine ignored Elizabeth's questions. "Miss Bennet, I am well known amongst my friends and acquaintances for my frankness, so I won't mince words with you." She paused, Elizabeth supposed, for dramatic effect. "You're ruining this ballet company."

"I'm sorry?" Elizabeth nearly laughed at the suggestion that she, an insignificant *corps de ballet* dancer, could be at all responsible for the demise of one of the oldest and most respected dance companies in the country.

"No need to play dumb. I know your game, but I simply can't figure out how you've managed to play it so well. But you *do* know you're shooting yourself in the foot, don't you?"

Elizabeth finally mustered a reply. "I'm sorry. I really don't know what you mean."

"You don't? One would think that, to get your way with William Darcy, he would have to remain in New York."

"My way with Mr. Darcy?" repeated Elizabeth. Her eyes narrowed as she finally understood Catherine's meaning.

"You won't deny it, will you? I have it on good authority that you and William Darcy are having an affair."

Starting, Elizabeth opened her mouth to reply, but she was cut off.

"I refused to believe it myself at first. I could scarcely *believe* William Darcy would be interested in a woman like you. But then, well, how could it be denied? After he gave that role to your sister... and what it cost him! And for what?" Catherine stared down her nose at Elizabeth, a sneer twisting up the corner of her lips.

"You must know that William is already engaged to my daughter. He's an extremely loyal fiancé. They've been together for years. And I know he's not usually so easily tempted by girls like you. So you can see how I would dismiss the rumors for as long as I did."

Elizabeth bristled. "He must not be so dedicated to Anne if you think he's having an affair with me."

Catherine glared at the *corps* girl and then reached into a sleek, leather bag lying beside her and pulled out a silver cigarette holder. Plucking a cigarette from within, Catherine lit it, inhaled long, and then blew a stream of smoke straight into Elizabeth's face.

"I know about *you*, Miss Bennet."

"Really."

"I know that you were in William's piece. I know you rehearsed privately with him. And I also know that your sister expected Anne's promotion for herself. Is this what the affair is all about? Taking revenge on your sister's behalf? Getting him to cast her since she was passed over for the soloist promotion? No, don't deny it. I've been in the arts for years. I know all the games dancers play. And I know that trading sex for professional favors isn't below many a *corps* girl."

Elizabeth swallowed down a growing lump of fury in her throat. "Perhaps you're right."

Catherine waited and then waved her cigarette around in a gesture of frustration. "And that's all you have to say for yourself?"

"I don't think I have to say anything for myself! I don't see how my sex life affects you at all."

"I give this company a lot of money to ensure that it remains the best in the nation, uncompromised by anything less than the highest artistic standards! And so I don't enjoy seeing that money wasted because some vulgar *corps de ballet* dancer has the star choreographer wrapped around her finger."

Elizabeth raised an eyebrow. "Vulgar?

"Would *you* describe using sex to get your way any differently?"

"No, but it also nicely describes using *money* to get your way."

Catherine's face went black. She took another long drag of her cigarette. "You *cannot* be insinuating that supporting the arts and sleeping with the choreographer are the same thing!"

"According to you, I'm also doing my part to *support the arts*," Elizabeth retorted with the same black glint in her eyes.

Catherine struggled to rein in the emotion in her voice. "You saw what happened with his last piece. It was a critical disaster. I've heard this new work is a horror and your sister incompetent in it."

Elizabeth pressed her lips together. Seeing this, Catherine relaxed and added, "And Webster fired him over it! I care very deeply for William, and I don't want to see his reputation as a legendary dancer and choreographer tarnished by you."

Fired? thought Elizabeth. She steeled her face and tried to make her voice even. "I don't hand out the pink slips—unless you think I'm sleeping with Sir Webster, too."

Catherine snorted. "You know perfectly well what I'm talking about. Who convinced Darcy to go modern; who convinced him to cast your sister as the lead in his piece? You must have woven quite a potent spell over him. Not even Webster could change the man's mind, even after I withdrew my pledge to the company. I refuse—*refuse*, Miss Bennet—to support the kind of modern, *avant-garde garbage* that William Darcy is creating. And I *refuse* to support a company that gives lead roles to unworthy *corps de ballet* dancers when there are much worthier people in the soloist ranks."

Elizabeth breathed deeply once then twice before she answered. "Your money doesn't buy his principles."

"I'm sorry?" Catherine said.

"Mr. Darcy isn't the kind of man who allows anyone to compromise his integrity."

"Is that so? Then, how did *you* manage it?"

Was this really happening? Did Catherine Boroughs think she was so high and mighty that she didn't need to care for anyone else's feelings—for decency and respect? Did she think her net worth exempted her from manners? Elizabeth—exhausted after a day of relentless rehearsals in which she'd been on her feet for five hours and endured two bloodied toes and a creaky ankle—couldn't take much more. Gripped by a sadomasochistic urge, Elizabeth smirked, narrowed her eyes, and replied with the first thing that popped into her head.

"It's simple; I have no gag reflex."

Catherine first looked puzzled, but when the words sank in, her mouth fell open, and she turned a regal shade of violet. She sputtered, rendered speechless for the first time in this conversation and possibly, Elizabeth thought, this decade.

"Disgusting!" Catherine gasped. "Shameful and disgusting! I don't think I've met a girl so vulgar in all my life. You call yourself a dancer? An artist?! You're a *slut.* Wait until Webster hears about this. There's no place for dancers like you at Ballet Theater."

Then, Elizabeth saw red. "Look, I've had too long a week for this. I don't care who you are, how much money you donate, or how many artistic directors and finance directors and managers and artists you have chained to you and your money. It doesn't matter to me. The only reason I'm talking to you at all is because I love this company and because I want to move up in it, and I want to tell you that neither you nor anyone is going to stop me from at least trying."

Catherine narrowed her eyes. "So you did have an affair with Darcy?"

Elizabeth snapped forward so fast that Catherine jerked back in her seat. "Maybe I should be more explicit. I will work my ass off, but I will not, do not, and have never had sex for my roles or anyone else's. And this conversation is over." Scooting over on the leather seat, Elizabeth grabbed the door handle. Catherine's arm shot out to still her.

"I want to hear that you'll stay away from Darcy."

Balling her fist, Elizabeth swallowed down an explosion of rage and answered in a voice so calm, it made Catherine's grip falter.

"This conversation is over because you're not going to hear that." Elizabeth yanked her hand away and pushed open the door.

"Miss Bennet!" Catherine yelled.

Leaping out of the car, Elizabeth's feet hit the pavement, and she slammed the door, startling Catherine Borough's chauffeur from his halcyon cigarette break. She tossed her bag onto her shoulder and thundered away from the car as fast as she could.

"Dumb bitch!"

Elizabeth had never felt so insulted. Anything William, or even Caroline, had ever said to her paled in comparison to this tirade. Sleeping with William Darcy so that she would get a better part? The irony was that she *had* slept with him and then gotten demoted for it. Sleeping with William Darcy to get her sister a better part? The greater irony was that *Jane* now had a better part and Elizabeth could have strangled her. She should have told Catherine *that*! The old hag would have choked on her Virginia Slim.

And William fired from BTNY? That was crazy talk. William Darcy was the golden goose; Lucas would never fire him. Truly, Catherine Boroughs must have been abusing drugs or suffering from a mental disorder—schizophrenia perhaps.

But at least Elizabeth had stood up to her. She hadn't trembled in intimidation, protested her innocence, or even cried tears of rage. Elizabeth knew Catherine Boroughs' reputation. Not many *corps de ballet* dancers —hell, not many *people*—could say they had gone up against the dragon and come away uncharred.

Of course, Elizabeth thought, she still might get burned. She would probably be fired, perhaps even blacklisted from other dance companies in New York. She should have been quaking with fear and regret. Perhaps it was the adrenaline, but Elizabeth couldn't find the fear. She had withstood Caroline Bingley and William Darcy. What was one more self-righteous millionaire to her?

So much for all of that hard work, she thought. But the memory of Boroughs' face twisted in rage was worth it. She'd probably get a stern talking-to from her cosmetic surgeon about the ruin that emotions could wreak on one's face. That thought made Elizabeth burst into laughter. Someone passing her on the sidewalk, a tourist probably, smiled in return. Elizabeth could always go back to Berlin or maybe Japan, somewhere far away from the stupid politics of Ballet Theater. As William said, *fuck them.* And fuck Catherine Boroughs especially.

Elizabeth went into work the next day expecting a summons from Sir Webster Lucas. It never came. Elizabeth was not fired that day or the day after that. The remainder of the week passed by normally—classes, rehearsals, costume fittings, performances. No one glanced at her strangely. She did not hear her name whispered in the halls. Caroline barely acknowledged her.

The end of the fall season was several weeks away, and after that, *Nutcracker*, and then the winter season. In the halls and locker rooms of Ballet Theater, dancers hummed with casting speculations as they always did. According to Charlotte, who'd had it from Cassandra and Robbie, who'd overheard a conversation between Charles and Webster, Lydia was pinned for the Chinese variation. It was rumored Jane would be dancing Arabian. Everyone wondered whether Caroline would be healthy enough to perform in *Nutcracker* after the "injury" that had kept her from dancing in the fall season.

Elizabeth wondered when she would face the consequences of her interaction with Catherine Boroughs, and when several weeks passed, she gradually forgot about it. Life at Ballet Theater whirled by as it always did, and then on an ordinary Tuesday during the dancers' lunch break, another cast list went up.

Elizabeth pushed herself off the floor downstairs and took a deep breath. She removed the headphones from her ears, tossed them in her bag, and prepared to go upstairs for her afternoon rehearsal. The hall was quiet.

As she pulled open the door, two fellow company members brushed past. They smiled at her. One patted her shoulder.

"Nice one, Liz," she said.

Elizabeth frowned in confusion and continued up the stairs. Another late dancer ran down the steps, smiled at her, and called out, "Congrats!" before streaking to the locker room so as not to be late.

Elizabeth's heart began beating a mazurka rhythm. Something was happening. She walked slowly down a hall that would typically be crowded with dancers. No one was around, and she felt an eerie anticipation like the opening of a horror movie. Checking the clock, she wondered where everyone could be.

Just then, Charlotte ambled by and stopped when she spied Elizabeth. "Hey!" she said, smiling, "I bet you feel like a million bucks."

"Uh, no," Elizabeth replied, "I'm exhausted, and I want to know why everyone keeps smiling at me."

Charlotte's face soured. "They're just being nice, Lizzy. Would you rather they take a crowbar to your kneecaps?"

"Huh?"

"Huh? Have you even seen the board?"

"No."

"*Nutcracker* casting is up."

Suddenly, Elizabeth understood. Her eyes widened, and she straightened her spine. Without a word of good-bye, she pushed past Charlotte.

Elizabeth saw a small crowd gathered in front of the company bulletin board. She began scanning the list.

She found her name towards the bottom of the page, in a cluster of *corps* dancers' names, for Waltz of the Snowflakes. Skipping over the Act Two variations, she saw that she'd also been chosen to dance in the Waltz of the Flowers and understudy the Dance of the Reed Pipes. Elizabeth smiled. She had not even been in Act Two the year before. It was progress but certainly no reason for all the congratulations. About to turn away from the board, she gasped when Lydia catapulted onto her in a bear hug.

"Woo-hoo!" she cried.

"Thanks," Elizabeth sputtered. "You're choking me."

"Sorry." Lydia giggled, releasing her. "So, how many times did you have to blow Lucas to get that part?"

Elizabeth guffawed. "First, that's just sick. Second, screw you. And third, you're in the same dances as me."

Lydia looked at Elizabeth strangely. She pointed at the list. "Why don't you take another look, Lizzy?"

Elizabeth turned around and skimmed the list again. She ran her index finger up the list of names for Waltz of the Flowers. She saw herself and nodded. Continuing upwards, she saw that her sister had been cast in the Dance of the Reed Pipes. Caroline's name was listed under Sugar Plum Fairy, along with two other principals. Elizabeth's finger continued the journey upwards to the cast list for Act One. The list for Waltz of the Snowflakes took up an entire page in itself. Elizabeth found herself and nodded again. Finally, simply to be thorough, she looked down again to the Act Two variations.

And then her finger stopped.

"You're kidding," she exhaled.

But there it was, in that staid, Times New Roman font, the one she had always hated, her name written under the heading "Arabian," one of the prime soloist roles in the second act. Elizabeth whirled around to gawk at Lydia, who simply grinned. Turning back, Elizabeth looked again, studying the words "Elizabeth Bennet."

And then, she smiled. Everything in her body turned warm and light. She saw that Jane had also been chosen to dance the role, most likely in a different cast, because it was a part for one. In spite of rank or experience, for the first time ever on any cast list, in a fluke of alphabetical serendipity, Elizabeth Bennet's name appeared above that of her sister, Jane.

Chapter 25

The next week, as the company's fall season wound down, rehearsals for *Nutcracker* began. It was Elizabeth's first time returning to a ballet. Thus far, everything in the company's repertoire had been new to her. As a result, rehearsals for Waltz of the Snowflakes felt easier. She knew all of the steps, and with each new sequence the rehearsal director re-taught, the next simply sprang from her legs. In rehearsals, the dormant steps began to reawaken.

Her Arabian rehearsals were another matter. Jane and the two other soloists in the role seemed equipped for it in a way Elizabeth was not. The languid, sensuous movements looked natural coming from their three tall, long bodies. They seduced their audience when they arched their backs and twirled their wrists in the Arabian flourish. Elizabeth felt squat and clumsy by comparison, unable to achieve the same degree of sexiness with her shorter torso, legs, and arms. The rehearsal director implored her to reach and preen more, but Elizabeth's body couldn't produce the movement that he wanted. Because of that, she feared she might be cast only in Tuesday evening performances.

That day, after a particularly disheartening rehearsal in which she'd struggled to nail a double *pique attitude* turn with the same fluidity as the other three dancers, Elizabeth went downstairs to her locker to find a text message waiting for her.

Heyyy! It's G! How are you? Guess what?

Elizabeth smiled. It was the first time she'd heard from Georgiana Darcy since returning from Miami three months ago. She typed a reply. *I'm good! You? What's going on?*

Georgiana replied immediately. *I'm coming to NYC to watch Dub's new piece! Let's hang out while I'm there!*

Swallowing down a lump of nervousness in her throat, Elizabeth knew that if Georgiana were coming then her brother would be, too. She wasn't sure if she wanted to see William, fearing that all of the old melancholy would return. She missed him too much to have only a taste of his company.

I'd love to see you, G. Maybe we can get a drink while you're here. There. She knew William didn't drink. She hoped it was clear that he wasn't invited.

Cool! ☺ *I'll text you when I'm there so we can figure out plans. Can't wait!!!!*

Sighing, Elizabeth tucked her phone back into her bag. She slumped onto a bench in the locker room, still in her leotard, sweats, and pointe shoes. Her thoughts meandered to the past, and she felt sad all over again.

William heard his sister yell something about peas. He frowned and yelled back, "What?"

From the den, Georgiana shouted something again, and William thought back to a time long ago when she'd been five and yelled for their father from across the house. Their father, sixty years her senior at the time, had chided her about children being seen and not heard. It had been William's job, as her fifteen-year-old brother, to explain on their father's behalf that, if she wanted something from someone in another room, she should come and tell them rather than screaming it across the house. Clearly, the lesson hadn't sunk in for either of them.

He closed the kitchen cabinet. He didn't need anything in it anyway. Other than a few suitcases of clothes and some random boxes that included his favorite coffee mug, his good kitchen knife, and a ridiculously expensive blender, there wasn't much in William's New York apartment that he considered necessary to ship down to Miami. It didn't surprise him. He'd lived a nomadic life for five years. While he thought returning to Ballet Theater and New York would change the impermanence in his life, it hadn't.

Walking to the den, William appeared in the doorway to see his sister peering at his CD collection and Anne sprawled on her back next to her. "I can't hear anything you're saying," he said.

"You should take your CDs," Georgiana said, exasperated.

William made a face. "I've burned them all. I don't need to take them."

"Then why do you still have them?" Anne asked, opening her eyes.

"Sentimental value," he answered. "I thought you were going to help."

"I'm helping."

"She's helping, Dub. She's keeping me company," explained Georgiana.

"I tried helping you before," Anne said to William, "but you wouldn't let me touch any of your stuff."

"You need to put glass items in bubble-wrap," he explained.

Anne lifted her hand to wave him off and closed her eyes again.

Ignoring the spat between the two, Georgiana looked to her brother with twinkling eyes. "I still can't believe that you're actually moving back to Miami, Dub."

"Seasonally," added William.

"What*ever*. At least we get to live together for *four* whole months!" Georgiana said.

He nodded and smiled, feeling both a surge of excitement and a twinge of sadness. Living with his sister again would be a relief. She wouldn't be alone anymore, and they could spend more time together. But moving back to Miami, even temporarily, also meant leaving the life he'd only started to rebuild in New York. He was leaving behind Charles, Ballet Theater, walks through Central Park, his favorite Italian restaurant and, even though he still hated himself for wanting her, Elizabeth. William wondered whether he was truly doing the right thing.

Georgiana's phone chirped then. Twisting behind her, she grabbed it. "It's Elizabeth!"

William's heart skipped, and then he chastised himself. He had to stop having these automatic reactions whenever he heard her name.

"Oh, I meant to tell you something about her," Anne said, eyes closed again and voice monotone.

"Cool! She's performing tonight! I'll get to see her dance again," Georgiana exclaimed.

"She's performing in something else, though, G."

Georgiana shrugged. "That doesn't matter. Although I don't understand why you didn't put her in your piece."

At this point, William couldn't figure it out either. If he could have done it all over again, he would have selfishly cast her in the lead role. Self-sacrifice had never been his thing.

"Should we go out again after the show? We could take her to La Fiore!

I know it's your favorite," Georgiana asked.

"I've already taken Elizabeth there, and the last time we were supposed to take her out after a show, you got a headache, remember?" said William.

"That wasn't my fault!" Georgiana waved him off. "Besides, you know you appreciated it."

William had, but he didn't want to admit to his sister that he needed her machinations to help him get an audience with a girl he liked. It made him feel prepubescent. He turned to Anne. "You said something before?"

Anne barely opened her eyes. "Yeah. I forgot to tell you that Elizabeth and my mother had a little chat the other day."

"Elizabeth and your mother?" William was stunned. There would be no reason for the two to fall into the same social circles; egomaniacal millionaires rarely deigned to mingle amongst the plebeians. "Why?"

"Who knows?" Anne inhaled slowly, as if she were trying to re-center herself into a meditation. Anne could sometimes be too like her mother, feigning indifference to get attention. It was infuriating.

"And that's it?" he snapped.

Anne shrugged.

"Anne, can you get up off the floor and come with me?" His sister looked alarmed. "Sorry, G. I'll fill you in later."

Annoyance flashed across Anne's face. Ignoring this, William walked into the kitchen. As it was, any mention of Catherine made him want to punch something, particularly after the shit she'd pulled with Charles and Webster over William's contract. What was she trying to do to Elizabeth now? He took steadying breaths, but he couldn't stop his mind from spinning. When Anne appeared in the kitchen, he turned to face her, folded his arms, and glared.

"Why didn't you tell me about this sooner?"

She glared back. "Because, thanks to Elizabeth, I had to come out to my mother, so I've kinda been dealing with some other stuff these last few weeks."

William was too astonished to reply.

"I finally told her that you and I weren't engaged—never were and never would be. She wasn't pleased."

"Shit. I'm sorry, Anne."

Anne ran her finger over the patterns in the granite countertop. "I'm not sure what pissed her off more: the fact that I'm gay, the fact that I was lying to her all these years, or the fact that she'll never get to call you her son-in-law."

William waited to reply. "What does this have to do with Elizabeth?"

Anne winced and held up her hands. "Just don't kill the messenger, okay?"

William's face darkened. Anne recounted what her mother had relayed: She wanted the truth from Elizabeth, she wanted to know how Elizabeth had manipulated him into getting everything she wanted, and she wanted to warn Elizabeth that her money was far more powerful than any *corps de ballet* dancer's influence. William listened, his rage rising to an angry boil in his chest. He waited for Anne to finish so he could gather his keys and coat, storm up to Catherine's townhouse only a few blocks away, and unleash a tirade about decorum and class warfare that he was already planning in his head.

"...and when she finally tried to get Elizabeth to promise to stay away from you, Elizabeth said she would never promise that and then got out of the car and left."

William's thoughts of vengeance cooled. He thought he'd misheard. "She said what?"

"Mother said that Elizabeth wouldn't promise to stay away from you."

"Wait. Did she say it just to piss off your mother, or did she say it because she meant something else?" A cocktail of emotions made his voice shaky and shrill.

Anne shrugged. "I don't know. I wasn't there."

Suddenly, William's thoughts careened in a completely different direction. Covering his mouth with a balled fist, he struggled to make sense of what he'd learned. He knew that if Elizabeth still hated him, she wouldn't have said that. Even if she'd wanted to piss off Catherine by being contrary, she would have mouthed off something in that smart-ass way of hers like *You might have asked me to do something more challenging than stay away from William Darcy,* or *I'll promise to stay away from him if he promises to stay away from me.* His mouth twitched into a smile as he imagined what she could have said and what she hadn't.

William walked past Anne and into the den, where his sister pretended to be absorbed in wrapping a picture frame in bubble wrap.

"I assume you heard everything," William said.

Looking guilty, Georgiana nodded.

"Why don't you go out with her after the show?"

"So you'll come?"

"No. You go. I need some time to think through all of this."

The reality was he needed to see Elizabeth alone on his own terms, not with his sister playing matchmaker.

Georgiana picked up her phone and sent Elizabeth a reply.

"Okay, last time, and then I think we're good for tonight," Patti, their rehearsal director, announced from her place at the edge of the stage.

The recorded music for Bach's *Partita* filled the empty space of the theater, which would be packed in just a few hours with ballet aficionados. They wouldn't be there to see *Partita* though, thought Elizabeth. They would be there for William Darcy's premiere.

As she waited in the wings stage left, Elizabeth saw the dancers for William's piece warming up in the wings on the opposite side of the stage. Jane was there, alone, jumping up and down to bring the blood back to her feet. She radiated focus. Elizabeth could only imagine what might have been going through Jane's thoughts on the eve of her debut as a principal dancer. Was she cycling through the steps for the three-hundredth time or imagining the blare of the lights in her first moments on stage? Was she conjuring up horrors like a ripped costume or a crash landing after a turn? If she were Elizabeth, she'd probably be dry heaving in a corner at this point.

From across the stage, she sent her sister a thought of comfort. Jane grew still then and breathed deeply as if she sensed it.

Elizabeth's run-through ended, and Patti dismissed them. In the few minutes of transition between rehearsals, Elizabeth approached Jane in the wings.

"*Merde*, Jane," said Elizabeth, wrapping her arms around her sister's shoulders and kissing her cheek.

Jane whispered her thanks and then turned to Elizabeth. The muscles around her lips were taught, and her eyes betrayed a wild fear that surprised Elizabeth.

"You'll be great," Elizabeth assured her.

Jane nodded and frowned as if she didn't believe her. "I just don't want to let Will down."

"You won't."

"He'll be here."

"I know."

"You do?" Jane looked surprised.

"I'm hanging out with his sister after the show."

Jane's mouth tightened again. "Lizzy, would it be too much trouble if I asked you to stay and watch? I know you haven't wanted much to do with me or this piece, but I need you to be here. Will you stay? Please?" She tried to maintain the evenness of her voice, but failed towards the very end.

Elizabeth squeezed her sister's hand. "I'll stay. And I'll tell you that you looked beautiful afterwards because you always do."

Jane cracked a smile. "You can lie to me just this once."

"It won't be a lie."

At that moment, Susan, the rehearsal director for Darcy's piece, called for places. Elizabeth wished her sister luck one last time and then disappeared back into the bowels of the theater to begin her own preparations for that evening's performance.

William shifted from side-to-side as he watched from the downstage right wing. It was the last thing he should have done in his nervous state—to watch Elizabeth dance. Already, he had a dozen concerns whirling through his head. Would Jane be able to nail the lift in the third movement that had always given her trouble? Would the costumes look garish brown in the lighting? Would the audience boo him permanently away from New York?

Did he really need to add *Does Elizabeth like me?* to the list? Did he really need to come watch her dance right before his piece premiered?

He'd always been fascinated with the Twyla Tharp choreography in *Bach Partita*. He admired how the music and dance seemed simultaneously to match and clash. None of the steps seemed to follow the severe violin, until they did in a flash of harmony and relief. The dissonance made those moments of accord all the more satisfying.

William watched Elizabeth execute a jump and turn sequence. The large rhinestone studs in her ears glinted in the bright stage lights, and the false eyelashes made her eyes seem especially large and expressive. It was a throwaway role; the *corps de ballet* was background décor, mere curtains for the soloists and principal dancers on stage. Elizabeth danced it cleanly, but a piece like this one wasted her talent. Perhaps it was like that for all of the *corps de ballet*. What hidden wonders could each artist bring to a dance if the dance had been choreographed just for her?

William had little time to muse on this question. The *corps de ballet* rushed off into the wings, Elizabeth straight into his. She met his eyes, and they went round. He smiled but knew better than to do or say anything. A performer needed her focus. But just being near her, hearing her harsh breathing next to him, made the left side of his body tingle. They stood together in the wing, silent, watching the *pas de deux* on stage for a long time. Each moment of the dance felt chaotic, relentless, and disappearing.

He hazarded a glance to his left where she stood. She glanced back up at him. The music ended, replaced by the stark opening trills of the *Chaconne* movement. And so they stood, silent and contemplative, until it was time for Elizabeth to reappear on stage. William remained in the wings, feeling a calm that lasted until the curtain rose on his new, final piece with Ballet Theater.

If it had not been for Jane's request, Elizabeth would not be there. It stirred up too many emotions to be near William, particularly now at the premiere of his piece. When she'd stood next to him in the wings during *Partita*, the plaintive moments of the violin solo had voiced all the turmoil in her heart.

She glanced around at the dancers in their unusual black costumes, shoulders bared, hair pulled taut and high, eyes smudged with black eye shadow. Stagehands moved with purpose, speaking into headsets. The stage manager stood in the far right wing in a relaxed conversation with the choreographer himself. Elizabeth did not want to display the longing and loss that she'd endured as she stood next to William before, so she tucked herself into a corner of the backstage area, watching her sister walk meditatively through the steps of the piece on stage.

"Places," the stage manager called to the dancers and again into his headset.

The lights on and backstage went dark, and the curtain whooshed up. She heard a cough in the audience and a few lone squeaks as patrons shifted in seats. The stage turned a brilliant orange, and the first deep notes of the music reverberated throughout the theater.

Elizabeth blinked. They were not the strings or winds of classical music, as she would have expected from William Darcy. The notes were electronic; they pulsed like a heartbeat. When a syncopated bongo joined in and then the first chords of a jazz piano, Elizabeth frowned. She'd heard this somewhere before. In her confusion, she couldn't remember where. And then, inhaling sharply, she remembered. She'd heard this music in William's BMW on a causeway in Miami.

She rushed to a stagehand several feet away.

"Do you have a program?" she asked. He looked at her as if he hadn't heard, and Elizabeth repeated the request. Her voice must have sounded urgent, because he fumbled for the rolled up program in his back pocket and pushed it at her. Flipping through the curled pages, Elizabeth finally stopped on the page for William's piece. She sucked in a breath. *The Muse*, his piece was called. Music by Georgiana Darcy.

She remembered the advice she'd given him that night in his car. *You have to choreograph something to this music. It just speaks to the soul.* She'd thought he'd dismissed it. She thought he'd been annoyed.

Elizabeth approached the stage and gaped at the dancers. Their movements, balletic yet unstructured, belied the ease of the music. They twisted, turned, and jumped, caught up in the pulse of the underlying beat, and just when the movement seemed to work itself into a fury, they seized up and seemed to melt into the mellow piano. The dance transfixed Elizabeth, and the audience sat entranced as well. She could not hear a single cough, seat shift, or crinkle of a candy wrapper.

Jane's solo arrived. Fierce and cat-like, she stretched and turned in a way that was unlike her usual dancing. Had William teased that out of her? She reached her hand and radiated strength, put it down and communicated vulnerability. Elizabeth tore her eyes from the stage to stare at William Darcy in the first wing. This piece was so radically unlike him. Where had all of this come from?

This is interesting and new, Elizabeth had told him that night. *You could do so much with rhythm and syncopation with this music.*

She knew, then. The music, the dancing, the inspiration—it had come from her. The muse was Elizabeth.

She gasped shakily and wiped at her wet eyes. It was beautiful but also cruel. He'd choreographed this piece yet cut her out of it. He was stupid, and she was, too. Because if he could feel this depth of emotion for her and if she could only stand there and sob, then what the hell were they doing?

Elizabeth watched the rest of the piece, a resolution taking hold.

As the end of the dance neared, instruments disappeared until only a quiet, constant beat remained. The movements quieted, too, leaving only Jane on stage. The lights faded to black. Elizabeth inhaled in that silent pause before the audience's applause overwhelmed the theater. The lights came up, and the dancers took their bows. Backstage, the stagehands clapped. Elizabeth's eyes sought William and found him receiving his congratulations from the stage manager.

Go, Elizabeth's head said.

Go where? She didn't know, but she couldn't bring herself to move.

Jane stepped forward to take her bow, and the audience responded in applause and shouts of "Brava!"

Jane gestured for William Darcy to come on stage for his bow. He did, and the theater pounded with applause.

Elizabeth stumbled back and ran to the dressing rooms. She let herself into Jane's, sat down on the empty sofa, put her face in her hands, and cried again out of gratitude for the dance that was hers.

In her remaining minutes of solitude, Elizabeth composed herself so that, when her sister burst into the dressing room, Elizabeth greeted her with a genuine, joyful shriek. She began to cry again, and so did Jane; they hugged and cried and laughed.

Even when they heard polite knocking, Elizabeth could not stop laughing her praises. It was Charles and William at the door, each with an enormous bouquet of roses for Jane. Both men hugged her, and then Charles hugged Elizabeth although she didn't know why. Other dancers pushed in to congratulate both the star and choreographer. Amidst the chaos, Elizabeth managed to catch William's eye. He gave her a small smile, and she found herself weaving around bodies to get closer to him. She stood next to William and looked up at him, feeling both sure and insecure under his gaze.

"I need to talk to you," she said. The voices around them cocooned their conversation.

He didn't seem surprised. "I wanted to talk to you, too."

"I'm going out with your sister now," she said.

"I know. We'll talk tomorrow, then."

"I'll be in rehearsals until three."

He nodded. "I'll find you."

Elizabeth nodded. Sir Webster Lucas interrupted then, gripping William's shoulder and pulling him into a teary hug. Elizabeth smiled, kissed Jane on the cheek one last time, and then slipped out to meet Georgiana Darcy for dinner.

Chapter 26

The next afternoon, when William approached Studio D, he found Elizabeth alone in it, marking through a series of steps and turns. He was nervous, and he sent a prayer up to whatever god was listening that he wasn't mistaken by his hunch. He'd been wrong before.

William stood at the half-open door and watched Elizabeth dance. Her legs only walked through the steps, but her arms and face performed full-out. Even without music, he could tell from the sensuous movements and rolls of her wrists that she was practicing the Arabian variation. William smiled, feeling a warm pride. He could claim no credit for Elizabeth's getting that role, but it satisfied him nonetheless because that was a role she could dance credibly. She tried a sequence of kicks and *chassés* several times, experimenting with different dynamics of the legs and arms. Finally discovering one she liked, she repeated it a few times.

Only then did William knock softly on the door. Elizabeth whipped her head back to him, glanced at the clock, and then smoothed her hands over her hair.

"Hey, I'm sorry," she said. "I completely lost track of time."

Her chest moved in quick breaths. Sweat beaded at her temples, strands of hair sprang out from her messy bun, and her cheeks were flushed pink. Still, to William, she looked beautiful, vibrant, and warm.

"That's okay," he responded. "Arabian?"

She smiled. "Yes."

"It's looking good."

"Really?" She frowned. "I'm just not sure."

William stepped into the studio, closed the door, and walked towards her. He saw Elizabeth glance back at the door and swallow.

"Alan keeps telling me that this part needs to be sexy, but I don't know. I'm just not getting *sexy* from it," Elizabeth added.

William pushed his hands into the front pockets of his jeans. Given the way Elizabeth looked, flushed and tussled and sexy, he wasn't sure whether this was the conversation to be having at the moment.

"I mean," Elizabeth continued, "she's dancing to celebrate the return of her boy-prince and his twelve-year-old girlfriend. Why would she be *sexy*? I guess I'm getting strong and powerful and *I am woman, hear me roar!* Which *is* sexy, but I don't think she would actively be trying, you know?"

"Okay. Why don't you let me see what you've got?"

Elizabeth swallowed again, hesitating for a beat, and then she nodded once.

She prepared and began to dance. Despite the silence of the studio, William could practically hear the music coming from her steps. Elizabeth danced, and although the movements were sultry, she performed them with power. Her eyes radiated a strength that seduced, and the pounding of his heart reminded William why he fell in love with her in the first place. When she finished, he nodded, even more nervous than before.

"I like it," he said.

Breathing hard, Elizabeth took a long sip of water and laughed. "That's it?"

He understood what she implied. Wasn't he going to give her more feedback? He hadn't come there, though, to be a choreographer.

"Yes, it looks really great, Elizabeth. Congratulations, by the way, on getting the part."

"Thanks." She smiled. "I don't know what Lucas was thinking, though. Sometimes I don't feel up for this role."

"He wouldn't have cast you if he didn't think you could dance it."

Elizabeth shrugged. "I can't get any of the turns when they have to be so slow."

He waited. She looked at him expectantly. Then, he realized she *wanted* his input.

"Just *plié* more," he said. "That should get you around for the turns."

"You and your *pliés*."

"It's all in your supporting leg."

Placing her water down on the floor, Elizabeth raised an eyebrow. "Let's see about that." She walked to the center of the room and picked up dancing from the middle of the variation. Preparing for the achingly slow *piqué attitude* turn, she called out, "Okay, here's your *plié*."

William smiled for encouragement but then watched in satisfaction as Elizabeth glided through the turn and ended in a clean *chasé*. She, too, seemed surprised.

Elizabeth blinked and stared at the edge of the mirror, thinking. Her face clouded over. Finally, she looked at him. "Sometimes, I get so mad at you."

Her voice had turned soft and serious. It took him aback.

"I've noticed." He waited for her to qualify her comment.

"You just come in here and tell me to *plié* and then, boom! Perfect turn. As if *you* did it."

"But I didn't."

"I know! But it's like..." She struggled to find the words. "I don't want to need *you* to be a better dancer."

"I don't think you need me to be a better dancer."

"But you make me a better dancer. I don't know why. You just do."

Elizabeth's forehead wrinkled as a storm cloud of feeling passed across her face. William waited. There were things he wanted to say to her, but he'd learned about the art of timing when he'd last had this conversation with her, so he decided to be patient. Let the storm die out.

She looked at him again, pain palpable on her face. In a small voice, she asked, "Why didn't you cast me in your piece?"

He let her question sink in, trying to understand exactly what she was asking. He'd thought she wanted nothing to do with him, but her voice and her eyes mirrored heartbreak. "I... I didn't think you'd want to be in it."

"Why? Are you kidding me?" The hurt in her voice had turned to anger.

"Why?" William repeated. "Because you resented it last time. You resented the meddling, I thought. I just couldn't bear your hatred again."

"But I didn't hate you! Couldn't you tell from Miami?"

William raised his hands in defeat. "Elizabeth, I had imagined so much before."

"You said I inspired you, and you chose Jane instead!"

His eyes widened in surprise. He *knew* this decision would come back to haunt him. Fearing that all of his hope would again be trampled, he exclaimed, "I chose Jane for you! I wanted to redeem myself. Don't get me wrong; your sister is an excellent dancer. But I thought this opportunity for Jane would mean something to *you* since you'd been so upset about her being passed over for promotion."

A kaleidoscope of emotions passed over Elizabeth's face. William watched it, hoping and fearful. Finally, Elizabeth buried her face in her hands and moaned, "Oh, God!"

Her shoulders shook and she made quiet noises. Thinking she was crying, William reached out to touch her shoulder in comfort. She lifted her face, the picture of a tragicomic mask. On the one hand, tears streamed from her eyes. On the other, she laughed. With both of his hands on her shoulders, he watched her in confusion. Elizabeth wiped her eyes and groaned.

"I'm an idiot! I'm an idiot. Don't listen to anything I say again. Ever."

He gave her an incredulous look. "Can I get that in writing?"

She laughed and looked up at him, abashed. Her eyes had softened. William took his chance. "So even the thing you said to me that night outside the theater... should I ignore that, too?" he asked.

Her face sobered, and a leftover tear streaked down her cheek. William knew she understood that he was referring to the night on Columbus Avenue when he botched his confession of love.

Elizabeth pressed her lips together and nodded. Her eyes shone. "Yeah," she whispered. "Everything. Ignore everything I said that night."

That was enough for him. William drew her close and kissed her.

They came up for air some time later, wild-eyed and flushed. William's heart thrummed in his ears. Relief and desire made it hard to speak. His forehead resting against Elizabeth's, he finally murmured, "We probably shouldn't be making out here."

"Let's go to your place, then," Elizabeth said.

William sighed and thought of Georgiana in dismay. "My sister's there."

"Then come to my place."

His heart leapt. He realized then it was the invitation that he wanted most. He pulled back, studied her face, and then asked, "Should I be ignoring this, too?"

She pressed her mouth to his, and they both sank into their desire again. When they parted, William replied, "I need to be at the theater by eight."

Elizabeth grinned. "Then we should go soon. Give me ten minutes." She pulled away from him and jogged to the side of the room to get her dance bag. He watched her go, and before she disappeared out the door, she looked back at William. She grinned and he returned the smile.

When she was gone, he caught a glimpse of himself in the mirror. With the goofy smile on his face, he hardly seemed the same person. He chuckled and shook his head, breathed deeply, and then went downstairs to wait for Elizabeth.

In retrospect, Elizabeth realized she had made a foolish and irrational decision.

How was ten minutes enough time to pretty herself after hours of dancing? She should have said twenty.

"Dammit!" she cursed, trying to run a comb through her wet hair. She was now at—she checked the clock on the back wall—thirteen minutes and counting. Knowing how William hated tardiness, Elizabeth flew through her preparations. Just a dab of gloss, a swipe of deodorant, a comb to get the tangles out. Lurching for her dance bag, she stubbed her toe on the bench and cursed again.

Throwing her dance clothes into her bag, she tossed the strap onto her shoulder and sprinted from the dressing room, up the stairs, and into the cool evening air. She didn't see him immediately because he waited for her several yards away. Hands tucked into the pockets of his pea coat, William radiated calm. He saw her, and his look changed. It sharpened and deepened. Months ago, she would have called his expression disapproval. Now she realized it meant just the opposite.

"Sorry," she said, blushing.

"For what?"

"I'm a little late."

He raised the corner of his mouth, his gaze constant and penetrating. "Let's get a cab."

Elizabeth nodded, and he hailed one. Once inside, they sat in a silence laden with uncertainty and expectation. Elizabeth didn't know what to say. Should she make small talk about Philadelphia? Should she ask him what he'd wanted to say to her? He'd never actually said it. Should she talk about the weather, unseasonably cool for October? Should she take his hand? Should she ask what they planned on doing once they got to her apartment, even though she knew?

"Are you hungry?" asked William.

Elizabeth didn't know. She was too nervous. "No."

They passed the remainder of the cab ride in silence. Elizabeth tried to ignore the electric charge between them. She worried about the state of her apartment. Cringing, she remembered that her bra and underwear from the day before were still crumpled in a pile on the floor in her room. Neither she nor Jane had done dishes in two days. She hadn't dusted the coffee table in weeks.

The cab flew uptown until the Manhattan landscape grew hillier, the high-rises shrunk to low-rises, and the language of the storefronts changed from English to Spanish. Instructing the taxi driver which building was hers, Elizabeth dug through her bag to find her wallet, but William had already snapped a crisp twenty from his. He handed it over and told the driver to keep the change. The cab pulled away.

Elizabeth had never thought much about the façade or foyer of her building, but now she was aware of the cracks in the old marble and the flickering fluorescent lights as she fumbled in her bag for her keys. She opened the first two doors, glancing over her shoulder at William, who remained quiet.

"I'm on the fourth floor," Elizabeth apologized. "It's a walk-up."

"I think I'll manage."

He said it lightly, but Elizabeth remembered the elevator that opened onto the penthouse of the Pemberley Building.

Reaching the fourth floor, she looked back at him and smiled timidly. He smiled back.

"Prepare yourself to be underwhelmed," she said, unlocking her front door and letting them both in. As Elizabeth feared, they walked into a scene of several days' worth of bowls and mugs piled in the sink. Elizabeth winced.

"Jane and I don't get much time to clean during the season," she explained. William merely smiled and shrugged.

"Okay, so let me give you the tour," she stumbled. "You've already seen the kitchen, unfortunately. And this is our living room."

"It's nice," he said, and it almost sounded like he meant it. He stared for a moment at some framed family pictures on a shelf.

"This is the bathroom." Elizabeth cringed inside at her dingy bathroom that needed new grout, a new vanity light bulb, and tile from the last quarter-century. "That's Jane's bedroom. Down there is mine. And that's about it. It's small. And outdated. But it's home."

She shrugged and couldn't meet his eyes. Nodding, William looked around, shoved his hands in his pockets, and said nothing.

"Can you give me a minute?" she asked. Not waiting for his reply, Elizabeth about-faced and scurried into her bedroom. She shut the door and then raced around the room, hiding her dirty clothes and straightening the clutter on her dresser. She cursed herself again for bringing him there.

Damn her libido! In the studio, she could only think of sliding all over his hard, naked body, but that was the problem with doing this thing sober. Now she regretted inviting him to her Harlem rat's nest when he was used to much nicer, fancier places.

"Ugh." She groaned and ran her hands over her face. She had not thought this through. Counting to ten and breathing deeply three times, she opened the door and walked down the hallway, expecting to find William sitting uncomfortably in her living room.

He was standing, however, leaning one arm against the wall. Turning his head towards her, he grinned. Elizabeth stopped, speechless and confused.

"I love your choice of artwork." He rapped his knuckles against the tack board where Jane and Elizabeth hung their calendar, reminder notes, important phone numbers, and...

Elizabeth's mouth fell open, and a volcanic blush erupted over her whole body.

"Oh, God!" She dashed over to the board and ripped down the crumpled magazine clipping of Perfection by Hermes.

William laughed. "No, I like it! You should keep it up."

"Will you shut up? Oh, my *God*, I'm going to die of embarrassment."

"No, I like it!"

William darted his hand out, trying to snatch the photo from her. Elizabeth scurried aside and hid it behind her back. After a short wrestling match, Elizabeth ended up pressed into a corner of the room. Their game had calmed her nerves, and she giggled.

William grinned. "If I'd known you liked that picture so much, I could have sent you a much nicer copy."

He was teasing her. Never one to be bested, Elizabeth arched an eyebrow. "Forget the copy. I've got the real thing right here."

His eyes darkened with desire, and that was how they ended up making out in the corner of her living room, squished in between the bookshelf and dining room table. They kissed messily until Elizabeth pulled away and uttered, "Bedroom."

That was where they went.

William was the first male visitor to Elizabeth's bed since she moved to New York. As such, she'd never realized how small a full-sized bed actually was. William was sprawled in hers, eyes closed, his breathing deep and calm. Meanwhile, Elizabeth twisted like a tuna caught in a net, trying to get comfortable and untangle her legs from the sheet. Catching her waist, William stilled her and dragged her on top of him. She laughed as she untwisted herself and placed a languid kiss where his ear, throat, and jaw met. The hairs on his chest tickled her skin, and she sighed in contentment on top of him.

Running his fingers through her hair, William stared back at her. She examined each feature of his face—his dark eyebrows, thick, short eyelashes, the ring of light brown around the gray of his eyes. She saw anxiety under their surface.

"Are you okay?" she asked.

He nodded. "Elizabeth, I need to be clear about what that was."

Her heart thumped. "Okay."

William waited.

"Are you asking *me*?"

"Yeah," he said.

Elizabeth feigned lightness. "Well, you see, William, when a man and a woman desire each other, they both get excited and the man's—"

"I know that much," he said, laughing. His face grew serious after that. "What I mean is—I probably should have had this conversation with you before we had sex, but you know how I feel about you. Nothing's changed since the spring."

His face was so plaintive and hopeful. Elizabeth wilted, knowing she was the reason for his insecurity. Until then, she hadn't been able to put words to the longings and confusions of her own heart. But she knew then that she cared for William and wanted this—wanted this being on top of him, this being naked together, this closeness to all the features of his face.

"I already told you," she said. "Everything for me has changed."

His eyes darted over her face while he considered this. Then he smiled and pulled her down to his lips, where it was warm and soft. They had three more hours before curtain, and they spent most of them tangled together in the too-small bed, which, for their purposes, served them well.

If anyone wondered why Elizabeth Bennet was in the downstage wing that night, they didn't ask. She stood in street clothes next to William Darcy, watching his piece performed. She cried again, but this time, he pulled her to him and held his arm around her shoulders for the rest of the work. The audience, having read the laudatory review in *The New York Times*, held their collective breaths with anticipation until the dance ended and then gave the dancers and choreographer a thundering ovation.

After the show, Elizabeth congratulated her sister, but Jane sensed that Elizabeth hadn't been there for her. Elizabeth confirmed the hunch when she asked whether Jane would be staying at Charles's that night and she could have the apartment to herself. Jane looked from Elizabeth to where William stood a few yards off, and she and the choreographer shared a smile. Then Jane nodded and kissed her sister on the cheek.

Idly stroking Elizabeth's waist as she dozed in front of the television, William finally began to feel the exhaustion of the weekend. It was Sunday evening, normally when he sprawled into his leather recliner, listened to Coltrane in his plush, finely decorated den, and read *The New York Times*.

That night, he lay cramped on a sofa barely big enough for one, much less two, watching reruns of a reality TV show. Yet William wouldn't have traded that moment in a small, cluttered Harlem apartment for anything.

That weekend he had discovered the joys of small beds, cramped shower stalls, and eating meals at a coffee table on the living room floor. Spending two nights with Elizabeth in her home, waking up with her in the morning, and going to sleep next to her at night, William had made fascinating discoveries.

For example, Elizabeth held a complete conversation with herself as she walked around the house searching for a misplaced leotard. She scrunched up her face when she brushed out the knots in her hair, but once her hair was smooth, he liked the erotic way she cast her head back as the brush went through her hair. She ate too much take-out; the Chinese place downstairs was on her speed dial. She wore old, oversized t-shirts to bed and still made them sexy.

They barely had any time together. On Sunday, Elizabeth still had to go to company class and rehearsals. She had to perform again that evening in *Partita*. While she was at work, William went home and explained his curious disappearance to Georgiana. She was thrilled for him, of course, and thrilled for Elizabeth. That night, the three of them went out after the performance, but they parted ways afterwards: Georgiana returned to Central Park West, and Elizabeth and William went uptown to Harlem.

Despite five, nearly six, years on the road as a choreographer, in his heart, William called New York home. He knew by heart in which direction the avenues ran, had been to every museum, and knew every shortcut through Central Park. Yet being with Elizabeth the next day made him see his city differently.

After a late breakfast on Monday afternoon, they huddled together on a bench in Central Park making out, something he never would have done months ago. Elizabeth forced him to take the subway back to her apartment and teased him relentlessly the entire way there, laughing as he gawked like a tourist at the train evangelist making his way down the aisle preaching redemption. They'd eaten roast pork so succulent, William couldn't believe the *Times* hadn't yet discovered the unassuming Dominican cafeteria a few blocks from Elizabeth's apartment. Elizabeth just laughed.

And, of course, there had been sex—the gut-shaking, seeing-stars kind and the whispered, reverent kind, too. William's knees still burned from their last go on the carpet several hours ago, the consequence of which now had Elizabeth dozing on the couch, curled into the shape of his body, breathing slowly. Her hair fell over his forearm, and she smelled fruity like the body lotion he'd watched her rub onto her legs. In her t-shirt and socks, she was the sweetest thing he had ever laid eyes on, and it made him smile like a cat on a sunny windowsill.

Tomorrow morning he'd have to wake up before sunrise to make it to Philadelphia in time for his rehearsal. It disappointed him, having to leave. He and Elizabeth hadn't worked out the logistics of what would inevitably be a long-distance relationship. It was still too new. They would figure out how to see each other despite rehearsal schedules and distance later. First, they needed to build the relationship before they could figure out how to sustain it. The thought of waiting an entire week before getting to do this again depressed him. But what was a week when there had been nothing in his life for so long? At least, that's what he tried to tell himself.

William heard a key turn in the lock of the door. Moments later, it opened, and he heard a loud exhalation followed by the lugging of bags.

"Lizzy?" Jane called.

Elizabeth didn't stir, and William didn't want to wake her. He heard Jane heft up a plastic bag onto the kitchen counter, the sound of cans and jars thudding against each other.

"I stopped at the grocery store and picked up more tuna and applesauce. Oh, thanks for doing the dishes. I'll do them next time."

Still, Elizabeth did not wake. William wondered whether he should wake her or at least answer on her behalf.

"Lizzy?" Jane called out. William heard her footsteps on the tile before she appeared in the doorway of the living room. Jane's eyes widened and her mouth fell open.

"Oh! Hey, Will." Her face took on a tinge of bafflement as she saw the choreographer curled up so intimately with her sister on the sofa. William merely smiled, put a finger to his lips, and then pointed down to Elizabeth.

Jane nodded. She stared at the scene for a few seconds longer and then retreated to the kitchen. William let her go, figuring the explanations could come later. Right now, he had only a few minutes more of a sleeping Elizabeth to enjoy, and he intended to enjoy them thoroughly.

Epilogue

William sighed in frustration, stared down at the carpet, and then swept the red, lacy bit of fabric from the floor. Frowning, he strode down the hall, down the stairs, and into his den, where Elizabeth reclined on the leather sofa. Her feet were propped up on the armrest and his cat, Austin, dozed on her stomach.

"We have a problem," he said.

Lowering the crossword puzzle of Thursday's *Times,* Elizabeth peered curiously at William. He waved her underwear in his hand.

"I thought you liked it when I wore the sexy ones," retorted Elizabeth.

William sighed. "I also like it when you put your laundry in the laundry basket."

"Oh, no," Elizabeth cried, in mock-horror, "something in William Darcy's life isn't tidy and in order. The world has begun to spin backwards on its axis!"

Rolling his eyes, William walked into the den and stood over Elizabeth. He hooked a finger under her impertinently raised chin and lowered his face down to hers.

"There are punishments for not cleaning your room."

"Ooh, yes, please," moaned Elizabeth.

Glancing quickly down to the crossword puzzle, William smiled devilishly. "Forty-eight across—Derbyshire."

"William!" Elizabeth cried. "I told you to stop doing that!"

"Next time, pick your underwear up off the floor." William straightened himself.

"Next time, I won't even let you take them off of me."

"Empty threats." William laughed, walking to the door.

"You won't be saying that when you're forced to sleep in an *empty* bed!"

Chuckling to himself, William strolled out of the den, his irritation dissipating. Staying mad at Elizabeth was an exercise in futility. Going back up the stairs, William returned to their room.

He paused and considered his choice of pronoun. *Their* room. When had it ceased to be his? With his hands on his hips, he scanned the master bedroom. Perhaps since she had insisted they paint the wall behind the bed a startling shade of green. Since she had bought him the fabulous purple orchid sitting on his nightstand. Since she stayed over so often that two drawers in his dresser were filled with her socks, t-shirts, and jeans, and a shelf in the medicine chest held her moisturizers and makeup. And since he started finding her panties strewn on the floor.

He took it for granted now, but in the beginning, he'd craved those little intimacies because they'd been impossible to come by. They'd suffered through the two-hour distance between New York and Philadelphia, but when William moved to Miami after Thanksgiving, the distance became a torture. Between William's erratic schedule, the little frustrations of trying to get a dance company off the ground, and Elizabeth's intense performance and rehearsal schedule for *The Nutcracker* and the winter season, they had little time or energy to cultivate a relationship. Much of their early relationship developed through stolen phone calls between rehearsals for Elizabeth and donor lunches for William. Sometimes, he was able to take a long weekend in New York, but even then, their schedules prevented them from having time to indulge in each other.

There were spats. But somehow the trial solidified what he already sensed: Together they made a great team. William discovered that one of Elizabeth's quips could lighten his mood for days. She instinctively seemed to know when he needed an unprompted text message, just to say she missed him. During a three-week break after her winter season, Elizabeth visited William in Miami and watched his company perform. It was the longest stretch of time they spent together. And though he'd been secretly nervous to suddenly spend so much time with her, the weeks flowed by in a haze. They sipped their morning coffee in silence on the patio. They went into the studio together. They ate sushi on Miami Beach. They made love—a lot. The night before Elizabeth's return to New York, she whispered her love to William as she drifted off to sleep, and that made all of the stress and the longing and the melancholy of separation bearable.

Several weeks later, after a successful company debut and a promise to his freelance dancers to see them next winter, he'd packed up a few boxes and moved back to New York, unemployed but eager to finally be in the same city as Elizabeth.

WILLIAM SMILED AND SHOOK HIS head. What had he been doing? Then, he remembered that he had come upstairs to search for his bow tie and cummerbund. Now that Elizabeth had all but moved in and replaced his things with hers, he didn't know where he kept anything anymore.

He heard the apartment buzzer. Seconds later, Elizabeth, who refused to use the expensive room-to-room intercom system, bellowed from below, "I'll get that."

William frowned. It was Saturday morning, and they weren't expecting anyone. Leaving the bedroom, William stood on the landing to the stairs, listening for who was at the door. He heard Elizabeth open it and gasp.

"Oh, my God, Jerome, what are these?" Jerome was the ancient doorman who had worked in the Pemberley Building since William's boyhood.

"Card's addressed to you, darlin'. They were just delivered."

"Oh, wow! Thank you."

"You have a good day, now."

"Yes. Yes, you, too."

Curious about the mysterious delivery, William descended the stairs and made his way into the foyer to find Elizabeth holding a mountain of lilies. She beamed.

"From G!" Elizabeth exclaimed.

William smiled. "That was nice of her. Is there a message?"

Setting the enormous arrangement on the kitchen counter, Elizabeth plucked a card from atop the flowers and read.

Dear Lizzy,

Congrats x 1,000,000! Sorry I couldn't come tonight, but I'll see you and Dub soon for spring break. Did you like the CD?

Love,

Georgiana Inez Darcy (aka G)

"That was so sweet of her. I should text to say thanks," said Elizabeth.

"I'm sure she'd be happy to know you liked them."

"Where should we put them?"

"Up in the bedroom?" William offered.

Nodding, Elizabeth grinned and lifted the arrangement. William followed her up the stairs and into the master bedroom, where Elizabeth set the flowers on the dresser.

"I could get used to all of this fuss," laughed Elizabeth.

"You deserve it."

Elizabeth shrugged. "Do I? I feel bad that Jane never got the same treatment."

"She had bad timing."

"And a less than god-like boyfriend," she said, approaching William and slipping her arms around his neck.

"God-*like*?" he teased, flashing a smile.

"You haven't been chosen for the pantheon yet," Elizabeth pecked William on the lips and then unraveled herself from his grasp. "And I have a hair appointment in thirty minutes. This is so exciting! It's like the prom I never went to."

William couldn't suppress a smile. "Okay, you'd better go before you're late."

"Oh! Yeah. See you at my place at seven." Snatching her bag from the chair in the corner, Elizabeth kissed him before bidding him good-bye. William listened as she cooed farewell to Austin and then closed the door softly behind her. Sighing, he looked around his very green room and smiled. It was the first time in his nearly thirty-year dancing career that he was looking forward to a Netherfield Gala.

As her hair stylist pulled out another hot roller, Elizabeth smiled dreamily into the mirror. The night promised to be perfect—perfect dress, perfect weather, perfect career, and perfect boyfriend. The dopey grin hadn't left her face since that morning.

For the past six months since she had begun seeing William, everything had been perfect. In the beginning, she had not expected them to work so well together. Elizabeth worried that the differences between them—age, income, experience, and personality—would be too much to overcome. She worried that William would be too serious and intense, that he could never withstand her teasing and propensity for the dramatic. But, to her surprise, he hid a mellow wit of his own, could tease in return, and tempered her emotional sensitivity with equal measures rationality and compassion. She made him laugh, and he made her think.

Not that William was all levelheadedness and logic. With choreography, especially, he often over-analyzed, lost himself, despaired. Elizabeth marveled that, with nothing more than a quiet embrace or stroke of his cheek, she could settle him.

William needed her. More than once, he jokingly begged her to give up Ballet Theater and to come dance with his company. He would make her prima ballerina and let her act like Caroline Bingley if she wanted. Elizabeth understood, in spite of his teasing, that every time she turned him down, he was secretly disappointed. For the meantime, however, Elizabeth knew that she belonged in Ballet Theater. She wanted to find her bearings in the ballet world without the name of William Darcy pinned to her leotard like an audition number. And fortunately, he respected and even encouraged those wishes. William wanted her to succeed, not so that he could live vicariously through her or make her his token Tallchief or LeClercq, but because he loved her and wanted her to be happy. That, in turn, made her want to succeed, not only for glory and gratification, but to please him as well. And so it was to William that Elizabeth had first revealed her news three weeks earlier.

She had sat in Sir Webster Lucas's office, speechless. Finally, when reality sank in, Elizabeth laughed. At seeing her strange reaction, the artistic director chuckled too, and then sat back in his chair with an expectant expression.

"Elizabeth, love, do you not want to be a soloist?" he asked.

She had nodded her head furiously and laughed some more. "I do! But this is so, oh my God, I can't believe—this is unreal. Thank you!"

Lucas had thanked her in return, embraced her, and wished her luck as she embarked for the upper echelons of the company. Leaving the office in a daze, Elizabeth paused for a moment in the hall, collecting herself, wondering whether this weren't some cruel practical joke orchestrated by Caroline Bingley.

No, Elizabeth remembered all of the rehearsal breaks she'd sacrificed to learn every part, all of those hours spent alone in studios, refining steps. They had paid off. But she had never expected that her return on investment would come this soon.

She had shot down the stairs and to the locker room to grab her cell phone. She called William and waited for his voice.

"Elle?" he asked in that endearment only he used. "Is everything okay?"

"Yes! Guess what?" It was hard keeping her voice down when she just wanted to shriek.

"What?"

"No, you have to guess!"

William chuckled and then paused. "You've been promoted to soloist."

That killed some of her excitement. "Wait, how'd you know?"

"Well, it's the second week in February, and there's no other reason for you to call me at this time of day," he chuckled.

"I could have called to say I love you."

"You're not Jane."

Elizabeth just laughed.

"Plus, Charles told me but swore me to secrecy," William added.

"No fair," Elizabeth clucked but quickly recovered her spirits. "But can you believe it? Soloist! And they're going to announce it at the gala!"

"That's great, Elizabeth. Congratulations." His voice was so calm, but she could feel the pride in it.

"Will you come with me? To the gala?"

"Of course, I will."

"I know how much you hate those things."

"Elle, for you, not only will I go to the gala, I'll even be pleasant to Lucas and Boroughs."

Elizabeth paused. "You really do love me."

"I do," he laughed.

"Okay, I gotta go. I have rehearsal in five."

Before hanging up the phone, William congratulated her again. Elizabeth could hear the smile on his face. She beamed back.

"Big night, tonight?" the hairstylist asked, snapping Elizabeth back to reality. Her hair was a mess of big curls that the stylist was smoothing into an upswept bun.

"Yeah. Work function."

"Ooh, very nice. I thought maybe you were getting married, judging from that big smile on your face."

Elizabeth bit her lip and grinned. "It's an important work function."

The hairdresser nodded knowingly and smiled in the mirror. "Well, then. We're going to have to make you ravishing, aren't we? Are you going with anyone special?"

Elizabeth laughed. "Am I that obvious?"

"Just a little."

"Actually," explained Elizabeth, "I'm getting promoted."

"That would also explain the smile. And so you're the guest of honor tonight?" The words came out slightly muffled as the stylist held three bobby pins between her lips.

"Yes, something like that. I'll be the one everyone's scrutinizing tonight."

"Some people make it a hobby to criticize and judge others, don't they?" joked the stylist.

Elizabeth rolled her eyes. "What else is there to do at a black-tie party?"

The woman laughed. "You've got that right. Don't worry. I'm going to make you gorgeous. Get everyone fired up and jealous of you."

That thought disheartened her as she remembered everyone she had already gotten fired up and jealous that year. At the gala, she would face many who she had no desire to see, mainly Catherine Boroughs. She would be surrounded by William's bourgeois peers, the ones she met at fundraising galas and penthouse gatherings, who dismissed her as William Darcy's trophy girlfriend or patronized her as a charity case. She would be required to smile and make chitchat, feigning interest she didn't feel. She understood a little better why William had cultivated a habit of brooding and frowning along the outer peripheries of parties. It kept people away.

Despite the drudgeries she'd have to perform that evening, Elizabeth remembered last year's Netherfield Gala, with its crushed hopes and humiliations. A year ago, she had gotten belligerently drunk and made a fool of herself with William. Her cheeks still burned a little at the memory, but as William said, he'd enjoyed his fair share of humiliations with her; they were even. The past, they both decided, was something to learn from and reminisce over, not to feel ashamed by.

"There," the hair stylist proclaimed, holding a mirror behind Elizabeth's head for her to see the sophisticated up-do. "How do you like it?"

Twisting her neck left and right, Elizabeth grinned at herself in the mirror. "I feel perfect."

"Jane," Elizabeth called from her room, "I need your opinion." Elizabeth plodded to Jane's room, taking small, penguin-like steps to avoid stamping on the hem of her dress. When Elizabeth reached the doorway of Jane's bedroom, she turned and looked over her shoulder. "Shawl or no?"

Jane gasped. "Oh, Lizzy! That dress!"

"Too slutty?" The dress, a tight, black number, deeply V'ed in both the front and back, revealing cleavage and a wide expanse of Elizabeth's back.

"No, it's perfect. Oh, it's gorgeous. When did you get that?"

Elizabeth turned around to face her sister and grinned. "William gave it to me for Valentine's Day."

"The man's got great taste." Jane shook her head.

"It's my taste, actually. But I can't afford my tastes, and fortunately, he can."

Jane giggled. "You shouldn't joke like that. People might think you're only dating him for his money."

"Like they don't already?"

Jane looked whimsically at her sister and sighed. "Aw, man. Why'd they have to promote me after *Nutcracker*? My timing sucks."

Swallowing down a surge of guilt, Elizabeth frowned sympathetically. "Don't think like that. You're already dancing soloist roles this season. I'd trade that for the Netherfield Gala any day."

Jane shrugged her assent reluctantly. Going over to her, Elizabeth wrapped her arms around Jane's shoulders and squeezed them.

"Janey, it's just a bunch of rich people. They don't care about me any more than they care about their next good cause. Besides, you look beautiful as always."

"Not as nice as you." Jane pouted. "I'm going to give real meaning to the expression 'plain Jane' tonight."

Elizabeth laughed. "Tonight you can feel what it's like to be me all the time."

Jane playfully rolled her eyes at her sister's silliness. Elizabeth kissed the top of Jane's head and was about to turn away when the glimmer of a precious stone made her stop.

"What the heck is this!?" she asked, grabbing Jane's left hand.

Looking up, Jane colored and then laughed.

"'Plain Jane,' my ass! What is this?" Elizabeth repeated.

Jane sighed and turned to face her sister. "I really wanted to wait to tell you."

"You're kidding! You're kidding! Oh, my Lord! He asked you to marry him?"

Jane nodded with a huge grin on her face. "I wanted to wait—"

"When?" asked Elizabeth, her eyes glittering.

"Valentine's Day."

"Valentine's Day! Valentine's Day? And you waited a month to tell me?"

"Well, you've been so happy, and I didn't want to take away from that," Jane explained.

Elizabeth sighed. "Oh, Jane. No, that was wrong. You should have said something. We could have been happy together."

Admiring her ring, Jane smiled and whispered, "I've really wanted to wear it."

"I would, too. Damn, that thing is *huge*!"

Jane only giggled. "Don't worry, Lizzy. We won't say anything until after tonight."

"Jane, I don't think you could hide that ring if you wanted to."

"Should I not wear it?"

"No, wear it. And if anyone asks, be honest. Oh, Jane, congratulations! I'm happy for you and Charles."

"Thanks, Lizzy." Jane squeezed Elizabeth's hand and smiled into her eyes. For a brief moment, the two sisters simply gazed at each other. Feeling suddenly teary, Elizabeth looked away first.

"Now, come on and get ready. The guys will be here in ten minutes," Elizabeth said.

"Oh, crap. I haven't even put on my makeup yet."

Elizabeth walked slowly back to her room, disbelieving, but happy for her sister. The past year had perhaps been just as hard for Jane with her jilted promotion and subsequent rejection by Elizabeth, and she deserved her happiness. Elizabeth entered her room, closed the door, and put on Georgiana's music, something she always did when she needed to collect her thoughts.

Jane married? It was strange to imagine. Elizabeth still felt sometimes as if she were twelve years old, Jane thirteen, and they were still dancing together in an unknown dance studio in Kalamazoo, Michigan. Elizabeth paced. She sat on the edge of her bed, but feeling unsettled, went to the window and peered at the small section of street not hidden by the opposing building.

It was not jealousy. Those days were over. Months ago, an announcement like this might have devastated Elizabeth—losing a sister, a roommate, a best friend to Prince Charming. But Elizabeth had nothing to envy. Leaning her forehead against the glass, she smiled softly and sadly. She was happy for Jane but felt like something had ended.

A knock on the door stole her from her thoughts.

"Are they here?" she called out.

The door opened. "They are."

"William!" She turned to see her boyfriend decked out in a sharply cut tuxedo. "I didn't hear the buzzer."

"Jane answered the door." His eyes roamed down the length of her body. "Wow, Elle. You look…"

William's words trailed off there, and Elizabeth laughed. "Any compliment will do."

He smiled, his eyes looking bright and youthful. "That's the best gift I've ever given myself."

Elizabeth laughed again, trying to push away her sadness. "Ah, your motives become clear. Are we leaving?"

"Apparently, Jane is still getting ready. What are you doing in here?" He looked around and frowned. "Georgiana's music? What happened?"

"Nothing. I was just thinking."

"Contemplating your big night?" Reaching out, William stroked her cheek.

"Not really."

"No? What, then?"

"My sister's getting married."

William nodded. "I heard."

"You heard? When?"

"A week ago. Charles let it slip. They didn't want to say anything until after tonight."

Elizabeth sighed in frustration. "So you were all in on it, then?"

"Not 'in on it.' They wanted to wait, and it wasn't my place to say anything." William paused. "Are you angry?"

Elizabeth thought about it and shook her head. "No, just surprised. My sister's getting *married*. Jane Bingley. That sounds weird."

William replied, "She might keep her name for the stage. Plenty of dancers do that."

"It's not about the name."

He sighed gently. "Didn't you ever consider the possibility of this happening?"

"I did. I just didn't think it would happen so soon." Elizabeth shrugged, her face taking on a tinge of melancholy. "I wonder when they'll have the wedding."

"Charles told me they're thinking of having it before the fall season."

"Before the fall season!" cried Elizabeth. "So soon? Our lease on the apartment isn't up for another year! Crap."

William laughed. "Ever the practical girl."

Accepting his criticism, Elizabeth smiled in spite of herself. "Sorry, this is a lot for me to digest: Jane married and me living with another roommate."

"I'll try not to take that as an insult."

Elizabeth stared at him. "What does that mean?"

"What do you mean, 'what does that mean'? Why would you need a roommate?"

"How else am I supposed to afford the rent?"

"Elizabeth," William said in what she called his "Dad" voice.

"No, William, I'm not letting you pay my rent."

"I don't want to pay your rent."

Elizabeth frowned and scanned his face. It took her several seconds to finally understand his meaning. When she did, her eyes widened. "You mean live together?"

William nodded.

"I thought you didn't like it when I left my laundry on the floor," she said.

"I don't."

"I . . . I just didn't think we'd live well together."

William frowned. "So we'd just never live together?"

She didn't reply. They'd only been together in the same area code for two months, so it wasn't something she'd needed to consider yet.

"I couldn't hope for that yet," she said. "You being in New York—even that's too tenuous."

William searched her eyes. "We can figure that out."

"And the laundry?"

He laughed, grabbed her hand, and pulled her to him. "I love you and can learn to tolerate your strewn laundry if it means I get everything else that comes with it."

"When?"

"Whenever."

She considered this. "Are you sure? If I take you up on your offer, your entire universe may implode on itself."

"Like it hasn't already?"

Chuckling, Elizabeth kissed his jaw. She breathed him in, the scent of wool, the whisper of aftershave. Closing her eyes, she nuzzled the skin of his neck. "All right, then. I'll move in. But Elsa's going to really hate you for it," she joked, referring to William's housekeeper.

Saying nothing, he lifted her chin, smiled down into her face, and then kissed her.

"Hey, you two!" called Charles from the living room. "Stop making out. The car's waiting."

William and Elizabeth laughed and untangled themselves from each other.

"You're wearing my lip gloss." Elizabeth rubbed his lips with her thumb.

He pecked her lips once more. Straightening his tuxedo jacket, he took Elizabeth's hand. "So, are you ready to be crowned queen of the evening?"

Smiling, Elizabeth grabbed her purse off the bed and nodded. "I've been ready for ages, William. Come on, let's not keep them waiting."